CHILDREN'S CLASSICS

The Children of the New Forest

CAPTAIN MARRYAT

The Children
of the
New Forest

PARRAGON

The Children of the New Forest
A Parragon Classic

This edition published in 1999 by
Parragon
Queen Street House
4 Queen Street
Bath
BA1 1HE

Printed and bound in the UK

CHAPTER 1

The circumstances which I am about to relate to my juvenile readers took place in the year 1647. By referring to the history of England of that date, they will find that King Charles the First, against whom the Commons of England had rebelled, after a civil war of nearly five years, had been defeated, and was confined as a prisoner at Hampton Court. The Cavaliers, or the party who fought for King Charles, had all been dispersed, and the Parliamentary army under the command of Cromwell were beginning to control the Commons.

It was in the month of November in this year that King Charles, accompanied by Sir John Berkely, Ashburnham, and Legg, made his escape from Hampton Court, and rode as fast as the horses could carry them towards that part of Hampshire which led to the New Forest. The King expected that his friends had provided a vessel in which he might escape to France; but in this he was disappointed. There was no vessel ready, and after riding for some time along the shore, he resolved to go to Titchfield, a seat belonging to the Earl of Southampton. After a long consultation with those who attended him, he yielded to their advice, which was, to trust to Colonel Hammond, who was governor of the Isle of Wight for the Parliament, but who was supposed to be friendly to the King. Whatever might be the feelings of commiseration of Colonel Hammond towards a king so unfortunately situated, he was firm in his duties towards his employers, and the consequence was, that King Charles found himself again a prisoner in Carisbrook Castle.

But we must now leave the King, and retrace history to the commencement of the civil war. A short distance from the town of Lymington, which is not far from Titchfield, where the King took shelter, but on the other side of the Southampton Water, and south of the New Forest, to which it adjoins, was a property called Arnwood, which belonged to a Cavalier of the name of Beverley. It was at that time a property of considerable value, being very extensive, and the park ornamented with valuable timber; for it abutted on the New Forest, and might have been supposed to have been a continuation of it. This Colonel Beverley, as we must call him, for he rose to that rank in the King's army, was a valued friend and companion of Prince Rupert's, and commanded several troops of cavalry. He was ever at his side in the brilliant charges made by his gallant prince, and at last fell in his arms at the battle of Naseby. Colonel Beverley had married into the family of the Villiers, and the issue of his marriage was two sons and two daughters; but his zeal and sense of duty had induced him, at the commencement of the war, to leave his wife and family at Arnwood, and he was fated never to meet them again. The news of his death had such an effect upon Mrs Beverley, already worn with anxiety on her husband's account, that a few

5

months afterwards she followed him to an early tomb, leaving the four children under the charge of an elderly relative, till such time as the family of the Villiers could protect them; but, as will appear by our history, this was not at that period possible. The life of a king and many other lives were in jeopardy, and the orphans remained at Arnwood, still under the care of their elderly relations, at the time that our history commences.

The New Forest, my readers are perhaps aware, was first enclosed by William the Conqueror as a royal forest for his own amusement, for in those days most crowned heads were passionately fond of the chase; and they may also recollect that his successor, William Rufus, met his death in this forest by the glancing of an arrow shot by Sir Walter Tyrrell. Since that time to the present day, it has continued a royal domain. At the period of which we are writing, it had an establishment of verderers and keepers, paid by the Crown, amounting to some forty or fifty men. At the commencement of the civil war they remained at their posts, but soon found, in the disorganized state of the country, that their wages were no longer to be obtained; and then, when the King had decided upon raising an army, Beverley, who held a superior office in the forest, enrol led all the young and athletic men who were employed in the forest, and marched them away with him to join the King's army. Some few remained, their age not rendering their services of value, and among them was an old and attached servant of Beverley's, a man above sixty years of age, whose name was Jacob Armitage, and who had obtained the situation through Colonel Beverley's interest. Those who remained in the forest lived in cottages many miles asunder, and indemnified themselves for the non-payment of their salaries by killing the deer for sale and for their own subsistence.

The cottage of Jacob Armitage was situated on the skirts of the New Forest, about a mile and a half from the mansion of Arnwood; and when Colonel Beverley went to join the King's troops, feeling how little security there would be for his wife and children in those troubled times, he requested the old man, by his attachment to the family, not to lose sight of Arnwood, but to call there as often as possible to see if he could be of service to Mrs Beverley. The colonel would have persuaded Jacob to have altogether taken up his residence at the mansion; but to this the old man objected. He had been all his life under the greenwood tree, and could not bear to leave the forest. He promised the colonel that he would watch over his family, and ever be at hand when required; and he kept his word. The death of Colonel Beverley was a heavy blow to the old forester, and he watched over Mrs Beverley and the orphans with the greatest solicitude; but when Mrs Beverley followed her husband to the tomb, he then redoubled his attentions, and was seldom more than a few hours at a time away from the mansion. The two boys were his inseparable companions, and he instructed them, young as they were, in all the secrets of his own calling. Such was the state of affairs at the time that King Charles made his escape from Hampton Court; and I now shall resume my narrative from where it was broken off.

As soon as the escape of Charles I was made known to Cromwell and the Parliament, troops of horse were dispatched in every direction to the southwards, towards which the prints of the horses' hoofs proved that he had gone. As they found that he had proceeded in the direction of the New Forest, the troops were subdivided and ordered to scour the forest, in parties of twelve to twenty, while others hastened down to Southampton Lymington, and every other seaport or part of the coast from which the King might be likely to embark. Old Jacob had been at Arnwood on the day before, but on this day he had made up his mind to procure some venison, that he might not go there again empty-handed; for Miss Judith Villiers was very partial to venison, and was not slow to remind Jacob, if the larder was for many days deficient in that meat. Jacob had gone out accordingly; he had gained his leeward position of a fine buck, and was gradually nearing him by stealth, now behind a huge oak-tree, and then crawling through the high fern, so as to get within shot unperceived, when on a sudden the animal, which had been quietly feeding, bounded away and disappeared in the thicket. At the same time, Jacob perceived a small body of horse galloping through the glen in which the buck had been feeding. Jacob had never yet seen the Parliamentary troops, for they had not during the war been sent to that part of the country, but their iron skull-caps, their buff accoutrements, and dark habiliments, assured him that such these must be; so very different were they from the gaily-equipped Cavalier cavalry commanded by Prince Rupert. At the time that they advanced, Jacob had been lying down in the fern near to some low black-thorn bushes; not wishing to be perceived by them, he drew back between the bushes, intending to remain concealed until they should gallop out of sight; for Jacob thought, 'I am a king's forester, and they may consider me as an enemy; and who knows how I may be treated by them?' But Jacob was disappointed in his expectations of the troops riding past him; on the contrary, as soon as they arrive at an oak-tree within twenty yards of where he was concealed, the order was given to halt and dismount; the sabres of the horsemen clattered in their iron sheaths as the order was obeyed, and the old man expected to be immediately discovered; but one of the thorn-bushes was directly between him and the troopers, and effectually concealed him. At last Jacob ventured to raise his head and peep through the bush, and he perceived that the men were loosening the girths of their black horses, or wiping away the perspiration from their sides with hand-fuls of fern.

A powerfully-framed man, who appeared to command the others, was standing with his hand upon the arched neck of his steed, which appeared as fresh and vigorous as ever, although covered with foam and perspiration. 'Spare not to rub down, my men,' said he, 'for we have tried the mettle of our horses, and have now but one half-hour's breathing-time. We must be on, for the work of the Lord must be done.'

'They say that this forest is many miles in length and breadth,' observed another of the men, 'and we may ride many a mile to no purpose; but here

7

is James Southwold, who once was living in it as a verderer; nay, I think he said that he was born and bred in these woods. – Was it not so, James Southwold?'

'It is even as you say,' replied an active-looking young man; 'I was born and bred in this forest, and my father was a verderer before me.'

Jacob Armitage, who listened to the conversation, immediately recognized the young man in question. He was one of those who had joined the King's army with the other verderers and keepers. It pained him much to perceive that one who had always been considered a frank, true-hearted young man, and who left the forest to fight in defence of his king, was now turned a traitor, and had joined the ranks of the enemy; and Jacob thought how much better it had been for James Southwold, if he had never quitted the New Forest, and had not been corrupted by evil company. 'He was a good lad,' thought Jacob, 'and now he is a traitor and a hypocrite.'

'If born and bred in this forest, James Southwold,' said the leader of the troop, 'you must fain know all its mazes and paths. Now call to mind – are there no secret hiding-places in which people may remain concealed; no thickets which may cover both man and horse? Peradventure thou mayest point out the very spot where this man Charles may be hidden.'

'I do know one dell, within a mile of Arnwood,' replied James Southwold, 'which might cover double our troop from the eyes of the most wary.'

'We will ride there then,' replied the leader. 'Arnwood, sayest thou? is not that the property of the Malignant Cavalier Beverley, who was shot down at Naseby?'

'Even so,' replied Southwold; 'and many is the time – that is, in the olden time, before I was regenerated – many is the day of revelry that I have passed there; many the cup of good ale that I have quaffed.'

'And thou shalt quaff it again,' replied the leader. 'Good ale was not intended only for Malignants, but for those who serve diligently. After we have examined the dell which thou speakest of, we will direct our horses' heads towards Arnwood.'

'Who knows but what the man Charles may be concealed in the Malignant's house?' observed another.

'In the day, I should say no,' replied the leader; 'but in the night the Cavaliers like to have a roof over their heads; and therefore at night, and not before, will we proceed thither.'

'I have searched many of their abodes,' observed another; 'but search is almost in vain. What with their spring panels, and secret doors, their false ceilings, and double walls, one may ferret for ever and find nothing.'

'Yes,' replied the leader, 'their abodes are full of these Popish abominations; but there is one way which is sure; and if the man Charles be concealed in any house, I venture to say that I will find him. Fire and smoke will bring him forth; and to every Malignant's house within twenty miles will I apply the torch; but it must be at night, for we are not sure of his being housed during the day. James Southwold, thou knowest well the mansion of Arnwood?'

'I know well my way to all the offices below – the buttery, the cellar, and the kitchen; but I cannot say that I have ever been into the apartments of the upper house.'

'That it needeth not; if thou canst direct us to the lower entrance, it will be sufficient.'

'That can I, Master Ingram,' replied Southwold, 'and to where the best ale used to be found.'

'Enough, Southwold, enough; our work must be done, and diligently. Now, my men, tighten your girths; we will just ride to the dell; if it conceals not whom we seek, it shall conceal us till night, and then the country shall be lighted up with the flames of Arnwood, while we surround the house and prevent escape. – Levellers, to horse!'

The troopers sprang upon their saddles, and went off at a hard trot, Southwold leading the way. Jacob remained among the fern until they were out of sight, and then rose up. He looked for a short time in the direction in which the troopers had gone, stooped down again to take up his gun, and then said, 'There's providence in this; yes, and there's providence in my not having my dog with me, for he would not have remained quiet for so long a time. Who could ever have thought that James Southwold would have turned a traitor! more than traitor, for he is now ready to bite the hand that has fed him, to burn the house that has ever welcomed him. This is a bad world, and I thank heaven that I have lived in the woods. But there is no time to lose'; and the old forester threw his gun over his shoulder and hastened away in the direction of his own cottage.

'And so the King has escaped,' thought Jacob, as he went along, 'and he may be in the forest! Who knows but he may be at Arnwood, for he must hardly know where to go for shelter! I must haste and see Miss Judith immediately. "Levellers, to horse!" the fellow said. What's a leveller?' thought Jacob.

As perhaps my readers may ask the same question, they must know that a large portion of the Parliamentary army had at this time assumed the name of Levellers, in consequence of having taken up the opinion that every man should be on an equality, and property should be equally divided. The hatred of these people to any one above them in rank or property, especially towards those of the King's party, which mostly consisted of men of rank and property, was unbounded, and they were merciless and cruel to the highest degree, throwing off much of that fanatical bearing and language which had before distinguished the Puritans. Cromwell had great difficulty in eventually putting them down, which he did at last accomplish by hanging and slaughtering many. Of this Jacob knew nothing; all he knew was, that Arnwood was to be burnt down that night, and that it would be necessary to remove the family. As for obtaining assistance to oppose the troopers, that he knew to be impossible. As he thought of what must take place, he thanked God for having allowed him to gain the knowledge of what was to happen, and hastened on his way. He had been about eight miles from Arnwood when he had concealed himself in the fern. Jacob first went to his cottage to deposit his gun, saddled his forest pony, and set off for Arnwood. In less than two hours the old man was at the door of the mansion; it was then about three o'clock in the afternoon, and being in the month of November, there was not so much as two hours of daylight remaining. 'I shall have a difficult job with the stiff old lady,' thought Jacob, as he rang the bell; 'I don't believe that she would rise out of her high chair for old Noll and his whole army at his back. But we shall see.'

CHAPTER 2

Before Jacob is admitted to the presence of Miss Judith Villiers, we must give some account of the establishment at Arnwood. With the exception of one male servant, who officiated in the house and stables as his services might be required, every man of the household of Colonel Beverley had followed the fortunes of their master; and as none had returned, they, in all probability, had shared his fate. Three female servants, with the man above mentioned, composed the whole household. Indeed, there was every reason for not increasing the establishment; for the rents were either paid in part, or not paid at all. It was generally supposed that the property, now that the Parliament had gained the day, would be sequestrated, although such was not yet the case; and the tenants were unwilling to pay to those who were not authorized to receive the rents which they might be again called upon to make good. Miss Judith Villiers, therefore, found it difficult to maintain the present household; and although she did not tell Jacob Armitage that such was the case, the fact was that very often the venison which he brought to the mansion was all the meat that was in the larder. The three female servants held the offices of cook, attendant upon Miss Villiers, and housemaid; the children being under the care of no particular servant, and left much to themselves. There had been a chaplain in the house, but he had quitted before the death of Mrs Beverley, and the vacancy had not been filled up; indeed, it could not well be, for the one who left had not received his salary for many months, and Miss Judith Villiers, expecting every day to be summoned by her relations to bring the children and join them, sat in her high chair waiting for the arrival of this summons, which from the distracted state of the times had never come.

As we have before said, the orphans were four in number; the two eldest were boys, and the youngest were girls. Edward, the eldest boy, was between thirteen and fourteen years old; Humphrey, the second, was twelve; Alice, eleven; and Edith, eight. As it is the history of these young persons which we are about to narrate, we shall say little about them at present, except that for many months they had been under little or no

10

restraint, and less attended to. Their companions were Benjamin, the man who remained in the house, and old Jacob Armitage, who passed all the time he could spare with them. Benjamin was rather weak in intellect, and was a source of amusement rather than otherwise. As for the female servants, one was wholly occupied with her attendance on Miss Judith, who was very exacting, and had a high notion of her own consequence. The other two had more than sufficient employment; as, when there is no money to pay with, everything must be done at home. That, under such circumstances, the boys became boisterous and the little girls became romps, is not to be wondered at; but their having become so was the cause of Miss Judith seldom admitting them into her room. It is true that they were sent for once a day, to ascertain if they were in the house, or in existence, but soon dismissed and left to their own resources. Such was the neglect to which these young orphans were exposed. It must, however, be admitted that this very neglect made them independent and bold, full of health from constant activity, and more fitted for the change which was soon to take place.

'Benjamin,' said Jacob, as the other came to the door, 'I must speak with the old lady.'

'Have you brought any venison, Jacob?' said Benjamin, grinning, 'else, I reckon, you'll not be over welcome.'

'No, I have not; but it is an important business, so send Agatha to her directly.'

'I will; and I'll not say anything about the venison.'

In a few minutes Jacob was ushered up by Agatha into Miss Judith Villiers's apartment. The old lady was about fifty years of age, very prim and starched, sitting in a high-backed chair, with her feet upon a stool, and her hands crossed before her, her black mittens reposing upon her snow-white apron.

The old forester made her obeisance.

'You have important business with us, I am told,' observed Miss Judith.

'Most important, madam,' replied Jacob. 'In the first place, it is right that you should be informed that his Majesty King Charles has escaped from Hampton Court.'

'His Majesty escaped!' replied the lady.

'Yes; and is supposed to be secreted somewhere in this neighbourhood. His Majesty is not in this house, madam, I presume?'

'Jacob, his Majesty is not in this house; if he were, I would suffer my tongue to be torn out sooner than I would confess it, even to you.'

'But I have more for your private ear, madam.'

'Agatha, retire; and, Agatha, be mindful that you go downstairs, and do not remain outside the door.'

Agatha, with this injunction, bounced out of the room, slamming-to the door so as to make Miss Judith start from her seat.

'Ill-mannered girl!' exclaimed Miss Judith. 'Now, Jacob Armitage, you may proceed.'

11

Jacob then entered into the detail of what he had overheard that morning, when he fell in with the troopers, concluding with the information that the mansion would be burnt down that very night. He then pointed out the necessity of immediately abandoning the house, as it would be impossible to oppose the troopers.

'And where am I to go to, Jacob?' said Miss Judith calmly.

'I hardly know, madam; there is my cottage, it is but a poor place, and not fit for one like you.'

'So I should presume, Jacob Armitage; neither shall I accept your offer. It would ill befit the dignity of a Villiers to be frightened out of her abode by a party of rude soldiers. Happen what will, I shall not stir from this – no, not even from this chair. Neither do I consider the danger so great as you suppose. Let Benjamin saddle, and be prepared to ride over to Lymington immediately. I will give him a letter to the magistrate there, who will send us protection.'

'But madam, the children cannot remain here. I will not leave them here. I promised the colonel . . .'

'Will the children be in more danger than I shall be, Jacob Armitage?' replied the old lady stiffly. 'They dare not ill-treat me – they may force the buttery and drink the ale – they may make merry with that and the venison which you have brought with you, I presume, but they will hardly venture to insult a lady of the house of Villiers.'

'I fear they will venture anything, madam. At all events, they will frighten the children, and for one night they will be better in my cottage.'

'Well, then, be it so; take them to your cottage, and take Martha to attend upon the Miss Beverleys. Go down now, and desire Agatha to come to me, and Benjamin to saddle as fast as he can.'

Jacob left the room, satisfied with the permission to remove the children. He knew that it was useless to argue with Miss Judith, who was immovable when once she had declared her intentions. He was debating in his own mind whether he should acquaint the servants with the threatened danger; but he had no occasion to do so, for Agatha had remained at the door while Jacob was communicating the intelligence, and as soon as he had arrived at that portion of it by which she learnt that the mansion was to be burnt down that night, had run off to the kitchen to communicate the intelligence to the other servants.

'I'll not stay to be burnt to death,' exclaimed the cook, as Jacob came in. 'Well, Mr Armitage, this is pretty news you have brought. What does my lady say?'

'She desires that Benjamin saddles immediately, to carry a letter to Lymington; and you, Agatha, are to go upstairs to her.'

'But what does she mean to do? Where are we to go?' exclaimed Agatha.

'Miss Judith intends to remain where she is.'

'Then she will remain alone, for me,' exclaimed the housemaid, who was admired by Benjamin. 'It's bad enough to have little victuals and no wages; but as for being burnt to death – Benjamin, put a pillion behind your saddle,

12

and I'll go to Lymington with you. I won't be long in getting my bundle.'

Benjamin, who was in the kitchen with the maids at the time that Jacob entered, made a sign significant of consent, and went away to the stable. Agatha went up to her mistress in a state of great perturbation, and the cook also hurried away to her bedroom.

'They'll all leave her,' thought Jacob; 'well, my duty is plain! I'll not leave the children in the house.' Jacob then went in search of them, and found them playing in the garden. He called the two boys to him, and told them to follow him. 'Now, Master Edward,' said he, 'you must prove yourself your father's own son. We must leave this house immediately; come up with me to your rooms, and help me to pack up yours and your sisters' clothes, for we must go to my cottage this night. There is no time to be lost.'

'But why, Jacob? I must know why.'

'Because the Parliamentary troopers will burn it down this night.'

'Burn it down! Why, the house is mine, is it not? Who dares to burn down this house?'

'They will dare it, and will do it.'

'But we will fight them, Jacob; we can bolt and bar; I can fire a gun, and hit too, as you know; then there's Benjamin and you.'

'And what can you and two men do against a troop of horse, my dear boy? If we could defend the place against them, Jacob Armitage would be the first; but it is impossible, my dear boy. Recollect your sisters. Would you have them burnt to death, or shot by these wretches? No, no, Master Edward, you must do as I say, and lose no time. Let us pack up what will be most useful, and load White Billy with the bundles; then you must all come to the cottage with me, and we will make it out how we can.'

'That will be jolly!' said Humphrey; 'come, Edward.'

But Edward Beverley required more persuasion to abandon the house; at last old Jacob prevailed, and the clothes were put up in bundles as fast as they could collect them.

'Your aunt said Martha was to go with your sisters, but I doubt if she will,' observed Jacob, 'and I think we shall have no room for her, for the cottage is small enough.'

'Oh, no, we don't want her,' said Humphrey; 'Alice always dresses Edith and herself too, ever since mamma died.'

'Now we will carry down the bundles, and you make them fast on the pony while I go for your sisters.'

'But where does Aunt Judith go?' inquired Edward.

'She will not leave the house, Master Edward; she intends to stay and speak to the troopers.'

'And so an old woman like her remains to face the enemy, while I run away from them!' replied Edward. 'I will not go.'

'Well, Master Edward,' replied Jacob, 'you must do as you please; but it will be cruel to leave your sisters here; they and Humphrey must come with me, and I cannot manage to get them to the cottage without you go with us; it is not far, and you can return in a very short time.'

To this Edward consented. The pony was soon loaded, and the little girls, who were still playing in the garden, were called in by Humphrey. They were told that they were going to pass the night in the cottage, and were delighted at the idea.

'Now, Master Edward,' said Jacob, 'will you take your sisters by the hand and lead them to the cottage? Here is the key of the door; Master Humphrey can lead the pony; and Master Edward,' continued Jacob, taking him aside, 'I'll tell you one thing which I will not mention before your brother and sisters: the troopers are all about the New Forest, for King Charles has escaped, and they are seeking for him. You must not, therefore, leave your brother and sisters till I return. Lock the cottage door as soon as it is dark. You know where to get a light, over the cupboard; and my gun is loaded, and hangs above the mantelpiece. You must do your best, if they attempt to force an entrance; but above all, promise me not to leave them till I return. I will remain here to see what I can do with your aunt; and when I come back, we can then decide how to act.'

This latter ruse of Jacob's succeeded. Edward promised that he would not leave his sisters, and it wanted but a few minutes of twilight when the little party quitted the mansion of Arnwood. As they went out of the gates they were passed by Benjamin, who was trotting away with Martha behind him on a pillion, holding a bundle as large as herself. Not a word was exchanged, and Benjamin and Martha were soon out of sight.

'Why, where can Martha be going?' said Alice. 'Will she be back when we come home tomorrow?'

Edward made no reply, but Humphrey said, 'Well, she has taken plenty of clothes in that huge bundle, for one night, at least.'

Jacob, as soon as he had seen the children on their way returned to the kitchen, where he found Agatha and the cook collecting their property, evidently bent upon a hasty retreat.

'Have you seen Miss Judith, Agatha?'

'Yes; and she told me that she should remain, and that I should stand behind her chair, that she might receive the troopers with dignity; but I don't admire the plan. They might leave her alone, but I am sure that they will be rude to me.'

'When did Benjamin say he would be back?'

'He don't intend coming back. He said he would not, at all events, till tomorrow morning, and then he would ride out this way, to ascertain if the report was false or true. But Martha has gone with him.'

'I wish I could persuade the old lady to leave the house,' said Jacob thoughtfully. 'I fear they will not pay her the respect that she calculates upon. Go up, Agatha, and say I wish to speak with her.'

'No, not I; I must be off, for it is dark already.'

'And where are you going, then?'

'To Gossip Allwood's. It's a good mile, and I have to carry my things.'

'Well, Agatha, if you'll take me up to the old lady, I'll carry your things for you.'

Agatha consented, and as soon as she had taken up the lamp, for it was now quite dark, Jacob was once more introduced.

'I wish, madam,' said Jacob, 'you would be persuaded to leave the house for this night.'

Jacob Armitage, leave this house I will not, if it were filled with troopers; I have said so.'

'But, madam –'

'No more, sir; you are too forward,' replied the old lady haughtily.

'But, madam –'

'Leave my presence, Jacob Armitage, and never appear again. Quit the room, and send Agatha here.'

'She has left, madam, and so has the cook, and Martha went away behind Benjamin; when I leave, you will be alone.'

'They have dared to leave?'

'They dared not shy, madam.'

'Leave me, Jacob Armitage, and shut the door when you go out.' Jacob still hesitated. 'Obey me instantly,' said the old lady; and the forester, finding all remonstrance useless, went out, and obeyed her last commands by shutting the door after him.

Jacob found Agatha and the other maid in the courtyard; he took up their packages, and, as he promised, accompanied them to Gossip Allwood, who kept a small ale-house about a mile distant.

'But, mercy on us! what will become of the children?' said Agatha, as they walked along, her fears for herself having, up to this time, made her utterly forgetful of them. 'Poor things! and Martha has left them.'

'Yes, indeed; what will become of the dear babes?' said the cook, half crying.

Now, Jacob, knowing that the children of such a Malignant as Colonel Beverley would have sorry treatment if discovered, and knowing also that women were not always to be trusted determined not to tell them how they were disposed of. He therefore replied, –

'Who would hurt such young children as those? No, no, they are safe enough; even the troopers would protect them.'

'I should hope so,' replied Agatha.

'You may be sure of that; no man would hurt babies,' replied Jacob. 'The troopers will take them with them to Lymington, I suppose. I've no fear for them; it's the proud old lady whom they will be uncivil to.'

The conversation here ended, and in due time they arrived at the inn. Jacob had just put the bundles down on the table, when the clattering of horses' hoofs was heard. Shortly afterwards, the troopers pulled their horses up at the door, and dismounted. Jacob recognized the party he had met in the forest and among them Southwold. The troopers called for ale, and remained some time in the house, talking and laughing with the women, especially Agatha, who was a very good-looking girl. Jacob would have retreated quietly, but he found a sentinel posted at the door to prevent the egress of any person. He reseated himself, and while he was listening to the conversation of the troopers, he was recognized by Southwold, who accosted him. Jacob did not pretend not to know him, as it would have been useless; and Southwold put many questions to him as to who were resident at Arnwood. Jacob replied that the children were there, and a few servants, and he was about to mention Miss Judith Villiers, when a thought struck him – he might save the old lady.

'You are going to Arnwood, I know,' said Jacob, 'and I have heard who you are in search of. Well, Southwold, I'll give you a hint. I may be wrong; but if you should fall in with an old lady or something like one when you go to Arnwood, mount her on your crupper, and away with her to Lymington as fast as you can ride. You understand me.' Southwold nodded significantly, and squeezed Jacob's hand.

'One word, Jacob Armitage; if I succeed in the capture by your means, it is but fair that you should have something for your hint. Where can I find you the day after tomorrow?'

'I am leaving the country this night, and go I must. I am in trouble, that's the fact; when all is blown over I will find you out. Don't speak to me any more just now.' Southwold again squeezed Jacob's hand, and left. Shortly afterwards the order was given to mount, and the troopers set off.

Armitage followed slowly and unobserved. They arrived at the mansion and surrounded it. Shortly afterwards he perceived the glare of torches, and in a quarter of an hour more thick smoke rose up in the dark but clear sky; at last the flames burst forth from the lower windows of the mansion, and soon afterwards they lighted up the country round to some distance.

'It is done,' thought Jacob, and he turned to bend his hasty steps towards his own cottage, when he heard the galloping of a horse and violent screams; a minute afterwards James Southwold passed him with the old lady tied behind him, kicking and struggling as hard as she could. Jacob smiled, as he thought that he had by his little stratagem saved the old woman's life, for that Southwold imagined that she was King Charles dressed up as an old woman was evident; and he then returned as fast as he could to the cottage.

In half an hour Jacob had passed through the thick woods which were between the mansion and his own cottage, occasionally looking back, as the flames of the mansion rose higher and higher, throwing their light far and wide. He knocked at the cottage door; Smoker, a large dog, cross-bred between the fox and bloodhound, growled till Jacob spoke to him, and then Edward opened the door.

'My sisters are in bed and fast asleep, Jacob,' said Edward, 'and Humphrey has been nodding this half-hour; had he not better go to bed before we go back?'

'Come out, Master Edward,' replied Jacob, 'and look.' Edward beheld the flames and fierce light between the trees, and was silent.

'I told you that it would be so, and you would all have been burnt in your beds, for they did not enter the house to see who was in it, but fired it as soon as they had surrounded it.'

'And my aunt!' exclaimed Edward, clasping his hands.

'Is safe, Master Edward, and by this time at Lymington.'

'We will go to her tomorrow. '

'I fear not; you must not risk so much, Master Edward. These Levellers spare nobody, and you had better let it be supposed that you are all burnt in the house.'

'But my aunt knows the contrary, Jacob.'

'Very true; I quite forgot that. ' And so Jacob had. He expected that the old woman would have been burnt, and then nobody would have known of the existence of the children; he forgot, when he planned to save her, that she knew where the children were.

'Well, Master Edward, I will go to Lymington tomorrow and see the old lady; but you must remain here, and take charge of your sisters till I come back, and then we will consider what is to be done. The flames are not so bright as they were.'

'No. It is my house that these Roundheads have burned down,' said Edward, shaking his fist.

'It was your house, Master Edward, and it was your property – but how long it will be so remains to be seen. I fear it will be forfeited.'

'Woe to the people who dare take possession of it!' cried Edward; 'I shall, if I live, be a man one of these days.'

'Yes, Master Edward, and then you will reflect more than you do now, and not be rash. Let us go into the cottage, for it's no use remaining out in the cold; the frost is sharp tonight.'

Edward slowly followed Jacob into the cottage. His little heart was full. He was a proud boy and a good boy, but the destruction of the mansion had raised up evil thoughts in his heart – hatred to the Covenanters, who had killed his father, and now burnt the property – revenge upon them (how, he knew not); but his hand was ready to strike, young as he was. He lay down on the bed, but he could not sleep. He turned and turned again, and his brain was teeming with thoughts and plans of vengeance. Had he said his prayers that night, he would have been obliged to repeat, 'Forgive us, as we forgive them who trespass against us.' At last he fell fast asleep, but his dreams were wild, and he often called out during the night, and woke his brothers and sisters.

CHAPTER 3

The next morning, as soon as Jacob had given the children their breakfast, he set off towards Arnwood. He knew that Benjamin had stated his intention to return with the horse and see what had taken place, and he knew him well enough to feel sure that he would do so. He thought it better to see him, if possible, and ascertain the fate of Miss Judith. Jacob arrived at the still smoking ruins of the mansion, and found several people there, mostly residents within a few miles, some attracted by curiosity, others busy in collecting the heavy masses of lead which had been melted from the roof, and appropriating them to their own benefit; but much of it was still too hot to be touched, and they were throwing snow on it to cool it, for it had snowed during the night. At last, Jacob perceived Benjamin on horseback riding leisurely towards him, and immediately went up to him.

'Well, Benjamin, this is a woeful sight. What is the news from Lymington?'

'Lymington is full of troopers, and they are not over civil,' replied Benjamin.

'And the old lady – where is she?'

'Ah, that's a sad business,' replied Benjamin, 'and the poor children, too. Poor Master Edward! he would have made a brave gentleman.'

'But the old lady is safe?' rejoined Jacob. 'Did you see her?'

'Yes, I saw her; they thought she was King Charles – poor old soul.'

'But they have found out their mistake by this time?'

'Yes, and James Southwold has found it out too,' replied Benjamin; 'to think of the old lady breaking his neck!'

'Breaking his neck? You don't say so! How was it?'

'Why, it seems that Southwold thought that she was King Charles dressed up as an old woman, so he seized her and strapped her fast behind him, and galloped away with her to Lymington; but she struggled and kicked so manfully, that he could not hold on, and off they went together, and he broke his neck.'

'Indeed! – a judgement – a judgement upon a traitor,' said Jacob.

'They were picked up, strapped together as they were, by the other troopers, and carried to Lymington.'

'Well, and where is the old lady, then? Did you see and speak to her?'

'I saw her, Jacob, but I did not speak to her. I forgot to say, that when she broke Southwold's neck she broke her own too.'

'Then the old lady is dead?'

'Yes, that she is,' replied Benjamin; 'but who cares about her? It's the poor children that I pity. Martha has been crying ever since.'

'I don't wonder.'

'I was at the Cavalier, and the troopers were there, and they were boasting of what they had done, and called it a righteous work. I could not stand that, and I asked one of them if it were a righteous work to burn poor children in their beds? So he turned round, and struck his sword upon the floor, and asked me whether I was one of them. "Who are you then?" and I – all my courage went away, and I answered I was a poor rat-catcher. "A rat-catcher; are you? – Well then, Mr Rat-catcher, when you are killing rats, if you find a nest of young ones, don't you kill them too? or do you leave them to grow, and become mischievous, eh?" "I kill the young ones, of course," replied I. "Well, so do we Malignants wherever we find them." I didn't say a word more, so I went out of the house as fast as I could.'

'Have you heard anything about the King?' inquired Jacob.

'No, nothing; but the troopers are all out again, and I hear are gone to the forest.'

'Well, Benjamin, good-bye; I shall be off from this part of the country – it's no use my staying here. Where's Agatha and cook?'

'They came to Lymington early this morning.'

'Wish them good-bye for me, Benjamin.'

'Where are you going then?'

'I can't exactly say, but I think London way. I only stayed here to watch over the children; and now that they are gone, I shall leave Arnwood for ever.'

Jacob, who was anxious, on account of the intelligence he had received of the troopers being in the forest, to return to the cottage, shook hands with Benjamin, and hastened away. 'Well,' thought Jacob, as he wended his way, 'I'm sorry for the poor old lady; but still, perhaps, it's all for the best. Who knows what they might do with these children! – Destroy the nest as well as the rats, indeed! – they must find the nest first.' And the old forester continued his journey, in deep thought.

We may here observe that, bloodthirsty as many of the Levellers were, we do not think that Jacob Armitage had grounds for the fears which he expressed and felt; that is to say, we believe that he might have made known the existence of the children to the Villiers family, and that they would never have been harmed by anybody. That by the burning of the mansion they might have perished in the flames had they been in bed, as they would have been at that hour, had he not obtained intelligence of what was about to be done, is true, but that there was any danger to them on account of their father having been such a staunch supporter of the King's cause is very unlikely, and not borne out by the history of the times; but the old forester thought otherwise. He had a hatred of the Puritans, and their deeds had been so exaggerated by rumour that he fully believed that the lives of the children were not safe. Under this conviction, and feeling himself bound by his promise to Colonel Beverley to protect them, Jacob resolved that they should live with him in the forest, and be brought up as his own grandchildren. He knew that there could be no better place for concealment; for, except the keepers, few people knew where his cottage was; and it was so out of the usual paths, and so embosomed in lofty trees, that there was little chance of its being seen, or being known to exist. He resolved, therefore, that they should remain with him till better times; and then he would make known their existence to the other branches of the family, but not before. 'I can hunt for them, and provide for them,' thought he, 'and I have a little money when it is required; and I will teach them to be useful – they must learn to provide for themselves. There's the garden, and the patch of land: in two or three years the boys will be able to do something. I can't teach them much, but I can teach them to fear God.

19

We must get on how we can, and put our trust in Him who is a Father to the fatherless.'

With such thoughts running in his head, Jacob arrived at the cottage, and found the children outside the door, watching for him. They all hastened to him, and the dog rushed before them to welcome his master. 'Down, Smoker, good dog! Well, Master Edward, I have been as quick as I can. How have Master Humphrey and your sisters behaved? But we must not remain outside today, for the troopers are scouring the forest, and may see you. Let us come in directly; for it would not do that they should come here.'

'Will they burn the cottage down?' inquired Alice, as she took Jacob's hand.

'Yes, my dear, I think they would, if they found that you and your brothers were in it; but we must not let them see you.'

They all entered the cottage, which consisted of one large room in front, and two back rooms for bedrooms. There was also a third bedroom, which was behind the other two, but which had not any furniture in it.

'Now let's see what we can have for dinner – there's venison left, I know,' said Jacob. 'Come, we must all be useful. Who will be cook?'

'I will be cook,' said Alice, 'if you will show me how.'

'So you shall, my dear,' said Jacob, 'and I will show you how. There's some potatoes in the basket in the corner – and some onions hanging on the string. We must have some water – who will fetch it?'

'I will,' said Edward, who took up a pail, and went out to the spring.

The potatoes were peeled and washed by the children – Jacob and Edward cut the venison into pieces – the iron pot was cleaned – and then the meat and potatoes put with water into the pot, and placed on the fire.

'Now I'll cut up the onions, for they will make your eyes water.'

'I don't care,' said Humphrey, 'I'll cut and cry at the same time.'

And Humphrey took up a knife, and cut away most manfully, although he was obliged to wipe his eyes with his sleeve very often.

'You are a fine fellow, Humphrey,' said Jacob. 'Now we'll put the onions in, and let it all boil up together. Now, you see you have cooked your own dinner; ain't that pleasant?'

'Yes,' cried they all; 'and we will eat our own dinner as soon as it is ready.'

'Then, Humphrey, you must get some of the platters down which are on the dresser; and, Alice, you will find some knives in the drawer. And let me see, what can little Edith do? Oh, she can go to the cupboard and find the salt-cellar. Edward, just look out, and if you see anybody coming or passing, let me know. We must put you on guard till the troopers leave the forest. '

The children set about their tasks, and Humphrey cried out, as he very often did, 'Now, this is jolly!'

While the dinner was cooking, Jacob amused the children by showing them how to put things in order; the floor was swept, the hearth was made tidy. He showed Alice how to wash out a cloth, and Humphrey how to dust the chairs. They all worked merrily, while little Edith stood and clapped her hands.

But just before dinner was ready, Edward came in and said, 'Here are troopers galloping in the forest!' Jacob went out, and observed that they were coming in a direction that would lead them near to the cottage.

He walked in, and after a moment's thought he said – 'My dear children, those men may come and search the cottage; you must do as I tell you, and mind that you are very quiet. Humphrey, you and your sisters must go to bed, and pretend to be very ill. Edward, take off your coat and put on this old hunting-frock of mine; you must be in the bedroom attending your sick brother and sisters. Come, Edith, dear, you must play at going to bed, and have your dinner afterwards.'

Jacob took the children into the bedroom, and removing the upper dress, which would have betrayed that they were not the children of poor people, put them in bed, and covered them up to the chins with the clothes. Edward had put on the old hunting-shirt, which came below his knees, and stood with a mug of water in his hand by the bedside of the two girls. Jacob went to the outer room, to remove the platters laid out for dinner; and he had hardly done so, when he heard the noise of the troopers, and soon afterwards a knock at the cottage-door.

'Come in,' said Jacob.

'Who are you, my friend?' said the leader of the troop, entering the door.

'A poor forester, sir,' replied Jacob, 'under great trouble.'

'What trouble, my man?'

'I have the children all in bed, with the small-pox.'

'Nevertheless, we must search your cottage.'

'You are welcome,' replied Jacob; 'only don't frighten the children if you can help it.'

The man, who was now joined by others, commenced his search. Jacob opened all the doors of the rooms, and they passed through. Little Edith shrieked when she saw them; but Edward patted her, and told her not to be frightened. The troopers, however, took no notice of the children; they searched thoroughly, and then came back to the front room.

'It's no use remaining here,' said one of the troopers. 'Shall we be off? I'm tired and hungry with the ride.'

'So am I, and there's something that smells well,' said another. 'What's this, my good man?' continued he, taking off the lid of the pot.

'My dinner for a week,' replied Jacob. 'I have no one to cook for me now, and can't light a fire every day.'

'Well, you appear to live well, if you have such a mess as that every day in the week. I should like to try a spoonful or two.'

'And welcome, sir,' replied Jacob; 'I will cook some more for myself.'

The troopers took him at his word; they sat down to the table, and very soon the whole contents of the kettle had disappeared. Having satisfied themselves, they got up, told him that his rations were so good that they

21

hoped to call again, and, laughing heartily, they mounted their horses and rode away.

'Well,' said Jacob, 'they are very welcome to the dinner; I little thought to get off so cheap.' As soon as they were out of sight, Jacob called to Edward and the children to get up again, which they soon did. Alice put on Edith's frock, Humphrey put on his jacket, and Edward pulled off the hunting-shirt.

'They're gone now,' said Jacob, coming in from the door.

'And our dinners are gone,' said Humphrey, looking at the empty pot and dirty platters.

'Yes; but we can cook another: and that will be more play, you know,' said Jacob. 'Edward, go for the water; Humphrey, cut the onions; Alice, wash the potatoes; and, Edith, help everybody, while I cut up some more meat.'

'I hope it will be as good,' observed Humphrey; 'that other did smell so nice!'

'Quite as good, if not better; for we shall improve by practice, and we shall have a better appetite to eat it with,' said Jacob.

'Nasty men eat our dinner,' said Edith. 'Shan't have any more. Eat this ourselves.'

And so they did as soon as it was cooked; but they were very hungry before they sat down.

'This is jolly!' said Humphrey, with his mouth full.

'Yes, Master Humphrey. I doubt if King Charles eats so good a dinner this day. Master Edward, you are very grave and silent.'

'Yes, I am, Jacob. Have I not cause? Oh! if I could but have mauled those troopers!'

'But you could not, so you must make the best of it. They say that every dog has his day, and who knows but King Charles may be on the throne again!'

There were no more visits to the cottage that day, and they all went to bed and slept soundly.

The next morning, Jacob, who was most anxious to learn the news, saddled the pony, having first given his injunctions to Edward how to behave in case any troopers should come to the cottage. He told him to pretend that the children were in bed with the small-pox, as they had done the day before. Jacob then travelled to Gossip Allwood's, and he there learnt that King Charles had been taken prisoner, and was at the Isle of Wight, and that the troopers were all going back to London as fast as they came. Feeling that there was now no more danger to be apprehended from them, Jacob set off as fast as he could for Lymington. He went to one shop and purchased two peasant dresses which he thought would fit the two boys, and at another he bought similar apparel for the two girls. Then with several other ready-made articles, and some other things which were required for the household, he made a large package, which he put upon the pony, and taking the bridle, set off home, and arrived in time to superintend the cooking of the dinner, which was this day venison steaks fried in a pan and boiled potatoes.

When dinner was over, he opened his bundle, and told the little ones that now they were to live in a cottage they ought to wear cottage clothes, and that he had brought them some to put on, in which they might rove about the woods, and not mind tearing them. Alice and Edith went into the bedroom, and Alice dressed Edith and herself, and came out quite pleased with their change of dress. Humphrey and Edward put theirs on in the sitting-room, and they all fitted pretty well, and certainly were very becoming to the children.

'Now, recollect, you are all my grandchildren,' said Jacob; 'for I shall no longer call you Miss and Master – that we never do in a cottage. You understand me, Edward, of course?' added Jacob.

Edward nodded his head, and Jacob telling the children that they might now go out of the cottage and play, they all set off, quite delighted with clothes which procured them their liberty.

We must now describe the cottage of Jacob Armitage, in which the children have in future to dwell. As we said before, it contained a large sitting-room, or kitchen, in which were a spacious hearth and chimney, table, stools, cupboards, and dressers; the two bedrooms which adjoined it were now appropriated, one for Jacob, and the other for the two boys; the third, or inner bedroom, was arranged for the two girls, as being more retired and secure. But there were outhouses belonging to it; a stall, in which White Billy, the pony, lived during the winter; a shed and pig-sty rudely constructed, with an enclosed yard attached to them; and it had, moreover, a piece of ground of more than an acre, well fenced in to keep out the deer and game, the largest portion of which was cultivated as a garden and potato-ground, and the other, which remained in grass, contained some fine old apple and pear trees. Such was the domicile. The pony, a few fowls, a sow and two young pigs, and the dog Smoker, were the animals on the establishment. Here Jacob Armitage had been born – for the cottage had been built by his grandfather – but he had not always remained at the cottage. When young, he felt an inclination to see more of the world, and had for several years served in the army. His father and brother had lived in the establishment at Arnwood, and he was constantly there as a boy. The chaplain of Arnwood had taken a fancy to him, and taught him to read – writing he had not acquired. As soon as he grew up, he served, as we have said, in the troop commanded by Colonel Beverley's father; and after his death, Colonel Beverley had procured him the situation of forest ranger, which had been held by his father, who was then alive, but too aged to do the duty. Jacob Armitage married a good and devout young woman, with whom he lived several years, when she died, without bringing him any family; after which, his father being also dead, Jacob Armitage had lived alone until the period at which we have commenced this history.

23

CHAPTER 4

The old forester lay awake the whole of this night, reflecting how he should act relative to the children; he felt the great responsibility that he had incurred, and was alarmed when he considered what might be the consequences if his days were shortened. What would become of them – living in so sequestered a spot that few knew even of its existence – totally shut out from the world, and left to their own resources? He had no fear if his life was spared, that they would do well; but if he should be called away before they had grown up and were able to help themselves, they might perish. Edward was not fourteen years old. It was true that he was an active, brave boy, and thoughtful for his years; but he had not yet strength or skill sufficient for what would be required. Humphrey, the second, also promised well; but still they were all children. 'I must bring them up to be useful – to depend on themselves; there is not a moment to be lost, and not a moment shall be lost; I will do my best, and trust to God. I ask but two or three years, and by that time I trust that they will be able to do without me. They must commence tomorrow the life of forester's children.'

Acting upon this resolution, Jacob, as soon as the children were dressed and in the sitting-room, opened his Bible, which he had put on the table, and said –

'My dear children, you know that you must remain in this cottage, that the wicked troopers may not find you out; they killed your father, and if I had not taken you away they would have burnt you in your beds. You must therefore live here as my children, and you must call yourselves by the name of Armitage, and not that of Beverley; and you must dress like children of the forest, as you do now, and you must do as children of the forest do – that is, you must do everything for yourselves, for you can have no servants to wait upon you. We must all work; but you will like to work if you all work together, for then the work will be nothing but play. Now, Edward is the oldest, and he must go out with me in the forest, and I must teach him to kill deer and other game for our support; and when he knows how, then Humphrey shall come out and learn how to shoot.'

'Yes,' said Humphrey, 'I'll soon learn.'

'But not yet, Humphrey, for you must do some work in the meantime; you must look after the pony and the pigs, and you must learn to dig in the garden with Edward and me when we do not go out to hunt; and sometimes I shall go by myself, and leave Edward to work with you when there is work to be done. Alice, dear, you must, with Humphrey, light the fire and clean the house in the morning. Humphrey will go to the spring for water, and do all the hard work; and you must learn to wash, my dear Alice – I will show you how; and you must learn to get dinner ready with Humphrey, who will assist you; and to make the beds. And little Edith

24

shall take care of the fowls, and feed them every morning, and look for the eggs – will you, Edith?'

'Yes,' replied Edith, 'and feed all the little chickens when they are hatched, as I did at Arnwood.'

'Yes, dear, and you'll be very useful. Now you know that you cannot do all this at once. You will have to try and try again; but very soon you will, and then it will be all play. I must teach you all, and every day you will do it better, till you want no teaching at all. And now, my dear children, as there is no chaplain here, we must read the Bible every morning. Edward can read, I know; can you, Humphrey?'

'Yes, all except the big words.'

'Well, you will learn them by-and-by. And Edward and I will teach Alice and Edith to read in the evenings, when we have nothing to do. It will be an amusement. Now, tell me, do you all like what I have told you?'

'Yes,' they all replied; and then Jacob Armitage read a chapter in the Bible, after which they all knelt down and said the Lord's Prayer. As this was done every morning and every evening, I need not repeat it again. Jacob then showed them again how to clean the house, and Humphrey and Alice soon finished their work under his directions; and then they all sat down to breakfast, which was a very plain one, being generally cold meat, and cakes baked on the embers, at which Alice was soon very expert; and little Edith was very useful in watching them for her, while she busied herself about her other work. But the venison was nearly all gone; and after breakfast Jacob and Edward, with the dog Smoker, went out into the woods. Edward had no gun, as he only went out to be taught how to approach the game, which required great caution; indeed Jacob had no second gun to give him, if he had wished so to do.

'Now, Edward, we are going after a fine stag, if we can find him – which I doubt not – but the difficulty is to get within shot of him. Recollect that you must always be hid, for his sight is very quick; never be heard, for his ear is sharp; and never come down to him with the wind, for his scent is very fine. Then you must hunt according to the hour of the day. At this time he is feeding; two hours hence he will be lying down in the high fern. The dog is of no use unless the stag is badly wounded, when the dog will take him. Smoker knows his duty well, and will hide himself as close as we do. We are now going into the thick wood ahead of us, as there are many little spots of cleared ground in it where we may find the deer; but we must keep more to the left, for the wind is to the eastward, and we must walk up against it. And now that we are coming into the wood, recollect not a word must be said, and you must walk quietly as possible, keeping behind me. – Smoker, to heel!' They proceeded through the wood for more than a mile, when Jacob made a sign to Edward and dropped down into the fern, crawling along to an open spot, where, at some distance, were a stag and three deer grazing. The deer grazed quietly, but the stag was ever and anon raising up his head and snuffing the air as he looked round, evidently acting as a sentinel for the females.

The stag was perhaps a long quarter of a mile from where they had crouched down in the fern. Jacob remained immovable till the animal began to feed again, and then he advanced crawling through the fern, followed by Edward and the dog, who dragged himself on his stomach after Edward. This tedious approach was continued for some time, and they had neared the stag to within half the original distance, when the animal again lifted up his head and appeared uneasy. Jacob stopped and remained without motion. After a time the stag walked away, followed by the does, to the opposite side of the clear spot on which they had been feeding, and, to Edward's annoyance, the animal was now half a mile from them. Jacob turned round and crawled into the wood, and when he knew that they were concealed, he rose on his feet and said, –

'You see, Edward, that it requires patience to stalk a deer. What a princely fellow! but he has probably been alarmed this morning, and is very uneasy. Now we must go through the woods till we come to the lee of him on the other side of the dell. You see he has led the does close to the thicket, and we shall have a better chance when we get there, if we are only quiet and cautious.'

'What startled him, do you think?' said Edward.

'I think, when you were crawling through the fern after me, you broke a piece of rotten stick that was under you, did you not?'

'Yes, but that made but little noise.'

'Quite enough to startle a red deer, Edward, as you will find out before you have been long a forester. These checks will happen, and have happened to me a hundred times, and then all the work is to be done over again. Now then to make a circuit – we had better not say a word. If we get safe now to the other side, we are sure of him.'

They proceeded at a quick walk through the forest, and in half an hour had gained the side where the deer were feeding. When about three hundred yards from the game Jacob again sank down on his hands and knees, crawling from bush to bush, stopping whenever the stag raised his head, and advancing again when it resumed feeding. At last they came to the fern at the side of the wood, and crawled through it as before, but still more cautiously as they approached the stag. In this manner they arrived at last to within eighty yards of the animal, and then Jacob advanced his gun ready to put it to his shoulder, and as he cocked the lock, raised himself to fire. The click occasioned by the cocking of the lock roused up the stag instantly, and he turned his head in the direction from whence the noise proceeded. As he did so, Jacob fired, aiming behind the animal's shoulder; the stag made a bound, came down again, dropped on his knees, attempted to run, and fell dead, while the does fled away with the rapidity of the wind.

Edward started up on his legs with a shout of exultation. Jacob commenced reloading his gun, and stopped Edward as he was about to run up to where the animal lay.

'Edward, you must learn your craft,' said Jacob; 'never do that again;

26

never shout in that way. On the contrary, you should have remained still in the fern.'

'Why so? the stag is dead.'

'Yes, my dear boy, that stag is dead; but how do you know but that there may be another lying down in the fern close to us, or at some distance from us, which you have alarmed by your shout? Suppose that we both had had guns, and that the report of mine had started another stag lying in the fern within shot, you would have been able to shoot it; or if a stag was lying at a distance, the report of the gun might have startled him so as to induce him to move his head without rising. I should have seen his antlers move and have marked his lair, and we should then have gone after him and stalked him too.'

'I see,' replied Edward, 'I was wrong; but I shall know better another time.'

'That's why I tell you, my boy,' replied Jacob; 'now let us go to our quarry. Ay, Edward, this is a noble beast. I thought that he was a hart royal, and so he is.'

'What is a hart royal, Jacob?'

'Why, a stag is called a brocket until he is three years old; at four years he is a staggart; at five years a warrantable stag; and after five years he becomes a hart royal.'

'And how do you know his age?'

'By his antlers. You see that this stag has nine antlers; now, a brocket has but two antlers, a staggart three, and a warrantable stag but four; at six years old, the antlers increase in number until they sometimes have twenty or thirty. This is a fine beast, and the venison is now getting very good. Now you must see me do the work of my craft.'

Jacob then cut the throat of the animal, and afterwards cut off its head, and took out its bowels.

'Are you tired, Edward?' said Jacob, as he wiped his hunting-knife on the coat of the stag.

'No, not the least.'

'Well, then, we are now, I should think, about four or five miles from the cottage. Could you find your way home? But that is of no consequence, Smoker will lead you home by the shortest path. I will stay here, and you can saddle White Billy and come back with him, for he must carry the venison back. It's more than we can manage – indeed, as much as we can manage with White Billy to help us. There's more than twenty stone of venison lying there, I can tell you.'

Edward immediately assented, and Jacob, desiring Smoker to go home, set about flaying and cutting up the animal for its more convenient transportation. In an hour and a half, Edward, attended by Smoker, returned with the pony, on whose back the chief portion of the venison was packed. Jacob took a large piece on his own shoulders, and Edward carried another, and Smoker, after regaling himself with a portion of the inside of the animal, came after them. During the walk home, Jacob initiated Edward into the terms of venery and many other points connected with deer-stalking, with which we shall not trouble our readers. As soon as they arrived at the cottage, the venison was hung up, the pony put in the stable, and then they sat down to dinner with an excellent appetite after their long morning's walk. Alice and Humphrey had cooked the dinner themselves, and it was in the pot, smoking hot, when they returned; and Jacob declared he never ate a better mess in his life. Alice was not a little proud of this, and of the praises she received from Edward and the old forester. The next day Jacob stated his intention of going to Lymington to dispose of a large portion of the venison, and bring back a sack of oatmeal for their cakes. Edward asked to accompany him, but Jacob replied, –

'Edward, you must not think of showing yourself at Lymington, or anywhere else, for a long while, until you are grown out of memory. It would be folly, and you would risk your sisters' and brother's lives, perhaps, as well as your own. Never mention it again: the time will come when it will be necessary perhaps; if so, it cannot be helped. At present you would be known immediately. No, Edward, I tell you what I do mean to do: I have a little money left, and I intend to buy you a gun, that you may learn to stalk deer yourself without me; for recollect if any accident should happen to me, who is there but you to provide for your brother and sisters? At Lymington I am known to many, but out of all who know me there is not one who knows where my cottage is; they know that I live in the New Forest, and that I supply them venison, and purchase other articles in return. That is all that they know; and I may therefore go without fear. I shall sell the venison tomorrow, and bring you back a good gun; and Humphrey shall have the carpenter's tools which he wishes for – for I think, by what he does with his knife, that he has a turn that way, and it may be useful. I must also get some other tools for Humphrey and you, as we then shall be able to work all together; and some threads and needles for Alice, for she can sew a little, and practice will make her more perfect.'

Jacob went off to Lymington as he had proposed, and returned late at night with White Billy well loaded: he had a sack of oatmeal, some spades and hoes, a saw and chisels, and other tools; two scythes and two three-pronged forks; and when Edward came to meet him, he put into his hand a gun with a very long barrel.

'I believe, Edward, that you will find that a good one, for I know where it came from. It belonged to one of the rangers, who was reckoned the best shot in the forest. I know the gun, for I have seen it on his arm, and have taken it in my hand to examine it, more than once. He was killed at Naseby, with your father, poor fellow! and his widow sold the gun to meet her wants.'

'Well!' replied Edward, 'I thank you much, Jacob, and I will try if I cannot kill as much venison as will pay back the purchase-money – I will, I assure you.'

'I shall be glad if you do, Edward; not because I want the money back, but because then I shall be more easy in my mind about you all if anything happens to me. As soon as you are perfect in your woodcraft, I shall take Humphrey in hand, for there is nothing like having two strings to your bow. Tomorrow we will not go out: we have meat enough for three weeks or more; and now the frost has set in, it will keep well. You shall practise at a mark with your gun, that you may be accustomed to it; for all guns, even the best, require a little humouring.'

Edward, who had often fired a gun before, proved the next morning that he had a very good eye, and after two or three hours' practice, hit the mark at a hundred yards almost every time.

'I wish you would let me go out by myself,' said Edward, overjoyed at his success.

'You would bring home nothing, boy,' replied Jacob. 'No, no, you have a great deal to learn yet. But I tell you what you shall do: any time that we are not in great want of venison, you shall have the first fire.'

'Well, that will do,' replied Edward.

The winter now set in with great severity, and they remained almost altogether within doors. Jacob and the boys went out to get firewood, and dragged it home through the snow.

'I wish, Jacob,' said Humphrey, 'that I was able to build a cart, for it would be very useful, and White Billy would then have something to do; but I can't make the wheels, and there is no harness.'

'That's not a bad idea of yours, Humphrey,' replied Jacob; 'we will think about it. If you can't build a cart, perhaps I can buy one. It would be useful if it were only to take the dung out of the yard on to the potato-ground; for I have hitherto carried it out in baskets, and it's hard work.'

'Yes, and we might saw the wood into billets, and carry it home in the cart instead of dragging it this way: my shoulder is quite sore with the rope, it cuts me so.'

'Well, when the weather breaks up, I will see what I can do, Humphrey; but just now the roads are so blocked up that I do not think we could get a cart from Lymington to the cottage, although we can a horse, perhaps.'

But if they remained indoors during the inclement weather, they were not idle. Jacob took this opportunity to instruct the children in everything. Alice learnt how to wash and how to cook. It is true that sometimes she scalded herself a little, sometimes burnt her fingers; and other accidents did occur, from the articles employed being too heavy for them to lift by themselves; but practice and dexterity compensated for want of strength, and fewer accidents happened every day. Humphrey had his carpenter's tools; and although at first he had many failures, and wasted nails and wood, by degrees he learnt to use his tools with more dexterity, and made several little useful articles. Little Edith could now do something, for she made and baked all the oatmeal cakes, which saved Alice a good deal of time and trouble in watching them. It was astonishing how much the children could do now there was no one to do it for them; and they had daily instruction from Jacob. In the evenings Alice sat down with her needle and thread to mend the clothes. At first they were not very well done, but she improved every day. Edith and Humphrey learnt to read while Alice worked, and then Alice learnt; and thus the winter passed away so rapidly that, although they had been five months at the cottage, it did not appear as if they had been there as many weeks. All were happy and contented, with the exception, perhaps, of Edward, who had fits of gloominess, and occasionally showed signs of impatience as to what was passing in the world, of which he remained in ignorance.

That Edward Beverley had fits of gloominess and impatience is not surprising. Edward had been brought up as the heir of Arnwood; and a boy at a very early age imbibes notions of his position, if it promises to be a high one. He was not two miles from that property which by right was his own. His own mansion had been reduced to ashes, he himself was hidden in the forest, and he could not but feel his position. He sighed for the time when the King's cause should be again triumphant, and his arrival at that age when he could in person support and uphold the cause. He longed to be in command, as his father had been – to lead his men on to victory – to recover his property, and to revenge himself on those who had acted so cruelly towards him. This was human nature; and much as Jacob Armitage would expostulate with him, and try to divert his feelings into other channels, long as he would preach to him about forgiveness of injuries, and patience until better times should come, Edward could not help brooding over these thoughts, and if ever there was a breast animated with intense hatred against the Puritans, it was that of Edward Beverley. Although this was to be lamented, it could not create surprise or wonder in the old forester. All he could do was as much as possible to reason with him, to soothe his irritated feelings, and by constant employment try to make him forget for a time the feelings of ill-will which he had conceived.

One thing was, however, sufficiently plain to Edward, which was, that whatever might be his wrongs, he had not the power at present to redress them; and this feeling, perhaps, more than any other, held him in some sort of check; and as the time when he might have an opportunity appeared far distant, even to his own sanguine imagination, so by degrees did he contrive to dismiss from his thoughts what it was no use to think about at present.

CHAPTER 5

As we have before said, time passed rapidly; with the exception of one or two excursions after venison, they remained in the cottage, and Jacob never went to Lymington. The frost had broken up, the snow had long disappeared, and the trees began to bud. The sun became powerful, and in the month of May the forest began again to look green.

'And now, Edward,' said Jacob Armitage, one day at breakfast, 'we will try for venison again to sell at Lymington, for I must purchase Humphrey's cart and harness; so let us get our guns and go out this fine morning. The stags are mostly by themselves at this season, for the does are with their young calves. We must find the slot of a deer, and track him to his lair, and you shall have the first shot if you like; but that, however, depends more upon the deer than upon me.'

They had walked four or five miles when they came upon the slot or track of a deer; but Jacob's practised eye pointed out to Edward that it was the slot of a young one, and not worth following. He explained to Edward the difference in the hoofmarks and other signs by which this knowledge was gained, and they proceeded onwards until they found another slot, which Jacob declared to be that of a warrantable stag – that is, one old enough to kill and to be good venison.

'We must now track him to his lair, Edward.'

This took them about a mile further, when they arrived at a small thicket of thorns about an acre in extent.

'Here he is, you see, Edward; let me now see if he is harboured.'

They walked round the thicket, and could not find any slot or track by which the stag had left the covert, and Jacob pronounced that the animal must be hid in it.

'Now, Edward, do you stay here while I go back to the lee side of the covert: I will enter it with Smoker, and the stag will, in all probability, when he is roused, come out to breast the wind. You will then have a good shot at him. Recollect to fire so as to hit him behind the shoulder; if he is moving quick, fire a little before the shoulders; if slow, take aim accurately; but recollect, if I come upon him in the covert, I shall kill him if I can, for we want the venison, and then we will go after another to give you a chance.'

Jacob then left Edward, and went down to the lee side of the covert, where he entered it with Smoker. Edward was stationed behind a thorn-bush, which grew a few yards clear of the covert, and he soon heard the creaking of the branches.

A short time elapsed, and a fine stag came out at a trot; he turned his head, and was just bounding away, when Edward fired, and the animal fell. Remembering the advice of Jacob, Edward remained where he was, in silence reloading his piece, and was soon afterwards joined by Jacob and the dog.

'Well done, Edward!' said the forester, in a low voice, and covering his forehead to keep off the glare of the sun, he looked earnestly at a high brake between some thorn-trees, about half a mile to windward. 'I think I see something there – look, Edward, your eyes are younger than mine. Is that the branch of a tree in the fern, or is it not?'

'I see what you mean,' replied Edward. 'It is not; it moves.'

'I thought so, but my eyes are not so good as they once were. It's another stag, depend upon it; but how to get near him – we never can get across this patch of dear grass without being seen.'

'No, we cannot get at him from this spot,' replied Edward; 'but if we were to fall back to leeward, and gain the forest again, I think that there are thorns sufficient from the forest to where he lies to creep from behind one to the other, so as to get a shot at him; don't you?'

'It will require care and patience to manage that; but I think it might be done. I will try; it is my turn now, you know. You had better stay here with the dog, for only one can hide from thorn to thorn.'

Jacob, ordering Smoker to remain, then set off. He had to make a circuit of three miles to get to the spot where the thorns extended from the forest and Edward saw no more of him, although he strained his eyes, until the stag sprung out, and the gun was discharged. Edward perceived that the stag was not killed, but severely wounded, running towards the covert near which he was hid. 'Down, Smoker,' said he, as he cocked his gun. The stag came within shot, and was coming nearer, when, seeing Edward, it turned. Edward fired, and then cheered on the dog, who sprang after the wounded animal, giving tongue as he followed him. Edward, perceiving Jacob hastening towards him, waited for him.

'He's hard hit, Edward,' cried Jacob, 'and Smoker will have him; but we must follow as fast as we can.'

They both caught up their guns and ran as fast as they could, when, as they entered the wood, they heard the dog at bay.

'We shan't have far to go, Edward; the animal is done up, Smoker has him at bay.'

They hastened on another quarter of a mile, when they found that the stag had fallen on his knees, and had been seized by the throat by Smoker.

'Mind, Edward, now how I go up to him, for the wound from the horn of the deer is very dangerous.'

Jacob advanced from behind the stag, and cut his throat with his hunting-knife. 'He is a fine beast, and we have done well today; but we shall have two journeys to make to get all this venison home. I could not get a fair shot at him – and see, I have hit him here in the flank.'

'And here is my ball in his throat,' said Edward.

'So it is. Then it was a good shot that you made, and you are master of the hunt this day, Edward. Now, I'll remain, and you go home for White Billy. Humphrey is right about the cart. If we had one, we could have carried all home at once; but I must go now and cut the throat of the other stag which you killed so cleverly. You will be a good hunter one of these days, Edward. A little more knowledge, and a little more practice, and I will leave it all to you, and hang my gun up over the chimney.'

It was late in the evening before they had made their two trips and taken all the venison home, and very tired were they before it was all safely housed. Edward was delighted with his success, but not more so than was old Jacob. The next morning, Jacob set off for Lymington, with the pony loaded with venison, which he sold, as well as two more loads which he promised to bring the next day, and the day after. He then looked out for a cart, and was fortunate in finding a small one just fitted to the size of the pony, who was not tall, but very strong, as all New Forest ponies are. He also procured harness, and then put Billy in the cart to draw him home; but Billy did not admire being put in a cart, and for some time was very restive, and backed and reared, and went every way but the right. But by dint of coaxing and leading, he at last submitted, and went straight on; but then the noise of the cart behind him frightened him, and he ran away. At last, having tired himself out, he thought that he might as well go quietly in harness, as he could not get out of it; and he did so, and arrived safe at the cottage. Humphrey was delighted at the sight of the cart, and said that now he should get on well. The next day, Jacob contrived to put all the remainder of the venison in the cart, and White Billy made no more difficulty; he dragged it all to Lymington, and returned with the cart as quietly and cleverly as if he had been in harness all his life.

'Well, Edward, the venison paid for the cart, at all events,' said Jacob; 'and now I will tell you all the news I collected while I was as Lymington. Captain Burly, who attempted to incite the people to rescue the King, has been hung, drawn, and quartered, as a traitor.'

'They are traitors who condemned him,' replied Edward in wrath.

'Yes, so they are; but there is better news, which is, that the Duke of York has escaped to Holland.'

'Yes, that is good news; and the King?'

'He is still a prisoner in Carisbrook Castle. There are many rumours and talks, but no one knows what is true, and what is false; but depend upon it, this cannot last long, and the King will have his rights yet.'

Edward remained very grave for some time.

'I trust in Heaven we all shall have our rights yet, Jacob,' said he at last. 'I wish I was a man!'

Here the conversation ended, and they went to bed.

This was now a busy time at the cottage. The manure had to be got out of the stable and pig-sties, and carried out to the potato-ground and garden; the crops had to be put in; and the cart was now found valuable. After the manure had been carried out and spread, Edward and Humphrey helped Jacob to dig the ground, and then to put in the seed. The cabbage-plants of last year were then put out, and the turnips and carrots sown. Before the month was over, the garden and potato-field were cropped, and Humphrey took upon himself to weed and keep it clean. Little Edith had also employment now; for the hens began to lay eggs, and as soon as she heard them cackling, she ran for the eggs and brought them in; and before the month was over, Jacob had set four hens upon eggs. Billy, the pony, was now turned out to graze in the forest; he came home every night of his own accord.

'I'll tell you what we want,' said Humphrey, who took the command altogether over the farm; 'we want a cow.'

'Oh, yes, a cow,' cried Alice; 'I have plenty of time to milk her.'

'Whose cows are those which I see in the forest sometimes?' said Humphrey to Jacob.

'If they belong to anybody, they belong to the King,' replied Jacob; 'but they are cattle which have strayed and found their way to the forest, and have remained here ever since. They are rather wild and savage, and you must be careful how you go too near them, as the bulls will run at you. They increase very fast; there were but six a few years ago, and now there are at least fifty in the herd.'

'Well, I'll try and get one, if I can,' said Humphrey.

'You will be puzzled to do that, boy,' replied Jacob; 'and as I said before, beware of the bulls.'

'I don't want a bull,' replied Humphrey; 'but a cow would give us milk, and then we should have more manure for the garden. My garden will then grow more potatoes.'

'Well, Humphrey, if you can catch a cow, no one will interfere; but I think you will not find it very easy, and you may find it very dangerous.'

'I'll look out for one,' replied Humphrey, 'anyhow. Alice, if we only had a cow, wouldn't that be jolly?'

The crops were now all up, and as the days began to be long, the work became comparatively light and easy. Humphrey was busy making a little wheelbarrow for Edith, that she might barrow away the weeds as he hoed them up; and at last this great performance was completed, much to the admiration of all, and much to his own satisfaction. Indeed, when it is recollected that Humphrey had only the handsaw and axe, and that he had to cut down the tree, and then to saw it into plank, it must be acknowledged that it required great patience and perseverance even to make a wheelbarrow; but Humphrey was not only persevering, but was full of invention. He had built up a hen-house with fir poles, and made the nests for the hens to lay and hatch in, and they now had between forty and fifty chickens running about. He had also divided the pig-sty, so that the sow might be kept apart from the other pigs; and they expected very soon to have a litter of young pigs. He had transplanted the wild strawberries from the forest, and had, by manure, made them large and good; and he had also a fine crop of onions in the garden, from seed which Jacob had bought at Lymington; now Humphrey was very busy cutting down some poles in the forest to make a cow-house, for he declared that he would have a cow somehow or another. June arrived, and it was time to mow down grass to make into hay for the winter, and Jacob had two scythes. He showed the boys how to use them, and they soon became expert; and as there was plenty of long grass at this time of the year, and they could mow when they pleased, they soon had White Billy in full employment carrying the hay home. The little girls helped to make it, for Humphrey had made them two rakes. Jacob thought that there was hay enough made, but Humphrey said that there was enough for the pony, but not enough for the cow.

'But where is the cow to come from, Humphrey?'

'Where the venison comes from,' replied he – 'out of the forest.'

So Humphrey continued to mow and make hay, while Edward and Jacob went out for venison. After all the hay was made and stacked,

Humphrey found out a method of thatching with fern, which Jacob had never thought of, and when that was done, they commenced cutting down fern for fodder. Here again Humphrey would have twice as much as Jacob had ever cut before, because he wanted litter for the cow. At last it became quite a joke between him and Edward, who, when he brought home more venison than would keep in the hot weather, told Humphrey that the remainder was for the cow. Still Humphrey would not give up the point, and every morning and evening he would be certain to be absent an hour or two, and it was found out he was watching the herd of wild cattle who were feeding: sometimes they were very near, at others a long way off. He used to get up into the trees, and examine them as they passed under him, without perceiving him. One night Humphrey returned very late, and the next morning he was off before daylight. Breakfast was over, and Humphrey did not make his appearance, and they could not tell what was the matter. Jacob felt uneasy, but Edward laughed, and said, –

'Oh, depend upon it, he'll come back and bring the cow with him.'

Hardly had Edward said these words, when in came Humphrey red with perspiration.

'Now then, Jacob and Edward, come with me; we must put Billy in the cart, and take Smoker and a rope with us. Take your guns too, for fear of accident.'

'Why, what's the matter?'

'I'll tell you as we go along; but I must put Billy in the cart, for there is no time to be lost.'

Humphrey disappeared, and Jacob said to Edward, –

'What can it be?'

'It can be nothing but the cow he is so mad about,' replied Edward. 'However, when he comes with the pony, we shall know; let us take our guns and the dog Smoker as he wishes.'

Humphrey now drove up the pony and cart, and they set off.

'Well, I suppose you'll tell us now what we are going for?' said Edward.

'Yes, I will. You know I've been watching the cattle for a long while, because I wanted a cow. I have been in a tree when they have passed under me several times, and I observed that one or two of the heifers were very near calving. Yesterday evening I thought one could not help calving very soon indeed, and as I was watching, I saw that she was uneasy, and that she at last left the herd and went into a little copse of wood. I remained three hours to see if she came out again, and she did not. It was dark when I came home, as you know. This morning I went before daylight and found the herd. She is very remarkable, being black and white spotted; and, after close examination, I found that she was not with the herd, so I am sure that she went into the copse to calve, and that she has calved before this.

'Well, that may be,' replied Jacob; 'but now I do not understand what we are to do.'

'Nor I,' replied Edward.

'Well, then, I'll tell you what I hope to do. I have got the pony and cart to take the calf home with us, if we can get it – which I think we can. I have got Smoker to worry the heifer and keep her employed while we put the call in the cart; a rope that we may tie the cow, if we can; and you with your guns must keep off the herd, if they come to her assistance. Now do you understand my plan?'

'Yes, and I think it very likely to succeed, Humphrey,' replied Jacob, 'and I give you credit for the scheme. We will help you all we can. Where is the copse?'

'Not half a mile further,' replied Humphrey. 'We shall soon be there.'

On their arrival, they found that the herd were feeding at a considerable distance from the copse, which was perhaps as well.

'Now,' said Jacob, 'I and Edward will enter into the copse with Smoker, and you follow us, Humphrey. I will make Smoker seize the heifer if necessary; at all events he will keep her at bay – that is, if she is here. First let us walk round the copse and find her slot, as we call the track of a deer. See, here is her footing. Now let us go in.'

They advanced cautiously into the thicket, following the track of the heifer, and at last came upon her. Apparently she had not calved more than an hour, and was licking the calf, which was not yet on its legs. As soon as the animal perceived Jacob and Edward she shook her head, and was about to run at them; but Jacob told Smoker to seize her, and the dog flew at her immediately. The attack of the dog drove back the heifer quite into the thicket, and as the dog bounded round her, springing this way and that way to escape her horns, the heifer was soon separated from the calf.

'Now then, Edward and Humphrey,' said Jacob, advancing between the heifer and the calf, 'lift up the call between you and put it in the cart. Leave Smoker and me to manage the mother.'

The boys put their arms under me stomach of the call and carried it away. The heifer was at first too busy defending herself against the dog to perceive that the call was gone; when she did, Jacob called Smoker to him, so as to bring him between the heifer and where the boys were going out of the thicket. At last the heifer gave a loud bellow, and rushed out of the thicket in pursuit of her calf, checked by Smoker, who held on to her ear, and sometimes stopped her from advancing.

'Hold her, Smoker,' said Jacob, who now went back to help the boys. 'Hold her, boy. – Is the calf in the cart?'

'Yes, and tied fast,' replied Edward; 'and we are in the cart, too.'

'That's right,' replied Jacob. 'Now I'll get in too, and let us drive off. She'll follow us, depend upon it. – Here, Smoker! Smoker! let her alone.'

Smoker, at this command, came bounding out of the copse, followed by the heifer, lowing most anxiously. Her lowing was responded to by the calf in the cart, and she ran wildly up to it.

'Drive off, Humphrey,' said Jacob; 'I think I heard the lowing of the heifer answered by some of the herd, and the sooner we are off the better.'

Humphrey, who had the reins, drove off; the heifer followed, at one time running at the dog, at another putting her head almost into the hind part of the cart; but the lowing of the heifer was now answered by deeper tones, and Jacob said, –

'Edward, get your gun ready, for I think the herd is following. Do not fire, however, till I tell you. We must be governed by circumstances. It won't do to lose the pony, or to run any serious risk, for the sake of the heifer and calf. Drive fast, Humphrey.'

A few minutes afterwards they perceived at about a quarter of a mile behind them, not the whole herd, but a single bull, who was coming up at a fast trot with his tail in the air, and tossing his head, lowing deeply in answer to the heifer.

'There's only one, after all,' said Jacob; 'I suppose the heifer is his favourite. Well, we can manage him. – Smoker, come in. Come in, sir, directly,' cried Jacob, perceiving that the dog was about to attack the bull.

Smoker obeyed, and the bull advanced till he was within a hundred yards.

'Now, Edward, do you fire first – aim for his shoulder. Humphrey, pull up.'

Humphrey stopped the pony, and the bull continued to advance, but seemed puzzled whom to attack, unless it was the dog. As soon as the bull was within sixty yards, Edward fired, and the animal fell down on its knees, tearing the ground with its horns.

'That will do,' said Jacob. 'Drive on again, Humphrey; we will have a look at that fellow by-and-by. At present we had better get home, as others may come. He's up again, but he is at a standstill. I have an idea that he is hit hard.'

The cart drove on, followed by the heifer; but no more of the wild herd made their appearance, and they very soon gained the cottage.

'Now, then, what shall we do?' said Jacob. 'Come, Humphrey, you have had all the ordering of this, and have done it well.'

'Well, Jacob, we must now drive the cart into the yard, and shut the gate upon the cow, till I am ready.'

'That's easy done, by setting Smoker at her,' replied Jacob; 'but mercy on us, there's Alice and Edith running out! – the heifer may kill them! Go back, Alice! run quite into the cottage, and shut the door till we come.'

Alice and Edith hearing this, and Edward also crying out to them, made a hasty retreat to the cottage. Humphrey then packed the cart against the paling of the yard, so as to enable Edward to get on the other side of it, ready to open the gate. Smoker was set at the heifer, and, as before, soon engaged her attention; so that the gate was opened and the cart drove in, and the gate closed again, before the heifer could follow.

'Well, Humphrey, what next?'

'Why, now lift the calf out and put it into the cow-house. I will go into the cow-house with a rope and a slip-knot at the end of it, get upon the beam above, and drop it over her horns as she's busy with the calf, which she will be as soon as you let her in. I shall pass the end of the rope outside, for you to haul up when I am ready, and then we shall have her fast, till we can secure her properly. When I call out "ready" do you open the gate and let her in. You can do that and jump into the cart afterwards, for fear she may run at you; but I don't think that she will, for it's the calf she wants, and not either of you.'

As soon as Humphrey was ready with the rope, he gave the word, and the gate was opened; the cow ran in immediately, and hearing her calf bleat, went into the cow-house, the door of which was shut upon her. A minute afterwards Humphrey cried out to them to haul upon the rope, which they did.

'That will do,' said Humphrey from the inside: 'now make the rope fast, and then you may come in.'

They went in, and found the heifer drawn close to the side of the cow-house by the rope which was round her horns, and unable to move her head.

'Well, Humphrey, that's very clever; but now what's to be done?'

'First I'll saw off the tips of her horns, and then if she does run at us, she won't hurt us much. Wait till I go for the saw.'

As soon as the ends of her horns were sawed off, Humphrey took another piece of rope, which he fastened securely round her horns, and then made the other end fast to the side of the building, so that the animal could move about a little and eat out of the crib.

'There,' said Humphrey, 'now time and patience will do the rest. We must coax her, and handle her, and soon shall tame her. At present let us leave her with the calf. She has a yard of rope, and that is enough for her to lick her calf, which is all she requires at present. Tomorrow we will cut some grass for her.'

They then went out, shutting the cow-house door.

'Well, Humphrey, you've beat us, after all, and have the laugh on your side now,' said Jacob. '"Where there's a will, there's a way," that's certain; and I assure you, that when you were making so much hay, and gathering so much litter, and building a cow-house, I had no more idea that we should have a cow than that we should have an elephant; and I will say that you deserve great credit for your way of obtaining it.'

'That he certainly does,' replied Edward. 'You have more genius than I have, brother. But dinner must be ready if Alice has done her duty. What think you, Jacob, shall we after dinner go and look after that bull?'

'Yes, by all means. He will not be bad eating, and I can sell all I can carry in the cart at Lymington. Besides, the skin is worth money.'

CHAPTER 6

Alice and Edith were very anxious to see the cow, and especially to see the calf; but Humphrey told them that they must not go near till he went with them, and then they should see it. After dinner was over, Jacob and Edward took their guns, and Humphrey put Billy in the cart and followed them. They found the bull where they left him, standing quite still. He tossed his head when they approached him, which they did carefully, but he did not attempt to run at them.

'It's my idea that he has nearly bled to death,' said Jacob; 'but there's nothing like making sure. Edward, put a bullet just three inches behind his shoulder, and that will make all safe.'

Edward did so, and the animal fell dead. They went up to the carcass, which they estimated to weigh at least fifty stone.

'It is a noble beast,' said Edward; 'I wonder we never thought of killing one before.'

'They aren't game, Edward,' replied Jacob.

'No, they are not now, Jacob,' said Humphrey. 'As you and Edward claim all the game, I shall claim the cattle as my portion of the forest. Recollect, there are more, and I mean to have more of them yet.'

'Well, Humphrey, I give you up all my rights, if I have any.'

'And I all mine,' added Edward.

'Be it so. Some day you'll see what I shall do,' replied Humphrey. 'Recollect, I am to sell the cattle for my own self-advantage until I buy a gun, and one or two things which I want.'

'I agree to that too, Humphrey,' replied Jacob; 'and now to skin the beast.'

The skinning and quartering took up the whole afternoon, and Billy was heavily laden when he drew his cart home. The next day Jacob went to Lymington to sell the bull and the skin, and returned home well satisfied with the profit he had made. He had procured, as Humphrey requested, some milk-pans, a small churn, and milk-pail, out of the proceeds, and had still money left. Humphrey told them that he had not been to see the heifer yet, as he thought it better not.

'She will be tame tomorrow morning depend upon it,' said he.

'But if you give her nothing to eat, will not the calf die?'

'Oh no, I should think not. I shall not starve her, but I will make her thankful for her food before she gets it. I shall cut her some grass tomorrow morning.'

We may as well here say that the next morning Humphrey went in to the heifer. At first she tossed about and was very unruly. He gave her some grass, and patted her and coaxed her for a long while, till at last she allowed him to touch her gently. Every day for a fortnight he brought her

her food, and she became quieter every day, till at last, if he went up to her, she never pushed with her horns. The calf became quite tame, and as the helper perceived that the calf was quiet, she became more quiet herself. After the fortnight, Humphrey would not allow the heifer to receive anything except from the hand of Alice, that the animal might know her well; and when the calf was a month old, Humphrey made the first attempt to milk her. This was resisted at first by kicking, but in the course of ten days she gave down her milk. Humphrey then let her loose for a few days to run about the yard, still keeping the calf in the cowhouse, and putting the heifer in to her at night, milking her before the calf was allowed to suck. After this, he adventured upon the last experiment, which was to turn her out of the yard to graze in the forest. She went away to some distance, and he was fearful that she would join the herd, but in the evening she came back again to her calf. After this he was satisfied, and turned her out every day, and they had no further trouble with her. He would not, however, wean the calf till the winter time, when she was shut up in the yard and fed on hay. He then weaned the calf, which was a cow calf, and they had no more trouble with the mother. Alice soon learnt to milk her, and she became very tractable and good-tempered. Such was the commencement of the dairy at the cottage.

'Jacob,' said Humphrey, 'when do you go to Lymington again?'

'Why, I do not know. The end of August as it is now, and the month of September is not good for venison, and therefore I do not see what I shall have to go for.'

'Well, I wish, when you do go, you would get something for Alice and something for me.'

'And what is it that Alice wants?'

'She wants a kitten.'

'Well, I think I may find that. And what do you want, Humphrey?'

'I want a dog. Smoker is yours altogether; I want a dog for myself, to bring up after my own fashion.'

'Well, I ought to look out for another dog; although Smoker is not old, yet one ought to have two dogs to one's gun, in case of accident.'

'I think so too,' replied Edward. 'See if you can get two puppies, one for Humphrey, and one for myself.'

'Well, I must not go to Lymington for them. I must cross the forest, to see some friends of mine whom I have not seen for a long while, and I may get some of the right sort of puppies there, just like Smoker. I'll do that at once, as I may have to wait for them, even if I do have the promise.'

'May I go with you, Jacob?' said Edward.

'Why, I would rather not; they may ask questions.'

'And so would I rather he would not, for he will shirk his work here.'

'Why, what is there to do, Humphrey?'

'Plenty to do, and hard work, Edward; the acorns are fit for beating down, and we want a great many bushels for the pigs. We have to fatten three, and to feed the rest during the winter. I cannot get on well with only

Alice and Edith; so if you are not very lazy, you will stay with us and help us.'

'Humphrey, you think of nothing but your pigs and farmyard.'

'And you are too great a hunter to think of anything but a stag; but a bird in the hand's worth two in the bush, in my opinion; and I'll make more by my farmyard than you ever will by the forest.'

'Humphrey has nothing to do with the poultry and eggs, has he, Edward? They belong to Edith and me; and Jacob shall take them to Lymington and sell them for us, and get us some new clothes for Sunday, for these begin to look rather worn – and no wonder.'

'No, dearest, the poultry are yours, and I will sell them for you as soon as you please, and buy what you wish with the money,' replied Jacob. 'Let Humphrey make all the money he can with his pigs.'

'Yes; and the butter belongs to me, if I make it,' said Alice.

'No, no,' replied Humphrey, 'that's not fair; I find cows, and get nothing for them. We must go halves, Alice.'

'Well, I have no objection to that,' said Alice, 'because you find the cows and feed them. I made a pound of butter yesterday, just to try what I could do; but it's not firm, Jacob. How is that?'

'I have seen the women make butter, and know now, Alice so next time I will be with you. I suppose you did not wash your buttermilk well out, nor put any salt in it.'

'I did not put any salt in it. '

'But you must, or the butter will not keep.'

It was arranged that Edward should stay at home to assist in collecting the acorns for the pigs, and that Jacob should cross the forest alone to see after the puppies; and he set off the next morning. He was away two days, and then returned; said that he had a promise of two puppies, and that he had chosen them; they were of the same breed as Smoker, but they were only a fortnight old, and could not be taken from the mother yet awhile, so that he had arranged to call again when they were three or four months old, and able to follow him across the forest. Jacob also said that he was very near being hurt by a stag that had made at him – for at that season of the year the stags were very dangerous and fierce – but that he had fired, and struck off one of the animal's horns, which made it turn.

'You must be careful, Edward, how you go about the forest now.'

'I have no wish to go,' replied Edward; 'as we cannot hunt, it is no use; but in November we shall begin again.'

'Yes,' replied Jacob, 'that will be soon enough. Tomorrow I will help you with the acorns, and the day afterwards, if I am spared, I will take Alice's poultry to Lymington for her.'

'Yes, and when you come back you will help me to churn, for then I shall have a good deal of cream.'

'And don't forget to buy the kitten, Jacob,' said Edith.

'What's the good of a kitten?' said Humphrey, who was very busy making a birdcage for Edith, having just finished one for Alice; 'she will only steal your cream and eat up your birds.'

'No, she won't; for we'll shut the door fast where the milk and cream is, and we'll hang the cages so high that Miss Puss won't be able to get at them.'

'Well, then, a kitten will be useful,' said Edward, 'for she will teach you to be careful.'

'My coat is a little the worse for wear, and so is yours, Edward. We must try if we cannot, like Alice, find means to pay for another.'

'Humphrey,' said Jacob, 'I'll buy all you want, and trust to you for paying me again as soon as you can.'

'That's just what I want,' replied Humphrey. 'Then you must buy me a gun and a new suit of clothes first; when I've paid for them, I shall want some more tools, and some nails and screws, and two or three other things; but I will say nothing about them just now. Get me my gun, and I'll try what the forest will do for me – especially after I have my dog.'

'Well, we shall see; perhaps you'll like to come out with me sometimes and learn woodcraft, for Edward knows as much as I do now, and can go out by himself.'

'Of course I will, Jacob; I want to learn everything.'

'Well, there's a little money left in the bag yet, and I will go to Lymington tomorrow. Now I think it is time that we went to bed; and if you are all as tired as I am, you will sleep soundly.'

Jacob put into the cart the next day about forty of the chickens which Alice had reared; the others were kept to increase the number in the poultry-yard. They had cost little or nothing bringing up; for when quite young they had only a little oatmeal cake, and afterwards, with the potatoes which were left, they found themselves, as fowls can always do when they have a great range of ground to go over.

Jacob came back at sunset with all the articles. He brought a new suit for Alice and Edith, with some needles, and thread, and worsted, and gave Alice some money which was left from the sale of the chickens, after he had made the purchases. He also bought a new suit for Edward and Humphrey, and a gun, which was much approved of by Humphrey, as it had a larger bore and carried a heavier bullet than either Jacob's or Edward's; and there was a white kitten for Alice and Edith. There was no news, only that the Levellers had opposed Cromwell, and he had put them down with the other troops, and Jacob said that it appeared that they were all squabbling and fighting with each other.

Time passed, the month of November came on without anything to disturb the daily employments of the family in the forest, when one evening Jacob, who had returned from hunting with Edward (the first time they had been out since the season commenced), told Alice that she must do all she could to give them a good dinner the next day, as it was to be a feast.

'Why, so, Jacob?'

'If you cannot guess, I won't tell you till the time comes,' replied Jacob.

'Well, then, Humphrey must help us,' replied Alice, 'and we will do what we can. I will try, now that we have some meat, to make a grand dinner.'

Alice made all the preparations, and had for dinner the next day, a piece of baked venison, a venison stew, a pair of roast chickens, and an apple pie – which, for them, was a very grand dinner indeed. And it was very well dressed: for Jacob had taught her to cook, and by degrees she improved upon Jacob's instruction. Humphrey was quite as clever at it as she was; and little Edith was very useful, as she plucked the fowls, and watched the things while they were cooking.

'And now I'll tell you,' said Jacob, after saying grace, 'why I asked you for a feast this day. It is because exactly on this day twelvemonth I brought you all to the cottage. Now you know.'

'I did not know it certainly, but I dare say you are right,' replied Edward.

'And now, children, tell me,' said Jacob, 'has not this year passed very quickly and very happily – quite as quickly and quite as happily as if you had been staying at Arnwood?'

'Yes, more so,' replied Humphrey; 'for then very often I did not know what to do to amuse myself, and since I have been here the days have always been too short.'

'I agree with Humphrey,' said Edward.

'And I am sure I do,' replied Alice; 'I'm always busy, and always happy, and I'm never scolded about dirtying my clothes or tearing them, as I used to be.'

'And what does little Edith say?'

'I like to help Alice, and I like to play with the kitten,' replied Edith.

'Well, my children,' said Jacob, 'depend upon it, you are most happy when your days pass quickest, and that is only the case when you have plenty to do. Here you are in peace and safety; and may it please God that you may continue so! We want very few things in this world – that is, we really want very few things, although we wish and sigh for many. You have health and spirits, which are the greatest blessings in life. Who would believe, to look at you all, that you were the same children that I brought away from Arnwood? You were then very different from what you are now. You are strong and healthy, rosy and brown, instead of being fair and delicate. Look at your sisters, Edward. Do you think that any of your former friends – do you think that Martha, who had the care of them, would know them?'

Edward smiled, and said, 'Certainly not; especially in their present dresses.'

'Nor would, I think, Humphrey be known again. You, Edward, were always a stout boy; and, except that you have grown very much, and are more brown, there is no great difference. You would be known again, even in your present forester's dress; but what I say is, that we ought to be thankful to the Almighty that you, instead of being burnt in your beds, have found

43

health, and happiness, and security, in a forester's hut; and I ought to be, and am, most thankful to heaven, that it has pleased it to spare my life, and enable me to teach you all to the present how to gain your own livelihoods after I am called away. I have been able so far to fulfil my promise to your noble father; and you know not what a heavy load on my mind is every day lessened, as I see each day that you are more and more able to provide for yourselves. God bless you, dear children, and may you live to see many returns, and happy returns, of the day'; and Jacob was so much moved as he said this, that a tear was seen rolling down his furrowed cheek.

The second winter now came on. Jacob and Edward went out hunting usually about twice a week; for the old forester complained of stiffness and rheumatism, and not feeling so active as he used to be. Humphrey now accompanied Edward perhaps one day in the week, but not more, and they seldom returned without having procured venison, for Edward knew his business well, and no longer needed the advice of Jacob. As the winter advanced, Jacob gave up going out altogether. He went to Lymington to sell the venison and procure what was necessary for the household; such as oatmeal and flour, which were the principal wants; but even these journeys weakened him, and it was evident that the old man's constitution was breaking fast. Humphrey was always busy. One evening he was making something which puzzled them all. They asked him what it was for, but he would not tell them.

'It's an experiment that I am trying,' said he, as he was bending a hazel stick. 'If it answers, you shall know; if it does not, I've only had a little trouble for nothing. Jacob, I hope you will not forget the salt tomorrow when you go to Lymington, for my pigs are ready for killing, and we must salt the greatest part of the pork. After the legs and shoulders have lain long enough in salt, I mean to try if I cannot smoke them, and if I do, I'll then smoke some bacon. Won't that be jolly, Alice? Won't you like to have a great piece of bacon hanging up there, and only to have to get on a stool to cut off what you want, when Edward and I come home hungry, and you've nothing to give us to eat?'

'I shall be very glad to have it, and I think so will you too, by the way you talk.'

'I shall, I assure you. – Jacob, didn't you say the ash sticks were the best to smoke bacon with?'

'Yes, boy: when you are ready, I'll tell you how to manage. My poor mother used to smoke very well up this very chimney.'

'I think that will do,' said Humphrey, letting his hazel stick spring up, after he had bent it down, 'but tomorrow I shall find out.'

'But what is it for, Humphrey?' said Edith.

'Go away, puss, and play with your kitten,' replied Humphrey, putting away his tools and his materials in a corner. 'I've a great deal on my hands now, but I must kill my pigs before I think of anything else.'

The next day Jacob took the venison into Lymington, and brought back the salt and other articles required. The pigs were then killed, and salted down under Jacob's directions; his rheumatism did not allow him to assist, but Humphrey and Edward rubbed in the salt, and Alice took the pieces of pork away to the tub when they were finished. Humphrey had been out the day before with the unknown article he had been so long about. The next morning he went out early before breakfast, and when he returned he brought a hare in his hand, which he laid on the table.

'There,' said he, 'my spring has answered, and this is the fruits of it. Now I'll make some more, and we will have something by way of a change for dinner.'

They were very much pleased with Humphrey's success, and he was not a little proud of it.

'How did you find out how to make it?'

'Why, I read in the old book of travels, which Jacob brought home with him last summer, of people catching rabbits and hares in some way like this; I could not make it out exactly, but it gave me the idea.'

We ought to have told the reader that Jacob had more than once brought home an old book or two which he had picked up, or had given him, and that these had been occasionally looked into by Humphrey and Edward, but only now and then, as they had too much to do to find much time for reading, although sometimes, in the evening, they did take them up. When it is considered how young they were and what a practical and busy life they led, this cannot be surprising.

CHAPTER 7

Humphrey was now after something else. He had made several traps, and brought in rabbits and hares almost every day. He had also made some bird-traps, and had caught two goldfinches for Alice and Edith, which they put in the cages he had made for them. But as we said, Humphrey was about something else: he was out early in the morning, and in the evening, when the moon was up, he came home late, long after they had all gone to bed; but they never knew why, nor would he tell them. A heavy fall of snow took place, and Humphrey was more out than ever. At last, about a week after snow had lain on the ground, one morning he came in with a hare and rabbit in his hand, and said, –

'Edward, I have caught something larger than a hare or a rabbit, and you must come and help me, and we must take our guns. – Jacob, I suppose your rheumatism is too bad to let you come too?'

'No; I think I can manage. It's the damp that hurts me so much. This frosty air will do me good, perhaps. I have been much better since the snow fell. Now, then, let us see what you have caught.'

'You will have to walk two miles,' said Humphrey, as they went out.

'I can manage it, Humphrey; so lead the way.'

Humphrey went on till they came close to a clump of large trees, and then brought them to a pitfall which he had dug, about six feet wide and eight feet long and nine feet deep.

'There's my large trap,' said Humphrey, 'and see what I have caught in it.'

They looked down into the pit, and perceived a young bull in it. Smoker, who was with them, began to bark furiously at it.

'Now, what are we to do? I don't think it is hurt. Can we get it out?' said Humphrey.

'No, not very well. If it was a calf, we might; but it is too heavy: and if we were to get it out alive, we must kill it afterwards, so we had better shoot it at once.'

'So I think,' replied Humphrey.

'But how did you catch him?' said Edward.

'I read of it in the same book I did about the traps for hares,' replied Humphrey. 'I dug out the pit and covered it with brambles, and then put snow at the top. This is the thicket that the herd comes to chiefly in winter-time – it is large and dry, and the large trees shelter it; so that is why I chose this spot. I took a large bundle of hay, put some on the snow about the pit, and then strewed some more about in small handfuls, so that the cattle must find it, and pick it up, which I knew they would be glad to do, now that the snow is on the ground. And now, you see, I have succeeded.'

'Well, Humphrey, you beat us, I will say,' said Edward. 'Shall I shoot him?'

'Yes, now that he is looking up.'

Edward shot his ball through the forehead of the animal, which fell dead. But they were then obliged to go home for the pony and cart, and ropes to get the animal out of the pit, and a hard job they had of it too; but the pony helped them, and they did get it out at last.

'I will do it easier next time,' said Humphrey. 'I will make a windlass as soon as I can, and we will soon hoist out another, like they turn a bucket of water up from a well.'

'It's nice young meat,' said Jacob, who was skinning the bull, 'not above eighteen months old, I should think. Had it been a full-grown one, like that we shot, it must have remained where it was, for we never could have got it out.'

'Yes, Jacob, we should; for I should have gone down and cut it up in the pit, so that we would have handed it out by bits, if we could not have managed him whole.'

They loaded the cart with the skin and quarters of the animal, and then drove home.

'This will go far to pay for the gun, Humphrey,' said Jacob, 'if it don't pay for more.'

46

'I'm glad of it,' said Humphrey; 'but I hope it will not be the last which I take.'

'That reminds me, Humphrey, of one thing. I think you must come back with the cart and carry away all the entrails of the beast, and remove all the blood which is on the snow, for I've observed that cattle are very scared with the smell and sight of blood. I found that out by once or twice seeing them come to where I have cut the throat of a stag, and as soon as they have put their noses down to where the blood was on the ground, they have put their tails up and galloped away, bellowing at a terrible rate. Indeed I've heard say that if a murder has been committed in a wood, and you want to find the body, that a herd of cattle drove into it will serve you better than even a bloodhound.'

'Thank you for telling me that, Jacob, for I should never have supposed it; and I'll tell you what I'll do. I'll load the cart with fern litter, and put it at the bottom of the pit; so that if I could get a heifer or calf worth taking, it may not be hurt by the fall.'

'It must have taken you a long while to dig that pit, Humphrey.'

'Yes, it did, and as I got deeper the work was harder, and then I had to carry away all the earth and scatter it about. I was more than a month about it from the time that I began till it was finished, and I had a ladder to go up and down by at last, and carried the baskets of earth up, for it was too deep to throw it out.'

'Nothing like patience and perseverance, Humphrey. You've more than I have.'

'I'm sure he has more than I have, or shall ever have, I'm afraid,' replied Edward.

During this winter, which passed rapidly away, very few circumstances of any consequence occurred. Old Jacob was more or less confined to the cottage by the rheumatism, and Edward hunted either by himself or occasionally with Humphrey. Humphrey was fortunate enough to take a bull and cow calf in his pitfall, both of them about a year and fifteen months old, and by a rude invention of his, by way of windlass, contrived, with the assistance of Edward, to hoist them uninjured out of the pit. They were put into the yard, and after having been starved till they were tamed, they followed the example of the heifer and calf, and became quite tame. These were an important addition to their stock, as may well be imagined. The only mishap under which they laboured was old Jacob's confinement to the cottage, which, as the winter advanced, prevented him from going to Lymington; they could not, therefore, sell any venison, and Humphrey, by way of experiment, smoked some venison hams, which he hung up with the others. There was another point on which they felt anxiety, which was that Jacob could not cross the forest to get the puppies which had been promised them; and the time was passed, for it was now January, when he was to have called for them. Edward and Humphrey pressed the old man very hard to let one of them go; but the only answer they could obtain was, 'that he'd be better soon'. At last, finding that he got worse instead of better, he consented that Edward should go. He gave directions how to proceed, the way he was to take, and a description of the keeper's lodge; cautioned him to call himself by the name of Armitage, and describe himself as his grandson. Edward promised to obey Jacob's directions, and the next morning he set off, mounted upon White Billy, with a little money in his pocket, in case he should want it.

'I wish I was going with you,' said Humphrey, as he walked by the side of the pony.

'I wish you were, Humphrey: for my part, I feel as if I were a slave set at liberty. I do justice to old Jacob's kindness and good will, and acknowledge how much we are indebted to him; but still, to be housed up here in the forest, never seeing or speaking to any one, shut out from the world, does not suit Edward Beverley. Our father was a soldier, and a right good one, and if I were old enough, I think even now I should escape and join the royal party, broken as it may be, and by all accounts is, at this moment. Deer-stalking is all very well, but I fly at higher game.'

'I feel the same as you do,' replied Humphrey; 'but recollect, Edward, that the old man's very infirm; and what would become of our sisters if we were to leave them?'

'I know that well, Humphrey – I have no idea lf leaving them, you may be sure – but I wish they were with our relations in safety, and then we should be free to act.'

'Yes, we should, Edward; but recollect that we are not yet men, and boys of fifteen and thirteen cannot do much, although they may wish to do much.'

'It's true that I am only fifteen,' replied Edward, 'but I am strong enough, and so are you. I think if I had a fair cut at a man's head, I would make him stagger under it, were he as big as a buffalo. As young as I have been to the wars, that I know well; and I recollect my father promising me that I should go with him as soon as I was fifteen.'

'What puzzles me,' replied Humphrey, 'is the fear that old Jacob has of our being seen at Lymington.'

'Why, what fear is there?'

'I cannot tell more than you; in my opinion, the fear is only in his own imagination. They surely would not hurt us (if we walked about without arms like other people) because our father had fought for the King? That they have beheaded some people is true; but then they were plotting in the King's favour, or in other ways opposed to Parliament. This I have gathered from Jacob; but I cannot see what we have to fear, if we remain quiet. But now comes the question, Edward (for Jacob has, I believe, said more to me on one subject than he has to you): Suppose you were to leave the forest, what would be the first step which you would take?'

'I should of course state who I was, and take possession of my father's property at Arnwood, which is mine by descent.'

'Exactly; so Jacob thinks, and he says that would be your ruin, for the property is sequestered, as they call it, or forfeited to the Parliament, in consequence of your father having fought against it on the Kings side. It no longer belongs to you, and you would not be allowed to take it; on the contrary, you would, in all probability, be imprisoned, and who knows what might then take place? You see there is danger.'

'Did Jacob say this to you?'

'Yes, he did: he told me he dare not speak to you on the subject, you were so fiery; and if you heard that the property was confiscated, you would certainly do some rash act and that anything of the kind would be a pretence for laying hold of you; and then he said that he did not think that he would live long, for he was weaker every day, and that he only hoped his life would be spared another year or two, that he might keep you quiet till better times came. He said that if they supposed that we were all burnt in the house when it was fired, it would give them a fair opportunity of calling you an impostor and treating you accordingly, and that there were so many anxious to have a gift of the property, that you would have thousands of people compassing your death. He said that your making known yourself and claiming your property would be the very conduct that your enemies would wish you to follow, and would be attended with most fatal consequences; for he said, to prove that you were Edward Beverley, you must declare that I and your sisters were in the forest with him, and this disclosure would put the whole family in the power of their bitterest enemies; and what would become of your sisters it would be impossible to say, but most likely they would be put under the charge of some Puritan family, who would have a pleasure in ill-treating and humiliating the daughters of such a man as Colonel Beverley.'

'And why did he not tell me all this?'

'He was afraid to say anything to you – he thought that you would be so mad at the idea of this injustice, that you would do something rash; and he said, "I pray every night that my otherwise useless life may be spared, for were I to die, I know that Edward would quit the forest."'.

'Never, while my sisters are under my protection,' replied Edward; 'were they safe, I would be out of it tomorrow.'

'I think, Edward, that there is great truth in what Jacob says; you could do no good (for they would not restore your property) by making your seclusion known at present, and you might do a great deal of harm. "Bide your time" is good advice in such troubled times. I therefore think that I should be very wary if I were you; but I still think that there is no fear of either you or me going out of the forest in our present dresses and under the name Armitage. No one would recognize us: you are grown tall, and so am I, and we are so tanned and sunburnt with air and exercise, that we do look more like children of the forest than the sons of Colonel Beverley.'

'Humphrey, you speak very sensibly, and I agree with you. I am not quite so fiery as the old man thinks; and if my bosom burns with indignation, at all events I have sufficient power to conceal my feelings when it is necessary. I can oppose art to art if it becomes requisite, and which, from what you have said, I believe now is really so. One thing is certain, that while King Charles is a prisoner, as he now is, and his party dispersed or gone abroad, I can do nothing, and to make myself known would only be to injure myself and all of us. Keep quiet, therefore, I certainly shall, and also remain as I am now under a false name; but still I must and will mix up with other people and know what is going on. I am willing to live in this forest and protect my sisters as long as it is necessary so to do; but although I will reside here, I will not be confined to the forest altogether.'

'That's exactly what I think, too, Edward, what I wish myself; but let us not be too hasty even in this. And now I will wish you a pleasant ride, and, Edward, if you can, procure of the keepers some small shot for me; I much wish to have some.'

'I will not forget; good-bye, brother.'

Humphrey returned home to attend his farmyard, while Edward continued his journey through the forest. Some estimate of the character of the two boys may be formed from the above conversation. Edward was courageous and impetuous – hasty in his resolves, but still open to conviction. Brought up as the heir to the property, he felt, more than Humphrey could be expected to do, the mortification of being left a pauper, after such high prospects in his early days; his vindictive feelings against the opposite party were therefore more keen, and his spirit mounted more under the conviction which he laboured. His disposition was naturally warlike, and this disposition had been fostered by his father when he was a child; still a kinder heart or a more generous lad never existed.

Humphrey was of a much more subdued and philosophical temperament, not perhaps so well calculated to lead as to advise; there was great prudence in him united with courage, but his was a passive courage rather than an active one – a courage which if assailed would defend itself valiantly, but would be wary and reflective before it would attack. Humphrey had not that spirit of chivalry possessed by Edward. He was a younger son, and had to earn, in a way, his own fortune, and he felt that his inclinations were more for peace than strife. Moreover, Humphrey had talents which Edward had not – a natural talent for mechanics, and an inquisitive research into science, as far as his limited education would permit him. He was more fitted for an engineer or an agriculturist than for a soldier, although there is no doubt that he would have made a very brave soldier, if such was to have become his avocation.

For kindness and generosity of nature he was equal to his brother, and this was the reason why an angry word never passed between them; for the question between them was, not which should have his way, but which should give up most to the wishes of the other. We hardly need say that there never were two brothers who were more attached, and who so mutually respected each other.

CHAPTER 8

Edward put the pony to a trot, and in two hours was on the other side of the New Forest. The directions given to him by Jacob were not forgotten, and before it was noon he found himself at the gate of the keeper's house. Dismounting, and hanging the bridle of the pony over the rail, he walked through a small garden, neatly kept, but, so early in the year, not over gay, except that the crocus and snowdrops were peeping. He rapped at the door with his knuckles, and a girl of about fourteen, very neatly dressed, answered the summons.

'Is Oswald Partridge at home, maiden?' said Edward.

'No, young man, he is not. He is in the forest.'

'When will he return?'

'Towards the evening is his time, unless he is more than usually successful.'

'I have come some distance to find him,' replied Edward; 'and it would vex me to return without seeing him. Has he a wife, or any one that I could speak to?'

'He has no wife but I am willing to deliver a message.'

'I am come about some dogs which he promised to Jacob Armitage, my relation; but the old man is too unwell, and has been for some time, to come himself for them, and he has sent me.'

'There are dogs, young and old, large and small, in the kennels; so far do I know, and no more.'

'I fear then I must wait till his return,' replied Edward.

'I will speak to my father,' replied the young girl, 'if you will wait one moment.'

In a minute or two the girl returned, saying that her father begged that he would walk in, and he would speak with him, Edward bowed, and followed the young girl, who led the way to a room, in which was seated a man dressed after the fashion of the Roundheads of the day. His steeple-crowned hat lay on the chair, with his sword beneath it. He was sitting at a table covered with papers.

'Here is the youth, father,' said the girl; and having said this, she crossed the room and took a seat by the side of the fire. The man, or we should rather say gentleman – for he had the appearance of one, notwithstanding the sombre and peculiar dress he wore – continued to read a letter which he had just opened; and Edward, who feared himself the prisoner of a Roundhead, when he only expected to meet a keeper, was further irritated by the neglect shown towards him by the party. Forgetting that he was, by his own assertion, not Edward Beverley, but the relative of one Jacob Armitage, he coloured up with anger as he stood at the door. Fortunately the time that it took the other party to read through the letter gave Edward

51

also time for recollecting the disguise under which he appeared; the colour subsided from his cheeks, and he remained in silence, occasionally meeting the look of the little girl, who, when their eyes met, immediately withdrew her glance.

'What is your business, young man?' at last said the gentleman at the table.

'I came, sir, on private business with the keeper, Oswald Partridge, to obtain two young hounds, which he promised to my grandfather, Jacob Armitage.'

'Armitage!' said the other party, referring to a list on the table; 'Armitage – Jacob – yes – I see he is one of the verderers. Why has he not been here to call me?'

'For what reason should he call upon you, sir?' replied Edward.

'Simply, young man, because the New Forest is, by the Parliament, committed to my charge. Notice has been given for all those who were employed to come here, that they might be permitted to remain, or be discharged, as I may deem most advisable.'

'Jacob Armitage has heard nothing of this, sir,' replied Edward. 'He was a keeper, appointed under the King. For two or three years his allowances have never been paid, and he has lived in his own cottage which was left to him by his father, being his own property. '

'And pray, may I ask, young man, do you live with Jacob Armitage?'

'I have done so for more than a year.'

'And as your relation has received no pay and allowances, as you state, pray, by what means has he maintained himself ?'

'How have the other keepers maintained themselves?' replied Edward.

'Do not put questions to me, sir,' replied the gentleman: 'but be pleased to reply to mine. What has been the means of subsistence of Jacob Armitage?'

'If you think that he has no means of subsistence, sir, you are mistaken,' replied Edward. 'We have land of our own, which we cultivate; we have our pony and our cart; we have our pigs and our cows.'

'And they have been sufficient?'

'Had the patriarchs more?' replied Edward.

'You are pithy at reply, young man; but I know something of Jacob Armitage, and we know,' continued he, putting his finger close to some writing opposite the name on the list, 'with whom he has associated, and with whom he has served. Now allow me to put one question. You have come, you say, for two young hounds. Are their services required for your pigs and cows, and to what uses are they to be put?'

'We have as good a dog as there is in the forest,' replied Edward, 'but we wished to have others, in case we should lose him.'

'As good a dog as in the forest – good for what?'

'For hunting.'

'Then you acknowledge that you do hunt?'

'I acknowledge nothing for Jacob Armitage, he may answer for himself,' replied Edward; 'but allow me to assure you, that if he has killed venison, no one can blame him.'

'Perhaps you will explain why?'

'Nothing is more easy. Jacob Armitage served King Charles, who employed him as a verderer in the forest, and paid him his wages. Those who should not have done so, rebelled against the King, took his authority from him, and the means of paying those he employed. They were still servants of the King, for they were not dismissed; and, having no other means of support, they considered that their good master would be but too happy that they should support themselves by killing, for their subsistence, that venison which they could no longer preserve for him without eating some themselves.'

'Then you admit that Jacob Armitage has killed the deer in the forest?'

'I admit nothing for Jacob Armitage.'

'You admit that you have killed it yourself.'

'I shall not answer that question, sir. In the first place, I am not here to criminate myself; and, in the next, I must know by what authority you have the right to inquire.'

'Young man,' replied the other in a severe tone, 'if you wish to know my authority, malapert as you are' (at this remark Edward started, yet, recollecting himself, he compressed his lips and stood still), 'this is my commission, appointing me the agent of Parliament to take charge and superintend the New Forest, with power to appoint and dismiss those whom I please. I presume you must take my word for it, as you cannot read and write.'

Edward stepped up to the table, and very quietly took up the paper and read it. 'You have stated what is correct, sir,' said he, laying it down; 'and the date of it is, I perceive, on the 20th of the last month of December. It is, therefore, but eighteen days old.'

'And what inference would you draw from that, young man?' replied the gentleman, looking up to him with some astonishment.

'Simply this, sir – that Jacob Armitage has been laid up with rheumatism for three months, during which time he certainly has not killed any venison. Now, sir, until the Parliament took the forest into their hands, it undoubtedly belonged to his Majesty, if it does not now; therefore Jacob Armitage, for whatever slaughter he may have committed, is, up to the present, only answerable to his sovereign, King Charles.'

'It is easy to perceive the school in which you have been brought up, young man, even if there was not evidence on this paper that your forefather served under the cavalier Colonel Beverley, and has brought you up to his way of thinking.'

'Sir, it is a base dog that bites the hand that feeds him,' replied Edward with warmth. 'Jacob Armitage, and his father before him, were retainers in the family of Colonel Beverley; they were indebted to him for the situation they now hold in the forest; indebted to him for everything; they revere his name, they uphold the cause for which he fell, as I do.'

'Young man, if you do not speak advisedly, at all events you speak gratefully; neither have I a word of disrespect to offer to the memory of Colonel Beverley, who was a gallant man, and true to the cause which he espoused, although it was not a holy one; but in my position, I cannot, in justice to those whom I serve, give places and emolument to those who have been, and still are, as I may judge by your expressions, adverse to the present government.'

'Sir,' replied Edward, 'your language, with respect to Colonel Beverley, has made me feel respect for you, which I confess I did not at first; what you say is very just; not that I think you harm Jacob Armitage; as, in the first place, I know that he would not serve under you; and, in the next, that he is too old and infirm to hold the situation; neither has he occasion for it, as his cottage and land are his own, and you cannot remove him.'

'He has the title, I presume?' replied the gentleman.

'He has the title given to his grandfather, long before King Charles was born, and I presume the Parliament do not intend to invalidate the acts of former kings.'

'May I inquire what relation you are to Jacob Armitage?'

'I believe, I have before said, his grandson.'

'You live with him?'

'I do.'

'And if the old man dies, will inherit his property?'

Edward smiled, and looking at the young girl, said, –

'Now, I ask you, maiden, if your father does not presume upon his office.'

The young girl laughed, and said, –

'He is in authority.'

'Not over me, certainly, and not over my grandfather, for he dismissed him.'

'Were you brought up at the cottage, young man?'

'No, sir, I was brought up at Arnwood. I was a playmate of the children of Colonel Beverley.'

'Educated with them?'

'Yes, for, as far as my wilfulness would permit, the chaplain was always ready to give me instruction.'

'Where were you when Arnwood was burnt down?'

'I was at the cottage at that time,' replied Edward, grinding his teeth and looking wildly.

'Nay, nay, I can forgive any expression of feeling on your part, my young man, when that dreadful and disgraceful deed is brought to your memory. It was a stain that can never be effaced – a deed most diabolical, and what we thought would call down the vengeance of Heaven. If prayers could avert, or did avert it, they were not wanting on our side.'

Edward remained silent: this admission on the part of the Roundhead prevented an explosion on his part. He felt that all were not so bad as he had imagined. After a long pause, he said, –

54

'When I came here, sir, it was to seek Oswald Partridge, and obtain the hounds which he had promised us; but I presume that my journey is now useless.'

'Why so?'

'Because you have the control of the forest, and will not permit dogs for the chase to be given away to those who are not employed by the powers that now govern.'

'You have judged correctly, in so far that my duty is to prevent it; but as the promise was made previous to the date of my commission, I presume,' said he, smiling, 'you think I have no right to interfere, as it will be an *ex post facto* case, if I do: I shall not therefore interfere, only I must point out to you, that the laws are still the same relative to those who take the deer in the forest by stealth – you understand me?'

'Yes, sir, I do; and if you will not be offended, I will give you a candid reply.'

'Speak then.'

'I consider that the deer in this forest belong to King Charles, who is my lawful sovereign, and I own no authority but from him. I hold myself answerable to him alone for any deer I may kill, and I feel sure of his permission and full forgiveness for what I may do.'

'That may be your opinion, my good sir, but it will not be the opinion of the ruling powers; but if caught, you will be punished, and that by me, in pursuance of the authority vested in me.'

'Well, sir; if so, so be it. You have dismissed the Armitages on account of their upholding the King, and you cannot, therefore, be surprised that they uphold him more than ever. Nor can you be surprised if a dismissed verderer becomes a poacher.'

'Nor can you be surprised, if a poacher is caught, that he incurs the penalty,' replied the Roundhead. 'So now there's an end of our argument. If you go into the kitchen, you will find wherewithal to refresh the outward man, and if you wish to remain till Oswald Partridge comes home, you are welcome.'

Edward, who felt indignant at being dismissed to the kitchen, nodded his head and smiled upon the little girl, and left the room. 'Well,' thought he, as he went along the passage, 'I came here for two puppies, and I have found a Roundhead. I don't know how it is, but I am not so angry with him as I thought I should be. That little girl had a nice smile – she was quite handsome when she smiled. Oh, this is the kitchen, to which,' thought he, 'the lord of Arnwood is dismissed by a Covenanter and Roundhead, probably a tradesman or outlaw, who has served the cause. Well, be it so; as Humphrey says, "I'll bide my time". But there is no one here, so I'll try if there is a stable for White Billy, who is tired, I presume, of being at the gate.'

Edward returned by the way he came, went out of the front door, and through the garden to where the pony was made fast, and led him away in search of a stable. He found one behind the house, and filling the rack with hay, returned to the house, and seated himself at a porch which was at the door which led to the back premises – for the keeper's house was large and commodious. Edward was in deep thought, when he was roused by the little girl, the daughter of the newly-appointed Intendant of the forest, who said, –

'I am afraid, young sir, you have had but sorry welcome in the kitchen, as there was no one to receive you. I was not aware that Phœbe had gone out. If you will come with me, I may, perhaps, find you refreshment.'

'Thanks, maiden; you are kind and considerate to an avowed poacher,' replied Edward.

'Oh, but you will not poach, I'm sure; and if you do, I'll beg you off if I can,' replied the girl, laughing.

Edward followed her into the kitchen, and she soon produced a cold fowl and a venison pasty, which she placed on the table; she then went out and returned with a jug of ale.

'There,' said she, putting it on the table, 'that is all that I can find.'

'Your father's name is Heatherstone, I believe. It was on the warrant.'

'Yes, it is.'

'And yours?'

'The same as my father's, I should presume.'

'Yes, but your baptismal name?'

'You ask strange questions, young sir; but still I will answer you that. My baptismal name is Patience.'

'I thank you for your condescension,' replied Edward. 'You live here?'

'For the present, good sir; and now I leave you.'

'That's a nice little girl,' thought Edward, 'although she is the daughter of a Roundhead; and she calls me "sir". I cannot, therefore, look like Jacob's grandson, and must be careful.' Edward then set to with a good appetite at the viands which had been placed before him, and had just finished a hearty meal when Patience Heatherstone again came in and said, –

'Oswald Partridge is now coming home.'

'I thank you, maiden,' replied Edward. 'May I ask a question of you? Where is the King now?'

'I have heard that he resides at Hurst Castle,' replied the girl; 'but,' added she in a low tone, 'all attempts to see him would be useless, and only hurt him and those who made the attempt.' Having said this, she left the room.

CHAPTER 9

Edward having finished his meal, and had a good pull at the jug of ale, which was a liquor he had not tasted for a long while, rose from the table and went out of the back door and found there Oswald Partridge. He accosted him, stating the reason for his coming over to him. 'I did not know that Jacob had a grandson; indeed I never knew that he had a son. Have you been living with him long?'

'More than a year,' replied Edward; 'before that I was in the household at Arnwood.'

'Then you are of the King's side, I presume?' replied Oswald.

'To death,' replied Edward, 'when the time comes.'

'And I am also; that you may suppose, for never would I give a hound to any one that was not. But we had better go to the kennels; dogs may hear, but they can't repeat.'

'I little thought to have met any one but you here when I came,' said Edward; 'and I will now tell you all that passed between me and the new Intendant.' Edward then related the conversation.

'You have been bold,' said Oswald; 'but perhaps it is all the better. I am to retain my situation, and so are two others; but there are many new hands coming in as rangers. I know nothing of them but that they are little fitted for their places, and rail against the King all day long, which I suppose is their chief merit in the eyes of those who appoint them. However, one thing is certain, that if those fellows cannot stalk a deer themselves, they will do all they can to prevent others; so you must be on the alert, for the punishment is severe.'

'I fear them not; the only difficulty is that we shall not be able to find a sale for the venison now,' replied Edward.

'Oh, never fear that; I will give you the names of those who will take all your venison off your hands without any risk on your part, except in the killing of it. They will meet you in the park, lay down ready money, and take it away. I don't know, but I have an idea that this new Intendant, or what you may call him, is not so severe as he pretends to be. Indeed, his permitting you to say what he did, and his own words relative to the colonel, convince me that I am right in the opinion that I formed.'

'Do you know who he is?'

'Not much about him, but he is a great friend of General Cromwell's, and they say has done good service to the Parliamentary cause. But we shall meet again, for the forest is free, at all events'.

'If you come here,' continued Oswald, 'do not carry your gun, and see that you are not watched home. There are the dogs for your grandfather. Why, how old must you be? for Jacob is not more than sixty or thereabout.'

'I am fifteen past, nevertheless.'

'I should have put you down for eighteen or nineteen at least. You are well grown indeed for that age. Well, nothing like a forest life to turn a boy into a man! Can you stalk a deer?'

'I seldom go out without bringing one down.'

'Indeed! That Jacob is a master of his craft is certain. But you are young to have learnt it so soon. Can you tell the slot of a brocket from a stag?'

'Yes, and the slot of a brocket from a doe.'

57

'Better still. We must go out together; and besides, I must know where the old man's cottage is (for I do not exactly): in the first place, because I may want to come to you; and in the next, that I may put others on a false scent. – Do you know the clump of large oaks which they call the Clump Royal?'

'Yes, I do.'

'Will you meet me there the day after tomorrow at early dawn?'

'If I live and do well.'

'That's enough. Take the dogs on the leashes, and go away now.'

'Many thanks. But I must not leave the pony; he is in the stable.'

The keeper nodded adieu to Edward, who left him to go to the stable for the pony. Edward saddled White Billy, and rode away across the forest with the dogs trotting at the pony's heels.

Edward had much to reflect upon as he rode back to the cottage. He felt that his position was one of more difficulty than before. That old Jacob Armitage would not last much longer he was convinced; even now the poor old man was shrunk away to a skeleton with pain and disease. That the livelihood to be procured from the forest would be attended with peril, now that order had been restored and the forest was no longer neglected, was certain; and he rejoiced that Humphrey had, by his assiduity and intelligence, made the farm so profitable as it promised to be. Indeed he felt that, if necessary, they could live upon the proceeds of the farm, and not run the risk of imprisonment by stalking the deer. But he had told the Intendant that he considered the game as the King's property, and he was resolved that he would at all events run the risk, although he would no longer permit Humphrey so to do. 'If anything happens to me,' thought Edward, 'Humphrey will still be at the cottage to take care of my sisters, and if I'm obliged to fly the country, it will suit well my feelings, as I can then offer my services to those who still support the King.' With these thoughts, and many others, he amused himself until, late in the evening, he arrived at the cottage. He found all in bed except Humphrey, who had waited for him, and to whom he narrated all that had passed. Humphrey said little in reply; he wished to think it over before he gave any opinion. He told Edward that Jacob had been very ill the whole of the day, and had requested Alice to read the Bible to him during the evening.

The next morning Edward went to Jacob, who for the last ten days had altogether kept his bed, and gave him the detail of what had happened at the keeper's lodge.

'You have been more bold than prudent, Edward,' replied Jacob; 'but I could not expect you to have spoken otherwise. You are too proud and too manly to tell a lie, and I am glad that it is so. As for your upholding the King, although he is now a prisoner in their hands, they cannot blame you or punish you for that, as long as you have not weapons in your hands; but now that they have taken the forest under their jurisdiction, you must be careful, for they are the ruling powers at present, and must be obeyed, or the forfeit must be paid. Still I do not ask you to promise me this or that;

I only point out to you that your sisters will suffer by any imprudence on your part; and for their sakes be careful. I say this, Edward, because I feel that my days are numbered, and that in a short time I shall be called away. You will then have all the load on your shoulders which has been latterly on mine. I have no fear for the result if you are prudent; these few months past, during which I have only been a burden to you, have proved that you and Humphrey can find a living here for yourselves and your sisters; and it is fortunate, now that the forest laws are about to be put in force, that you have made the farm so profitable. If I might advise, let your hunting in the forest be confined to the wild cattle; they are not game, and the forest laws do not extend to them, and the meat is as valuable as venison – that is to say, it does not sell so dear, but there is more of it. But stick to the farm as much as you can; for you see, Edward, you do not look like a low-born forester, nor ought you to do so, and the more quiet you keep the better. As for Oswald Partridge, you may trust him; I know him well, and he will prove your friend for my sake as soon as he hears that I am dead. Leave me now; I will talk to you again in the evening. Send Alice to me, my dear boy.'

Edward was much distressed to perceive the change which had taken place in old Jacob. He was evidently much worse, but Edward had no idea how much worse he was. Edward assisted Humphrey in the farm, and in the evening again went to Jacob, and then told him of the arrangement he had made to meet Oswald Partridge on the following morning.

'Go, my boy,' said Jacob; be as intimate with him as you can, and make a friend of him – nay, if it should be necessary, you may tell him who you are. I did think of telling him myself, as it might be important to you one day as evidence. I think you had better bring him here tomorrow night, Edward; tell him I am dying, and wish to speak to him before I go. Alice will read the Bible to me now, and I will talk with you another time.'

Early the next morning Edward set off to the appointed rendezvous with Oswald Partridge. The Clump Royal, as it was called, from the peculiar size and beauty of the oaks, was about seven miles from the cottage; and at the hour and time indicated Edward, with his gun in his hand and Smoker lying beside him, was leaning against one of those monarchs of the forest. He did not wait long. Oswald Partridge, similarly provided, made his appearance, and Edward advanced to meet him.

'Welcome, Oswald,' said Edward.

'And welcome to you also, my fine lad,' replied Oswald. 'I have been hard questioned about you since we parted – first, by the Roundhead Heatherstone, who plied me in all manner of ways to find out whether you are what you assert, the grandson of Jacob – or some other person. I really believe that he fancies you are the Duke of York. But he could not get any more from me than what I knew. I told him that your grandfather's cottage was his own property, and a grant to his forefathers; that you were brought up at Arnwood, and had joined your grandfather after the death of the colonel, and the murderous burning of the house and all within it by his

59

party. But the pretty little daughter was more curious still. She cross-questioned me in every way when her father was not present, and at last begged me as a favour to tell you not to take the deer, as her father was very strict in his duty, and, if caught, you would be imprisoned.'

'Many thanks to her for her caution, but I hope to take one today, nevertheless,' replied Edward; 'a hart royal is not meat for Roundheads, although the King's servants may feast on them.'

'That's truly said. Well, now I must see your woodcraft. You shall be the leader of the chase.'

'Think you we can harbour a stag about here?'

'Yes, in this month, no doubt.'

'Let us walk on,' said Edward. 'The wind is fresh from the eastern quarter: we will face it, if you please – or rather, keep it blowing on our right cheek for the present.'

''Tis well,' replied Oswald; and they walked for about half an hour.

'This is the slot of a doe,' said Edward in a low voice, pointing to the marks; 'yonder thicket is a likely harbour for the stag.' They proceeded, and Edward pointed out to Oswald the slot of the stag into the thicket. They then walked round, and found no marks of the animal having left his lair.

'He is here,' whispered Edward; and Oswald made a sign for Edward to enter the thicket, while he walked to the other side. Edward entered the thicket cautiously. In the centre he perceived, through the trees, a small cleared spot, covered with high fern, and felt certain that the stag was lying there. He forced his way on his knees till he had a better view of the place, and then cocked his gun. The noise induced the stag to move his antlers, and discover his lair. Edward could just perceive the eye of the animal through the heath; he waited till the beast settled again, took steady aim, and fired. At the report of the gun another stag sprang up and burst away. Oswald fired and wounded it, but the animal made off, followed by the dogs. Edward, who hardly knew whether he had missed or not, but felt almost certain that he had not, hastened out of the thicket to join in the chase; and as he passed through the fern patch, perceived that his quarry lay dead. He then followed the chase, and being very fleet of foot, soon came up with Oswald, and passed him without speaking. The stag made for a swampy ground, and finally took to the water beyond it, and stood at bay. Edward then waited for Oswald, who came up with him.

'He has soiled,' said Edward, 'and now you may go in and kill

Oswald, eager in the chase, hastened up to where the dogs and stag were in the water, and put a bullet through the animal's head.

Edward went to him, assisted to drag the stag out of the water, and then Oswald cut its throat, and proceeded to perform the usual offices.

'How did you happen to miss him?' said Oswald, 'for these are my shots?'

'Because I never fired at him,' said Edward; 'my quarry lies dead in the fern – and a fine fellow he is. '

'This is a warrantable stag,' said Oswald.

'Yes, but mine is a hart royal, as you will see when we go

As soon as Oswald had done his work, he hung the quarters of the animal on an oak-tree, and went back with Edward.

'Where did you hit him, Edward?' said Oswald, as they walked along.

'I could only see his eye through the fern, and I must have hit him thereabouts.'

On their arrival at the spot Oswald found that Edward had put the ball right into the eye of the stag.

'Well,' said he, 'you made me suppose that you know something of our craft, but I did not believe that you were so apt as you thought yourself to be. I now confess that you are a master, as far as I can see, in all branches of the craft. This is indeed a hart royal. Twenty-five antlers, as I live! Come, out with your knife, and let us finish; for if we are to go to the cottage, we have no time to lose. It will be dark in half an hour.' They hung all the quarters of the stag as before, and then set off for Jacob's cottage, Edward proposing that Oswald should take the cart and pony to carry the meat home the next morning, and that he would accompany him to bring it back.

'That will do capitally,' said Oswald; 'and here we are, if I recollect right, and I hope there is something to eat.'

'No fear of that – Alice will be prepared for us,' replied Edward.

Their dinner was ready for them; and Oswald praised the cooking. He was much surprised to find that Jacob had four grandchildren. After dinner he went into Jacob's room, and remained with him more than an hour. During this conference Jacob confided to Oswald that the four children were the sons and daughters of Colonel Beverley, supposed to have been burnt in the firing of Arnwood. Oswald came out, much surprised as well as pleased with the information, and with the confidence reposed in him. He saluted Edward and Humphrey respectfully, and said, 'I was not aware with whom I was in company, sir, as you may well imagine; but the knowledge of it has made my heart glad.'

'Nay, Oswald,' replied Edward, 'remember that I am still Edward Armitage, and that we are the grandchildren of old Jacob.'

'Certainly, sir, I will, for your own sake, not forget that such is to be supposed to be the case. I assure you I think it very fortunate that Jacob has confided the secret to me, as it may be in my power to be useful. I little thought that I should ever have had my dinner cooked by a daughter of Colonel Beverley.'

They then entered into a long conversation, during which Oswald expressed his opinion that the old man was sinking fast, and would not last more than three or four days. Oswald had a bed made up for him on the floor of the room where Edward and Humphrey slept, and the next morning they set off, at an early hour, with the pony and cart, loaded it with the venison, and took it across the forest to the keeper's lodge. It was so late when they arrived that Edward consented to pass the night there, and return home on the following morning. Oswald went into the sitting-

61

room to speak with the Intendant of the forest, leaving Edward in the kitchen with Phœbe, the maid-servant. He told the Intendant that he had brought home some fine venison, and wished his orders about it. He also stated that he had been assisted by Edward Armitage, who had brought the venison home for him in his cart, and who was now in the kitchen, as he would be obliged to pass the night there; and on being questioned, he was lavish in his praises of Edward's skill and knowledge of woodcraft, which he declared to be superior to his own.

'It proves that the young man has had much practice, at all events,' replied Mr Heatherstone, smiling. 'He has been living at the King's expense, but he must not follow it up at the cost of the Parliament. It would be well to take this young man as a ranger if we could; for although he is opposed to us, yet, if he once took our service, he would be faithful, I am sure. You can propose it to him, Oswald. The haunches of that hart royal must be sent up to General Cromwell tomorrow – the remainder we will give directions for, as soon as I have made up my mind how to dispose of it.'

Oswald left the room, and came back to Edward. 'General Cromwell is to have the haunches of your stag,' said he to Edward, smiling; 'and the Intendant proposes that you should take service as one of the rangers.'

'I thank you,' replied Edward, 'but I've no fancy to find venison for General Cromwell and his Roundheads, and so you may tell the Intendant, with many thanks for his goodwill towards me, nevertheless.'

'I thought as much; but the man meant kindly, that I really think. – Now, Phœbe, what can you give us to eat, for we are hungry?'

'You shall be served directly,' replied Phœbe. 'I have some steaks on the fire.'

'And you must find a bed for my young friend here.'

'I have none in the house, but there is plenty of good straw over the stables.'

'That will do,' replied Edward; 'I'm not particular.'

'I suppose not. Why should you be?' replied Phœbe, who was rather old and rather cross, 'If you mount the ladder that you will see against the wall, you will find a good bed when you are at the top of it.'

Oswald was about to remonstrate, but Edward held up his finger, and no more was said.

As soon as they had finished their supper Phœbe proposed that they should go to bed. It was late, and she would sit up no longer. Edward rose and went out, followed by Oswald, who had given up the keeper's house to the Intendant and his daughter, and slept in the cottage of one of the rangers, about a quarter of a mile off. After some conversation they shook hands and parted, as Edward intended returning very early the next morning, being anxious about old Jacob.

Edward went up the ladder into the loft. There was no door to shut out the wind, which blew piercingly cold, and after a time he found himself so chilled that he could not sleep. He rose to see if he could not find some protection from the wind, by getting more into a corner; for although Phœbe had told him that there was plenty of straw, it proved that there was very little indeed in the loft, barely enough to lie down upon. Edward, after a time, descended the ladder to walk in the yard, that by exercise he might recover the use of his limbs. At last, turning to and fro, he cast his eyes up to the window of the bedroom above the kitchen, where he perceived a light was still burning. He thought it was Phœbe, the maid, going to bed; and with no very gracious feelings towards her for having deprived him of his own night's rest, he was wishing that she might have the toothache or something else to keep her awake, when suddenly through the white window curtain he perceived a broad light in the room. It increased every moment; and he saw the figure of a female rush past it, and attempt to open the window; the drawing of the curtains showed him that the room was on fire. A moment's thought, and he ran for the ladder by which he had ascended to the loft, and placed it against the window. The flames were less bright, and he could not see the female who had been at the window when he went for the ladder. He ascended quickly and burst open the casement: the smoke poured out in such volume that it nearly suffocated him, but he went in; and as soon as he was inside, he stumbled against the body of the person who had attempted to open the window, but who had fallen down senseless. As he raised the body the fire, which had been smothered from want of air when all the windows and doors were closed, now burst out, and he was scorched before he could get on the ladder again, with the body in his arms; but he succeeded in getting it down safe. Perceiving that the clothes were on fire, he held them till they were extinguished, and then, for the first time, discovered that he had brought down the daughter of the Intendant of the forest. There was no time to be lost, so Edward carried her into the stable and left her there, still insensible, upon the straw, in a spare stall, while he hastened to alarm the house. The watering butt for the horses was outside the stable, Edward caught up the pail, filled it, and hastening up the ladder threw it into the room, and then descended for more.

By this time Edward's continual calls of 'Fire! fire!' had aroused the people of the house, and also of the cottages adjacent. Mr Heatherstone came out half dressed, and with horror on his countenance. Phœbe followed screaming, and the other people now hastened from the cottages.

'Save her! my daughter is in the room!' exclaimed Mr Heatherstone. 'Oh, save her, or let me do so!' cried the poor man in agony; but the fire burst out of the window in such force that any attempt would have been in vain.

'Oswald,' cried Edward to him, 'let the people pass the water up to me as fast as possible. They can do no good looking on.'

Oswald set the men to the work, and Edward was now supplied with water so fast that the fire began to diminish. The window was now approachable, and a few more buckets enabled him to put one foot into the room, and then every moment the flames and smoke decreased.

Meanwhile it would be impossible to describe the agony of the Intendant, who would have rushed up the ladder into the flames, had he not been held by some of the men. 'My daughter! my child! – burnt – burnt to death!' exclaimed he, clasping his hands.

At that moment a voice in the crowd called out, 'There were four burnt at Arnwood!'

'God of heaven!' exclaimed Mr Heatherstone, falling down into a swoon, in which state he was carried to a neighbouring cottage.

Meanwhile the supply of water enabled Edward to put out the fire altogether. The furniture of the room was burnt, but the fire had extended no further; and when Edward was satisfied that there was no more danger, he descended the ladder, and left it to others to see that all was safe. He then called Oswald to him, and desired that he would accompany him to the stable.

'O sir,' replied Oswald, 'this is dreadful! and such a sweet young lady too.'

'She is safe and well,' replied Edward; 'I think so, at least I brought her down the ladder, and put her in the stable before I attempted to put out the fire. See, there she is; she has not recovered yet from her swoon. Bring some water. She breathes! thank God! There, that will do, Oswald; she is recovering. Now let us cover her up in your cloak, and carry her to your cottage. We will recover her there.'

Oswald folded up the still unconscious girl in his cloak, and carried her away in his arms, followed by Edward.

As soon as they arrived at the cottage, the inmates of which were all busy at the keeper's lodge, they put her on a bed, and very soon restored her to consciousness.

'Where is my father?' cried Patience, as soon as she was sufficiently recovered.

'He is safe and well, miss,' replied Oswald.

'Is the house burnt down?'

'No. The fire is all out again. '

'Who saved me? Tell me.'

'Young Armitage, miss.'

'Who is he? Oh, I recollect now. But I must go to my father. Where is he?'

'In the other cottage, miss.'

Patience attempted to stand, but found that she was too much exhausted, and she fell back again on the bed. 'I can't stand,' said she. 'Bring my father to me.'

'I will, miss,' replied Oswald. – 'Will you stay here, Edward?'

'Yes,' replied Edward. He went out of the cottage door, and remained there while Oswald went to Mr Heatherstone.

Oswald found him sensible, but in deep distress, as may be imagined. 'The fire is out, sir,' said Oswald.

'I care not for that. My poor, poor child!'

'Your child is safe, sir,' replied Oswald.

'Safe, did you say?' cried Mr Heatherstone, starting up. 'Safe! Where?'

'In my cottage. She has sent me for you.'

Mr Heatherstone rushed out, passed by Edward, who was standing at the door of the other cottage, and was in his daughter's arms. Oswald came out to Edward, who then detailed to him the way in which he had saved the girl.

'Had it not been for the ill-nature of that girl Phœbe, in sending me to sleep where there was no straw, they would all have been burnt,' observed Edward.

'She gave you an opportunity of rewarding good for evil,' observed Oswald.

'Yes; but I am burnt very much in my arm,' said Edward. 'Have you anything that will be good for it?'

'Yes, I think I have. Wait a moment.'

Oswald went into the cottage and returned with some salve, with which he dressed Edward's arm, which proved to be very severely burnt.

'How grateful the Intendant ought to be – and will be, I have no doubt!' observed Oswald.

'And for that very reason I shall saddle my pony and ride home as fast as I can; and – do you hear, Oswald? – do not show him where I live.'

'I hardly know how I can refuse him if he requires it.'

'But you must not. He will be offering me a situation in the forest by way of showing his gratitude, and I will accept of none. I have no objection to save his daughter, as I would save the daughter of my worst enemy, or my worst enemy himself, from such a dreadful death; but I do not want their thanks or offers of service. I will accept nothing from a Roundhead; and as for the venison in the forest, it belongs to the King, and I shall help myself whenever I think proper. Good-bye, Oswald. You will call and see us when you have time?'

'I will be with you before the week is out, depend upon it,' replied Oswald.

Edward then asked Oswald to saddle his pony for him, as his arm prevented him from doing it himself, and as soon as it was done he rode away for the cottage.

Edward rode fast, for he was anxious to get home and ascertain the state of poor old Jacob; and, moreover, his burnt arm was very painful. He was met by Humphrey about a mile from the cottage, who told him that he did not think that the old man could last many hours, and that he was very anxious to see him. As the pony was quite tired with the fast pace that Edward had ridden, Edward pulled up to a walk, and, as they went along, acquainted Humphrey with what had passed.

'Is your arm very painful?'

'Yes, it is indeed,' replied Edward; 'but it can't be helped.'

'No, of course not; but it may be made more easy. I know what will do it some good; for I recollect when Benjamin burnt his hand at Arnwood what they applied to it, and it gave him great relief.'

'Yes, very likely; but I am not aware that we have any drugs or medicine in the cottage. But here we are: will you take Billy to the stable, while I go to old Jacob?'

'Thank God that you are come, Edward,' said the old forester, 'for I was anxious to see you before I die; and something tells me that I have but a short time to remain here.'

'Why should you say so? Do you feel very ill?'

'No, not ill; but I feel that I am sinking fast. Recollect that I am an old man, Edward.'

'Not so very old, Jacob. Oswald said that you were not more than sixty years old.'

'Oswald knows nothing about it. I am past seventy-six, Edward; and you know, Edward, the Bible says that the days of men are threescore years and ten; so that I am beyond the mark. And now, Edward, I have but few words to say. Be careful – if not for your own sake, at least for your little sisters'. You are young, but you are strong and powerful above your years, and can better protect them than I could. I see darker days yet coming; but it is His will, and who shall doubt that that is right? I pray you not to make your birth and lineage known as yet – it can do no good, and it may do harm – and if you can be persuaded to live in the cottage, and to live on the farm, which will now support you all, it will be better. Do not get into trouble about the venison, which they now claim as their own. You will find some money in the bag in my chest, sufficient to buy all you want for a long while; but take care of it, for there is no saying but you may require it. And now, Edward, call your brother and sisters to me, that I may bid them farewell. I am, as we all are, sinful, but I trust in the mercy of God through Jesus Christ. Edward, I have done my duty towards you as well as I have been able; but promise me one thing – that you will read the Bible and prayers every morning and evening, as I have always done, after I am gone. Promise me that, Edward.'

'I promise you that it shall be done, Jacob,' replied Edward, 'and I will not forget your other advice.'

'God bless you, Edward. Now call the children.'

Edward summoned his sisters, and Humphrey.

'Humphrey, my good boy,' said Jacob, 'recollect that in the midst of life we are in death, and that there is no security for young or old. You or your brother may be cut off in your youth; one may be taken and the other left. Recollect your sisters depend upon you, and do not therefore be rash. I fear that you will run too much risk after the wild cattle, for you are always scheming after taking them. Be careful, Humphrey, for you can ill be spared. Hold to the farm as it now is; it will support you all. – My dear Alice and Edith, I am dying; very soon I shall be laid by your brothers in my grave. Be good children, and look up to your brothers for everything. – And now kiss me, Alice. You have been a great comfort to me, for you have read the Bible to me when I could no longer read myself. May your deathbed be as well attended as mine has been, and may you live happily, and die the death of a Christian! Good-bye, and may God bless you! – Bless you, Edith; may you grow up as good and as innocent as you are now. – Farewell, Humphrey! – farewell, Edward! – my eyes are dim – pray for me, children. – O God of mercy, pardon my many sins, and receive my soul, through Jesus Christ! Amen, amen.'

These were the last words spoken by the old forester. The children, who were kneeling by the side of the bed, praying as he had requested, when they rose up found that he was dead. They all wept bitterly, for they dearly loved the good old man. Alice remained sobbing in Edward's arms, and Edith in Humphrey's, and it was long before the brothers could console them. Humphrey at last said to Alice, 'You hurt poor Edward's arm – you don't know how painful it is! – Come, dears, let us go into the other room and get something to take the pain away.'

These requests diverted the attention, at the same time that it roused fresh sympathy in the little girls. They all went into the sitting-room. Humphrey gave his sisters some potatoes to scrape upon a piece of linen, while he took off Edward's coat, and turned up his short sleeves. The scraped potatoes were then laid on the burn, and Edward said they gave him great relief. Some more were then scraped by the little girls, who could not, however, repress their occasional sobs. Humphrey then told them that Edward had had nothing to eat, and that they must get him some supper. This again occupied them for some time; and when the supper was ready they all sat down to it. They went to bed early, but not before Edward had read a chapter out of the Bible, and the prayers, as old Jacob had always done; and this again caused their tears to flow afresh.

'Come, Alice, dear, you and Edith must go to bed,' said Humphrey.

The little girls threw themselves into their brothers' arms; and having wept for some time, Alice raised herself, and taking Edith by the hand, led her away to the bedroom.

CHAPTER 10

'Humphrey,' said Edward, 'the sooner all this is over the better. As long as poor Jacob's body remain in the cottage, there will be nothing but distress with the poor girls.'

'I agree with you,' replied Humphrey. 'Where shall we bury him?'

'Under the great oak-tree, at the back of the cottage,' replied Edward. 'One day the old man said to me that he should like to be buried under one of the oaks of the forest.'

'Well, then, I will go and dig his grave tonight,' replied Humphrey. 'The moon is bright, and I shall have it finished before morning.'

'I am sorry that I cannot help you, Humphrey.'

'I am sorry that you are hurt; but I want to help, Edward. If you will like down a little, perhaps you will be able to sleep. Let us change the potato poultice before you go on.'

Humphrey put the fresh dressing on Edward's arm; and Edward, who was very much exhausted, lay down in his clothes on the bed. Humphrey went out, and having found his tools, set to his task. He worked hard, and before morning had finished. He then went in, and took his place on the bed by the side of Edward, who was in a sound sleep. At daylight Humphrey rose and waked Edward. 'All is ready, Edward; but I fear you must help me to put poor Jacob in the cart. Do you think you can?'

'Oh yes; my arm is much easier, and I feel very different from what I did last night. If you will go and get the cart, I will see what I can do in the meantime.'

When Humphrey returned, he found Edward had selected a sheet to wind the body in, but could not do more till Humphrey came to help him. They then wrapped it round the body, and carried it out of the cottage, and put it into the cart.

'Now, Edward, shall we call our sisters?'

'No, not yet. Let us have the body laid in the grave first, and then we will call them.'

They dragged the body on the cart to the grave, and laid it in it, and then returned back and put the pony in the stable again.

'Are there not prayers proper for reading over the dead?' said Humphrey.

'I do believe that there are, but they are not in the Bible; so we must read some portion of the Bible,' said Edward.

'Yes, I think there is one of the Psalms which it would be right to read, Edward,' said Humphrey, turning over the leaves. 'Here it is – the 90th, in which you recollect it says "that the days of man are threescore years and ten".'

'Yes,' replied Edward; 'and we will read this one also – the 146th.'

'Are our sisters risen, do you think?'

'I am sure that they are,' replied Humphrey, 'and I will go to them.'

Humphrey went to the door, and said, 'Alice – Alice and Edith – come out immediately.' They were both ready dressed.

Edward took the Bible under his arm, and Alice by the hand. Humphrey led Edith until they arrived at the grave, when the two little girls saw the covered body of Jacob lying in it.

'Kneel down,' said Edward, opening the Bible. And they all knelt by the grave. Edward read the two psalms, and then closed the book. The little girls took one last look at the body, and then turned away weeping to the cottage. Edward and Humphrey filled up the grave, and then followed their sisters home.

''I'm glad it's over,' said Humphrey, wiping his eyes. 'Poor old Jacob! I'll put a paling round his grave.'

'Come in, Humphrey,' said Edward.

Edward sat down upon old Jacob's chair, and took Alice and Edith to him. Putting his arm round each, he said, –

'Alice and Edith, my dear little sisters, we have lost a good friend, and one to whose memory we cannot be too grateful. He saved us from perishing in the flames which burnt down our father's house, and has protected us here ever since. He is gone; for it has pleased God to summon him to Him, and we must bow to the will of Heaven. And here we are, brothers and sisters, orphans, and with no one to look to for protection but Heaven. Here we are, away from the rest of the world, living for one another. What, then, must we do? We must love one another dearly, and help one another. I will do my part, if my life is spared, and so will Humphrey, and so will you, my dear sisters. I can answer for all. Now it is no use to lament – we must all work, and work cheerfully; and we will pray every morning and every night that God will bless our endeavours, and enable us to provide for ourselves, and live here in peace and safety. Kiss me, dear Alice and Edith, and kiss Humphrey, and kiss one another. Let these kisses be the seals to our bond; and let us put our trust in Him who only is a father to the widow and the orphan. And now let us pray.'

Edward and the children repeated the Lord's Prayer, and then rose up. They went to their respective employments, and the labour of the day soon made them composed, although then, for many days afterwards, it was but occasionally that a smile was seen upon their lips.

Thus passed a week, by which time Edward's arm was so far well that it gave him no pain, and he was able to assist Humphrey in the work on the farm. The snow had disappeared, and the spring, although it had been checked for a time, now made rapid advances. Constant occupation and the return of fine weather, both had the effect of restoring the serenity of their minds; and while Humphrey was preparing the paling to fix round the grave of old Jacob, Alice and Edith collected the wild violets which now peeped forth on sheltered spots, and planted the roots over the grave. Edward also procured all the early flowers he could collect, and assisted his sisters in their task; and thus, in planting it and putting up the paling, the grave of the old man became their constant work-ground; and when their labour was done, they would still remain there and talk over his worth. The Sunday following the burial, the weather being fine and warm, Edward proposed that they should read the usual service, which had been selected by old Jacob, at the grave, and not in the cottage as formerly; and this they continued afterwards to do whenever the weather would permit. Thus did old Jacob's resting-place become their church, and overpower them with those feelings of love and devotion which gave efficacy to prayer. As soon as the paling was finished, Humphrey put up a board against the oak-tree, with the simple words carved on it: 'Jacob Armitage.'

Edward had every day expected that Oswald Partridge would have called upon him, as he had promised to do before the week was out; but Oswald had not made his appearance, much to Edward's surprise. A month passed away; Edward's arm was now quite well, and still Oswald came not. One morning Humphrey and Edward were conversing upon many points – the principal of which was upon Edward going to Lymington, for they were now in want of flour and meal – when Edward thought of what old Jacob had told him relative to the money that he would find in his chest. He went into Jacob's room and opened the chest, at the bottom of which, under the clothes, he found a leather bag, which he brought out to Humphrey. On opening it they were much surprised to find in it more than sixty gold pieces, besides a great deal of silver coin.

'Surely this is a great sum of money,' observed Humphrey. 'I don't know what is the price of things, but it appears to me that it ought to last us a long while.'

'I think so too,' replied Edward. 'I wish Oswald Partridge would come, for I want to ask him many questions. I don't know the price of flour or anything else we have to purchase, nor do I know what I ought to be paid for venison. I don't like to go to Lymington till I see him, for that reason. If he does not come soon, I shall ride over and see what is the matter.'

Edward then replaced the money in the chest, and he and Humphrey then went out to the farmyard to go on with their work.

It was not until six weeks after the death of old Jacob that Oswald Partridge made his appearance.

'How is the old man, sir?' was his first question.

'He was buried a few days after you left,' replied Edward.

'I expected as much,' said the forester. 'Peace be with him – he was a good man. And how is your arm?'

'Nearly well,' replied Edward. 'Now, sit down, Oswald, for I have a great deal to say to you; and first let me ask you what has detained you from coming here according to your promise.'

'Simply, and in a few words – murder.'

'Murder!' exclaimed Edward.

'Yes, deliberate murder, sir. In short, they have beheaded the King – beheaded King Charles, our sovereign.'

'Have they dared to do it?'

'They have,' replied Oswald. 'We know little that is going on in the forest, but when I saw you last I heard that he was then in London, and was to be tried.'

'Tried!' exclaimed Edward. 'How could they try a king? By the laws of our country a man must be tried by his equals; and where were his equals?'

'Majesty becomes nought, I suppose,' replied Oswald; 'but still it is as I say. Two days after you left, the Intendant hastened up to London, and from what I have understood he was strongly opposed to the deed, and did all he could to prevent it, but it was of no use. When he left, he gave me strict injunctions not to go away from the cottage for an hour, as his daughter was left alone; and as I promised, I could not come to you; but, nevertheless, Patience received letters from him, and told me what I tell you.'

'You have not dined, Oswald?' said Edward.

'No, that I have not.'

'Alice, dear, get some dinner, will you? And, Oswald, while you dine, excuse me if I leave you for a while. Your intelligence has so astounded me that I can listen to nothing else till I have had a little while to commune with myself and subdue my feelings.'

Edward was indeed in a state of mind which required calming down. He quitted the cottage and walked out for some distance into the forest in deep thought.

'Murdered at last!' exclaimed he. 'Yes, well may it be called murder, and no one to save him – not a blow struck in his defence – not an arm raised. How much gallant blood has been shed in vain! Spirit of my fathers – didst thou leave none of thy mettle and thy honour behind thee? or has all England become craven! Well, the time will come, and if I can no longer hope to fight for my King, at all events I can fight against those who have murdered him.'

Such were Edward's thoughts as he wandered through the forest, and more than an hour elapsed before his impetuous blood could return to its usual flow. At last, more calm, he returned to the cottage, and listened to the details which Oswald now gave him of what he had heard.

When Oswald had finished, Edward asked him whether the Intendant had returned.

'Yes, or I should not have been here,' replied Oswald. 'He came back yesterday, looking most disconsolate and grave, and I hear that he returns to London in a few days. Indeed, he told me so himself, for I requested permission to come over to see your grandfather. He said that I might go, but must return soon, as he must go back to London. I believe from what Miss Patience told me, and what I have seen myself, that he is sincerely amazed and vexed at what has taken place; and so indeed are many more, who, although opposed to the King's method of government, never had an idea that things should have turned out as they had done. I have a message from him to you, which is, that he begs you will come to see him that he may thank you for the preservation of his child.'

'I will take his thanks from you, Oswald; that will do as well as if he gave them me in person.'

'Yes, perhaps so; but I have another message from another party, which is the young lady herself. She desires me to tell you that she will never be happy till she has seen you and thanked you for your courage and kindness; and that you have no right to put her under such an obligation, and not give her an opportunity of expressing what she feels. Now, Mr Edward, I am certain that she is earnest in what she says, and she made me promise that I would persuade you to come. I could not refuse her, for she is a dear little creature. As her father will go to London in a few days, you may ride over and see her without any fear of being affronted by any offers which he may make to you.'

'Well,' replied Edward, 'I have no great objection to see her again, for

71

she was very kind to me; and as you say that the Intendant will not be there, I perhaps may come. But now I must talk to you about other matters.'

Edward then put many questions to Oswald relative to the value of various articles, and to the best method of disposing of his venison.

Oswald answered all his questions, and Edward took down notes and directions on paper.

Oswald remained with them for two days, and then bade them farewell, exacting a promise from Edward that he would come to the ranger's cottage as soon as he could. 'Should the Intendant come back before he is expected, I will come over and let you know; but I think, from what I heard him say, he expected to be at least a month in London.'

Edward promised that Oswald should see him in less than ten days, and Oswald set out on his journey.

'Humphrey,' said Edward, as soon as Oswald was gone, 'I have made up my mind to go to Lymington tomorrow. We must have some flour, and many other articles, which Alice says she can no longer do without.'

'Why should we not both go, Edward?' replied Humphrey.

'No, not this time,' replied Edward. 'I have to find out many things and many people, and I had rather go by myself. Besides, I cannot allow my sisters to be left alone. I do not consider there is any danger, I admit, but something might happen to them. I should never forgive myself. Still, it is necessary that you should go to Lymington, with me some time or another, that you may know where to purchase and sell, if required. What I propose is, that I will ask Oswald to come and stay here a couple of days. We will then leave him in charge of our sisters, and go to Lymington together.'

'You are right, Edward; that will be the best plan.'

As Humphrey made this remark, Oswald re-entered the cottage.

'I will tell you why I have returned, Mr Edward,' said Oswald. 'It is of no consequence whether I return now or tomorrow. It is now early, and as you intend going to Lymington, it occurred to me that I had better go with you. I can then show you all you want, which will be much better than going by yourself.'

'Thank you, Oswald; I am much obliged to you,' said Edward. 'Humphrey, we will get the cart out immediately, or we shall be late. Will you get it, Humphrey? for I must go for some money, and speak to Alice.'

Humphrey went immediately to put the pony in the cart, when Edward said, –

'Oswald, you must not call me Mr Edward, even when we are alone. If you do, you will be calling me so before other people; and therefore recollect in future it must be plain Edward. '

'Since you wish it, certainly,' replied Oswald. 'Indeed, it would be better, for a slip of the tongue before other people might create suspicion.'

The pony and cart were soon at the door, and Edward, having received further instructions from Alice, set off for Lymington, accompanied by Oswald.

CHAPTER 11

'Would you have found your way to Lymington?' said Oswald, as the pony trotted along.

'Yes, I think so,' replied Edward; 'but I must have first gone to Arnwood. Indeed, had I been alone, I should have done so; but we have made a much shorter cut.'

'I did not think that you would have liked to have seen the ruin of Arnwood,' replied Oswald.

'Not a day passes without my thinking of them,' replied Edward. 'I should like to see them. I should like to see if any one has taken possession of the property, for they say it is confiscated.'

'I heard that it was to be, but not that it was yet,' said Oswald; 'but we shall know more when we get to Lymington. I have not seen it for more than a year. I hardly think that any one will recognize you.'

'I should think not; but I care little if they do. Indeed, who is there to know me?'

'Well, my introduction of you will save some surmises, probably. I shall not take you among those who may be inclined to ask questions. See, there is the steeple; we have not more than a quarter of an hour's drive.'

As soon as they arrived at Lymington, Oswald directed the way to a small hostelrie, to which the keepers and verderers usually resorted. In fact, the landlord was the party who took all the venison off their hands, and disposed of it. They drove into the yard, and giving the pony and cart in charge of the hostler, went into the inn, where they found the landlord, and one or two other people, who were drinking.

'Well, Master Andrew, how fare you?' said Oswald.

'Let me see,' said the corpulent landlord, throwing back his head and putting out his stomach as he peered at Oswald; 'why, Oswald Partridge, as I am a born man. Where have you been this many a day?'

'In the forest, Master Andrew, where there are no few chops and changes.'

'Yes, I heard you have a sort of Parliamentary keeper, I'm told. And who is this with you?'

'The grandson of an old friend of yours, now dead, poor old Jacob Armitage.'

'Jacob dead, poor fellow! As true as flint was Jacob Armitage, as I'm a born man! And so he is dead! Well, we all owe Heaven a death. Foresters and landlords, as well as kings, all must die!'

'I have brought Edward Armitage over here to introduce him to you, Master Andrew. Now that the old man is dead, you must look to him for forest meat.'

73

'Oh, well, well, it is scarce now. I have not had any for some time. Old Jacob brought me the last. You are not one of the Parliamentary foresters, then, I presume?' continued the landlord, turning to Edward.

'No,' replied Edward, 'I kill no venison for Roundheads.'

'Right, my sapling – right and well said. The Armitages were all good men and true, and followed the fortunes of the Beverleys; but there are no Beverleys to follow now. Cut off root and branch – more's the pity. That was a sad business. But come in; we must not talk here, for walls have ears, they say, and one never knows who one dares to speak before now.'

Oswald and Edward then entered with the landlord, and arrangements were made between Master Andrew and the latter for a regular supply of venison during the season at a certain price; but as it would now be dangerous to bring it into the town, it was agreed that when there was any ready Edward should come to Lymington and give notice, and the landlord would send out people to bring it in during the night. This bargain concluded, they took a glass with the landlord, and then went into the town to make the necessary purchases. Oswald took Edward to all the shops where the articles he required were to be purchased; some they carried away with them; others, which were too heavy, they left, to be called for with the cart as they went away. Among other articles, Edward required powder and lead, and they went to a gunsmith's where it was to be procured. While making his purchases, Edward perceived a sword, which he thought he had seen before, hanging up against the walk among other weapons.

'What sword is that?' said he to the man who was measuring out the powder.

'It's not my sword exactly,' replied the man, 'and yet I cannot return it to its owner or to the family. It was brought me to be cleaned by one of Colonel Beverleys people, and before it was called for the house was burnt and every soul perished. It was one of the colonel's swords, I am sure, as there is E. B. on a silver plate engraved on it. I have a bill owing me for work done at Arnwood, and I have no chance of its being paid now; so, whether I am to sell the sword, or what to do, I hardly know.'

Edward remained silent for some little while, for he could not trust himself to speak. At last he replied, 'To be candid with you, I am, and all my family have been, followers of the Beverley family, and I should be sorry if the colonel's sword was to fall into any other hands. I think, therefore, if I pay the bill which is due, you may safely let me hold the sword as a security for the money, with the express understanding that if it is ever claimed by the Beverley family I am to give it up.'

'Certainly,' said Oswald; 'nothing can be fairer or more clearly put.'

'I think so too, young man,' replied the shopkeeper. 'Of course you will leave your name and address?'

'Yes; and my friend here will vouch for its being correct,' replied Edward.

The shopkeeper then produced the account, which Edward paid; and giving on the paper the name of Edward Armitage, he took possession of the sword. He then paid for the powder and lead, which Oswald took charge of, and, hardly able to conceal his joy, hastened out of the shop.

'Oswald,' cried Edward, 'I would not part with it for thousands of pounds. I never will part with it but with my life.'

'I believe so,' replied Oswald. 'And I believe more, that it will never be disgraced in your hands. But do not talk so loud for there are listeners and spies everywhere. Is there anything else that you require?'

'No, I think not. The fact is, that this sword has put everything out of my head. If there was anything else, I have forgotten it. Let us go back to the inn, and we will harness the pony and call for the flour and oatmeal. '

When they arrived at the inn, Oswald went out to the yard to get the cart ready, while Edward went into the landlord's room to make inquiries as to the quantity of venison he would be able to take off his hands at a time. Oswald had taken the sword from Edward, and had put it in the cart while he was fastening the harness, when a man came up to the cart, and looked earnestly at the sword. He then examined it, and said to Oswald, –

'Why, that was Colonel Beverley's, my old master's, sword. I knowed it again directly. I took it to Phillips, the gunmaker, to be cleaned.'

'Indeed!' replied Oswald. 'I pray what may be your name?'

'Benjamin White,' replied the man. 'I served at Arnwood till the night it was burned down, and I have been here ever since.'

'And what are you doing now?'

'I'm tapster at the Commonwealth in Fish Street – not much of a place.'

'Well, well, you stand by the pony, and look that nobody takes anything out of the cart, while I go in for some parcels.'

'Yes, to be sure I will. But, I say, forester, how came you by that sword?'

'I will tell you when I come out again,' replied Oswald.

Oswald then went in to Edward, and told him what had occurred.

'He will certainly know you, sir, and you must not come out till I can get him away,' said he.

'You are right, Oswald. But before he goes, ask him what became of my aunt, and where she was buried, and also ask him where the other servants are – perhaps they are at Lymington as well as he.'

'I will find it all out,' replied Oswald, who then left Edward and returned to the landlord and recommenced conversation.

Oswald on his return told Benjamin in what manner the sword had been procured from the shopman by the grandson of old Armitage.

'I never knew that he had one,' replied Benjamin; 'nor did I know that old Jacob was dead.'

'What became of all the women who were at Arnwood?' inquired Oswald.

'Why, Agatha married one of the troopers, and went away to London.'

'And the others?'

'Why, cook went home to her friends, who live about ten miles from here, and I have never heard of her since.'

'But there were three of them,' said Oswald.

'Oh yes; there was Phœbe,' replied Benjamin, looking rather confused. 'She married a trooper – the jilt! – and went off to London when Agatha did. If I'd have thought that she would have done so, I would not have carried her away from Arnwood behind me, on a pillion, as I did; she might have been burnt with the poor children, for all as I cared.'

'Was not the old lady killed?'

'Yes; that is to say, she killed herself rather than not kill Southwold.'

'Where was she buried?'

'In the churchyard at St Faith's, by the mayor and corporation; for there was not money enough found upon her person to pay the expenses of her burial.'

'And so you are tapster at the Commonwealth. Is it a good inn?'

'Can't say much for it. I shan't stay longer than I can help, I can tell you.'

'Well, but you must have an easy place if you can stay away so long as you do now.'

'Won't I be mobbed when I go back! but that's always the case, make haste or not, so it's all one. However, I do think I must be a-going now, so good-bye, Mr Forester; and tell Jacob Armitage's grandson that I shall be glad to see him for old Jacob's sake; and it's hard but I'll find him something to drink when he calls.'

'I will: I shall see him tomorrow,' replied Oswald, getting into the cart; 'so good-bye, Benjamin,' much to the satisfaction of Oswald, who thought that he would never go.

They went away at a rapid pace to make up for lost time, and soon disappeared round the corner of the street. Oswald then got out again, summoned Edward, and having called for the flour and other heavy articles, they set off on their return.

During the drive Oswald made known to Edward the information which he had gained from Benjamin, and at a late hour they arrived safely at the cottage.

They stayed up but a short time, as they were tired; and Oswald had resolved upon setting off before daylight on the following morning, which he did without disturbing any one; for Humphrey was up and dressed as soon as Oswald was, and gave him something to eat as he went along. All the others remained fast asleep. Humphrey walked about a mile with Oswald, and was returning to the farm, when he thought, as he had not examined his pitfall for many days, that he might as well look at it before he went back. He therefore struck out in the direction in which it lay, and arrived there just as the day began to dawn.

It was the end of March, and the weather was mild for the season. Humphrey arrived at the pit, and it was sufficiently light for him to perceive that the covering had been broken in and therefore, in all probability, something must have been trapped. He sat down and waited for daylight, but at times he thought he heard a heavy breathing, and once a low groan. This made him more anxious, and he again and again peered into the pit, but could not for a long while discover any thing, until at last he thought that he could make out a human figure lying at the bottom. Humphrey called out, asking if there was any one there. A groan was the reply, and now Humphrey was horrified at the idea that somebody had fallen into the pit, and had perished, or was perishing for want of succour. Recollecting that the rough ladder, which he had made to take the soil up out of the pit was against an oak-tree close at hand, he ran for it and put it down the pit, and then cautiously descended. On his arrival at the bottom, his fears were found to be verified, for he found the body of a lad half-clothed lying there. He turned it up, as it was lying with its face to the ground, and attempted to remove it and to ascertain if there was life in it, which he was delighted to find was the case. The lad groaned several times, and opened his eyes. Humphrey was afraid that he was not strong enough to lift it on his shoulders and carry it up the ladder; but on making the attempt, he found out, from exhaustion, the poor lad was light enough for him to carry him, which he did, and safely landed him by the side of the pit.

Recollecting that the watering-place of the herd of cattle was not far off, Humphrey then hastened to it, and filled his hat half full of water. The lad, although he could not speak, drank eagerly, and in a few minutes appeared much recovered. Humphrey gave him some more, and bathed his face and temples. The sun had now risen, and it was broad daylight. The lad attempted to speak, but what he did say was in so low a tone, and evidently in a foreign language, that Humphrey could not make him out. He therefore made signs to the lad that he was going away, and would be back soon; and having, as he thought, made the lad comprehend this, Humphrey ran away to the cottage as fast as he could; and as soon as he arrived he called for Edward, who came out, and when Humphrey told him in few words what had happened, Edward went into the cottage again for some milk and some cake, while Humphrey put the pony into the cart.

In a few moments they were off again, and soon arrived at the pitfall, where they found the lad still lying where Humphrey had left him. They soaked the cake in the milk, and as soon as it was soft, gave him some; after a time he swallowed pretty freely, and was so much recovered as to be able to sit up. They then lifted him into the cart, and drove gently home to their cottage.

'What do you think he is, Edward?' said Humphrey.

'Some poor beggar lad who has been crossing the forest.'

'No, not exactly; he appears to me to be one of the Zingaros or gipsies, as they call them; he is very dark, and has black eyes and white teeth, just like those I saw once near Arnwood when I was out with Jacob. Jacob said that no one knew where they came from, but that they were all over the country, and that they were great thieves, and told fortunes and played all manner of tricks.'

'Perhaps it may be so; I do not think that he can speak English.'

'I am most thankful to Heaven that I chanced this morning to visit the pitfall. Only suppose that I had found the poor boy starved and dead! I should have been very unhappy, and never should have had any pleasure in looking at the cows, as they would always have reminded me of such a melancholy accident.'

'Very true, Humphrey; but you have been saved that misfortune, and ought to be grateful to Heaven that such is the case. What shall we do with him now we have him?'

'Why, if he chooses to remain with us, he will be very useful in the cow-yard,' said Humphrey.

'Of course,' replied Edward, laughing, 'as he was taken in the pitfall, he must go into the yard with all the others who were captured in the same way.'

'Well, Edward, let us get him all right again first, and then we will see what is to be done with him; perhaps he will refuse to remain with us.'

As soon as they arrived at the cottage they lifted the lad out of the cart, and carried him into Jacob's room, and laid him on the bed, for he was too weak to stand.

Alice and Edith, who were much surprised at the new visitor, and the way in which he had been caught, hastened to get some gruel ready for him. As soon as it was ready they gave it to the boy, who then fell back on the bed with exhaustion, and was soon in a sound sleep. He slept soundly all the night; and the next morning, when he awoke, he appeared much better, although very hungry. This last complaint was easy to remedy, and then the lad got up and walked into the sitting-room.

'What's your name?' said Humphrey to the lad.

'Pablo,' replied the lad.

'Can you speak English?'

'Yes, little,' replied he.

'How did you happen to fall into the pit?'

'Not see hole.'

'Are you a gipsy?'

'Yes, Gitano – same thing.'

Humphrey put a great many more questions to the lad, and elicited from him, in his imperfect English, the following particulars.

That he was in company with several others of his race, going down to the sea-coast on one of their usual migrations, and that they had pitched their tents not far from the pitfall. That during the night he had gone out to set some snares for rabbits, and going back to the tents, it being quite dark, he had fallen into the hole. That he had remained there three days and nights, having in vain attempted to get out. His mother was with the party of gipsies to which he belonged; but he had no father. He did not know where to follow the gang, as they had not said where they were going, further than to the sea-coast. That it was no use looking for them; and that he did not care much about leaving them, as he was very unkindly treated. In reply to the question as to whether he would like to remain with them, and work with them on the farm, he replied that he should like it very much if they would be kind to him, and not make him work too hard; that he would cook the dinner, and catch them rabbits and birds, and make a great many things.

'Will you be honest, if we keep you, and not tell lies?' said Edward.

The lad thought a little while, and then nodded his head in the affirmative.

'Well, Pablo, we will try you, and if you are a good lad, we will do all we can to make you happy,' said Edward; 'but if you behave ill, we shall be obliged to turn you out of doors: do you understand?'

'Be as good as I can,' replied Pablo; and here the conversation ended for the present.

Pablo was a very short-built lad, of apparently fifteen or sixteen years of age, very dark in complexion, but very handsome in features, with beautiful white teeth and large dark eyes; and there was certainly something in his intelligent countenance which recommended him, independent of his claim to their kindness from his having been left thus friendless in consequence of his misadventure. Humphrey was particularly pleased with and interested about him, as the lad had so nearly lost his life through his means.

'I really think, Edward,' said Humphrey, as they were standing outside of the door of the cottage, 'that the lad may be very useful to us, and I sincerely hope that he may prove honest and true. We must first get him into health and spirits, and then I will see what he can do.'

'The fact is, my dear Humphrey, we can do no otherwise: he is separated from his friends, and does not know where to go. It would be inhuman, as we have been the cause of his misfortune, to turn him away; but although I feel this, I do not feel much security as to his good behaviour and being very useful. I have always been told that these gipsies were vagrants, who lived by stealing all they could lay their hands upon; and if he has been brought up in that way I fear that he will not easily be reformed. However, we can but try, and hope for the best.'

'What you say is very just, Edward; at the same time there is an honest look about this lad, although he is a gipsy, that makes me put a sort of confidence in him. Admitting that he has been taught to do wrong, do you not think that, when told the contrary, he may be persuaded to do right?'

'It is not impossible, certainly,' replied Edward; 'but, Humphrey, be on the safe side, and do not trust him too far until you know more of him.'

'That I most certainly will not,' replied Humphrey. 'When do you purpose going over to the keeper's cottage, Edward?'

'In a day or two; but I am not exactly in a humour now to be very civil to the Roundheads, although the one I have promised to visit is a lady, and a very amiable, pretty little girl in the bargain.'

'Why, Edward, what has made you feel more opposed to them than usual?'

'In the first place, Humphrey, the murder of the King – for it was murder, and nothing better – I cannot get that out of my head; and yesterday I obtained what I consider as almost a gift from Heaven; and if it is so, it was not given but with the intention that I should make use of it.'

'And what was that, Edward?'

'Our gallant father's sword, which he drew so nobly and so well in defence of his sovereign, Humphrey, and which I trust his son may one day wield with equal distinction, and, it may be, better fortune. Come in with me, and I will show it to you.'

Edward and Humphrey went into the bedroom, and Edward brought out the sword, which he had placed by his side on the bed.

'See, Humphrey, this was our father's sword; and,' continued Edward, kissing the weapon, 'I trust I may be permitted to draw it to revenge his death, and the death of one whose life ever should have been sacred.'

'I trust that you will, my dear brother,' replied Humphrey; 'you will have a strong arm and a good cause. Heaven grant that both may prosper! But tell me how you came by it.'

Edward then related all that had passed during his visit with Oswald to Lymington, not forgetting to tell him of Benjamin's appearance, and the arrangements he had made relative to the sale of the venison.

As soon as dinner was over, Edward and Humphrey took down their guns, having agreed that they would go and hunt the wild cattle.

'Humphrey, have you any idea where the herd of cattle are feeding at this time?'

'I know where they were feeding yesterday and the day before, and I do not think that they will have changed their ground; for the grass is yet very young, and only grown on the southern aspects. Depend upon it, we shall fall in with them not four miles from where we now are, if not nearer.'

'We must stalk them as we do the deer, must we not? They won't allow us to approach within shot, Humphrey, will they?' said Edward.

'We have to take our chance, Edward; they will allow us to advance within shot, but the bulls will then advance upon us, while the herd increase their distance. On the other hand if we stalk them, we may kill one, and then the report of the gun will frighten the others away. In the first instance there is a risk; in the second there is none; but there is more fatigue and trouble. Choose as you please; I will act as you decide.'

'Well, Humphrey, since you give me the choice, I think that this time I shall take the bull by the horns, as the saying is – that is, if there are any trees near us, for if the herd are in an open place I would not run such a risk; but if we can fire upon them and fall back upon a tree in case of a bull charging, I will take them openly.'

'With all my heart, Edward: I think it will be very hard, if, with our two guns and Smoker to back us, we do not manage to be masters of the field. However, we must survey well before we make our approach; and if we can get within shot without alarming or irritating them, we of course will do so.'

'The bulls are very savage at this spring-time,' observed Edward.

'They are so at all times, as far as I can see of them,' replied Humphrey; 'but we are near to them now I should think – yes, there is the herd.'

'There they are, sure enough,' replied Edward: 'now we have not to do with deer, and need not be so very cautious; but still the animals are wary, and keep a sharp look-out. We must approach them quietly, by slipping from tree to tree. Smoker, to heel! – down – quiet, Smoker – good dog!'

Edward and Humphrey stopped to load their guns, and then approached the herd in the manner which had been proposed, and were very soon within two hundred yards of the cattle, behind a large oak, when they stopped to reconnoitre. The herd contained about seventy head of cattle of various sizes and ages. They were feeding in all directions, scattered, as the young grass was very short; but although the herd was spread over many acres of land, Edward pointed out to Humphrey that all the full-grown large bulls were on the outside, as if ready to defend the others in case of attack.

'Humphrey,' said Edward, 'one thing is clear – as the herd is placed at present we must have a bull or nothing. It is impossible to get within shot of the others without passing a bull and depend upon it our passage will be disputed; and moreover, the herd will take to flight, and we shall get nothing at all.'

'Well,' replied Humphrey, 'beef is beef; and, as they say, beggars must not be choosers, so let it be a bull, if it must be so.'

'Let us get nearer to them, and then we will decide what we shall do. Steady, Smoker!'

They advanced gradually, hiding from tree to tree, until they were within eighty yards of one of the bulls. The animal did not perceive them, and as they were now within range, they again stepped behind the tree to consult.

'Now, Edward, I think that it would be best to separate. You can fire from where we are, and I will crawl through the fern, and get behind another tree.'

'Very well, do so,' replied Edward; 'if you can manage, get to that tree with the low branches, and then perhaps you will be within shot of the white bull, which is coming down in this direction. Smoker, lie down! He cannot go with you, Humphrey; it will not be safe.'

The distance of the tree which Humphrey ventured to get to was about one hundred and fifty yards from where Edward was standing. Humphrey crawled along for some time in the fern, but at last he came to a bare spot of about ten yards wide, which they were not aware of, and where he could not be concealed. Humphrey hesitated, and at last decided upon attempting to cross it. Edward, who was one moment watching the motions of Humphrey and at another that of the two animals nearest to them, perceived that the white bull farthest from him, but nearest to Humphrey, threw its head in the air, pawed with its foot, and then advanced with a roar to where Humphrey was on the ground, still crawling towards the tree, having passed the open spot, and being now not many yards from the tree. Perceiving the danger that his brother was in, and that, moreover, Humphrey himself was not aware of it, he hardly knew how to act. The bull was too far from him to fire at it with any chance of success; and how to let Humphrey know that the animal had discovered him and was making towards him, without calling out, he did not know. All this was the thought of a moment, and then Edward determined to fire at the bull nearest to him, which he had promised not to do till Humphrey was also ready to fire; and after firing, to call Humphrey. He, therefore, for one moment turned away from his brother, and, taking aim at the bull, fired his gun; but probably from his nerves being a little shaken at the idea of Humphrey being in danger, the wound was not mortal, and the bull galloped back to the herd, which formed a close phalanx about a quarter of a mile distant. Edward then turned to where his brother was, and perceived that the bull had not made off with the rest of the cattle, but was within thirty yards of Humphrey, and advancing upon him, and that Humphrey was standing up beside the tree with his gun ready to fire. Humphrey fired, and, as it appeared, he also missed his aim; the animal made at him; but Humphrey, with great quickness, dropped his gun, and, swinging by the lower boughs, was into the tree, and out of the bull's reach in a moment. Edward smiled when he perceived that Humphrey was safe; but still he was a prisoner, for the bull went round and round the tree roaring and looking up at Humphrey. Edward thought a minute, then loaded his gun, and ordered Smoker to run in to the bull. The dog, who had only been restrained by Edward's keeping him down at his feet, sprang forward to the attack. Edward had intended, by calling to the dog, to induce the bull to follow it till within gunshot; but before the bull had been attacked, Edward observed that one or two more of the bulls had left the herd, and were coming at a rapid pace towards him. Under these circumstances Edward perceived that his only chance was to climb into a tree himself, which he did, taking good care to take his gun and ammunition with him. Having safely fixed himself in a forked bough, Edward then surveyed the position of the parties. There was Humphrey in the tree, without his gun. The bull who had pursued Humphrey was now running at Smoker, who appeared to be aware that he was to decoy the bull towards Edward, for he kept retreating towards him. In the meantime the two other bulls were quite close at hand, mingling their bellowing and roaring with the first; and one of them as near to Edward as the first bull, which was engaged with Smoker. At last one of the advancing bulls stood still, pawing the ground as if disappointed at not finding an enemy, not forty yards from where Edward was perched. Edward took good aim, and when he fired the bull fell dead. Edward was reloading his piece when he heard a howl, and looking round saw Smoker flying up in the air, having been tossed by the first bull; and at the same time he observed that Humphrey had descended from the tree, recovered his gun, and was now safe again upon the lower bough. The first bull was advancing again to attack Smoker, who appeared

82

incapable of getting away, so much was he injured by the fall, when the other bull, who apparently must have been an old antagonist of the first, roared and attacked him; and now the two boys were up in the tree, the two bulls fighting between them, and Smoker lying on the ground, panting and exhausted. As the bulls, with locked horns, were furiously pressing each other, both guns were discharged, and both animals fell. After waiting a little while to see if they rose again, or if any more of the herd came up, Edward and Humphrey descended from the trees and heartily shook hands.

CHAPTER 12

'A narrow escape, Humphrey!' said Edward, as he held his brother's hand.

'Yes, indeed; we may thank Heaven for our preservation,' replied Humphrey. 'And poor Smoker! Let us see if he is much hurt.'

'I trust not,' said Edward, going up to the dog, who remained quite still on the ground, with his tongue out, and panting violently.

They examined poor Smoker all over very carefully, and found that there was no external wound; but on Edward pressing his side, the animal gave a low howl.

'It is there where the horn of the bull took him,' observed Humphrey.

'Yes,' said Edward, pressing and feeling softly – 'and he has two of his ribs broken. Humphrey, see if you can get him a little water; that will recover him more than anything else. The bull has knocked the breath out of his body. I think he will soon be well again, poor fellow.'

Humphrey soon returned with some water from a neighbouring pool. He brought it in his hat, and gave it to the dog, who lapped it slowly at first, but afterwards much faster, and wagging his tail.

'He will do now,' said Edward; 'we must give him time to recover himself. Now then, let us examine our quarry. Why, Humphrey, what a quantity of meat we have here! It will take three journeys to Lymington at least.'

'Yes, and no time to lose, for the weather is getting warm already, Edward. Now, what to do? Will you remain while I go home for the cart?'

'Yes, it's no use both going. I will stay here and watch poor Smoker, and take off the skins ready by the time you are back again. Leave me your knife as well as my own, for one will soon be blunt.'

Humphrey gave his knife to Edward, and taking up his gun, set off for the cottage. Edward had skinned two of the bulls before Humphrey's return; and Smoker, although he evidently was in great pain, was on his legs again. As soon as they had finished and quartered the beasts, the cart was loaded, and they returned home; they had to return a second time, and both the pony and they were very tired before they sat down to supper. They found the gipsy boy very much recovered, and in good spirits. Alice said that he had been amusing Edith and her by tossing up three potatoes at a time, and playing them like balls; and that he had spun a platter upon an iron skewer and balanced it on his chin. They gave him some supper, which he ate in the chimney-corner, looking up and staring every now and then at Edith, to whom he appeared very much attached already.

'Is it good?' said Humphrey to the boy, giving him another venison steak.

'Yes; not have so good supper in pit-hole,' replied Pablo, laughing.

Early on the following morning Edward and Humphrey set off to Lymington with the cart laden with meat. Edward showed Humphrey all the shops and the streets they were in where the purchases were to be made – introduced him to the landlord of the hostelrie – and having sold their meat, they returned home. The rest of the meat was taken to Lymington and disposed of by Humphrey on the following day; and the day after that the three skins were carried to the town and disposed of.

'We made a good day's work, Edward,' said Humphrey, as he reckoned up the money they had made.

'We earned it with some risk, at all events,' replied Edward; 'and now, Humphrey, I think it is time that I keep my promise to Oswald, and go over to the Intendant's house, and pay my visit to the young lady, as I presume she is – and certainly she has every appearance of being one. I want the visit to be over, as I want to be doing.'

'How do you mean, Edward?'

'I mean that I want to go out and kill some deer; but I will not do it till after I have seen her. When my visit is over, I intend to defy the Intendant and all his verderers.'

'But why should this visit prevent you going out this very day, if so inclined?'

'I don't know, but she may ask me if I have done so, and I do not want to tell her that I have; neither do I want to say that I have not if I have; and therefore I shall not commence till after I have seen her.'

'When will you set off?'

'Tomorrow morning; and I shall take my gun, although Oswald desired me not; but, after the fight we had with the wild cattle the other day, I don't think it prudent to be unarmed – indeed, I do not feel comfortable without I have my gun at any time.'

'Well, I shall have plenty to do when you are away – the potatoes must be hoed up, and I shall see what I can make of Master Pablo. He appears well enough, and he has played quite long enough, so I shall take him with me to the garden tomorrow, and set him to work. What a quantity of fruit there is a promise of in the orchard this year! And, Edward, if this boy turns out of any use, and is a help to me, I think that I shall take all the orchard into garden, and then enclose another piece of ground, and see if we cannot

84

grow some corn for ourselves. It is the greatest expense that we have at present, and I should like to take my own corn to the mill to be ground.'

'But will not growing corn require plough and horses?' said Edward.

'No; we will till it by hand: two of us can dig a great deal at odd times, and we shall have a better crop with the spade than with the plough. We have now so much manure that we can afford it.'

'Well, if it is to be done, it should be done at once, Humphrey, before the people from the other side of the forest come and find us out, or they will dispute our right to the enclosure.'

'The forest belongs to the King, brother, and not to the Parliament; and we are the King's liege men, and only look to him for permission,' replied Humphrey. 'But what you say is true: the sooner it is done the better, and I will about it at once.'

'How much do you propose fencing in?'

'About two or three acres.'

'But that is more than you can dig this year or the next.'

'I know that; but I will manure it without digging, and the grass will grow so rich to what it will outside of the enclosure, that they will suppose it has been enclosed a long while.'

'That's not a bad idea, Humphrey; but I advise you to look well after that boy, for he is of a bad race, and has not been brought up, I am afraid, with too strict notions of honesty. Be careful, and tell your sisters also to be cautious not to let him suppose that we have any money in the old chest, till we find out whether he is to be trusted or not.'

'Better not let him know it under any circumstances,' replied Humphrey. 'He may continue honest if not tempted by the knowledge that there is anything worth stealing.'

'You are right, Humphrey. Well, I will be off tomorrow morning and get this visit over. I hope to be able to get all the news from her, now that her father is away.'

'I hope to get some work out of this Master Pablo,' replied Humphrey. 'How many things I could do, if he would only work! Now, I'll tell you one thing. I will dig a sawpit and get a saw, and then I can cut out boards, and build anything we want. The first time I go to Lymington I will buy a saw – I can afford it now; and I'll make a carpenter's bench for the first thing, and then, with some more tools, I shall get on; and then, Edward, I'll tell you what else I will do.'

'Then, Humphrey,' replied Edward, laughing, 'you must tell me some other time, for it is now very late, and I must go to bed, as I have to rise early. I know you have so many projects in your mind that it would take half the night to listen to them.'

'Well, I believe what you say is true,' replied Humphrey, 'and it will be better to do one thing at a time than to talk about doing a hundred; so we will, as you say, to bed.'

At sunrise Edward and Humphrey were both up. Alice came out when they tapped at her door, as she would not let Edward go without his breakfast. Edith joined them, and they went to prayers. While they were so employed, Pablo came out and listened to what was said. When prayers were over, Humphrey asked Pablo if he knew what they had been doing.

'No, not much; suppose you pray sun to shine.'

'No, Pablo,' said Edith; 'pray to God to make us good.'

'You bad then?' said Pablo. 'Me not bad.'

'Yes, Pablo, everybody very bad,' said Alice; 'but if we try to be good, God forgives us.'

The conversation was then dropped, and as soon as Edward had made his breakfast he kissed his sisters, and wished Humphrey farewell.

Edward threw his gun over his arm, and calling his puppy which he had named Holdfast, bade Humphrey and his sisters farewell, and set off on his journey across the forest.

Holdfast, as well as Humphrey's puppy, which had been named Watch, had grown very fine young animals. The first had been named Holdfast, because it would seize the pigs by the ears and lead them into the sty; and the other, because it was so alert at the least noise; but, as Humphrey said, Watch ought to have learnt to lead the pigs, it being more in his line of business than Holdfast's, which was to be brought up for hunting in the forest, while Watch was being educated as a house and farmyard dog.

Edward had refused to take the pony, as Humphrey required it for the farm work, and the weather was so fine that he preferred walking – the more so as it would enable him on his return across the forest to try for some venison, which he could not have done if he had been mounted on Billy's back. Edward walked quick, followed by his dog, which he had taught to keep to heel. He felt happy, as people do who have no cares, from the fine weather – the deep green of the verdure chequered by the flowers in bloom, and the majestic scenery which met his eye on every side. His heart was as buoyant as his steps, as he walked along, the light summer breeze fanning his face. His thoughts, however, which had been more of the chase than anything else, suddenly changed, and he became serious. For some time he had heard no political news of consequence, or what the Commons were doing with the King. This reverie naturally brought to his mind his father's death, the burning of his property, and its sequestration. His cheeks coloured with indignation, and his brow was moody. Then he built castles for the future. He imagined the King released from his prison, and leading an army against his oppressors; he fancied himself at the head of a troop of cavalry, charging the Parliamentary horse. Victory was on his side. The King was again on his throne, and he was again in possession of the family estate. He was rebuilding the hall, and somehow or another it appeared to him that Patience was standing by his side, as he gave directions to the artificers, when his reverie was suddenly disturbed by Holdfast barking and springing forward in advance.

Edward, who had by this time got over more than half his journey, looked up, and perceived himself confronted by a powerful man, apparently about forty years of age, and dressed as a verderer of the forest. He thought at the time that he had seldom seen a person with a more sinister and forbidding countenance.

'How now, young fellow, what are you doing here?' said the man, walking up to him, and cocking the gun which he held in his hand as he advanced.

Edward quietly cocked his own gun, which was loaded, when he perceived that hostile preparation on the part of the other person, and then replied, 'I am walking across the forest, as you may perceive.'

'Yes, I perceive you are walking, and you are walking with a dog and a gun; you will now be pleased to walk with me. Deer-stalkers are not any longer permitted to range this forest.'

'I am no deer-stalker,' replied Edward. 'It will be quite sufficient to give me that title when you find me with venison in my possession; and as for going with you, that I certainly shall not. Sheer off, or you may meet with harm.'

'Why, you young good-for-nothing, if you have not venison, it is not from any will not to take it; you are out in pursuit of it, that is clear. Come, come, you've the wrong person to deal with: my orders are to take up all poachers, and take you I will.'

'If you can,' replied Edward. 'But you must first prove that you are able to so do. My gun is as good and my aim is as sure as yours, whoever you may be. I tell you again I am no poacher, nor have I come out to take the deer, but to cross over to the Intendant's cottage, whither I am now going. I tell you thus much, that you may not do anything foolish; and having said this, I advise you to think twice before you act once. Let me proceed in peace, or you may lose your place, if you do not, by your own rashness, lose your life.'

There was something so cool and so determined in Edward's quiet manner that the verderer hesitated. He perceived that any attempt to take Edward would be at the risk of his own life; and he knew that his orders were to apprehend all poachers, but not to shoot people. It was true that resistance with firearms would warrant his acting in self-defence; but admitting that he should succeed, which was doubtful, still Edward had not been caught in the act of killing venison, and he had no witnesses to prove what had occurred. He also knew that the Intendant had given very strict orders as to the shedding of blood, which he was most averse to, under any circumstances; and there was something in Edward's appearance and manner so different from a common person that he was puzzled. Moreover, Edward had stated that he was going to the Intendant's house. All things considered, as he found that bullying would not succeed, he thought it advisable to change his tone, and therefore said, –

'You tell me that you are going to the Intendant's house; you have business there, I presume? If I took you prisoner, it is there I should have conducted you; so, young man, you may now walk on before me.'

'I thank you,' replied Edward, 'but walk on before you I will not; but if you choose to half-cock your gun again, and walk by my side, I will do the same. Those are my terms, and I will listen to no other; so be pleased to make up your mind, as I am in haste.'

The verderer appeared very indignant at this reply, but after a time said, Be it so.'

Edward then uncocked his gun, with his eyes fixed upon the man, and the verderer did the same; and then they walked side by side, Edward keeping at the distance of three yards from him, in case of treachery.

After a few moments' silence the verderer said, –

'You tell me you are going to the Intendant's house: he is not at home.'

'But young Mistress Patience is, I presume,' said Edward.

'Yes,' replied the man, who, finding that Edward appeared to know so much about the Intendant's family, began to be more civil – 'yes, she is at home, for I saw her in the garden this morning.'

'And Oswald, is he at home?' rejoined Edward.

'Yes, he is. You appear to know our people, young man. Who may you be, if it is a fair question?'

'It would have been a fair question had you treated me fairly,' replied Edward; 'but as it is no concern of yours, I shall leave you to find it out.'

This reply puzzled the man still more, and he now, from the tone of authority assumed by Edward, began to imagine that he had made some mistake, and that he was speaking to a superior, although clad in a forester's dress. He therefore answered humbly, observing that he had only been doing his duty.

Edward walked on without making any reply.

As they arrived within a hundred yards of the Intendant's house, Edward said, –

'I have now arrived at my destination, and am going into that house, as I told you. Do you choose to enter it with me, or will you go to Oswald Partridge and tell him that you have met with Edward Armitage in the forest, and that I should be glad to see him? I believe you are under his orders, are you not?'

'Yes, I am,' replied the verderer, 'and as I suppose that all's right, I shall go and deliver your message.'

Edward then turned away from the man, and went into the wicket-gate of the garden, and knocked at the door of the house. The door was opened by Patience Heatherstone herself, who said, 'Oh, how glad I am to see you! Come in.' Edward took off his hat and bowed. Patience led the way into her father's study, where Edward had been first received.

'And now,' said Patience, extending her hand to Edward, 'thanks, many thanks, for your preserving me from so dreadful a death. You don't know how unhappy I have been at not being able to give you my poor thanks for your courageous behaviour.'

Her hand still remained in Edward's while she said this.

'You rate what I did too highly,' replied Edward; 'I would have done the same for any one in such distress: it was my duty as a – man' – cavalier he was about to say, but he checked himself.

'Sit down,' said Patience, taking a chair; 'nay, no ceremony. I cannot treat as an inferior one to whom I owe such a debt of gratitude.'

Edward smiled as he took his seat.

'My father is as grateful to you as I am – I'm sure that he is; for I heard him when at prayer call down blessings on your head. What can he do for you? I begged Oswald Partridge to bring you here, that I might find out. O sir, do pray let me know how we can show our gratitude by something more than words.'

'You have shown it already, Mistress Patience,' replied Edward. 'Have you not honoured a poor forester with your hand in friendship, and even admitted him to sit down before you?'

'He who has preserved my life at the risk of his own becomes to me as a brother – at least I feel as a sister towards him. A debt is still a debt, whether indebted to a king or to a –'

'Forester, Mistress Patience – that is the real word that you should not have hesitated to have used. Do you imagine that I am ashamed of my calling?'

'To tell you candidly the truth, then,' replied Patience, 'I cannot believe that you are what you profess to be. I mean to say that, although a forester now, you were never brought up as such. My father has an opinion allied to mine.'

'I thank you both for your good opinion of me, but I fear that I cannot raise myself above the condition of a forester; nay, from your father's coming down here, and the new regulations, I have every chance of sinking down to the lower grade of a deer-stalker and poacher. Indeed, had it not been that I had my gun with me, I should have been seized as such this very day as I came over.'

'But you were not shooting the deer, were you, sir?' inquired Patience.

'No, I was not; nor have I killed any since I saw you.'

'I am glad that I can say that to my father,' replied Patience; 'it will much please him. He said to me that he thought you capable of much higher employment than any that could be offered here, and only wished to know what you would accept. He has interest – great interest – although just now at variance with the rulers of this country, on account of the –'

'Murder of the King you would or should have said, Mistress Patience. I have heard how much he was opposed to that foul deed, and I honour him for it.'

'How kind, how truly kind you are to say so!' said Patience, the tears starting in her eyes. 'What pleasure to hear my father's conduct praised by you!'

'Why, of course, Mistress Patience, all of my way of thinking must praise him. Your father is in London, I hear?'

'Yes, he is; and that reminds me that you must want some refreshment after your walk. I will call Phœbe.' So saying, Patience left the room.

The fact was, Mistress Patience was reminded that she had been sitting with a young man some time, and alone with him – which was not quite

89

proper in those times – and when Phœbe appeared with the cold viands she retreated out of hearing, but remained in the room.

Edward partook of the meal offered him in silence, Patience occupying herself with her work, and keeping her eyes fixed on it, unless when she gave a slight glance at the table to see if anything was required. When the meal was over Phœbe removed the tray, and then Edward rose to take his leave.

'Nay, do not go yet; I have much to say first. Let me again ask you how we can serve you.'

'I never can take any office under the present rulers of the nation. So that question is at rest.'

'I was afraid you would answer so,' replied Patience gravely. 'Do not think I blame you; for many are there already who would gladly retrace their steps if it were possible. They little thought, when they opposed the King, that affairs would have ended as they have done. Where do you live, sir?'

'At the opposite side of the forest, in a house belonging to me now, but which was inherited by my grandfather.'

'Do you live alone? surely not.'

'No, I do not.'

'Nay, you may tell me anything, for I would never repeat what might hurt you, or you might not wish to have known.'

'I live with my brother and two sisters, for my grandfather is lately dead.'

'Is your brother younger than you are?'

'He is.'

'And your sisters, what are their ages?'

'They are younger still.'

'You told my father that you lived upon your farm?'

'We do.'

'Is it a large farm?'

'No; very small.'

'And does that support you?'

'That and killing wild cattle has lately.'

'Yes, and killing deer also until lately?'

'You have guessed right.'

'You were brought up at Arnwood, you told my father; did you not?'

'Yes, I was brought up there, and remained there until the death of Colonel Beverley.'

'And you were educated, were you not?'

'Yes; the chaplain taught me what little I do know.'

'Then, if you were brought up in the house and educated by the chaplain, surely Colonel Beverley never intended you for a forester?'

'He did not. I was to have been a soldier as soon as I was old enough to bear arms.'

'Perhaps you are *distantly* related to the late Colonel Beverley?'

'No, I am not distantly related,' replied Edward, who began to feel uneasy at this close-examination; 'but still, had Colonel Beverley been alive, and the King still required his services, I have no doubt that I should have been serving under him at this time. And now, Mistress Patience, that I have answered so many questions of yours, may I be permitted to ask a little about yourself in return? Have you any brothers?'

'None; I am an only child.'

'Have you only one parent alive?'

'Only one.'

'What families are you connected with?'

Patience looked up with surprise at this last question.

'My mother's name was Cooper; she was sister to Sir Anthony Ashley Cooper, who is a person well known.'

'Indeed! Then you are of gentle blood?'

'I believe so,' replied Patience, with surprise.

'Thank you for your condescension, Mistress Patience. And now, if you will permit me, I will take my leave.'

'Before you go, let me once more thank you for saving a worthless life,' said Patience. 'Well, you must come again when my father is here. He will be but too glad to have an opportunity of thanking one who has preserved his only child. Indeed, if you knew my father, you would feel as much regard for him as I do. He is very good, although he looks so stern and melancholy; but he has seldom smiled since my poor mother's death.'

'As to your father, Mistress Patience, I will think as well as I can of one who is joined to a party which I hold in detestation. I can say no more.'

'I must not say all that I know, or you would perhaps find out that he is not quite so wedded to that party as you suppose. Neither his brother-in-law nor he are great friends of Cromwell's, I can assure you; but this in confidence.'

'That raises him in my estimation. But why, then, does he hold office?'

'He did not ask it – it was given to him, I really believe, because they wished him out of the way; and he accepted it because he was opposed to what was going on, and wished himself to be away. At least I infer so much from what I have learnt. It is not an office of power or trust which leagues him with the present Government.'

'No; only one which opposes him to me and my malpractices,' replied Edward, laughing. 'Well, Mistress Patience, you have shown great condescension to a poor forester, and I return you many thanks for your kindness towards me. I will now take my leave.'

'And when will you come and see my father?'

'I cannot say. I fear that I shall not to be able very soon to look in his injured face, and it will not be well for a poacher to come near him,' replied Edward. 'However, some day I may be taken and brought before you as a prisoner, you know, and then he is certain to see me.'

'I will not tell you to kill deer,' replied Patience; 'but if you do kill them, no one shall harm you – or I know little of my power or my father's. Farewell, then, sir; and once more gratitude and thanks.'

Patience held out her hand again to Edward, who this time, like a true Cavalier, raised it respectfully to his lips. Patience coloured a little, but did not attempt to withdraw it; and Edward, with a low obeisance, quitted the room.

CHAPTER 13

As soon as he was out of the Intendant's house, Edward hastened to the cottage of Oswald Partridge, whom he found waiting for him; for the verderer had not failed to deliver his message.

'You have had a long talk with Mistress Patience,' said Oswald, after the first greeting; 'and I am glad of it, as it gives you consequence here. The Roundhead rascal whom you met was inclined to be very precise about doing his duty, and insisted that he was certain that you were on the look-out for deer; but I stopped his mouth by telling him that I often took you out with me, as you were the best shot in the whole forest, and that the Intendant knew that I did so. I think that if you were caught in the act of killing a deer you had better tell them that you killed it by my request; and I will bear you out, if they bring you to the Intendant, who will, I'm sure, thank me for saying so. You might kill all the deer in the forest, after what you have done for him.'

'Many thanks; but I do not think I can take advantage of your offer. Let them catch me if they can, and if they do catch me, let them take me if they can.'

'I see, sir, that you will accept no favour from the Roundheads,' replied Oswald. 'However, as I am now head keeper, I shall take care that my men do not interfere with you, if I can help it. All I wish is to prevent any insult or indignity being offered to you – they not being aware who you are, as I am.'

'Many thanks, Oswald. I must take my chance.'

Edward then told Oswald of their having taken the gipsy boy in the pit, at which he appeared much amused.

'What is the name of the verderer whom I met in the forest?' inquired Edward.

'James Corbould. He was discharged from the army,' replied Oswald.

'I do not like his appearance,' said Edward.

'No; his face tells against him,' replied Oswald. 'But I know nothing of him; he has been here little more than a fortnight.'

'Can you give me a corner to put my head in tonight, Oswald? for I shall not start till tomorrow morning.'

'You may command all I have, sir,' replied Oswald. 'But I fear there is little more than a hearty welcome. I have no doubt that you could be lodged at the Intendant's house if you choose.'

'No, Oswald; the young lady is alone, and I will not trust to Phœbe's accommodation again. I will stay here, if you will permit me.'

'And welcome, sir. I will put your puppy in the kennel at once.'

Edward remained that night at Oswald's, and at daylight he rose, and having taken a slight breakfast, throwing his gun over his shoulder, went to the kennel for Holdfast, and set off on his return home.

'That's a very nice little girl,' were the words which Edward found himself constantly saying to himself as he walked along; 'and she is of a grateful disposition, or she would not have behaved as she has done towards me – supposing me to be of mean birth.' And then he thought of what she had told him relative to her father, and Edward felt his animosity against a Roundhead wasting fast away. 'I am not likely to see her again very soon,' thought Edward, 'unless, indeed, I am brought to the Intendant as a prisoner.' Thus thinking upon one subject or another, Edward had gained above eight miles of his journey across the forest, when he thought that he was sufficiently far away to venture to look out for some venison. Remembering there was a thicket not far from him, in which there was a clear pool of water, Edward thought it very likely that he might find a stag there cooling himself, for the weather was now very warm at noonday. He therefore called Holdfast to him, and proceeded cautiously towards the thicket. As soon as he arrived at the spot he crouched and crept silently through the underwood. At last he arrived close to the cleared spot by the pool. There was no stag there, but fast asleep upon the turf lay James Corbould, the sinister-looking verderer who had accosted him in the forest on the previous day. Holdfast was about to bark, when Edward silenced him, and then advanced to where the verderer was lying, and who, having no dog with him to give notice of Edward's approach, still remained snoring with the sun shining on his face. Edward perceived that his gun was under him on the grass. He took it up, gently opened the pan and scattered the powder, and then laid it down again; for Edward said to himself, 'That man has come out after me, that I am certain; and as there are no witnesses, he may be inclined to be mischievous, for a more wretched looking person I never saw. Had he been deer-hunting he would have brought his dog; but he is man-hunting, that is evident. Now I will leave him, and should he fall in with anything, he will not kill at first shot, that's certain; and if he follows me, I shall have the same chance of escape as anything else he may fire at.' Edward then walked out of the covert, thinking that if ever there was a face which proclaimed a man to be a murderer, it was that of James Corbould. As he was threading his way, he heard the howl of a dog, and on looking round, perceived that Holdfast was not with him. He turned back, and Holdfast came running to him. The fact was that Holdfast had smelt some meat in the pocket of the verderer, and had been putting his nose in to ascertain what it was. In so doing he had wakened up Corbould, who had saluted him with a heavy blow on the head. This occasioned the puppy to give the howl, and also occasioned Corbould to seize his gun and follow stealthily in the track of the dog, which he well knew to be the one he had seen the day before with Edward.

Edward waited for as short time, and not perceiving that Corbould made his appearance, continued on his way home, having now given up all thoughts of killing any venison. He walked fast, and was within six miles of the cottage, when he stopped to drink at a small rill of water, and then sat down to rest himself for a short time. While so doing, he fell into one of his usual reveries, and forgot how time passed away. He was, however, aroused by a low growl on the part of Holdfast, and it immediately occurred to him that Corbould must have followed him. Thinking it as well to be prepared, he quietly loaded his gun, and then rose up to reconnoitre. Holdfast sprang forward, and Edward, looking in the direction, perceived Corbould partly hidden behind a tree, with his gun levelled at him. He heard the trigger pulled, and snap of the lock, but the gun did not go off; and then Corbould made his appearance, striking at Holdfast with the butt-end of his gun. Edward advanced to him and desired him to desist, or it would be the worse for him.

'Indeed, younker! it may be the worse for you,' cried Corbould.

'It might have been if your gun had gone off,' replied Edward.

'I did not aim at you; I aimed at the dog, and I will kill the brute if I can.'

'Not without danger to yourself; but it was not him that you aimed at – your gun was not pointed low enough to hit the dog – it was levelled at me, you sneaking wretch; and I have only to thank my own prudence and your sleepy head for having escaped with my life. I tell you candidly that I threw the powder out of your pan while you were asleep. If I served you as you deserve, I should now put my bullet into you; but I cannot kill a man who is defenceless – and that saves your life. But set off as fast as you can away from me, for if you follow me I will show no more forbearance. Away with you directly,' continued Edward, raising his gun to his shoulder and pointing it to Corbould; 'if you do not be off, I'll fire.'

Corbould saw that Edward was resolute, and thought proper to comply with his request. He walked away till he considered himself out of gunshot, and then commenced a torrent of oaths and abusive language, with which we shall not offend our readers. Before he went further, he swore that he would have Edward's life before many days had passed, and then shaking his fist he went away. Edward remained where he was standing till the man was fairly out of sight, and then proceeded on his journey. It was now about four o'clock in the afternoon, and Edward, as he walked on, said to himself, 'That man must be of a very wicked disposition, for I have offended him in nothing except in not submitting to be made his prisoner; and is that an offence to take a man's life for? He is a dangerous man, and will be more dangerous after being again foiled by me as he has been today. I doubt if he will go home. I am almost sure that he will turn and follow me when he thinks that he can without my seeing him; and if he does, he will find out where our cottage is – and who knows what mischief he may not do, and how he may alarm my little sisters? I'll not go home till dark; and I'll now walk in another direction, that I may mislead him.' Edward then walked away more to the north, and every half-hour shifted his course, so as to be walking in a very different direction from where the cottage stood. In the meantime it grew gradually dark; and as it became so, every now and then when Edward passed a large tree, he turned round behind it and looked to see if Corbould was following him. At last, just as it was dark, he perceived the figure of a man at no great distance from him, who was following him, running from tree to tree, so as to make his approach. 'Oh, you are there!' thought Edward. 'Now will I give you a nice dance, and we will see whose legs are tired soonest. Let me see – where am I?' Edward looked round, and then perceived that he was close to the clump of trees where Humphrey had made his pitfall for the cattle, and there was a clear spot of about a quarter of a mile between it and where he now stood. Edward made up his mind, and immediately walked out to cross the clearing, calling Holdfast to heel. It was now nearly dark, for there was only the light of the stars; but still there was sufficient light to see his way. As Edward crossed the cleared spot, he once looked round, and perceived that Corbould was following him, and nearer than he was before, trusting probably to the increased darkness to hide his approach. 'That will do,' thought Edward. 'Come along, my fine fellow.' And Edward walked on till he came to the pitfall; there he stopped and looked round, and soon discovered the verderer at a hundred yards' distance. Edward held his dog by the mouth that he should not growl or bark, and then went on in a direction so as to bring the pitfall exactly between Corbould and himself. Having done so, he proceeded at a more rapid pace; and Corbould, following him, also increased his, till he arrived at the pitfall, which he could not perceive, and fell into it headlong; and as he fell into the pit, at the same time Edward heard the discharge of his gun, the crash of the small branches laid over it, and a cry on the part of Corbould. 'That will do,' thought Edward. 'Now you may lie there as long as the gipsy did, and that will cool your courage. Humphrey's pitfall is full of adventure. In this case it has done me a service. Now I may turn and go home as fast as I can. Come, Holdfast, old boy; we both want our suppers. I can answer for one, for I could eat the whole of that pasty which Oswald set before me this morning.' Edward walked at a rapid pace, quite delighted at the issue of the adventure. As he arrived near to the cottage, he found Humphrey outside, with Pablo, on the lookout for him. He soon joined them, and soon after embraced Alice and Edith, who had been anxiously waiting for his return, and who had wondered at his being out so late. 'Give me my supper, my dear girls,' said Edward, 'and then you shall know all about it.'

As soon as Edward had satisfied his craving appetite – for he had not, as my readers must recollect, eaten anything since his departure early in the morning from the house of Oswald Partridge – he entered into a narrative of the events of the day. They all listened with great interest; and when Edward had finished, Pablo, the gipsy boy, jumped up, and said, –

'Now he is in the pit, tomorrow morning I take gun and shoot him.'

'No, no, Pablo, you must not do that,' replied Edward, laughing.

'Pablo,' said little Edith, 'go and sit down; you must not shoot people.'

'He shoot Master then,' said Pablo. 'He very bad man.'

'But if you shoot him, you will be a bad boy, Pablo,' replied Edith, who appeared to have assumed an authority over him. Pablo did not appear to understand this, but he obeyed the order of his little mistress, and resumed his seat at the chimney-corner.

'But, Edward,' said Humphrey, 'what do you propose to do?'

'I hardly know. My idea was to let him remain there for a day or two, and then send to Oswald to let him know where the fellow was.'

'The only objection to that is,' replied Humphrey, 'that you say his gun went off as he fell into the pit. It may be probable that he is wounded, and if so he might die if he is left there.'

'You are right, Humphrey – that is possible; and I would not have the life of a fellow-creature on my conscience.'

'I think it would be advisable, Edward, that I should set off early tomorrow on the pony, and see Oswald, tell him all that has occurred, and show him where the pitfall it.'

'I believe that would be the best plan, Humphrey.'

'Yes,' said Alice; 'it would be dreadful that a man should die in so wicked a state. Let him be taken out, and perhaps he will repent.'

'Won't God punish him, brother?' said Edith.

'Yes, my dear, sooner or later the vengeance of Heaven overtakes the wicked. But I am very tired after so long a walk. Let us go to prayers, and then to bed.'

The danger that Edward had incurred that day was felt strongly by the whole party; and, with the exception of Pablo, there was earnest devotion and gratitude to Heaven when their orisons were offered up.

Humphrey was off before daybreak, and at nine o'clock had arrived at the cottage of Oswald, by whom he was warmly greeted before the cause of his unexpected arrival was made known. Oswald was greatly annoyed at Humphrey's narration, and appeared to be very much of the opinion of Pablo, which was to leave the scoundrel where he was; but on the remonstrance of Humphrey he set off with two of the other verderers, and before nightfall Humphrey arrived at the pitfall, where they heard Corbould groaning below.

'Who's there?' said Oswald, looking into the pit.

'It's me – it's Corbould,' replied the man.

'Are you hurt?'

'Yes, badly,' replied Corbould. 'When I fell, my gun went off, and the ball has gone through my thigh. I have almost bled to death.'

Humphrey went for the ladder, which was at hand, and with much exertion on the part of the whole four of them they contrived to drag out

Corbould, who groaned heavily with pain. A handkerchief was tied tightly round his leg to prevent any further bleeding, and they gave him some water, which revived him.

'Now, what's to be done?' said Oswald. 'We can never get him home.'

'I will tell you,' said Humphrey, walking with him aside. 'It will not do for any of these men to know our cottage, and we cannot take them there. Desire them to remain with the man, while you go for a cart to carry him home. We will go to the cottage, give Billy his supper, and then return with him in the cart, and bring your men something to eat. Then I will go with you, and bring the cart back again before daylight. It will be a night's walk, but it will be the safest plan.'

'I think so too,' replied Oswald, who desired the men to wait till his return, as he was going to borrow a cart; and then set off with Humphrey.

As soon as they arrived at the cottage, Humphrey gave the pony to Pablo to put into the stable and feed, and then communicated to Edward the state of Corbould.

'It's almost a pity that he had not killed himself outright,' observed Oswald. 'It would have been justice to him for attempting your life without any cause. He is a bloodthirsty scoundrel, and I wish he was anywhere but where he is. However, the Intendant shall know of it, and I have no doubt that he will be discharged.'

'Do nothing in a hurry, Oswald,' replied Edward. 'At present let him give his own version of the affair, for he may prove more dangerous when discharged than when under your control. Now sit down and take your supper. Billy must have an hour to get his, and therefore there is no hurry for you.'

'That is your gipsy lad, Edward, is he not?' said Oswald.

'Yes.'

'I like the boy's looks; but they are a queer race. You must not trust him too much,' continued Oswald, in an undertone, 'until you have tried him and are satisfied of his fidelity. They are very excitable, and capable of strong attachment if well treated. That I know, for I did a gipsy a good turn once, and it proved to be the saving of my life afterwards.'

'Oh, tell us how, Oswald,' said Alice.

'It is too long a story now, my dear little lady,' replied Oswald, 'but I will another time. Whatever he may do, do not strike him; for they never forgive a blow, I am told, by those who know them; and it never does them any good. As I said before, they are a queer race.'

'He will not be beaten by us,' replied Humphrey, 'depend upon it, unless Edith slaps him; for she is the one who takes most pains with him, and I presume he would not care much about her little hand.'

'No, no,' replied Oswald, laughing, 'Edith may do as she pleases. What does he do for you?'

'Oh, nothing as yet, for he is hardly recovered, poor fellow,' replied Humphrey. 'He follows Edith, and helps her to look for the eggs; and last night he set some springs after his own fashion, and certainly beat me, for he took three rabbits and a hare, while I, with all my traps, only took one rabbit.'

'I think you had better leave that part of your livelihood entirely to him. He has been bred up to it, Humphrey, and it will be his amusement. You must not expect him to work very hard; they are not accustomed to it. They live a roving life, and never speak if they can help it. Still, if you make him fond of you, he may be very useful, for they are very clever and handy.'

'I hope to make him useful,' replied Humphrey, 'but still I will not force him to do what he does not like. He is very fond of the pony already, and likes to take care of him.'

'Bring him over to me one of these days, so that he may know where to find me. It may prove of consequence if you have a message to send and cannot come yourselves.'

'That is very true,' replied Edward. 'I will not forget it.'

'Humphrey, shall you or I go with the cart?'

'Humphrey, by all means. It will not do for them to suppose I had the cart from you, Edward. They do not know Humphrey, and he will be off again in the morning before they are up.'

'Very true,' replied Edward.

'And it is time for us to set off,' replied Oswald. 'Will Mistress Alice oblige me with something for my men to eat, for they have fasted the whole day?'

'Yes,' replied Alice. 'I will have it ready before the pony is in the cart. — Edith, dear, come with me.'

Humphrey then went out to harness the pony, and when all was ready he and Oswald set off again.

When they arrived at the pitfall, they found Corbould lying between the two other verderers, who were sitting by his side. Corbould was much recovered since his wound had been bound up, and he was raised up and put on the fodder which Humphrey had put into the cart; and they proceeded on their journey to the other side of the forest, the verderers eating what Humphrey had brought for them as they walked along. It was a tedious and painful journey for the wounded man; who shrieked out when the cart was jolted by the wheel getting into a rut or hole; but there was no help for it, and he was very much exhausted when they arrived, which was not till past midnight. Corbould was then taken to his cottage and put on the bed, and another verderer sent for a surgeon. Those who had been with Oswald were glad to go to bed, for it had been a fatiguing day. Humphrey remained with Oswald for three hours, and then again returned with Billy, who, although he had crossed the forest three times in the twenty-four hours, appeared quite fresh and ready to go back again.

'I will let you know how he gets on, Humphrey, and what account he gives of his falling into the pit; but you must not expect me for a fortnight at least.'

Humphrey wished Oswald good-bye; and Billy was so anxious to get back to his stable that Humphrey could not keep him at a quiet pace.

'Horses, and all animals, indeed, know that there is no place like home. It is a pity that men, who consider themselves much wiser, have not the same consideration,' thought Humphrey as the pony trotted along. Humphrey thought a good deal about the danger that Edward had been subjected to, and said to himself, 'I really think that I should be more comfortable if Edward was away. I am always in a fidget about him. I wish the new king, who is now in France, would raise an army and come over. It is better that Edward should be fighting in the field than remain here and risk being shot as a deer-stealer, or put in prison. The farm is sufficient for us all; and when I have taken in more ground, it will be more than sufficient, even if I do not kill the wild cattle. I am fit for the farm, but Edward is not. He is thrown away, living in this obscurity, and he feels it. He will always be in hot water some way or another, that is certain. What a narrow escape he has had with that scoundrel, and yet how little he cares for it! He was intended for a soldier, that is evident; and if ever he is one, he will be in his element, and distinguish himself, if it pleases God to spare his life. I'll persuade him to stay at home a little while to help me to enclose the other piece of ground, and after that is done, I'll dig a sawpit, and see if I can coax Pablo to saw with me. I must go to Lymington and buy a saw. If I once could get the tree sawed up into planks, what a quantity of things I could make, and how I could improve the place!'

Thus thought Humphrey as he went along. He was all for the farm and improvements, and was always calculating when he should have another calf or a fresh litter of pigs. His first idea was that he would make Pablo work hard; but the advice he had received from Oswald was not forgotten, and he now was thinking how he should coax Pablo into standing below in the sawpit, which was not only hard work, but disagreeable, from the sawdust falling into the eyes. Humphrey's cogitations were interrupted by a halloo, and turning round in the direction of the voice, he perceived Edward, and turned the cart to join him.

'You're just in time, Humphrey; I have some provision for Alice's larder. I took my gun and came out on the path which I knew you would return on, and I have killed a young buck. He is good meat, and we are scarce of provisions.'

Humphrey helped Edward to put the venison in the cart, and they returned to the cottage, which was not more than three miles off. Humphrey told Edward the result of his journey, and then proposed that Edward should stop at home for a few days and help him with the new enclosure. To this Edward cheerfully consented; and as soon as they arrived at the cottage, and Humphrey had had his breakfast, they took their axes and went out to fell at a cluster of small spruce firs about a mile off.

CHAPTER 14

'Now, Humphrey, what do you propose to do?'

'This,' replied Humphrey: 'I have marked out three acres or thereabouts of the land running in a straight line behind the garden. There is not a tree on it, and it is all good feeding ground. What I intend to do is to enclose it with the spruce-fir posts and rails that we are about to cut down, and then set a hedge upon a low bank which I shall raise all round inside the rails. I know where there are thousands of seedling thorns, which I shall take up in the winter, or early in the spring, to put in, as the bank will be ready for them by that time.'

'Well, that's all very good; but I fear it will be a long while before you have such a quantity of land dug up.'

'Yes, of course it will; but, Edward, I have plenty of manure to spare, and I shall put it over all this land, and then it will become a rich pasture, and also an earlier pasture than what we can get from the forest, and will be very handy to turn the cows and the calves upon, or even Billy if we want him in a hurry.'

'All that is very true,' replied Edward, 'so that it will be useful at all events if you do not dig it up.'

'Indeed it will,' replied Humphrey. 'I only wish it were six acres instead of three.'

'I can't say I do,' replied Edward, laughing. 'You are too grand in your ideas. Only think what a quantity of spruces we shall have to cut down on it, to post and rail what you just propose. Let it be three acres first, Humphrey, and when they are enclosed you may begin to talk of three more.'

'Well, perhaps you are right, Edward,' said Humphrey. 'Why, here's Pablo coming after us. He's not coming to work, I presume, but to amuse himself by looking on.'

'I don't think he is strong enough to do much hard work, Humphrey, although he appears very ingenious.'

'No; I agree with you: and if he is to work, depend upon it, it must not be by having work set out for him. He would take a disgust to it directly. I have another plan for him.'

'And what is that, Humphrey?'

'I shall not set him anything to do, and shall make him believe that I do not think he is able to do anything. That will pique him, and I think by that means I shall get more work out of him than you would think, especially when, after he has done it, I express my wonder and give him praise.'

'Not a bad idea that. You will work upon his pride, which is probably stronger than his laziness.'

'I do not think him lazy, but I think him unused to hard work, and, having lived a life of wandering and idleness, not very easy to be brought to constant and daily work, except by degrees, and by the means which I propose. Here we are,' continued Humphrey, throwing his axe and bill-hook down and proceeding to take off his doublet. 'Now for an hour or two's fulfilment of the sentence of our first parents – to wit, "the sweat of the brow".'

Edward followed Humphrey's example in taking off his doublet. They selected the long thin trees most fitted for rails, and were hard at work when Pablo came up to them. More than a dozen trees had fallen, and lay one upon the other, before they stopped a while to recover themselves a little.

'Well, Pablo,' said Humphrey, wiping his forehead, 'I suppose you think looking on better than cutting down trees; and so it is.'

'What cut down trees for?'

'To make posts and rails to fence in more ground. I shall not leave the boughs on.'

'No; cut them off by-and-by, and then put poles on the cart and carry them home.'

Edward and Humphrey then recommenced their labour, and worked for another half-hour, when they paused to recover their wind.

'Hard work, Pablo,' said Humphrey.

'Yes, very hard work; Pablo not strong enough.'

'Oh no, you are not able to do anything of this kind, I know. No work this for gipsies: they take birds' nests and catch rabbits.'

'Yes,' replied Pablo, nodding, 'and you eat them.'

'So he does, Pablo,' said Edward; 'so you are useful in your way; for if he had nothing to eat he would not be able to work. Strong man cut down trees, weak man catch rabbits.'

'Both good,' said Pablo.

'Yes, but strong man like work; not strong man not like work, Pablo. So now look on again, for we must have another spell.'

'Strong man cut down trees, not strong man cut off branches,' said Pablo, taking up the billhook, and setting to work to cut off the boughs, which he did with great dexterity and rapidity.

Edward and Humphrey exchanged glances and smiles, and then worked away in silence till it was, as they supposed, dinner-time. They were not wrong in their supposition, although they had no other clock than their appetites, which, however, tell the time pretty correctly to those who work hard. Alice had the platters on the table and was looking out to see if they were coming.

'Why, Pablo, have you been at work?' said Edith.

'Yes, little missy – work all the morning.'

'Indeed he has, and has worked very well, and been very useful,' said Edward.

'It has given you an appetite for your dinner, Pablo has it not?' said Humphrey.

'Have that without work,' replied the boy.

'Pablo, you are a very good gipsy boy,' said Edith, patting his head with a patronizing air. 'I shall let you walk out with me and carry the basket to put the eggs in when you come home in the evening.'

'That is a reward,' said Humphrey, laughing.

After dinner they continued their labour, and by supper-time had so many trees cut down that they determined to carry home the next day, and lay them along, to see how many more they would want. While they put the trees in the cart and took them home, Pablo contrived to lop off the boughs and prepare the poles for them to take away. As soon as they had cut down sufficient and carted them home, they then selected shorter trees for posts; and when Pablo had cleared them of the boughs they sawed them out the proper lengths, and then carted them home. This occupied nearly the whole week, and then they proceeded to dig holes and set the posts in. The railing was then to be nailed to the posts, and that occupied them three days more; so that it was altogether a fortnight of hard work before the three acres were enclosed.

'There,' said Humphrey, 'that's a good job over. Many thanks, Edward, for your assistance – and thank you, too Pablo, for you really have helped us very much indeed, and are a very useful, good boy. Now for raising the bank – that I must do when I can spare time; but my garden is overrun with weeds, and I must get Edith and Alice to help me there.'

'If you don't want me any longer, Humphrey,' said Edward, 'I think I shall go over to see Oswald, and take Pablo with me. I want to know how that fellow Corbould is, and what he says; and whether the Intendant has come back – not that I shall go near him or his good little daughter, but I think I may as well go, and it will be a good opportunity of showing Pablo the way to Oswald's cottage.'

'I think so too; and when you come back, Edward, one of us must go to Lymington; for I require some tools, and Pablo is very ragged. He must have better clothes than these old ones of ours if he is to be sent messages. Don't you think so?'

'Certainly I do.'

'And I want a thousand things,' said Alice.

'Indeed, mistress, won't less than a thousand content you?'

'Yes, perhaps not quite a thousand; but I really do want a great many, and I will make you a list of them. I have not pans enough for my milk; I want salt; I want tubs: but I will make out a list, and you will find it a very long one.'

'Well, I hope you have something to sell to pay for them?'

'Yes; I have plenty of butter salted down.'

'What have you, Edith?'

'Oh, my chickens are not large enough yet: as soon as they are, Humphrey must get me some ducks and geese, for I mean to keep some; and by-and-by I will have some turkeys, but not yet. I must wait till Humphrey builds me the new house for them he has promised me.'

'I think you are right, Edith, about the ducks and geese: they will do well on the water behind the yard, and I will dig you out a bigger pool for them.'

'Edith, my dear, your little fingers are just made to weed my onions well, and I wish you would do it tomorrow morning, if you have time.'

'Yes, Humphrey, but my little fingers won't smell very nice afterwards.'

'Not till you have washed them, I guess; but there is soap and water, you know.'

'Yes, I know there is. But if I weed the onions, I cannot help Alice to make the butter; however, if Alice can do without me, I will do it.'

'I want some more seeds sadly,' said Humphrey, 'and I must make out my list. I must go to Lymington myself this time, Edward, for you will be puzzled with all our wants. '

'Not if I know exactly what you do want; but as I really do not, and probably should make mistakes, I think it will be better if you do go. But it is bedtime, and as I shall start early, good night, sisters. I beg you will let me have something to eat before I start. I shall try for some venison as I come back, and shall take Smoker with me. He is quite well again, and his ribs are as stout as ever.'

'And, Edward,' said Alice, 'I wish, when you kill any venison, that you would bring home some of those parts which you usually throw away; for I assure you, now that we have three dogs, I hardly know how to find enough for them to eat.'

'I'll not fail, Alice,' replied Edward; 'and now once more good night.'

Early the next morning Edward took his gun, and with Pablo and Smoker set off for Oswald's cottage.

Edward talked a great deal with Pablo relative to his former life, and, by the answers which the boy gave him, was satisfied that, notwithstanding his doubtful way of bringing-up, the lad was not corrupted, but was a well-minded boy. As they walked through a grove of trees, Edward still talking, Pablo stopped and put his hand before Edward's mouth, and then stooping down, at the same time seizing Smoker by the neck, he pointed with his finger. Edward at first could see nothing, but eventually he made out the horns of an animal just rising above a hillock. It was evidently one of the wild cattle. Edward cocked his gun and advanced cautiously, while Pablo remained where he was, holding Smoker. As soon as he was near enough to hit the head of the animal, Edward levelled and fired, and Pablo let Smoker loose, who bounded forward over the hillock. They followed the dog, and found him about to seize a calf which stood by a heifer that Edward had shot. Edward called him over, and went up to the animal: it was a fine young heifer, and the calf was not more than a fortnight old.

'We cannot stop now, Pablo,' said Edward. 'Humphrey would like to have the calf, and we must take our chance of its remaining by its mother till we come back. I think it will for a day or two, so let us push on.'

No further adventure happened, and they arrived a little after noon at Oswald's cottage. He was not at home, his wife saying that she believed that he was with the Intendant, who had come back from London the day before.

'But I will put on my hood and see,' said the young woman.

In a few minutes she returned with Oswald.

'I am glad that you have come, sir,' said Oswald, as Edward extended his hand, 'as I have just seen the Intendant, and he has been asking many questions about you. I am certain he thinks that you are not the grandson of Jacob Armitage, and that he supposes I know who you are. He asked me where your cottage was, and whether I could not take him to it, as he wished to speak to you, and said that he felt great interest about you.'

'And what did you say?'

'I said that your cottage was a good day's journey from here, and I was not certain that I knew the exact way, as I had been there but seldom; but that I knew where to find it after I saw the forests of Arnwood. I told him about Corbould and his attempt upon you, and he was very wroth. I never saw him moved before; and young Mistress Patience, she was indeed angry and perplexed, and begged her father to send the assailant away as soon as he could be moved.'

'Master Heatherstone replied, "Leave it to me, my dear," and then asked me what account Corbould gave of himself and his falling into the pit. I told him that Corbould stated that he was following a deer which he had severely wounded about noonday, and having no dog with him he could not overtake it, although he knew by its bleeding track that it could not hold out much longer; that he followed it until nightfall, and had it in view and close to him, when he fell into the pit.'

'Well, the story was not badly made up,' said Edward, 'only for a stag read man. And what did the Intendant say to that?'

'He said that he believed you, and that Corbould's story was false, as, if it had been a stag that he was following, no one would have known that he had fallen into the pit, and he would have remained there till now. I quite forgot to say that when the Intendant said that he wished to call at your cottage, the young mistress said that she would go with him, as you had told her that you had two sisters living with you, and she wished very much to see them and make their acquaintance.'

'I am afraid that we shall not be able to prevent this visit, Oswald,' replied Edward. 'He is in command here, and the forest is in his charge. We must see to it. I only should like, if possible, to have notice of his coming, that we may be prepared.'

'You need no preparation, sir, if he should come,' replied Oswald.

'Very true,' said Edward – 'we have nothing to conceal; and if he finds us in a pickle, it is of no consequence.'

'Rather the better, sir, ' replied Oswald. 'Let your sisters be at the wash-tub, and you and your brother carting manure; he will then be more likely to have no suspicion of your being otherwise than what you assume to be.'

'Have you heard any news from London, Oswald?'

'Not as yet. I was away yesterday evening, when Master Heatherstone came back, and I have not seen his man this morning. While you eat your dinner I will go into the kitchen and if he is not there, Phœbe will be sure to tell me all that she has heard.'

'Do not say that I am here, Oswald, as I do not wish to see the Intendant.'

'Mum's the word, sir; but you must stay in the cottage, or others will see you, and it may come to his ears.'

Oswald's wife then put before him a large pie and some wheaten bread, with a biggin of good beer. Edward helped Pablo to a large allowance, and then filled his own platter. While thus occupied, Oswald Partridge had left the cottage as agreed.

'What do you say, Pablo? Do you think you can walk back tonight?'

'Yes. Like walking at night. My people always do; sleep in the daytime.'

'Well, I think it will be better to go home. Oswald has only one bed, and I do not wish them to know that I am here; so, Pablo, eat heartily, and then we shall not be so tired. I want to get home, that I may send Humphrey after the calf.'

'One bed here; you stay,' replied Pablo. 'I go home, and tell Master Humphrey.'

'Do you think you would be able to find your way, Pablo?'

'Once go one way, always know same way again.'

'You are a clever fellow, Pablo, and I have a mind to try you. Now drink some beer. I think, Pablo, you shall go home and tell Humphrey that I and Smoker will be where the heifer lies dead, and have it skinned by nine o'clock tomorrow morning; so if he comes he will find me there.'

'Yes, I go now.'

'No, not now; you must rest yourself a little more.'

'Pablo not tired,' replied the gipsy, getting up; 'be back before supper. As I go along, look at calf and dead cow – see if calf stay with mother.'

'Very well then, if you wish it you may go now, ' said Edward.

Pablo nodded his head, and disappeared.

A few minutes afterwards Oswald made his appearance.

'Is the boy gone?'

'Yes; he is gone back to the cottage,' and Edward then stated how he had killed the heifer, and wanted to obtain the calf.

'I've an idea that you will find that boy very useful if he is properly managed.'

'I think so too,' replied Edward; 'and I am glad to perceive that he is already attached to all of us. We treat him as ourselves.'

'You are right. And now for the news that I have to tell you. The Duke of Hamilton, the Earl of Holland, and Lord Capel have been tried, condemned, and executed.'

Edward sighed. 'More murder! But we must expect it from those who have murdered their King. Is that all?'

'No. King Charles the Second has been proclaimed in Scotland, and invited to come over.'

'That is indeed news,' replied Edward. 'Where is he now?'

'At the Hague; but it was said that he was going to Paris.'

'That is all that you have heard?'

'Yes; that was what was current when Master Heatherstone was in town. His man Samson gave me the news; and he further said "that his master's journey to London was to oppose the execution of the three lords, but it was all in vain".'

'Well,' replied Edward, after a pause, 'if the King does come over, there will be some work cut out for some of us, I expect. Your news has put me in a fever,' continued Edward, taking up the biggin and drinking a large draught of beer.

'I thought it would,' replied Oswald: 'but until the time comes, the more quiet you keep the better.'

'Yes, Oswald. But I can't talk any more; I must be left alone to think. I will go to bed, as I shall be off early in the morning. Is that fellow Corbould getting well?'

'Yes, sir: he is out of bed, and walks a little with a stick; but he is still very lame, and will be for some time.'

'Good night, Oswald; if I have anything to say, I will write and send the boy. I do not want to be seen here any more.'

'It will be best, sir. Good night, I will put Smoker in the kennel to the right, as he will not be friendly with the other dogs.'

Edward retired to bed, but not to sleep. The Scots had proclaimed the King, and invited him over. 'He will surely come,' thought Edward, 'and he will have an army round him as soon as he lands.' Edward made up his resolution to join the army as soon as he had heard that the King had landed, and what with considering how he should be able so to do, and afterwards building castles as to what he would do, it was long before he fell asleep; and when he did, he dreamt of battles and victory; he was charging at the head of his troops; he was surrounded by the dying and the dead; he was wounded, and he was somehow or another well again, as if by magic. And then the scene was changed, and he was rescuing Patience Heatherstone from his own lawless men, and preserving the life of her father, which was about to be sacrificed. And at last he awoke and found that the daylight peeped through the windows, and that he had slept longer than he intended to do. He arose and dressed himself quickly, and not waiting for breakfast, went to the kennel, released Smoker from his durance, and set off on his return.

Before nine o'clock he had arrived at the spot where the heifer lay dead. He found the calf still by its side, bleating and walking round uneasily. As he approached with the dog it went to a farther distance, and there remained. Edward took out his knife, and commenced skinning the heifer, and then took out the inside. The animal was quite fresh and good, but not very fat, as may be supposed. While thus occupied Smoker growled and then sprang forward, bounding away in the direction of the cottage, and Edward thought Humphrey was at hand. In a few minutes the pony and cart appeared between the trees, with Humphrey and Pablo in it, and

106

Smoker leaping up at his friend Billy.

'Good morning, Humphrey,' said Edward. 'I am almost ready for you; but the question is, how are we to take the calf? It is as wild as a deer.'

'It will be a puzzler, without Smoker can run it down,' said Humphrey.

'I take him with Smoker,' said Pablo.

'How will you take it, Pablo?'

Pablo went to the cart, and took out a long small cord which Humphrey had brought with them, and made a noose at one end; he coiled the rope in his hand, and then threw it out to its full length, by way of trial. 'This way I take him, suppose I get near enough. This way take bulls in Spain – call him lasso. Now come with me.' Pablo had his rope again coiled in his hand, and then went round to the other side of the calf, which still remained lowing at about two hundred yards' distance.

'Now tell Smoker,' cried Pablo.

Humphrey set Smoker upon the calf, which retreated from the dog, presenting his head to run at it; and Pablo kept behind the animal, while Smoker attacked it, and drove it near to him.

As soon as the calf, which was so busy with the dog that it did not perceive Pablo, came sufficiently near to him, Pablo threw his rope, and caught the loop round the animal's neck. The calf set off galloping towards Humphrey, and dragging Pablo after him, for the latter was not strong enough to hold it.

Humphrey went to his assistance, and then Edward, and the calf was thrown down by Smoker, who seized it by the neck, and it was tied and put on the cart in a few minutes.

'Well done, Pablo! You are a clever fellow,' said Edward, 'and this calf shall be yours.'

'It is a cow calf,' said Humphrey, 'which I am glad of. – Pablo, you did that well, and, as Edward says, the calf belongs to you.'

Pablo looked pleased, but said nothing.

The meat and hide were put into the cart with some of the offal which Alice had asked for the dogs, and they set off on their return home.

Humphrey was very anxious to go to Lymington, and was not sorry that he had some meat to take with him. He determined to get off the next morning; and Edward proposed that he should take Pablo with him, that he might know the way there in case of any emergency, for they both felt that Pablo could be trusted. Edward said he would remain at home with his sisters, and see if he could be of any use to Alice; if not, there would be work in the garden. Humphrey and Pablo went away after breakfast, with Billy, and the meat and skin of the heifer in the cart. Humphrey had also a large basket of eggs, and three dozen of chickens from Alice, to be disposed of, and a list, as long as the tail of a kite, of articles which she and Edith required. Fortunately there was nothing very expensive on the list, long as it was; but women in those days required needles, pins, buttons, tapes, thread, worsted, and a hundred other little necessaries, as they do now. As soon as they were gone Edward, who was still castle-building instead of offering his services to Alice, brought out his father's sword and commenced cleaning it. When he had polished it up to his satisfaction he felt less inclined than ever to do anything; so after dinner he took his gun and walked out into the forest, that he might indulge in his reveries. He walked on, quite unconscious of the direction in which he was going, and more than once finding his hat knocked off his head by the branch of a tree which he had not perceived – for the best of all possible reasons, because his eyes were cast on the ground – when his ears were saluted with the neighing of a horse. He looked up, and perceived that he was near to a herd of forest ponies, the first that he had seen since he had lived in the forest.

This roused him, and he looked about him. 'Where can I have been wandering to?' thought Edward. 'I never fell in with any of the forest ponies before; I must therefore have walked in a direction quite contrary to what I usually do. I do not know where I am; the scenery is new to me. What a fool I am! It's lucky that nobody except Humphrey digs pitfalls, or I should probably have been in one by this time; and I've brought out my gun and left the dog at home. Well, I suppose I can find my way back.' Edward then surveyed the whole herd of ponies, which were at no great distance from him. There was a fine horse or two among them, which appeared to be the leaders of the herd. They allowed Edward to approach to within two hundred yards, and then, with manes and tails streaming in the air, they darted off with the rapidity of the wind.

'Now I'll puzzle Humphrey when I go back,' thought Edward. 'He says that Billy is getting old, and that he wishes he could get another pony. I will tell him what a plenty there are, and propose that he should invent some way of catching one. That will be a poser for him; yet I'm sure that he'll try, for he is very ingenious. And now which way am I to turn to find my way home? I think it ought to be to the north; but which is north? for there is no sun out, and now I perceive it looks very like rain. I wonder how long I have been walking! I'm sure I don't know.' Edward then hurried in a direction which he considered might lead him homeward, and walked fast; but he once more fell into his habit of castle-building, and was talking to himself: 'The King proclaimed in Scotland! He will come over of course. I will join his army, and then . . .' Thus he went on, again absorbed in the news which he had gained from Oswald, till on a sudden he again recollected himself, and perceived that he had lost sight of the copse of trees on a high hill, to which he had been directing his steps. Where was it? He turned round and round, and at last found out that he had been walking away from it. 'I must dream no more,' thought he; 'or if I do indulge in any more day-dreams, I certainly shall neither sleep nor dream tonight. It is getting dark already, and here am I lost in the forest, and all through my own foolishness. If the stars do not shine, I shall not know how to direct my steps; indeed, if they do, I don't know whether I have walked south or north, and I am in a pretty pickle – not that I care for being out in the forest on a night like this; but my sisters and Humphrey will be alarmed at my absence. The best thing I can do is to decide upon taking some straight line, and continue in it. I must then get out of the forest at last, even if I walk right across it. That will be better than going backwards and forwards, or round and round, as I otherwise shall do, just like a puppy running after its own tail. So now shine out, stars!' Edward waited until he could make out Charles's Wain, which he well knew, and then the Polar Star. As soon as he was certain of that, he resolved to travel by it due north, and he did so, sometimes walking fast, and at others keeping up a steady trot for half a mile without stopping. As he was proceeding on his travels he observed under some trees ahead of him a spark of fire emitted. He thought it was a glowworm at first, but it was more like the striking of a flint against steel; and as he saw it a second time, he stopped that he might ascertain what it might be before he advanced further.

CHAPTER 15

It was now very dark, as there was no moon, and the stars were often obscured by the clouds, which were heavy, and borne along by the wind, which was very high. The light again appeared, and this time Edward heard the clash of the flint against the steel, and he was certain that it was somebody striking a light. He advanced very cautiously, and arrived at a large tree, behind which he remained to reconnoitre. The people, whoever they might be, were not more than thirty yards from him. A light spread its rays for a moment or two. and he could make out a figure kneeling and holding his hat to, protect it from the wind; then it burned brighter, and he saw that a lantern had been lighted, and then again, of a sudden, all was dark again: so Edward immediately satisfied himself that a dark lantern had been lighted and then closed. Who the parties might be he of course had no idea; but he was resolved that he would ascertain, if he could, before he accosted them and asked his way.

'They have no dog,' thought Edward, 'or it would have growled before this; and it's lucky that I have none either.' Edward then crept softly nearer to them. The wind, which was strong, blew from where they were to where Edward stood, so that there was less chance of their hearing his approach.

Edward went on his hands and knees, and crawled through the fern until he gained another tree, and within ten yards of them, and from where he could hear what they might say. He was thus cautious, as he had been told by Oswald that there were many disbanded soldiers who had taken up their quarters in the forest, and had committed several depredations upon the houses adjacent to it, always returning to the forest as a rendezvous. Edward listened, and heard one say, –

'It is not time yet! No, no; too soon by half an hour or more. The people from Lymington who buy him what he wants always bring it to him at night, that his retreat may not be discovered. They sometimes do not leave the cottage till two hours after dark, for they do not leave Lymington to go there till it is dark.'

'Do you know who it is who supplies him with food?'

'Yes; the people at the inn in Parliament Street – I forget the sign.'

'Oh, I know! Yes, the landlord is a downright Malignant in his heart! We might squeeze him well if we dared show ourselves in Lymington.'

'Yes, but they would squeeze our necks tighter than would be agreeable, I expect,' replied the other.

'Are you sure that he has money?'

'Quite sure; for I peeped through the chinks of the window-shutters, and I saw him pay for the things brought to him. It was from a canvas bag, and it was gold that he took out.'

'And where did he put the bag after he had paid them?'

'That I can't tell; for as I knew that they would come out as soon as they were paid, I was obliged to beat a retreat lest I should be seen.'

'Well, then, how is it to be managed?'

'We must first tap at the door, and try if we can get in as benighted travellers. If that won't do, and I fear it will not, while you remain begging for admittance at the door, and keep him occupied, I will try the door behind, that leads into the garden; and if not the door, I will try the window. I have examined them both well, and have been outside when he has shut up his shutters, and I know the fastenings. With a pane out I could open them immediately.'

'Is there anybody else besides him in the cottage?'

'Yes, a lad who attends him, and goes to Lymington for him.'

'No women?'

'Not one.'

'But do you think we two sufficient? Had we not better get more help? There is Broom, and Black, the gipsy, at the rendezvous. I can go for them, and be back in time. They are stout and true.'

'Stout enough, but not true. No, no, I want no sharers in this business, and you know how ill they behaved in the last affair. I'll swear that they only produced half the swag. I like honour between gentlemen and soldiers, and that's why I have chosen you. I know I can trust you, Benjamin. It's time now; what do you say? We are two to one, for I count the boy as nothing. Shall we start?'

'I am with you. You say there's a bag of gold, and that's worth fighting for.'

'Yes, Ben, and I'll tell you: with what I've got buried, and my share of that bag, I shall have enough, I think; and I'll start for the Low Countries, for England's getting rather too warm for me.'

'Well, I shan't go yet,' replied Benjamin. 'I don't like your foreign parts; they have no good ale, and I can't understand their talk. I'd sooner remain in jolly old England, with a halter twisted ready for me, than pass my life with such a set of chaps who drink nothing but Schiedam, and wear twenty pair of breeches. Come, let's be off. If we get the money, you shall go to the Low Countries, Will, and I'll start for the north, where they don't know me – for if you go, I won't stay here.'

The two men then rose up; and the one whose name appeared to be Will first examined if the candle in his dark-lantern burnt well, and then they both set off, followed by Edward, who had heard quite enough to satisfy him that they were bent upon a burglary – if not murder. Edward followed them, so as to keep their forms indistinctly in sight, which was as much as he could do at twenty yards' distance. Fortunately the wind was so high that they did not hear his footsteps, although he often trod upon a rotten stick, which snapped as it broke in twain. As near as Edward could guess, he had tracked them for about three miles, when they stopped, and he perceived that they were examining their pistols, which they took from their belts. They then went on again, and entered a small plantation of oak-trees, of about forty years' growth – very thick and very dark, with close undergrowth below. They followed each other through a narrow path, until they came to a cleared place in the middle of the plantation, in which here stood a low cottage, surrounded with covert on every side, with the exception of some thirty yards of land around it. All was still, and as dark as pitch. Edward remained behind the trees, and when the two men again stopped he was not six feet from them. They consulted in a low tone, but the wind was so high that he could not distinguish what they said. At last they advanced to the cottage, and Edward, still keeping within the trees, shifted his position so that he should be opposite the gable end of the cottage. He observed one man go up to the front door, while the other went round to the door behind, as had been agreed. Edward threw open the pan of the lock of his gun, and reprimed it, that he might be sure, and then waited for what was to follow. He heard the man Will at the front door, talking and asking for shelter in a plaintive but loud voice; and shortly afterwards he perceived a light through the chinks of the shutters – for Edward was continually altering his position to see what was going on in the front and in the back. At one time he thought of levelling his gun and killing one of the men at once; but he could not make up his mind to do that, as a burglary, although intended, had not yet been committed; so he remained passive until the attack was really made, when he resolved that he would come to the rescue. After some minutes of entreaty that they would open the door, the man in front commenced thumping and beating against it, as if he would make them open the door by force; but this was to attract the attention of those within, and divert it from the attempts that the other was making to get in behind. Edward was aware of this: he now kept his eye upon what was going on at the back. Advancing nearer, which he ventured to do now that both the men were so occupied, he perceived that the fellow had contrived to open the window close to the back door, and was remaining quite close to it with a pistol in his hand, apparently

111

not wishing to run the risk of climbing in. Edward slipped under the eaves of the cottage, not six feet from the man, who remained with his back partly turned towards him. Edward then finding he had obtained this position unperceived, crouched down with his gun ready pointed.

As Edward remained in this position, he heard a shrill voice cry out, 'They are getting in behind!' and a movement in the cottage. The man near him, who had his pistol in his hand, put his arm through the window, and fired inside. A shriek was given, and Edward fired his gun into the body of the man, who immediately fell. Edward lost no time in reloading his gun, during which he heard the bursting open of the front door and the report of firearms; then all was silent for a moment, excepting the wailing of somebody within. As soon as his gun was reloaded, Edward walked round to the front of the cottage, where he found the man who was called Ben lying across the threshold of the open door. He stepped across the body, and, looking into the room within, perceived a body stretched on the floor, and a young lad weeping over it.

'Don't be alarmed; I am a friend,' said Edward, going in to where the body lay; and taking the light which was at the farther end of the chamber, he placed it on the floor, that he might examine the state of the person, who was breathing heavily, and apparently badly wounded. 'Rise up, my lad,' said Edward, 'and let me see if I can be of any use.'

'Ah no!' cried the boy, throwing back his long hair from his temples; 'he bleeds to death!'

'Bring me some water, quick,' said Edward, 'there's a good lad, while I see where he is hurt.'

The boy ran up to fetch the water, and Edward discovered that the ball had entered the neck, above the collarbone, and that the blood poured out of the man's mouth, who was choking with the effusion. Although ignorant of surgery, Edward thought that such a wound must be mortal; but the man was not only alive, but sensible, and although he could not utter a word, he spoke with his eyes, and with signs. He raised his hand and pointed to himself first, and shook his head, as if to say that it was all over with him; and then he turned round his head, as if looking for the lad, who was now returning with the water. When the lad again knelt by his side, weeping bitterly, the man pointed to him, and gave such an imploring look that Edward immediately comprehended what he wished; it was to ask protection for the boy. It could not be misunderstood, and could Edward do otherwise than promise it to the dying man? His generous nature could not refuse it, and he said, 'I understand you; you wish me to take care of your boy when you are gone. Is it not so?'

The man signified assent.

'I promise you I will do so. I will take him into my own family and he shall share with us.'

The man raised his hand again, and a gleam of joy passed over his features as he took the hand of the lad and put it into that of Edward. His eyes were then fixed upon Edward, as if to scrutinise into his character by his features, while the former bathed his temples and washed the blood from his mouth with the water brought by the boy, who appeared in a state of grief so violent as to paralyse his senses. After a minute or two another effusion of blood choked the wounded man, who after a short struggle fell back dead.

'He is gone!' thought Edward. 'And now what is to be done? I must first ascertain whether the two villains are dead or not.'

Edward took a light and examined the body of Ben, lying over the threshold of the door: the man was quite dead, the ball having entered his brain. He was proceding round the outside of the cottage to examine the state of the other man, whom he had shot himself; but the wind nearly blew out the light, and he therefore returned to the chamber and placed it on the floor, near to where the boy lay insensible over the corpse of the man who had died in the arms of Edward, and then went out without a light, and with his gun, to the other side of the cottage, where the other robber had fallen. As he approached the man a faint voice was heard to say, –

'Ben, Ben, some water, for the love of God! Ben, I'm done for!'

Edward, without giving any answer, went back to the room for the water, which he took round to the man, and put it to his lips. He felt that he was bound by humanity so to do to a dying man, scoundrel though he might be. It was still dark, but not so dark as it had previously been, for the late moon was just rising.

The man drank the water eagerly, and said, 'Ben, I can speak now, but I shan't long.' He then pulled the basin towards him again, and after he had drunk, he said, in broken sentences, 'I feel – that I am bleeding to death – inside.' Then he paused. 'You know the oak – struck by lightning – a mile north – of this. Oh, I'm going fast! Three yards from it south – I buried all my – money; it's yours. Oh, another drink.'

The man again attempted to drink out of the basin proffered by Edward; but as he made the attempt he fell back with a groan.

Edward, perceiving that he was dead, returned to the cottage to look after the lad, who still remained prostrate, and embracing the corpse in the chamber. Edward then reflected upon what had best be done. After a time he decided upon dragging away the body of the robber named Ben outside of the threshold, and then securing the door. This, with some trouble, he effected, and he then made fast the window that had been forced open behind. Before he removed the boy, who lay with his face buried on the corpse, and appeared to be in a state of insensibility, Edward examined the corpse as it lay. Although plainly dressed, yet it was evident that it was not the body of a rustic. The features were fair, and the beard was carefully cut; the hands were white, and the fingers long, and evidently had never been employed in labour. That the body was that of some superior person disguised as a rustic was evident, and this was corroborated by the conversation which took place between the two robbers. 'Alas!' thought Edward, 'the family of Arnwood appear not to be the only people

113

who are in disguise in this forest. That poor boy! he must not remain there.' Edward looked round, and perceived that there was a bed in the adjoining room, the door of which was open; he lifted up the boy, and carried him, still insensible, into the room and laid him on the bed. He then went for some more water, which he found and threw into his face, and poured a little into his mouth. Gradually the boy stirred, and recovered from his stupor; and then Edward held the water to his mouth, and made him drink some, which he did, and then, suddenly aroused to a recollection of what had passed, the boy gave a shriek of woe and burst into a paroxysm of tears. This ended in convulsive sobbings and low moanings. Edward felt that he could do no more at present, and that it would be better if he was left for a time to give vent to his grief. Edward sat down on a stool by the side of the orphan, and remained for some time in deep and melancholy thought.

'How strange,' thought he at last, 'it is that I should feel so little as I do now, surrounded by death, compared to what I did when good old Jacob Armitage died! Then I felt it deeply, and there was an awe in death. Now I no longer dread it. Is it because I loved the good old man, and felt that I had lost a friend? No, that cannot be the cause; I may have felt more grief, but not awe or dread. Or is it because that was the first time that I had seen death, and it is the first sight of death which occasions awe? Or is it because that every day I have fancied myself on the battlefield, with hundreds lying dead and wounded around me, in my dreamings? I know not. Poor old Jacob died peaceably in his bed, like a good Christian, and trusting, after a blameless life, to find mercy through his Saviour. Two of these who are now dead, out of three, have been summoned away in the height of their wickedness, and in the very commission of crime; the third has been foully murdered; and out of the three lying dead, one has fallen by my own hand, and yet I feel not so much as when I attended the couch and listened to the parting words of a dying Christian! I cannot account for it, or reason why; I only know that it is so, and I now look upon death unconcerned. Well, this is a kind of preparation for the wholesale murder and horrors of the battlefield, which I have so long sighed for – God forgive me if I am wrong. And this poor boy! I have promised to protect him, and I will. Could I fail my promise, I should imagine the spirit of his father (as I presume he was) looking down and upbraiding me. No, no, I will protect him. I and my brother and sisters have been preserved and protected, and I were indeed vile if I did not do to others as I have been done by. And now let me reflect what is to be done. I must not take the boy away and bury the bodies; this person has friends at Lymington, and they will come here. The murder has taken place in the forest: then I must let the Intendant know what has occurred. I will send over to Oswald; Humphrey shall go. Poor fellow! what a state of anxiety must he and my little sisters be in at my not returning home! I had quite forgotten that; but it cannot be helped. I will wait till sunrise, and then see if the boy will be more himself, and probably from him I shall be able to find out what part of the forest I am in.'

Edward took up the candle and went into the room in which he had laid the boy on the bed. He found him in a sound sleep. 'Poor fellow,' said Edward, 'he has for a time forgotten his misery. What a beautiful boy he is! I long to know his history. Sleep on, my poor fellow; it will do you service.'

Edward then returned to the other room, and recollected, or rather was reminded, that he had had no supper, and it was nearly dawn of day. He looked into a cupboard, and found plenty of provisions and some flasks of wine. 'I have earned my supper,' thought he, 'and I will not, therefore, deny myself.' So he brought out the viands and a flask of wine, and made a hearty meal. 'It is long since I have tasted wine,' thought he, 'and it may be long ere I drink it again. I have little relish for it now; it is too fiery to the palate. I recollect, when a child, how my father used to have me at the table, and give me a stoup of claret, which I could hardly lift to my lips, to drink to the health of the King.' The memory of the King raised other thoughts in Edward's mind, and he again sank into one of his reveries, which lasted till he fell into a slumber. When he woke up, it was at the voice of the boy, who in his sleep had cried out, 'Father!' Edward started up, and found that the sun was an hour high, and that he must have slept some time. He gently opened the cottage door, looked at the bodies of the two men, and then walked out to survey the locality of the cottage, which he had but faintly made out during the night. He found that it was surrounded by a thicket of trees and underwood, so close and thick that there appeared to him no outlet in any direction. 'What a place for concealment!' thought Edward; 'but still these prowling thieves discovered it. Why, troops of horse might scour the forest for months, and never discover such a hiding-place.' Edward walked round by the side of the thicket, to find out the track by which the robbers had entered when he followed them, and at last succeeded in doing so. He followed the path through the thicket until he was clear of it, and again in the forest; but the scenery outside was unknown to him, and he had not an idea as to what part of the forest it was in. 'I must question the boy,' thought Edward. 'I will go back and wake him up, for it is time that I was moving.' As he was again turning into the thicket he heard a dog giving tongue, as if on a scent. It came nearer and nearer to him, and Edward remained to see what it might be. In a moment more he perceived his own dog, Smoker, come bounding out of a neighbouring copse, followed by Humphrey and Pablo. Edward hallooed. Smoker sprang towards him, leaping up, and loading him with caresses, and in another moment he was in Humphrey's arms.

'O Edward, let me first thank God!' said Humphrey, as the tears started and rolled down his cheeks. 'What a night we have passed! What has happened? That dear fellow Pablo thought of putting Smoker on the scent; he brought out your jacket and showed it to Smoker, and gave it him to smell, and then led him along till he was on your footsteps; and the dog followed him, it seems, although it has been round and round in every direction, till at last he has brought us to you.'

Edward shook hands with Pablo, and thanked him.

'How far are we from the cottage, Humphrey?'

'About eight miles, I should say, Edward – not more.'

'Well, I have much to tell you, and I must tell it to you in few words before I go farther, and afterwards I will tell you all in detail.'

Edward then gave a succinct narration of what had occurred, and having prepared Humphrey and Pablo for what they were to see, led the way back through the thicket to the cottage inside of it. Humphrey and Pablo were much shocked at the scene of slaughter which presented itself to their eyes; and after having viewed the bodies they began to consult what had best be done.

The proposal of Edward that Humphrey should go over and make known the circumstances to Oswald, that they might be communicated to the Intendant, was readily acceded to; and Pablo, it was agreed, should go home and tell Alice and Edith that Edward was safe.

'But now, Humphrey, about this boy. We cannot leave him here.'

'Where is he?'

'He still sleeps, I believe. The question is, whether you should ride over with the pony, or walk, and leave Pablo to return with the pony and cart; for I will not take the boy away, or leave the house myself, without removing the property, which belongs to the boy, and of which I will make inquiry when he wakes. Besides, there is money, by what the robbers stated, which of course must be taken care of for him.'

'I think it will be best for me to walk over, Edward. If I ride, I should arrive too late in the afternoon for anything to be done till next morning; and if I walk, I shall be in time enough, so that is settled. Besides, it will give you more time to remove the boy's property, which, as his father was in all probability a Malignant and a denounced man, they might think right to secure for the Government.'

'Very true; then be it so. Do you start for the Intendant's. – And, Pablo, go home and fetch the pony and cart, while I remain here with the boy, and get everything ready.'

Humphrey and Pablo both set off, and then Edward went to waken the boy, still lying on the bed.

'Come, you must get up now. You know that what's done cannot be undone; and if you are a good boy, and have read the Bible, you must know that we must submit to the will of God, who is our kind Father in heaven.'

'Ah me!' said the boy, who was awake when Edward went to him, 'I know well it is my duty, but it is a hard duty, and I am heart-broken. I have lost my father, the only friend I had in the world. Who is there to love and to cherish me now? What will become of me?'

'I promised your father before he died, that I would take care of you, my poor fellow; and a promise is sacred with me, even if it were not made to a dying man. I will do my best, depend upon it, for I have known myself what it is to want and to find a protector. You shall live with me and my brother and sisters, and you shall have all we have.'

116

'Have you sisters, then?' replied the boy.

'Yes. I have sent for the cart to take you away from this, and tonight you shall be in our cottage; but now tell me – I do not ask who your father was, or why he was living here in secret, as I found it out by what I overheard the robbers say to one another – but how long have you lived here?'

'More than a year.'

'Whose cottage is it?'

'My father bought it when he came, as he thought it safer so, that he might not be discovered or betrayed; for he had escaped from prison after having been condemned to death by the Parliament.'

'Then he was a loyal man to his King?'

'Yes, he was, and that was his only crime.'

'Then fear not, my good boy. We are all loyal as well as he was, and will never be otherwise. I tell you this that you may safely trust to us. Now, if the cottage was his, the furniture and property were his also.'

'Yes; all was his.'

'And it is now yours, is it not?'

'I suppose so,' said the boy, bursting into tears.

'Then listen to me. Your father is safe from all persecution now – he is, I trust, in heaven; and you they cannot touch, as you have done nothing to offend them; but still they will take possession of your father's property as soon as they know of his death and find out who he was. This, for your sake, I wish to prevent them from doing, and have therefore sent for the cart, that I may remove to my cottage everything that is of value, that it may be held for your benefit. Some day or another you may require it. The murder having been committed in the forest, and I having been a witness, and, moreover, having shot one of the robbers – I have considered it right to send over to the Intendant of the forest, to give him notice of what has taken place within his jurisdiction. I do not think he is so bad a man as the rest; but still, when he comes here, he may consider it his duty to take possession of everything for the Parliament, as I have no doubt such are his orders, or will be when he communicates with the Parliament. Now, this is a robbery which I wish to prevent by carrying away your property before they come over, which they will tomorrow; and I propose that you shall accompany me, with all that you can take away, or that may be useful this evening.'

'You are very kind,' replied the boy. 'I will do all you wish; but I feel very weak and very unwell.'

'You must exert yourself for your own sake, my poor fellow. Come now, sit up and put all your own clothes together. Collect everything in this room while I look about the house. And tell me, had not your father some money? for the robbers said that they saw him counting it out of a sack, through the chinks of the shutters, and that was why they made the attack.'

'Hateful money!' cried the boy. 'Yes; he had, I believe, a great deal of money, but I cannot say how much.'

117

'Now get up, and do as I request, my dear boy,' said Edward, raising him up in his arms. 'When your grief is lessened you may have many happy days yet in store for you. You have a Father in heaven that you must put your trust in, and with Him you will find peace.'

The boy rose up, and Edward closed the door of the chamber, that he might not see his father's corpse.

'I do put my trust in heaven, good sir,' replied the boy, 'for it has already sent me a kind friend in my distress. You are good, I am sure – I see that in your face. Alas! how much more wretched would have been my condition if you had not fortunately come to our assistance – too late, indeed, to save my poor father, but not too late to succour and console his child. I will go away with you, for I cannot stay here.'

CHAPTER 16

Edward then took the counterpane off the bed, and went with it into the next room. He gently drew the body to the corner of the room, and covered it up with the counterpane, and then proceeded to examine the cupboards, etc. In one he found a good store of books; in another there was linen of all sorts, a great many curious arms, two suits of bright armour such as worn in those times, pistols and guns and ammunition. On the floor of one of the cupboards was an iron chest about two feet by eighteen inches. It was locked. Edward immediately concluded that this chest held the money of the unfortunate man; but where was the key? Most likely about his person. He did not like to afflict the poor boy by putting the question to him, but he went to the body and examined the pockets of the clothes. He found a bunch of several keys, which he took, and then replaced the cover-lid. He tried one of the keys, which appeared to be of the right size, to the lock of the iron chest, and found that it fitted it. Satisfied with this, he did not raise the lid of the chest, but dragged it out into the centre of the room. There were many things of value about the room: the candlesticks were silver, and there were goblets of the same metal. Edward collected all these articles and a timepiece, and put them into a basket of which there were two large ones at the end of the room, apparently used for holding fire-wood. Everything that he thought could be useful or of value he gathered together for the benefit of the poor orphan boy. He afterwards went into another small room, where he found sundry small trunks and cases locked up. These he brought out without examining, as he presumed that they contained what was of value, or they would not be locked. When he had collected everything, he found that he had already more than the cart could carry in one trip; and he wanted to take some bedding with him, as he had

118

not a spare bed in the cottage to give to the boy. Edward decided in his own mind that he would take the most valuable articles away that night, and return with the cart for the remainder early on the following morning. It was now past noon, and Edward took out of the cupboard what victuals were left, and then went into the chamber where the boy was, and begged that he would eat something. The poor boy said that he had no appetite; but Edward insisted, and at last prevailed upon him to eat some bread and drink a glass of wine, which proved of great service to him. The poor fellow shuddered as he saw the body covered up in the corner of the room, but said nothing. Edward was trying to make him eat a little more, when Pablo made his appearance at the door.

'Have you put up all that you want in the bedchamber?' said Edward.

'Yes, I have put up everything.'

'Then we will bring them out. – Come, Pablo, you must help us.'

Pablo made signs, and pointed to the door. Edward went out.

'First pull body away from this.'

'Yes,' replied Edward; 'we must do so.'

Edward and Pablo pulled the body of the robber on one side of the doorway, and threw over it some dried fern which lay by; they then backed the cart down to the door; the iron chest was first got in, then all the heavy articles, such as armour, guns, and books, etc., and by that time the cart was more than half loaded. Edward then went into the chamber, and brought out the packages the boy had made up, and put them all in the cart, until it was loaded high up; they brought out some blankets, and laid over all, to keep things steady; and then Edward told the boy that all was ready, and that they had better go.

'Yes, I am willing,' replied he, with streaming eyes; 'but let me see him once more.'

'Come then,' said Edward, leading him to the corpse, and uncovering the face.

The boy knelt down, kissed the forehead and cold lips, covered up the face again, and then rose and wept bitterly on Edward's shoulder. Edward did not attempt to check his sorrow – he thought it better it should have vent – but after a time he led the boy by degrees till they were out of the cottage.

'Now then,' said Edward, 'we must go, or we shall be late. My poor little sisters have been dreadfully alarmed at my not having come home last night, and I long to clasp them in my arms.'

'Indeed you must,' replied the boy, wiping away his tears, 'and I am very selfish; let us go on.'

'No room for cart to get through wood,' said Pablo. 'Hard work, cart empty; more hard work, cart full.'

And so it proved to be, and it required all the united efforts of Billy, Edward, and Pablo to force a passage for the cart through the narrow pathway; but at last it was effected, and then they went on at a quick pace, and in less than two hours the cottage was in sight. When within two hundred yards of it Edith, who had been on the watch, came bounding out, and flew into Edward's arms, and covered him with kisses.

'You naughty Edward, to frighten us so!'

'Look, Edith, I have brought you a nice little play fellow. Welcome him, dearest.'

Edith extended her hand as she looked into the boy's face.

'He is a pretty boy, Edward – much prettier than Pablo.'

'No, Missy Edith,' said Pablo; 'Pablo more man than he.'

'Yes, you may be more man, Pablo; but you are not so pretty.'

'And where is Alice?'

'She was getting supper ready, and I did not tell her that I saw you coming, because I wanted first kiss.'

'You little jealous thing! But here comes Alice. – Dear Alice, you have been very uneasy, but it was not my fault,' said Edward, kissing her. 'If I had not been where I was, this poor boy would have been killed as well as his father. Make him welcome, Alice, for he is an orphan now, and must live with us. I have brought many things in the cart; and tomorrow we will bring more, for we have no bed for him, and tonight he must sleep with me.'

'We will make him as happy as we can, Edward, and we will be sisters to him,' said Alice, looking at the boy, who was blushing deeply. – 'How old are you, and what is your name?'

'I am thirteen years old next January,' replied the boy.

'And your Christian name?'

'I will tell you by-and-by,' replied he, confused.

They arrived at the cottage, and Edward and Pablo were busy unpacking the cart and putting all the contents into the inner chamber, where Pablo now slept, when Alice, who with Edith had been talking to the boy, came to Edward and said, –

'Edward, he's a girl!'

'A girl!' replied Edward, astonished.

'Yes, she has told me so, and wished me to tell you.'

'But why does she wear boy's clothes?'

'It was her father's wish, as he was very often obliged to send her to Lymington to a friend's house, and he was afraid of her getting into trouble. But she has not told me her story as yet; she says that she will tonight.'

'Well, then,' replied Edward, 'you must make up a bed for her in your room tonight. Take Pablo's bed, and he shall sleep with me. Tomorrow morning I will bring some more bedding from her cottage.'

'How Humphrey will be surprised when he comes back!' said Alice, laughing.

'Yes – she will make a nice little wife for him some years hence; and she may prove an heiress perhaps, for there is an iron chest with money in it.'

Alice returned to her new companion, and Edward and Pablo continued to unload the cart.

'Well, Pablo, I suppose you will allow that now that you know that she is a girl she is handsomer than you?'

'Oh yes,' replied Pablo; 'very handsome girl, but too much girl for handsome boy.'

At last everything was out of the cart, the iron chest dragged into Pablo's room, and Billy put into his stable and given his supper, which he had well earned, for the cart had been very heavily loaded. They then all sat down to supper, Edward saying to their new acquaintance,

'So I find that I am to have another sister instead of another brother. Now you will tell me your name?'

'Yes; Clara is my name.'

'And why did you not tell me that you are a girl?'

'I did not like, because I was in boy's clothes, and felt ashamed; indeed I was too unhappy to think about what I was. My poor dear father!' and she burst into tears.

Alice and Edith kissed her and consoled her, and she became calm again. After supper was over they busied themselves making arrangements for her sleeping in their room, and then they went to prayers.

'We have much to be thankful for, my dears,' said Edward. 'I am sure I feel that I have been in great danger, and I only wish that I had been more useful than I have been; but it has been the will of God, and we must not arraign His decrees. Let us return thanks for His great mercies, and bow in submission to His dispensations, and pray that He will give peace to poor little Clara, and soften her affliction.'

And as Edward prayed, little Clara knelt and sobbed, while Alice caressed her with her arm round her waist, and stopped at times her prayer to kiss and console her. When they had finished, Alice led her away to her bedroom, followed by Edith, and they put her to bed. Edward and Pablo also retired, both worn out by the fatigue and excitement of the day.

They were up on the following morning at day-dawn, and putting Billy in the cart, set off for the cottage of Clara. They found everything as they had left it, and having loaded the cart with what had been left behind the day before, and bedding for two beds, with several articles of furniture which Edward thought might be useful, there being still a little room left, Edward packed up in a wooden case with dried fern all the wine that was in the cupboard; and having assisted Pablo in forcing the cart once more through the path in the wood, he left him to return home with the cart, while he remained to wait the arrival of Humphrey, and whoever might come with him from the Intendant's. About ten o'clock, as he was watching outside of the wood, he perceived several people approaching him, and soon made out that Humphrey, the Intendant, and Oswald were among the number. When they came up to him, Edward saluted the Intendant in a respectful manner, and shook hands with Oswald, and then led the way by the narrow path which led through the wood to the cottage. The Intendant was on horseback, but all the rest were on foot.

The Intendant left his horse to the care of one of the verderers, and went through the wood on foot with the rest of the party, preceded by Edward. He appeared to be very grave and thoughtful, and Edward thought that there was a coolness in his manner towards himself – for it must be recollected that Mr Heatherstone had not seen Edward since he had rendered him such service in saving the life of his daughter. The consequence was that Edward felt somewhat indignant; but he did not express his feelings by his looks even, but conveyed the party in silence to the cottage. On their arrival Edward pointed to the body of the robber, which had been covered with fern, and the verderers exposed it.

'By whose hand did that man fall?' said the Intendant.

'By the hand of the party who lived in the cottage.' (Edward then led the way round to the back of the cottage, where the other robber lay.) 'And this man was slain by my hand,' replied Edward. – 'We have one more body to see,' continued Edward, leading the way into the cottage and uncovering the corpse of Clara's father.

Mr Heatherstone looked at the face, and appeared much moved. 'Cover it up,' said he, turning away; and then, sitting down on a chair, close to the table, –

'And how was this found?' he said.

'I neither saw this person killed, nor the robber you first saw, but I heard the report of the firearms at almost the same moment, and I presume that they fell by each other's hands.'

The Intendant called his clerk, who had accompanied him, and desired him to get ready his writing materials, and then said,-

'Edward Armitage, we will now take down your deposition as to what has occurred.'

When Edward then commenced by stating 'that he was out in the forest and had lost his way, and was seeking his way home-'

'You were out in the forest during the night?'

'Yes, sir, I was.'

'With your gun?'

'I always carry my gun,' replied Edward.

'In pursuit of game?'

'No, sir, I was not. I have never been out in pursuit of game during night time in my life.'

'What were you then about? You did not go out for nothing?'

'I went out to commune with my own thoughts. I was restless, and I wandered about without knowing where I went, and that is the reason why I lost my way.'

'And, pray, what may have excited you?'

'I will tell you. I was over with Oswald Partridge the day before; you had just arrived from London, and he gave me the news that King Charles had been proclaimed in Scotland, and that news unsettled me.'

'Well, proceed.'

Edward met with no more interruption in his narrative. He stated briefly all that had taken place, from the time he fell in with the robbers till the winding up of the catastrophe.

The clerk took down all that Edward had stated, and then read it over to him to ascertain if he had written it down correctly, and then inquired of Edward if he could read and write.

'I should hope so,' replied Edward, taking the pen and signing his name.

The clerk stared, and then said, 'People in your condition do not often know how to read and write, Mr Forester, and therefore you need not be offended at the question.'

'Very true,' replied Edward. 'May I ask if my presence is considered any longer to be necessary?'

'You stated that there was a boy in the house, young man,' said the Intendant. 'What has become of him?'

'He is removed to my cottage.'

'Why did you do so?'

'Because when his father died I promised to him that I would take care of his child; and I intend to keep my word.'

'You had spoken with him, then, before he died,' said the Intendant.

'Not so; it was all carried on by signs on his part, but it was as intelligible as if he spoke, and what I replied he well understood; and I really think I removed a great anxiety off his mind by giving him the promise.'

The Intendant paused, and then said, 'I perceive that some articles have been removed – the bedding, for instance. Have you taken anything away?'

'I have removed bedding, for I had no bed to offer to the lad: and he told me that the cottage and furniture belonged to his father. Of course by his father's death it became his, and I felt that I was warranted in so doing.'

'May I ask, did you remove any papers?'

'I cannot tell. The lad packed up his own things. There were some boxes removed, which were locked up, and the contents are to me wholly unknown. I could not leave the boy here in this scene of death, and I could not well leave the property belonging to him to be at the mercy of any other plunderers of the forest. I did as I considered right for the benefit of the boy, and in accordance with the solemn promise which I made to his father.'

'Still, the property should not have been removed. The party who now lies dead there is a well-known Malignant.'

'How do you know that, sir?' interrupted Edward. 'Did you recognize him when you saw the body?'

'I did not say that I did,' replied the Intendant.

'You either must have so done, sir,' replied Edward, 'or you must have been aware that he was residing in this cottage. You have to choose between.'

'You are bold, young man,' replied the Intendant, 'and I will reply to your observation. I did recognize the party when I saw his face, and I knew him to be one who was condemned to death, and who escaped from prison a few days before the one appointed for his execution. I heard search had been made for him, but in vain, and it was supposed that he had escaped beyond the seas. Now his papers may be the means of giving the Parliament information against others as well as himself.'

123

'And enable them to commit a few more murders,' added Edward.

'Silence, young man; the authorities must not be spoken of in so irreverent a manner. Are you aware that your language is treasonable?'

'According to Act of Parliament, as at present constituted, it may be,' replied Edward; 'but as a loyal subject of King Charles the Second I deny it.'

'I have no concern with your loyalty, young man, but I will not admit any language to be uttered in my presence against the ruling powers. The inquest is over. Let every one leave the house except Edward Armitage, to whom I would speak alone.'

'Excuse me one moment, sir,' said Edward, 'and I will return.'

Edward went out with the rest, and calling Humphrey aside, said to him, 'Contrive to slip away unperceived; here are the keys, haste to the cottage as fast as you can; look for all the papers you can find in the packages taken there; bury them in the iron chest in the garden, or anywhere where they cannot be discovered.'

Humphrey nodded and turned away, and Edward reentered the cottage.

He found the Intendant was standing over the corpse. He had removed the coverlid, and was looking mournfully down on the face disfigured with blood. Perceiving the entrance of Edward, he again took his seat at the table, and after a pause said, –

'Edward Armitage, that you have been brought up very superior to your station in life is certain; and that you are loyal, bold, and resolute is equally so. You have put me under an obligation which I never can repay, even if you allowed me to exert myself in your behalf. I take this opportunity of acknowledging it; and now allow me to say that for these times you are much too frank and impetuous. This is no time for people to give vent to their feelings and opinions. Even I am as much surrounded with spies as others, and am obliged to behave myself accordingly. Your avowed attachment to the King's cause has prevented me from showing that more than cordiality that I really feel for you, and to which you are in every way entitled.'

'I cannot conceal my opinions, sir. I was brought up in the house of a loyal Cavalier, and never will be otherwise.'

'Granted; why should you be? But do you not yourself see that you do the cause more harm than good by thus avowing your opinions when such avowal is useless? If every other man in the county who is of your opinion was to express himself, now that your cause is hopeless, as you have done, the prisons would be crowded, the executions would be daily, and the cause would be in proportion weakened by the loss of the most daring. "Bide your time," is a good motto, and I recommend it to you. You must feel that, however we may be at variance in our opinions, Edward Armitage, my hand and my authority never can be used against one to whom I am so indebted; and feeling this, you compel me in the presence of others to use a harshness and coldness towards you contrary – wholly contrary – to what, you may believe me when I say it, I really feel for one who so nobly rescued my only child.'

'I thank you, sir, for your advice, which I feel to be good; and for your good opinion, which I value.'

'And which I feel that you deserve. And you shall have, young as you are, my confidence, which I know you will not abuse. I did know this man who now lies dead before us, and I did also know that he was concealed in this cottage. Major Ratcliffe was one of my earliest and dearest friends, and until this unhappy civil war there never was any difference between us, and even afterwards only in politics and the cause we each espoused. I knew, before I came down here as Intendant, where his place of concealment was, and have been most anxious for his safety.'

'Excuse me, Mr Heatherstone, but each day I find more to make me like you than I did the day before. At first I felt most inimical; now I only wonder how you can be leagued with the party you now are.'

'Edward Armitage, I will now answer for myself and thousands more. You are too young a man to have known the cause of the insurrection, or rather opposition to the unfortunate King Charles. He attempted to make himself absolute, and to wrest the liberties from the people of England; that his warmest adherents will admit. When I joined the party which opposed him, I little thought that matters would have been carried so far as they have been. I always considered it lawful to take up arms in defence of our liberties, but at the same time I equally felt that the person of the King was sacred.'

'I have heard so, sir.'

'Yes, and in truth: for never did any people strive more zealously to prevent the murder of the King – for murder it was – than my relative Ashley Cooper and myself; so much so, indeed, as to have incurred not only the suspicion but the ill-will of Cromwell, who, I fear, is now making rapid advances towards that absolute authority for which the King has suffered, and which he would now vest in his own person. I considered that our cause was just; and had the power been left in the hands of those who would have exercised it with discretion and moderation, the King would even now have been on the throne, and the liberties of his subjects sacred; but it is easier to put a vast and powerful engine into motion than to stop it, and such has been the case in this unfortunate civil war. Thousands who took an active part against the King will, when the opportunity is ripe, retrace their steps; but I expect that we have much to suffer before that time will come. And now, Edward Armitage, I have said more to you than I have to any person breathing, except my own kinsman.'

'I thank you for your confidence, sir, which not only will not be betrayed, but will act as a warning to guide my future conduct.'

'I meant it should. Be no longer rash and careless in avowing your opinions. You can do no good to the cause, and may do yourself much harm. – And now I must ask you another question, which I could not before the other people. You have surprised me by stating that Major Ratcliffe had a son here. There must be some mistake, or the boy must be an impostor. He had a daughter – an only daughter, as I have – but he never had a son.'

'It is a mistake that I fell into, sir, by finding a boy here, as I stated to you at the inquest; and I considered it to be a boy until I brought her home, and then she discovered to my sisters that she was a girl dressed in boy's clothes. I did not give that as explanation at the inquest, as it was not necessary.'

'I am right, then. I must relieve you of that charge, Edward Armitage. She shall be to me as a daughter, and I trust that you will agree with me, without any disparagement to your feelings, that my house will be a more fit residence for her than your cottage.'

'I will not prevent her going if she wishes it, after your explanation and confidence, Mr Heatherstone.'

'One thing more. As I said to you before, Edward Armitage, I believe many of these verderers, all of whom have been selected from the army, are spies upon me; I must therefore be careful. You said that you were not aware that there were any papers?'

'I saw none, sir; but I suspect, from the many locked-up trunks and small boxes, that there may be. But when I went out with the others from the inquest, I dispatched my brother Humphrey to the cottage, advising him to open all the locks, and to remove any papers which he might find.'

The Intendant smiled.

'Well, if such is the case, we have only to go to your cottage and make an examination. We shall find nothing, and I shall have performed my duty. I was not aware that your brother was here. I presume it was the young man who walked with Oswald Partridge.'

'It was, sir.'

'By his appearance, I presume that he also was brought up at Arnwood?'

'He was, sir, as well as I,' replied Edward.

'Well, then, I have but one word more to say. Recollect, if I appear harsh and severe in the presence of others, it is only assumed towards you, and not real. You understand that?'

'I do, sir, and beg you will exercise your discretion.'

The Intendant then went out and said to the party, 'It appears, from what I can extract from this lad Armitage, that there are boxes which he removed to his cottage. We will go there to see what they may contain. It is now noon. – Have you any refreshment to offer us in your cottage, young man, when we arrive?'

'I keep no hostelrie, sir,' replied Edward somewhat gloomily. 'My own labour and my brother's is sufficient for the support of my own family, but no more.'

'Let us move on; and two of you keep your eye upon that young man,' said the Intendant, aside.

They then proceeded through the wood. The Intendant mounted his horse, and they set off for the cottage, where they arrived at about two o'clock in the afternoon.

CHAPTER 17

Humphrey came out as soon as he perceived the Intendant and his party approaching, and whispered to Edward that all was safe. The Intendant dismounted, and ordering everybody but his clerk to wait outside, was ushered into the cottage by Edward. Alice, Edith, and Pablo were in the room. The two girls were not a little flushed and frightened by the unusual appearance of so large a body of strangers.

'These are my sisters, sir,' said Edward. – 'Where is Clara, Alice?'

'She is alarmed, and has gone into our bedroom.'

'I hope you are not alarmed at my presence,' said the Intendant, looking earnestly at the two girls. 'It is my duty which obliges me to pay this visit; but you have nothing to fear. – Now, Edward Armitage, you must produce all the boxes and packages which you took from the cottage.'

'I will, sir,' replied Edward, 'and here are the keys. – Humphrey, do you and Pablo bring them out.'

The boxes were brought out, opened, and examined by the Intendant and his clerk, but of course no papers were found in them.

'I must now send in two of my people to search the house,' said the Intendant. 'Had you not better go to the little girl, that she may not be frightened?'

'I will go to her,' said Alice.

Two of the people, assisted by the clerk, then searched the house. They found nothing worthy of notice, except the weapons and armour which Edward had removed, and which he stated to the Intendant that he took away as valuable property belonging to the little girl.

'It is sufficient,' said the Intendant to his clerk – 'undoubtedly there are no papers; but I must, before I go, interrogate this child, who has been removed thus. But she will be frightened, and I shall obtain no answer from her, if we are so many, so let everybody leave the cottage while I speak to her.'

The clerk and the others left the cottage, and the Intendant desired Edward to bring Clara from the bedroom. She came out accompanied by, and clinging indeed to, Alice, for she was much alarmed.

'Come here, Clara,' said the Intendant gently. 'You do not know, perhaps, that I am your sincere friend; and now that your father is dead, I want you to come and live with my daughter, who will be delighted to have you as a companion. Will you go with me? and I will take care of you and be a father to you.'

'I do not like to leave Alice and Edith; they treat me so kindly and call me sister,' replied Clara, sobbing.

'I am sure they do, and that you must be fond of them already; but still it is your duty to come with me; and if your father could speak to you now, he would tell you so. I will not force you away; but remember you are born a lady, and must be brought up and educated as a lady, which cannot be the case in this cottage, although they are very kind to you and very nice young people. You do not recollect me, Clara, but you have often sat on my knee when you were a little girl, and when your father lived in Dorsetshire. You recollect the great walnut tree by the sitting-room window, which looked out in the garden don't you?'

'Yes,' replied Clara with surprise.

'Yes, so do I too, and how you used to sit on my knee. And do you remember Jason, the big mastiff, and how you used to ride upon his back?'

'Yes,' replied Clara, –'I do; but he died a long while ago.'

'He did, when you were not more than six years old. And now tell me, where did the old gardener bury him?'

'Under the mulberry tree,' replied Clara.

'Yes, so he did; and I was there when poor Jason was buried. You don't recollect me. But I will take off my hat, for I did not wear the same dress that I do now. Now look, Clara, and see if you remember me.'

Clara, who was no longer alarmed, looked on the Intendant's face, and then said, 'You called my father Philip, and he used to call you Charles.'

'You are right, my sweet one,' replied the Intendant, pressing Clara to his bosom; 'I did so and we were great friends. Now, will you come with me? and I have a little girl, older than you by three or four years, who will be your companion, and love you dearly.'

'May I come and see Alice and Edith sometimes?'

'Yes, you shall; and she will come with you and make their acquaintance, if their brother will permit it. I will not take you away now, dearest. You shall remain here for a few days, and then we will come over and fetch you. – I will send Oswald Partridge over to let you know the day, Edward Armitage, when we will come for her. – Good-bye, dear Clara; and good-bye, my little girls. – Humphrey Armitage, good-bye. – Who is this lad you have there?'

'He is a gipsy whom Humphrey trapped in his pitfall, sir, and we have soon tamed him,' replied Edward.

'Well, then, Edward Armitage, good-bye,' said the Intendant, extending his hand to him; 'we must meet soon again.'

The Intendant then went out of the cottage, and joined his people outside. Edward went out after him; and as the Intendant mounted his horse, he said very coldly to Edward, 'I shall keep a sharp lookout on your proceedings, sir, depend upon it. I tell you so decidedly, so fare you well.'

With these words the Intendant put the spurs to his horse and rode away.

'What made him speak so sharply to you, Edward?' said Humphrey.

'Because he means kindly, but does not want other people to know it, ' replied Edward. 'Come in, Humphrey; I have much to tell you and much to surprise you with.'

128

'I have been surprised already,' replied Humphrey. 'How did this Roundhead know Clara's father so well?'

'I will explain all before we go to bed,' replied Edward. 'Let us go in now.'

The two brothers had a long conversation that evening in which Edward made Humphrey acquainted with all that had passed between him and the Intendant.

'It's my opinion, Edward,' said Humphrey, 'that he thinks matters have been carried too far, and that he is sorry that he belongs to the Parliamentary party. He finds out, now that it is too late, that he has allied himself with those who have very different feelings and motives than his own, and has assisted to put power into the hands of those who have not the scruples which he has.'

'Yes; and in ridding themselves of one tyranny, as they considered it, they have every prospect of falling into the hands of a greater tyrant than before – for, depend upon it, Cromwell will assume the sovereign power, and rule this kingdom with a rod of iron.'

'Well, many more are, I have no doubt, or soon will be, of his opinion; and the time will come, be it sooner or later, when the King will have his own again. They have proclaimed him in Scotland already. Why does he not come over and show himself? His presence would, I think, induce thousands to flock to him; I'm sure that it would me.'

'I am very glad of this good intelligence with the Intendant, Edward, as it will not now be necessary for us to be so careful. We may go and come when we please. I almost wish you could be persuaded to accept any eligible offer he may make you. Many, no doubt, are in office and serving the present Government who have the same feelings as the Intendant, or even feelings as strong as your own.'

'I cannot bear the idea of accepting anything from them or their instruments, Humphrey; nor, indeed, could I leave my sisters.'

'On that score you may make your mind easy. Pablo and I are quite sufficient for the farm or anything else we may want to do. If you can be more useful elsewhere, have no scruple in leaving us. If the King was to come over and raise an army, you would leave us, of course; and I see no reason why, if an eligible offer is made you, you should not do it now. You and your talents are thrown away in this forest, and you might serve the King and the King's cause better by going into the world and watching the times than you ever can by killing his venison.'

'Certainly,' replied Edward, laughing, 'I do not much help his cause by killing his deer; that must be admitted. All I shall say is this – if anything is offered to me which I can accept without injury to my feelings and my honour, I shall not decline it, provided that I may, by accepting it, prove of service to the King's cause.'

'That is all I wish, Edward. And now I think we had better go to bed.'

The next day they dug up the iron chest and the box into which Humphrey had put all the papers he had collected together. Edward opened the iron chest, and found in it a considerable quantity of gold in bags, and many trinkets and jewels which he did not know the value of. The papers he did not open, but resolved that they should be given to the Intendant, for Edward felt that he could trust in him. The other boxes and trunks were also opened and examined, and many other articles of apparent value discovered.

'I should think all these jewels worth a great deal of money, Humphrey,' said Edward. 'If so, all the better for poor little Clara. I am sorry to part with her, although we have known her so short a time. She appears to be such an amiable and affectionate child.'

'That she is; and certainly the handsomest little girl I ever saw. What beautiful eyes! Do you know that on one of her journeys to Lymington she was very nearly taken by a party of gipsies? and by what Pablo can make out, it would appear that it was by the party which he belonged to.'

'I wonder at her father's permitting her to go alone such a distance.'

'Her father could not do otherwise. Necessity has no law. He could trust no other person, so he put her in boy's clothes that there might be less risk. Still, she must have been very intelligent to have done the office.'

'She is thirteen years old, although she is small,' replied Edward. 'And intelligent she certainly is, as you may see by her countenance. Who would ever have imagined that our sisters would have been able to do what they are doing now? It's an old saying, "We never know what we can do till we try." By-the-by, Humphrey, I met a famous herd of forest ponies the other day, and I said to myself, "I wonder whether Humphrey will be clever enough to take one of them, as he has the wild cattle? For Billy is getting old, and we want a successor."'

'We want more than a successor to Billy, Edward, we want two more to help him; and I have the means of maintaining two more ponies, if I could catch them.'

'I fear that you will never manage that, Humphrey,' said Edward, laughing.

'I know well what you mean,' replied Humphrey; 'you wish to dare me to do it. Well, I won't be dared to anything and I most certainly will try to catch a pony or two; but I must think about it first, and when I have arranged my plan in my mind I will then make the attempt.'

'When I see the ponies in the yard I will believe it, Humphrey. They are as wild as deer and as fleet as the wind, and you cannot catch them in a pitfall.'

'I know that, good brother; but all I can say is that I will try what I can do, and I can do no more – but not at present, for I am too busy.'

Three days after this conversation Oswald Partridge made his appearance, having been sent by the Intendant to tell Edward that he should come over on the following day to take away little Clara.

'And how is she to go?' said Edward.

'He will bring a little nag for her if she can ride; if she cannot, she must ride in the cart which will come for the baggage.'

'Clara, can you ride a horse?'

'Yes,' replied Clara, 'if it does not jump about too much. I always rode one when I lived in Dorsetshire.'

'This won't jump about, my little lady,' said Oswald, 'for he is thirty years old, I believe, and as steady as an old gentleman ought to be.'

'I have had some conversation with Master Heatherstone,' continued Oswald to Edward. 'He is much pleased with you, I can tell you. He said that in times like these he required young men like you about him; and that as you would not take the berth of verderer, he must find one better suited for you, for he said you were too good for such an office.'

'Many thanks to him for his good opinion,' replied Edward; 'but I do not think that he has any office in his gift which I can accept.'

'So I thought, but I said nothing. He again asked many questions relative to old Jacob Armitage, and he pressed me very hard. He said that Humphrey was as much above his position in appearance as you were; but as he was brought up at Arnwood, he presumed that he had had the same advantages. And then he said, "But were his two sisters brought up at Arnwood also?" I replied that I believed not, although they were often there, and were allowed to play with the children of the house. He looked at me steadfastly, as if he would read my thoughts, and then went on writing. I cannot help thinking that he has a suspicion that you are not the grandchildren of old Jacob; but at the same time I do not think that he has an idea who you really are.'

'You must keep our secret, Oswald,' replied Edward. 'I have a very good opinion of the Intendant, I acknowledge; but I will trust nobody.'

'As I hope for future mercy, sir, I never will divulge it until you bid me,' replied Oswald.

'I trust to you, Oswald, and so there's an end of the matter. But tell me, Oswald, what do they say about his taking charge of this little girl?'

'Why, they did begin to talk about it; but when he gave out that it was the order of Parliament that the child should remain with him until further directions, of course they said nothing, for they dared not. It seems that the Ratcliffe property is sequestrated, but not yet granted to any one; and the Parliament will most likely, as soon as she is old enough, give her as a wife, with the property, to one of their party. They have done it before now, as it secures the property under all changes.'

'I perceive,' replied Edward. 'When did you hear that the little girl was to live with him?'

'Not till yesterday morning and it was not till the evening that we knew it was the order of Parliament.'

Edward did not think it right to tell Oswald what he knew, as it was a secret confided to him by the Intendant, and therefore merely observed, 'I presumed that the child would not be left on our hands,' and then the conversation dropped.

As Oswald had informed them, the Intendant made his appearance in the forenoon of the following day, and was accompanied by his daughter, who rode by his side. A groom, on another horse, led a pony for Clara to ride; and a cart for the luggage followed at some distance. Edward went out to assist Miss Heatherstone to dismount, and she frankly extended her hand to him as she reached the ground. Edward was a little surprised as well as pleased at this condescension on her part towards a forester.

'You do me much honour, Mistress Patience,' said he, bowing.

'I cannot forget that I owe my life to you, Master Armitage,' replied Patience, 'and I cannot be too grateful. May I request another favour of you?'

'Certainly, if it is in my power to do as you wish.'

'It is this,' said she in a low voice – 'that you will not hastily reject any overtures which may be made to you by my father; that is all. And now let me go in and see your sisters, for my father has praised them very much, and I wish to know them.'

Edward led the way into the cottage, and Patience followed him, while the Intendant was in conversation with Humphrey. Edward, having introduced his sisters and Clara, then went out to pay his respects to the Intendant, who, now they were alone, was very candid towards both him and Humphrey.

Edward then told the Intendant that there was an iron chest with a good deal of money in it, and jewels also, and many other articles of value in the other boxes.

'I fear, sir, that the cart will hardly hold all the goods.'

'I do not intend to take away the heavy or more bulky articles, such as the bedding, armour, etc. I will only take Clara's own packages, and the valuables and papers. The remainder may stay here, as they can be of no use till they are demanded from you. Where is Oswald Partridge?'

'In the stable with the horses, sir,' replied Humphrey.

'Then, when the cart is loaded – and it had better be done by you while the men are in the stable – Oswald shall take charge of it, and take the things to my house.'

'Here are the keys, sir,' said Edward, presenting them.

'Good. And now, Edward Armitage, that we are alone I want to have a little conversation with you. You are aware how much I feel indebted to you for the service you have rendered me, and how anxious I am to show my gratitude. You are born for better things than to remain an obscure forester, and perhaps a deer-stalker. I have now an offer to make to you, which I trust, upon reflection, you will not refuse; and I say reflection, because I do not wish you to give an answer till you have well reflected. I know that you will not accept anything under the present Government, but a private situation you can raise no objection to; the more so as, so far from leaving your family, you will be more in a position to protect them. I am in want of a secretary, and I wish you to accept that office, to live entirely in my house, and to receive a handsome salary for your services, which will not, I trust, be too heavy. You will be near to your family here in the cottage, and be able to protect them and assist them; and what is more, you will mix with the world and know what is going on, as I am in the confidence of the Government. Of course I put implicit confidence in you, or I would not offer the situation. But you will not be always down here: I have my correspondents and friends, to whom I shall have to send you occasionally on most trusty commissions. You, I am sure, will suit me in every respect, and I hope you will undertake the post which I now offer you. Give me no answer just now; consult with your brother, and give the offer due consideration, and when you have made up your mind you can let me know.'

Edward bowed, and the Intendant went into the cottage.

Edward then assisted Humphrey and Pablo to get the iron chest on the cart, and covered it with the other packages and boxes, till the cart was well loaded. Leaving Pablo in charge till Oswald came from the stables, Edward and Humphrey then went into the cottage, where they found a very social party – Patience Heatherstone having succeeded in making great friends with the other three girls, and the Intendant, to Edward's surprise, laughing and joking with them. Alice and Edith had brought out some milk, biscuits, and all the fruit that was ripe, with some bread, a cold piece of salt beef, and a ham; and they were eating as well as talking.

'I have been praising your sisters' housekeeping, Armitage,' said the Intendant. 'Your farm appears to be very productive.'

'Alice expected Miss Heatherstone, sir,' replied Edward, 'and made an unusual provision. You must not think that we live on such fare every day.'

'No,' replied the Intendant dryly; 'on other days I dare say you have other fare. I would almost make a bet that there is a pasty in the cupboard which you dare not show to the Intendant of the New Forest.'

'You are mistaken, sir, for once,' replied Humphrey. 'Alice knows well how to make one, but she has not one just now.'

'Well, I must believe you, Master Humphrey,' replied the Intendant. – 'And now, my dear child, we must think of going, for it is a long ride, and the little girl is not used to a horse.'

'Mistress Alice, many thanks for your hospitality; and now, farewell. – Edith, good-bye, dear. – Now, Clara, are you quite ready?'

They all went out of the cottage. The Intendant put Clara on the pony after she had kissed Alice and Edith. Edward assisted Patience; and when she was mounted she said, –

'I hope you will accept my father's offer; you will oblige me so much if you do.'

'I will give it every consideration it deserves,' replied Edward. 'Indeed, it will depend more upon my brother than myself whether I accept it or not.'

'Your brother is a very sensible young man, sir, therefore I have hopes,' replied Patience.

'A quality which it appears you do not give me credit for Miss Heatherstone.'

'Not when pride or vindictive feelings obtain the mastery,' replied she.

'Perhaps you will find that I am not quite so proud, or bear such ill-will, as I did when I first saw your father, Miss Heatherstone; and some allowance should be made, even if I did show such feelings, when you consider that I was brought up at Arnwood.'

'True – most true, Master Armitage. I had no right to speak so boldly, especially to you, who risked your own life to save the daughter of one of those Roundheads who treated the family of your protector so cruelly. You must forgive me; and now, farewell!'

Edward bowed, and then turned to the Intendant, who had apparently been waiting while the conversation was going on. The Intendant bade him a cordial farewell; Edward shook Clara by the hand, and the cavalcade set off. They all remained outside of the cottage till the party were at some distance, and then Edward walked apart with Humphrey, to communicate to him the offer made by the Intendant, and asked his opinion.

'My opinion is made up, Edward; which is, that you should accept it immediately. You are under no obligation to the Government, and you have already conferred such an obligation upon the Intendant that you have a right to expect a return. Why stay here, when you can safely mix with the world and know how things are going on? I do not require your assistance, now that I have Pablo, who is more useful every day. Do not lose such an opportunity of making a friend for yourself and all of us – a protector, I may say; and who is, by what he has confided to you, anything but approving of the conduct of the present Government. He has paid you a deserved compliment by saying that he can and will trust you. You must not refuse the offer, Edward; it would really be folly if you did.'

'I believe you are right, Humphrey; but I have been so accustomed to range the forest – I am so fond of the chase – I am so impatient of control or confinement, that I hardly know how to decide. A secretary's life is anything but pleasing to me, sitting at a table writing and reading all day long. The pen is but a poor exchange for the long-barrelled gun.'

'It does more execution, nevertheless,' replied Humphrey, 'if what I have read is true. But you are not to suppose that your life will be such a sedentary one. Did he not say that he would have to trust you with missions of importance? Will you not, by going to London and other places, and mixing with people of importance, be preparing yourself for your proper station in life, which I trust that one day you will resume? And does it follow that, because you are appointed a secretary, you are not to go out in the forest and shoot a deer with Oswald, if you feel inclined – with this difference, that you may do it then without fear of being insulted or persecuted by such a wretch as that Corbould? Do not hesitate any longer, my dear brother; recollect that our sisters ought not to live this forest life as they advance in years – they were not born for it, although they have so well conformed to it. It depends upon you to release them eventually from their false position; and you can never have such an opening as is now offered you by one whose gratitude alone will make him anxious to serve you.'

134

'You are right, Humphrey, and I will accept the offer. I can but return to you if things do not go on well.'

'I thank you sincerely for your decision, Edward,' replied Humphrey. 'What a sweet girl that Patience Heatherstone is! I think I never saw such an enchanting smile!'

Edward thought of the smile she gave him when they parted but an hour ago, and agreed with Humphrey; but he replied, –

'Why, brother, you are really in love with the Intendant's daughter.'

'Not so, my dear fellow; but I am in love with her goodness and sweetness of disposition, and so are Alice and Edith, I can tell you. She has promised to come over and see them, and bring them flowers for their garden, and I hardly know what; and I am very glad of it, as my sisters have been buried here so long that they cannot but gain by her company now and then. No! I will leave Mistress Heatherstone for you; I am in love with little Clara.'

'Not a bad choice, Humphrey: we both aspire high, for two young foresters; do we not? However, they say "every dog has his day", and Cromwell and his Parliament may have theirs. King Charles may be on his throne again now, long before – you catch a forest pony, Humphrey.'

'I hope he will, Edward; but recollect how you laughed at the idea of my catching a cow – you may be surprised a second time. "Where there is a will there is a way," the saying is. But I must go and help Alice with the heifer; she is not very quiet yet, and I see her going out with her pail.'

The brothers then parted, and Edward walked about, turning over in his mind the events of the day, and very often finding his thoughts broken in upon by sudden visions of Patience Heatherstone; and certainly the remembrance of her was to him the most satisfactory and pleasing portion of the prospect in his offered situation.

'I shall live with her, and be continually in her company,' thought he. 'Well, I would take a less pleasing office if only for that. She requested me to accept it to oblige her, and I w ill do so. How hasty we are in our conclusions! When I first saw her father, what an aversion I felt for him! Now, the more I know him the more I like him – nay, more, respect him. He said that the King wished to be absolute and wrest the liberties from his subjects, and that they were justified in opposing him; I never heard that when at Arnwood.'

'If so, was it lawful so to do?'

'I think it was, but not to murder him – that I can never admit, nor does the Intendant; on the contrary, he hold his murderers in as great detestation as I do. Why, then, we do not think far apart from one another. At the commencement the two parties were – those who supported him, not admitting that he was right, but too loyal to refuse to figh¸ for their King; and those who opposed, hoping to force him to do right: the King for his supposed prerogatives, the people for their liberties. The King was obstinate, the people resolute, until virulent warfare inflamed both parties, and neither would listen to reason; and the people gained the upper hand, they wreaked their vengeance, instead of looking to the dictates of humanity and justice. How easy it had been to have deposed him and sent him beyond the seas! instead of which they detained him a prisoner and then murdered him. The punishment was greater than the offence, and dictated by malice and revenge; it was a diabolical act, and will soil the page of our nation's history.' So thought Edward as he paced before the cottage, until he was summoned in by Pablo to their evening meal.

CHAPTER 18

'Edward,' said Edith, 'scold Pablo; he has been ill-treating my poor cat. He is a cruel boy.'

Pablo laughed.

'See, Edward, he's laughing; put him in the pitfall again, and let him stay there till he says he is sorry.'

'I very sorry now, Missy Edith, but cat bite me,' said Pablo.

'Well, if pussy did, it didn't hurt you much; and what did I tell you this morning out of the Bible? – that you must forgive them who behave ill to you.'

'Yes, Missy Edith, you tell me all that, and so I do; I forgive pussy 'cause she bite me, but I kick her for it.'

'That's not forgiveness – is it, Edward? You should have forgiven it at once, and not kicked it at all.'

'Missy Edith, when pussy bite me, pussy hurt me, make me angry, and I give her a kick; then I think what you tell me, and I do as you tell me. I forgive pussy with all my heart.'

'I think you must forgive Pablo, Edith,' said Edward, 'if it is only to set him a good example.'

'Well, I will this time; but if he kicks pussy again, he must be put in the pitfall – mind that, Pablo.'

'Yes, Missy Edith, I go into pitfall, and then you cry, and ask Massa Edward to take me out. When you have me put in pitfall, then you not good Christian, 'cause you not forgive when you cry and take me out, then you good Christian once more.'

By this conversation it will appear to the reader that they had been trying to impress Pablo with the principles of the Christian religion, and such was the case, Edith having been one of the most active in the endeavour, although very young for missionary. However, Alice and Humphrey had been more successful, and Pablo was now beginning to comprehend what they had attempted to instil, and was really progressing ever day.

Edward remained at the cottage, expecting to hear some message from the Intendant. He was right in his conjecture, for on the third day Oswald Partridge came over to say that the Intendant would be happy to see him, if he could make it convenient to go over, which Edward assented to do on the following day. Oswald had ridden over on a pony. Edward arranged to take Billy and return with him. They started early the next morning, and Edward asked Oswald if he knew why the Intendant had sent for him.

'Not exactly,' replied Oswald; 'but I think, from what I heard Miss Patience say, it is to offer you some situation, if you could be prevailed upon to accept it.'

'Very true,' replied Edward; 'he offers me the post of secretary. What do you think?'

'Why, sir, I think I would accept it: at all events, I would take it on trial – there can be no harm done. If you do not like it, you can only go back to the cottage again. One thing I am sure of, which is, that Master Heatherstone will make it as pleasant to you as he can, for he is most anxious to serve you.'

'That I really believe,' replied Edward; 'and I have pretty well made up my mind to accept the office. It is a post of confidence, and I shall know all that is going on, which I cannot do while I am secluded in the forest; and depend upon it, we shall have stirrings news.'

'I suppose you think that the King will come over?' replied Oswald.

'I feel certain of it, Oswald; and that is the reason why I want to be where I can know all that is going on.'

'Well, sir, it is my opinion that the King will come over, as well as yours; yet I think at present he stands but a poor chance; but Master Heatherstone knows more on that score than any one, I should think; but he is very close.'

The conversation then changed, and after a ride of eight hours, they arrived at the Intendant's house. Edward gave Billy into Oswald's charge, and knocked at the door. Phœbe let him in, and asked him into the sitting-room, where he found the Intendant alone.

'Edward Armitage, I am glad to see you; and shall be still more so if I find that you have made up your mind to accept my proposition. What is your reply?'

'I am very thankful to you for the offer, sir,' replied Edward, 'and will accept it if you think that I am fitting for it, and if I find that I am equal to it: I can but give it a trial, and leave it if I find it too arduous or too irksome.'

'Too arduous it shall not be – that shall be my concern; and too irksome I hope you will not find it. My letters are not so many but that I could answer them myself, were it not that my eyes are getting weak, and I wish to save them as much as possible. You will therefore have to write chiefly what I shall dictate. But it is not only for that I require a person that I can confide in: I very often shall send you to London instead of going myself, and to that, I presume, you will have no objection?'

'Certainly none, sir.'

'Well, then, it is no use saying any more just now. You will have a chamber in this house, and you will live with me, and at my table altogether. Neither shall I say anything just now about remuneration, as I am convinced that you will be satisfied. All that I require now is to know the day that you will come, that everything may be ready.'

'I suppose, sir, I must change my attire!' replied Edward, looking at his forester's dress; 'that will hardly accord with the office of secretary.'

'I agree with you that it will be better to keep that dress for your forest excursions, as I presume you will not altogether abandon them,' replied the Intendant. 'You can provide yourself with a suit at Lymington. I will furnish you the means.'

'I thank you, sir; I have means, much more than sufficient,' replied Edward, 'although not quite so wealthy as little Clara appeared to be.'

'Wealthy, indeed!' replied the Intendant. 'I had no idea that poor Ratcliffe possessed so much ready money and jewels. Well, then, this is Wednesday; can you come over next Monday?'

'Yes, sir,' replied Edward. 'I see no reason to the contrary.'

'Well, then, that is settled; and I suppose you would like to see your accommodation. Patience and Clara are in the next room. You can join them, and you will make my daughter very happy by telling her that you are to become a resident with us. You will, of course, dine with us today, and sleep here tonight.'

Mr Heatherstone then opened the door, and saying to his daughter Patience, 'My dear, I leave you to entertain Edward Armitage till dinner-time,' he ushered Edward in, and closed the door again. Clara ran up to Edward as soon as he went in; and having kissed him, Edward then took Patience's offered hand.

'Then you have consented?' said Patience inquiringly.

'Yes, I could not refuse such kindness,' replied Edward.

'And when do you come?'

'On Monday night, if I can be ready by that time.'

'Why, what have you to get ready?' said Clara.

'I must not appear in a forester's dress, my little Clara. I can wear that with a gun in my hand, but not with a pen; so I must go to Lymington and see what a tailor can do for me.'

'You will feel as strange in a secretary's dress as I did in boys' clothes,' said Clara.

'Perhaps I may,' said Edward, although he felt that such would not be the case, having been accustomed to much better clothes when at Arnwood than what were usually worn by secretaries; and this remembrance brought back Arnwood in its train, and Edward became silent and pensive.

Patience observed it, and after a time said, –

'You will be able to watch over your sisters, Mr Armitage, as well here almost as if you were at the cottage. You do not return till tomorrow? How did you come over?'

'I rode the pony Billy, Mistress Patience.'

'Why do you call her Mistress Patience, Edward?' said Clara. 'You call me Clara; why not call her Patience?'

'You forget that I am only a forester, Clara,' replied Edward with a grave smile.

'No, you are a secretary now,' replied Clara.

'Mistress Patience is older than you by several years. I call you Clara because you are but a little girl; but I must not take that liberty with Mistress Heatherstone.'

'Do you think so, Patience?' said Clara.

'I certainly do not think that it would be a liberty in a person, after being well acquainted with me, to call me Patience,' replied she, 'especially when that person lives in the house with us, eats and associates with us as one of the family, and is received on an equality; but I dare say, Clara, that Master Armitage will be guided by his own feelings, and act as he considers to be proper.'

'But you give him leave, and then it is proper,' replied Clara.

'Yes, if he gave himself leave, Clara,' said Patience. 'But we will now show him his own room, Clara,' continued Patience, wishing to change the subject of conversation. – 'Will you follow us, sir?' said Patience, with a little mock ceremony.

Edward did so without replying, and was ushered into a large airy room, very neatly furnished.

'This is your future lodgings,' said Patience. 'I hope you will like it.'

'Why, he never saw anything like it before,' said Clara.

'Yes, I have, Clara,' replied Edward.

'Where did you?'

'At Arnwood; the apartments were on a much larger scale.'

'Arnwood! Oh yes, I have heard my father speak of it,' said Clara, with the tears starting in her eyes at his memory. 'Yes, it was burnt down, and all the children burnt to death.'

'So they say, Clara, but I was not there when it was burnt.'

'Where were you, then?'

'I was at the cottage where I now live,' Edward turned round to Patience, and perceived that her eyes were fixed upon him, as if she would have read his thoughts. Edward smiled, and said, –

'Do you doubt what I say?'

'No, indeed!' said she – 'I have no doubt that you were at the cottage at the time; but I was thinking that if the apartments at Arnwood were more splendid, those at your cottage are less comfortable. You have been used to better and to worse, and therefore will, I trust, be content with these.'

'I trust I have shown no signs of discontent. I should indeed be difficult to please if an apartment like this did not suit me. Besides, allow me to observe that, although I stated that the apartments at Arnwood were on a grander scale, I never said that I had ever been a possessor of one of them.'

Patience smiled and made no reply.

139

'Now that you know your way to your apartment, Master Armitage, we will, if you please, go back to the sitting-room,' she said. As they were going back into the sitting-room she said, 'When you come over on Monday, you will, I presume, bring your clothes in a cart? I ask it because I promised some flowers and other things to your sisters, which I can send back by the cart.'

'You are very kind to think of them, Mistress Patience,' replied Edward; 'they are fond of flowers, and will be much pleased with possessing any.'

'You sleep here tonight, I think my father said?' inquired Patience.

'He did make the proposal, and I shall gladly avail myself of it, as I am not to trust to Phœbe's ideas of comfort this time,' said Edward, smiling.

'Yes, that was a cross action of Phœbe's, and I can tell you, Master Armitage, that she is ashamed to look you in the face ever since. But how fortunate for me that she was cross, and turned you out as she did! You must forgive her, as she was the means of your performing a noble action; and I must forgive her, as she was the means of my life being saved.'

'I have no feeling except kindness towards Phœbe,' replied Edward. 'Indeed, I ought to feel grateful to her; for if she had not given me so bad a bed that night I never should have been so comfortably lodged as it is proposed that I shall be now.'

'I hope you are hungry, Edward,' said Clara. 'Dinner is almost ready.'

'I dare say I shall eat more than you do, Clara.'

'So you ought, a great big man like you. How old are you, Edward?' said Clara. 'I am thirteen; Patience is past sixteen; now how old are you?'

'I am not yet eighteen, Clara; so that I can hardly be called a man.'

'Why, you are as tall as Mr Heatherstone.'

'Yes, I believe I am.'

'And can't you do everything that a man can do?'

'I really don't know; but I certainly shall always try so to do.'

'Well, then, you must be a man.'

'Well, Clara, if it pleases you, I will be a man.'

'Here comes Mr Heatherstone, so I know dinner is ready. – Is it not, sir?'

'Yes, my child, it is,' replied Mr Heatherstone, kissing Clara; 'so let us all go in.'

Mr Heatherstone, as was usual at that time with the people to whose party he ostensibly belonged, said a grace before meat, of considerable length, and then they sat down to table. As soon as the repast was over, Mr Heatherstone returned to his study, and Edward went out to find Oswald Partridge, with whom he remained the larger portion of the afternoon, going to the kennel, and examining the dogs, and talking of matters connected with the chase.

'I have not two men that can stalk a deer,' observed Oswald. 'The men appointed here as verderers and keepers have not one of them been brought up to the business. Most of them are men who have been in the army, and I believe have been appointed to these situations to get rid of them, because they were troublesome; and they are anything but good characters. The consequence is that we kill but few deer, for I have so much to attend to here, as none of them know their duties, that I can seldom take my own gun out. I stated so to the Intendant, and he said that if you accepted an offer he had made you, and came over here, we should not want venison; so it is clear that he does not expect you to have your pen always in your hand.'

'I am glad to hear that,' replied Edward. 'Depend upon it, his own table, at all events shall be well supplied. Is not that fellow Corbould who is leaning against the wall?'

'Yes. He is to be discharged, as he cannot walk well, and the surgeon says he will always limp. He owes you a grudge, and I am glad that he is going away, for he is a dangerous man. But the sun is setting, Mr Edward, and supper will soon be on the table; you had better go back to the house.'

Edward bade Oswald farewell, and returned to the Intendant's, and found that Oswald was correct, as supper was being placed on the table.

Soon after supper, Phœbe and the menservants were summoned, and prayers offered up by the Intendant; after which Patience and Clara retired. Edward remained in conversation with the Intendant for about an hour, and then was conducted by him to his room, which had already been shown to him by Patience.

Edward did not sleep much that night. The novelty of his situation – the novelty of his prospects, and his speculations thereon – kept him awake till near morning. He was, however, up in good time, and having assisted at the morning prayers, and afterwards eaten a most substantial breakfast, he took his leave of the Intendant and the two girls, and set off on his return to the cottage, having renewed his promise of coming on the following Monday to take up his abode with them. Billy was fresh, and cantered gaily along, so that Edward was back early in the afternoon, and once more welcomed by his household. He stated to Humphrey all that had occurred, and Humphrey was much pleased at Edward having accepted the offer of the Intendant. Alice and Edith did not quite so much approve of it, and a few tears were shed at the idea of Edward leaving the cottage. The next day Edward and Humphrey set off for Lymington, with Billy in the cart.

'Do you know, Edward,' said Humphrey, 'what I am going to try and purchase? I will tell you: as many kids as I can, or goats and kids – I don't care which.'

'Why, have you not stock enough already? You will this year have four cows in milk, and you have two cow calves bringing up.'

'That is very true; but I do not intend to have goats for their milk, but simply for eating in lieu of mutton. Sheep I cannot manage, but goats with a little hay in winter will do well, and will find themselves in the forest all the year round. I won't kill any of the females for the first year or two, and after that I expect we shall have a stock sufficient to meet any demand upon it.'

'It is not a bad idea, Humphrey; they will always come home if you have hay for them during the winter.'

141

Yes, and a large shed for them to lie in when the snow is on the ground.'

'Now I recollect, when we used to go to Lymington, I saw a great many goats, and I have no doubt that they are to be purchased. I will soon ascertain that for you from the landlord of the hostelrie,' replied Edward. 'We will drive there first, as I must ask him to recommend me a tailor.'

On their arrival at Lymington they went straight to the hostelrie, and found the landlord at home. He recommended a tailor to Edward, who sent for him to the inn, and was measured by him for a plain suit of dark cloth. Edward and Humphrey then went out, as Edward had to procure boots, and many other articles of dress, to correspond with the one which he was about to assume.

'I am most puzzled about a hat, Humphrey,' said Edward. 'I hate those steeple-crowned hats worn by the Roundheads; yet the hat and feather is not proper for a secretary.'

'I would advise you to submit to wear the steeple-crowned hats, nevertheless,' said Humphrey. 'Your dress, as I consider, is a sort of disgrace to a Cavalier born, and the heir of Arnwood; why not, therefore, take its hat as well? As secretary to the Intendant, you should dress like him; if not, you may occasion remarks, especially when you travel on his concerns.'

'You are right, Humphrey; I must not do things by halves; and unless I wear the hat, I might be suspected.'

'I doubt if the Intendant wears it for any other reason,' said Humphrey.

'At all events I will not go to the height of the fashion,' replied Edward, laughing. 'Some of the hats are not quite so tall as the others.'

'Here is the shop for the hat and for the sword belt.'

Edward chose a hat and a plain sword-belt, paid for them, and desired the man to carry them to the hostelrie.

While all these purchases on the part of Edward, and many others by Humphrey, such as nails, saws, tools, and various articles which Alice required for the household, were gathered together, the landlord had sent out to inquire for the goats, and found out at what price they were to be procured. Humphrey left Edward to put away these in the cart, while he went out a second time to see the goats. He made an agreement with the man who had them for sale, for a male and three females with two kids each at their sides, and ten more female kids which had just been weaned.

The man engaged to drive them from Lymington, as far as the road went into the forest, on the following day; when Humphrey would meet them, pay him his money, and drive them to the cottage, which would be only three miles from the place agreed upon. Having settled that satisfactorily, he returned to Edward, who was all ready, and they went back home.

'We have dipped somewhat into the bag today, Edward,' said Humphrey; 'but the money is well spent.'

'I think so, Humphrey; but I have no doubt that I shall be able to replace the money very soon, as the Intendant will pay me for my services. The tailor has promised the clothes on Saturday without fail, so that you or I must go for them.'

'I will go, Edward; my sisters will wish you to stay with them now, as you are so soon lo leave them; and I will take Pablo with me, that he may know his way to the town, and I will show him where to buy things, in case he goes there by himself.'

'It appears to me to have been a most fortunate thing your having caught Pablo as you did, Humphrey, for I do not well know how I could have left you if you had not.'

'At all events I can do much better without you man I should have done,' replied Humphrey. 'Although I think now that I could get on by myself but still, Edward, you know we cannot tell what a day may bring forth, and I might fall sick, or something happen which might prevent my attending to anything; and then without you or Pablo everything might have gone to wrack and ruin. Certainly, when we think how we were left, by the death of old Jacob, to our own resources, we have much to thank God for in having got on so well.'

'I agree with you, and also that it has pleased Heaven to grant us all such good health. However, I shall be close at hand if you want me, and Oswald will always call and see how you get on.'

'I hope you will manage that he calls once a week.'

'I will if I can, Humphrey, for I shall be just as anxious as you are to know if all goes on well. Indeed, I shall insist upon coming over to you once a fortnight; and I hardly think the Intendant will refuse me – indeed I am sure that he will not.'

'So am I,' replied Humphrey. 'I am certain that he wishes us all well, and has, in a measure, taken us under his protection; but, Edward, recollect I shall never kill any venison after this, and so you may tell the Intendant.'

'I will, and that will be an excuse for him to send some over, if he pleases. Indeed, as I know I shall be permitted to go out with Oswald, it will be hard if a stray buck does not find its way to the cottage.'

Thus did they continue talking over matters till they arrived at the cottage. Alice came out to them, saying to Humphrey, –

'Well, Humphrey, have you brought my geese and ducks?'

Humphrey had forgotten them, but he replied, –

'You must wait till I go to Lymington again on Saturday, Alice, and then I hope to bring them with me. As it is, look how poor Billy is loaded. Where's Pablo?'

'In the garden. He has been working there all day, and Edith is with him.'

'Well, then, we will unload the cart while you get us something to eat, Alice, for we are not a little hungry, I can tell you.'

'I have some rabbit stew on the fire, Humphrey, all ready for you, and you will find it very good.'

'Nothing I like better, my dear girl. Pablo won't thank me for bringing this home,' continued Humphrey, taking the long saw out of the cart. 'He will have to go to the bottom of the pit again as soon as the pit is made.'

The cart was soon unloaded, Billy taken out and turned out to feed, and then they went in to the supper.

Humphrey was off the next morning with Pablo, at an early hour, to meet the farmer of whom he had purchased the goats and kids. He found them punctual to the time, at the place agreed upon; and being satisfied with the lot, paid the farmer his money, and drove them home through the forest.

'Goat very good, kid better; always eat kid in Spain,' said Pablo.

'Were you born in Spain, Pablo?'

'Not sure, but I think so. First recollect myself in that country.'

'Do you recollect your father?'

'No; never see him.'

'Did your mother never talk about him?'

'Call her mother, but think no mother at all. Custom with Gitanas.'

'Why did you call her mother?'

''Cause she feed me when little, beat me when I get big.'

'All mothers do that. What made you come to England?'

'I don't know, but I hear people say, Plenty of money in England – plenty to eat – plenty to drink; bring plenty money back in Spain.'

'How long have you been in England?'

'One, two, three year; yes, three year and a bit.'

'Which did you like best, England or Spain?'

'When with my people, like Spain best; warm sun – warm night. England little sun, cold night, much rain, snow, and air always cold; but now I live with you, have warm bed, plenty victuals, like England best.'

'But when you were with the gipsies, they stole everything, did they not?'

'Not steal everything,' replied Pablo, laughing; 'sometimes take and no pay when nobody there; farmer look very sharp – have big dog.'

'Did you ever go out to steal?'

'Make me go out. Not bring back something, beat me very hard; suppose farmer catch me, beat hard too; nothing but beat, beat, beat.'

'Then they obliged you to steal?'

'Suppose bring nothing home, first beat, and then not have to eat one, two, three days. How you like that, Massa Humphrey? I think you steal, after no victuals for three days?'

'I should hope not,' replied Humphrey, 'although I have never been so severely punished; and I hope, Pablo, you will never steal any more.'

'Why steal any more?' replied Pablo. 'I not like to steal; but because hungry I steal. Now I never hungry, always have plenty to eat; no one beat me now; sleep warm all night. Why I steal, then? No, Massa Humphrey, I never steal more, 'cause I have no reason why, and 'cause Missy Alice and Missy Edith tell me how the good God up there say must not steal.'

'I am glad to hear you give that as a reason, Pablo,' replied Humphrey, 'as it proves that my sisters have not been teaching you in vain.'

144

'Like to hear Miss Alice talk; she talk grave. Miss Edith talk too, but she laugh very much; very fond Miss Edith, very happy little girl; jump about just like one of these kids we drive home; always merry. Hah! see cottage now; soon get home, Massa Humphrey. Miss Edith like see kids very much. Where we put them?'

CHAPTER 19

'We will put them into the yard for the present; I mean that Holdfast shall take charge of them by-and-by. I will soon teach him.'

'Yes, he take charge of coat, or anything I tell him; why not take charge of goats? Clever dog, Holdfast. Massa Humphrey, you think Massa Edward take away born his dogs, Smoker and Watch? I say better not take puppy. Take Smoker, and leave puppy.'

'I agree with you, Pablo. We ought to have two dogs here. I will speak to my brother. Now run forward and open the gate of the yard, and throw them some hay, Pablo, while I go and call my sisters.'

The flock of goats were much admired, and the next morning were driven out into the forest to feed, attended by Pablo and Holdfast. When it was dinner-time Pablo drove the flock near to the cottage, telling the dog to mind them. The sensible animal remained at once with the goats until Pablo's return from dinner; and it may be as well to observe here that in a few days the dog took charge of them altogether, driving them home to the yard every evening; and as soon as the goats were put into the yard the dog had his supper; and the dog took care, therefore, not to be too late. To return to our narrative.

On Saturday Humphrey and Pablo went to Lymington to bring home Edward's clothes, and Humphrey made Pablo acquainted with all that he wanted to know, in case it might be necessary to send Pablo there alone.

Edward remained with his sisters, as he was to leave them on the Monday.

Sunday was passed as usual; they read the service at old Armitage's grave, and afterwards they walked in the forest; for Sunday was the only day on which Alice could find time to leave her duties in the cottage. They were more grave than usual at the idea of Edward's leaving them, but they kept up their spirits, as they were aware that it was for the advantage of all.

On Monday morning Edward, to please his sisters, put on his new clothes, and put his forester's dress in the bundle with his linen. Alice and Edith thought he looked very well in them, and said that it reminded them of the days of Arnwood. The fact was that Edward appeared as he was –

a gentleman born; that could not well be concealed under a forester's dress, and in his present attire it was undeniable. After breakfast Billy was harnessed and brought to the cottage door. Edward's linen was put in the cart, and as he had agreed with Humphrey, he took Smoker with him, leaving the puppy at the cottage. Pablo went with him to bring back the cart. Edward kissed his sisters, who wept at the idea of his leaving them, and shaking hands with Humphrey, he set off to cross the forest.

'Who would ever have believed this,' thought Edward, as he drove across the forest, 'that I should put myself under the roof and under the protection of a Roundhead? – one in outward appearance, and in the opinion of the world at least, if he is not so altogether in opinions. There is surely some spell upon me, and I almost feel as if I were a traitor to my principles. Why I know not; I feel a regard for that man, and a confidence in him. And why should I not? He knows my principles, my feelings against his party, and he respects them. Surely he cannot wish to gain me over to his party; that were indeed ridiculous – a young forester – a youth unknown. No, he would gain nothing by that, for I am nobody. It must be from good will, and no other feeling. I have obliged him in the service I rendered his daughter, and he is grateful.' Perhaps, had Edward put the question to himself, 'Should I have been on such friendly terms with the Intendant – should I have accepted his offer – if there had been no Patience Heatherstone?' he might then have discovered what was the 'spell upon him' which had rendered him so tractable; but of that he had no idea. He only felt that his situation would be rendered more comfortable by the society of an amiable and handsome girl, and he inquired no further.

His reverie was broken by Pablo, who appeared tired of holding his tongue, and said, 'Massa Edward, you not like leave home – you think very much. Why you go there?'

'I certainly do not like to leave home, Pablo, for I am very fond of my brother and sisters; but we cannot always do as we wish in this world, and it is for their sakes, more than from my own inclinations, that I have done so.'

'Can't see what good you do Missy Alice and Missy Edith 'cause you go away. How it possible do good, and not with them? Suppose bad accident, and you away, how you do good? Suppose bad accident, and you at cottage, then you do good. I think, Massa Edward, you very foolish.'

Edward laughed at this blunt observation of Pablo's and replied, 'It is very true, Pablo, that I cannot watch over my sisters and protect them in person when I am away; but there are reasons why I should go, nevertheless, and I may be more useful to them by going than by remaining with them. If I did not think so I would not leave them. They know nobody, and have no friends in the world. Suppose anything was to happen to me. Suppose both Humphrey and I were to die – for you know that we never know how soon that event may take place – who would there be to protect my poor sisters, and what would become of them? Is it not, therefore, wise that I should procure friends for them, in case of accident, who would look after them and protect them? And it is my hope that by leaving them now I shall make powerful and kind friends for them. Do you understand me?'

'Yes, I see now: you think more than me, Massa Edward. I say just now, you foolish; I say now, Pablo great fool.'

'Besides, Pablo, recollect that I never would have left them as long as there were only Humphrey and I to look after them, because an accident might have happened to one of us; but when you came to live with us, and I found what a good, clever boy you were, and that you were fond of us all, I then said, "Now I can leave my sisters, for Pablo shall take my place, and assist Humphrey to do what is required, and to take care of them." Am I right, Pablo?'

'Yes, Massa Edward,' replied Pablo, taking hold of Edward's wrist, 'you quite right. Pablo does love Missy Alice, Missy Edith, Massa Humphrey, and you, Massa Edward; he love you all very much indeed – he love you so much that he die for you! Can do no more.'

'That is what I really thought of you, Pablo, and yet I am glad to hear it from your own mouth. If you had not come to live with us, and had not proved so faithful, I could not have left to benefit my sisters; but you have induced me to leave, and they have to thank you if I am able to be of any service to them.'

'Well, Massa Edward, you go. Never mind us – we make plenty of work; do everything all the same as you.'

'I think you will, Pablo, and that is the reason why I have agreed to go away. But, Pablo, Billy is growing old, and you will want some more ponies.'

'Yes, Massa Edward; Massa Humphrey talk to me about ponies last night, and say, plenty in the forest. Ask me if I think us able catch them. I say yes, catch one, two, twenty, suppose want them.'

'Ah! how will you do that, Pablo?'

'Massa Edward, you ten Massa Humphrey no possible, so I no tell you how,' replied Pablo, laughing. 'Some day you come see us, see five ponies in the stable. Massa Humphrey and I, we talk about, find out how; you see.'

'Well, then, I shall ask no more questions, Pablo; and when I see the ponies in the stable, then I'll believe it, and not before.'

'Suppose you want big horse for ride, catch big horse, Massa Edward, you see. Massa Humphrey very clever – he catch cow.'

'Catch gipsy,' said Edward.

'Yes,' said Pablo, laughing; 'catch cow, catch gipsy, and by-and-by catch horse.'

When Edward arrived at the Intendant's house he was very kindly received by the Intendant and the two girls. Having deposited his wardrobe in his bedroom, he went out to Oswald and put Smoker in the kennel, and on his return found Pablo sitting on the carpet in the sitting-room, talking to Patience and Clara, and they all three appeared much amused. When Pablo and Billy had both had something to eat, the cart was filled with pots of flowers, and several other little things as presents from Patience Heatherstone, and Pablo set off on his return.

'Well, Edward, you do look like a . . .' said Clara, stopping.

'Like a secretary, I hope,' added Edward.

'Well, you don't look like a forester. – Does he, Patience?' continued Clara.

'You must not judge of people by their clothes, Clara.'

'Nor do I,' replied Clara. 'Those clothes would not look well upon Oswald or the other men, for they would not suit them; but they do suit you. – Don't they, Patience?'

Patience Heatherstone, however, did not make any answer to this second appeal made by Clara.

'Why don't you answer me, Patience?' said Clara.

'My dear Clara, it's not the custom for young maidens to make remarks upon people's attire. Little girls like you may do so.'

'Why, did you not tell Pablo that he looked well in his new clothes?'

'Yes, but Pablo is not Mr Armitage, Clara. That is very different.'

'Well, it may be, but still you might answer a question, if put to you, Patience; and I ask again, Does not Edward look much better in the dress he has on than in that he generally has worn?'

'I think it a becoming dress, Clara, since you will have an answer.'

'Fine feathers make fine birds, Clara,' said Edward, laughing; 'and so that is all we can say about it.'

Edward then changed the conversation. Soon afterwards dinner was announced, and Clara again observed to Edward, –

'Why do you always call Patience Mistress Heatherstone? – Ought he not to call her Patience, sir?' said Clara, appealing to the Intendant.

'That must depend upon his own feelings, my dear Clara,' replied Mr Heatherstone. 'It is my intention to waive ceremony as much as possible. Edward Armitage has come to live with us as one of the family, and he will find himself treated by me as one of us. I shall, therefore, in future address him as Edward and he has my full permission, and I may say it is my wish, that he should be on the same familiar terms with us all. When Edward feels inclined to address my daughter as he does you, by her name of baptism, he will, I dare say, now that he has heard my opinion, do so, and reserve "Mistress Heatherstone" for the time when they have a quarrel.'

'Then I hope he will never again address me that way,' observed Patience; 'for I am under too great obligations to him to bear even the idea of being on bad terms with him.'

'Do you hear that, Edward?' said Clara.

'Yes, I do, Clara; and after such a remark you may be sure that I shall never address her in that way again.'

In a few days Edward became quite at home. In the forenoon Mr Heatherstone dictated one or two letters to him, which he wrote, and after that his time was at his own disposal, and was chiefly passed in the company of Patience and Clara. With the first he had now become on the most intimate and brotherly footing; and when they addressed each other, Patience and Edward were the only appellations made use of. Once Mr Heatherstone asked Edward whether he would not like to go out with Oswald to kill a deer, which he did; but the venison was hardly yet in season. There was a fine horse in the stable at Edward's order, and he often rode out with Patience and Clara. Indeed, his time passed so agreeably that he could hardly think it possible that a fortnight had passed away when he asked permission to go over to the cottage and see his sisters.

With the Intendant's permission, Patience and Clara accompanied him; and the joy of Alice and Edith was great when they made their appearance. Oswald had, by Edward's request, gone over a day or two before to tell them that they were coming, that they might be prepared; and the consequence was that it was a holiday at the cottage. Alice had cooked her best dinner, and Humphrey and Pablo were at home to receive them.

'How pleasant it will be if we are to see you and Clara whenever we see Edward!' said Alice to Patience. 'So far from being sorry that Edward is with you, I shall be quite glad of it.'

'I water the flowers every day,' said Edith, 'and they make the garden look so gay.'

'I will bring you plenty more in the autumn, Edith; but this is not the right time for transplanting flowers yet, replied Patience. – 'And now, Alice, you must take me to see your farm, for when I was here last I had no time. Let us come now, and show me everything.'

'But my dinner, Patience; I cannot leave it, or it will be spoiled, and that will never do. You must either go with Edith now or wait till after dinner, when I can get away.'

'Well, then, we will stay till after dinner, Alice, and we will help you to serve it up. '

'Thank you; Pablo generally does that, for Edith cannot reach down the things. I don't know where he is.'

'He went away with Edward and Humphrey, I think,' said Edith. 'I'll scold him when he comes back for being out of the way.'

'Never mind, Edith; I can reach the dishes,' said Patience; 'and you and Clara can then take them, and the platters, and put them on the table for Alice.'

And Patience did as she proposed, and the dinner was soon afterwards on the table. There were a ham, and two boiled fowls, and a piece of salted beef, and some roasted kid, besides potatoes and green peas; and when it is considered that such a dinner was set on the table by such young people, left entirely to their own exertions and industry, it must be admitted that it did them and their farm great credit.

In the meantime Edward and Humphrey, after the first greetings were over, had walked out to converse, while Pablo had taken the horses into the stable.

'Well, Humphrey, how do you get on?'

'Very well, replied Humphrey. 'I have just finished a very tough job. I have dug out the sawpit, and have sawed the slabs for the sides of the pit, and made it quite secure. The large fir tree that was blown down is now at the pit, ready for sawing up into planks, and Pablo and I are to commence tomorrow. At first we made but a bad hand of sawing off the slabs, but before we had cut them all we got on pretty well. Pablo don't much like it, and indeed no more do I much – it is such mechanical work, and so tiring; but he does not complain. I do not intend that he shall saw more than two days in a week; that will be sufficient – we shall get on fast enough.'

'You are right, Humphrey; it is an old saying that you must not work a willing horse to death. Pablo is very willing, but hard work he is not accustomed to.'

'Well, now you must come and look at my flock of goats, Edward; they are not far off. I have taught Holdfast to take care of them, and he never leaves them now, and brings them home at night. Watch always remains with me, and is an excellent dog and very intelligent.'

'You have indeed a fine flock, Humphrey!' said Edward.

'Yes, and they are improved in appearance already since they have been here. Alice has got her geese and ducks, and I have made a place large enough for them to wash in until I have time to dig them out a pond.'

'I thought we had gathered more hay than you required, but with this addition I think you will find none to spare before the spring.'

'So far from it that I have been mowing down a great deal more, Edward, and it is almost ready to carry away. Poor Billy has had hard work of it, I assure you, since he came back, with one thing and another.'

'Poor fellow! But it won't last long, Humphrey,' said Edward, smiling; 'the other horses will soon take his place.'

'I trust they will,' said Humphrey; 'at all events by next spring. Before that I do not expect that they will.'

'By-the-by, Humphrey, you recollect what I said to you that the robber I shot told me just before he died?'

'Yes, I do recollect it now,' replied Humphrey; 'but I had quite forgot all about it till you mentioned it now, although I wrote it down that we might not forget it.'

'Well, I have been thinking all about it, Humphrey. The robber told me that the money was mine, taking me for another person; therefore I do not consider it was given to me, nor do I consider that it was his to give. I hardly know what to do about it, nor to whom the money can be said to belong.'

'Well, I think I can answer that question. The property of all malefactors belongs to the King, and therefore this money belongs to the King; and we may retain it for the King, or use it for his service.'

'Yes, it would have belonged to the King had the man been condemned and hung on the gallows as he deserved; but he was not, and therefore I think that it does not belong to the King.'

'Then it belongs to whoever finds it, and who keeps it till it is claimed – which will never be.'

'I think I must speak to the Intendant about it,' replied Edward. 'I should feel more comfortable.'

'Then do so,' replied Humphrey. 'I think you are right to have no concealments from him.'

'But Humphrey,' replied Edward, laughing, 'what silly fellows we are! We do not yet know whether we shall find anything. We must first see if there is anything buried there; and when we have done so, then we will decide how to act. I shall, if it please God, be over again in a fortnight, and in meantime do you find out the place, and ascertain if what the fellow said is true.'

'I will,' replied Humphrey. 'I will go tomorrow, with Billy and the cart, and take a spade and pickaxe with me. It may be a fool's errand, but still they are, and one would credit, for the honour of human nature, that the words of a dying man are those of truth. We had better go back now, for I think dinner must be ready.'

Now that they had become so intimate with Patience Heatherstone – and, I may add, so fond of her – there was no longer any restraint, and they had a very merry dinner-party; and after dinner Patience went out with Alice and Edith and looked over the garden and farm. She wished very much to ascertain if there was anything that they required, but she could discover but few things, and those only trifles; but she recollected them all, and sent them to the cottage a few days afterwards. But the hour of parting arrived; for it was a long ride back, and they could not stay any longer if they wished to get home before dark, as Mr Heatherstone had requested Edward that they should do. So the horses were brought out; and wishing good-bye, they set off again, little Edith crying after them, 'Come again soon! – Patience, you must come again soon!'

CHAPTER 20

The summer had now advanced, when Oswald one day said to Edward, –

'Have you heard the news, sir?'

'Nothing very particular,' replied Edward. 'I know that General Cromwell is over in Ireland, and they say very successful; but I have cared little for particulars.'

'They say a great deal more, sir,' replied Oswald. 'They say that the King is in Scotland, and that the Scotch have raised an army for him.'

'Indeed!' replied Edward; 'that is news indeed! The Intendant has never mentioned it to me.'

'I dare say not, sir, for he knows your feelings, and would be sorry to part with you.'

'I will certainly speak to him on the subject,' said Edward, 'at the risk of his displeasure; and join the army I will, if I find what you say is true. I should hold myself a craven to remain here while the King is fighting for his own, and not to be at his side.'

'Well, sir, I think it is true, for I heard that the Parliament had sent over for General Cromwell to leave Ireland and lead the troops against the Scotch army.'

'You drive me mad, Oswald! I will go to the Intendant immediately!'

Edward, much excited by the intelligence, went into the room where he usually sat with the Intendant. The latter, who was at his desk, looked up, and saw how flushed Edward was, and said very quietly, –

'Edward, you are excited, I presume, from hearing the news which has arrived?'

'Yes, sir, I am very much so; and I regret very much that I should be the last to whom such important news is made known.'

'It is, as you say, important news,' replied the Intendant; 'but if you will sit down, we will talk a little upon the subject.'

Edward took a chair, and the Intendant said, –

'I have no doubt that your present feeling is to go to Scotland and join in the army without delay?'

'Such is my intention, I candidly confess, sir. It is my duty.'

'Perhaps you may be persuaded to the contrary before we part,' replied the Intendant. 'The first duty you owe is to your family in their present position. They depend upon you, and a false step on your part would be their ruin. How can you leave them, and leave my employ, without it being known for what purpose you are gone? It is impossible! I must myself make it known; and even then it would be very injurious to me, the very circumstance of my having one of your party in my service. I am suspected by many already in consequence of the part I have taken against the murder of the late King, and also of the lords who have since suffered. But, Edward, I did not communicate this intelligence to you for many reasons. I knew that it would soon come to your ears, and I thought it better that I should be more prepared to show you that you may do yourself and me harm, and can do no good to the King. I will now show you that I do put confidence in you; and if you will read these letters they will prove to you that I am correct in what I assert.'

The Intendant handed three letters to Edward, by which it was evident that all the King's friends in England were of opinion that the time was not ripe for the attempt, and that it would be only a sacrifice to stir in the matter; that the Scotch army raised was composed of those who were the greatest enemies to the King, and that the best thing that could happen for the King's interest would be that they were destroyed by Cromwell; that it was impossible for the English adherents of Charles to join them, and that the Scotch did not wish them so to do.

'You are no politician, Edward,' said the Intendant, smiling as Edward laid the letters down on the table. 'You must admit that on showing you these letters I have put the utmost confidence in you?'

'You have indeed, sir; and thanking you for having so done, I hardly need add that your confidence will never be betrayed.'

'That I am sure of; and I trust you will now agree with me and my friends that the best thing is to remain quiet?'

'Certainly, sir, and for the future I will be guided by you.'

'That is all I require of you; and after that promise you shall hear all the news as soon as it arrives. There are thousands who are just as anxious to see the King on the throne again as you are, Edward – and you now know that I am one of them; but the time is not yet come, and we must bide our time. Depend upon it that General Cromwell will scatter that army like chaff. He is on his march now. After what has passed between us this day, Edward, I shall talk unreservedly to you on what is going on.' ·

'I thank you, sir, and I promise you faithfully, as I said before, not only to be guided by your advice, but to be most secret in all that you may trust me with.'

'I have confidence in you, Edward Armitage. And now we will drop the subject for the present. Patience and Clara want you to talk with them, so good-bye for the present.'

Edward left the Intendant, much pleased with the interview. The Intendant kept his word, and concealed nothing from Edward. All turned out as the Intendant had foretold. The Scotch army were cut to pieces by Cromwell, and the King retreated to the Highlands; and Edward now felt satisfied that he could do no better than be guided by the Intendant in all his future undertakings.

We must now pass over some time in a few words. Edward continued at the Intendant's, and gave great satisfaction to Mr Heatherstone. He passed his time very agreeably, sometimes going out to shoot deer with Oswald, and often supplying venison to his brothers and sisters at the cottage. During the autumn Patience very often went to the cottage, and occasionally Mr Heatherstone paid them a visit; but after the winter set in, Edward came over by himself, shooting as he went; and when he and Smoker came to the cottage, Billy always had a journey to go for the venison left in the forest. Patience sent Alice many little things for the use of her and Edith, and some very good books for them to read; and Humphrey, during the evenings, read with his sisters, that they might learn what he could teach them. Pablo also learned to read and write. Humphrey and Pablo had worked at the sawpit, and had sawed out a large quantity of boards and timber for building; but the building was put off till the spring.

The reader may recollect that Edward had proposed to Humphrey that he should ascertain whether what the robber had stated before his death, relative to his having concealed his ill-gotten wealth under the tree which was struck by lightning, was true. About ten days afterwards Humphrey set off on this expedition. He did not take Pablo with him, as, although he had a very good opinion of him, he agreed with Oswald that temptation should not be put in his way. Humphrey considered that it would be the best plan to go at once to Clara's cottage, and from that proceed to find the oak-tree mentioned by the robber. When he arrived at the thicket which surrounded the cottage, it occurred to him that he would just go through it and see if it was in the state which they had left it in; for after the Intendant had been there, he had given directions to his men to remain and bury the bodies, and then to lock up the doors of the cottage and bring the keys to him, which had been done. Humphrey tied Billy and the cart to a tree, and walked through the thicket. As he approached the cottage he heard voices; this induced him to advance very carefully, for he had not brought his gun with him. He crouched down as he came to the opening before the cottage. The doors and windows were open, and there were two men sitting outside, cleaning their guns; and in one of them Humphrey recognized the man Corbould, who had been discharged by the Intendant as soon as his wound had been cured, and who was supposed to have gone to London. Humphrey was too far off to hear what they said. He remained there some time, and three more men came out of the cottage. Satisfied with what he had seen, Humphrey cautiously retreated, and gaining the outside of the thicket, led away Billy and the cart over the turf, that the noise of the wheels might not be heard.

'This bodes no good,' thought Humphrey as he went along, every now and then looking back to ascertain if the men had come out and seen him. 'That Corbould, we know, has vowed vengeance against Edward, and all of us, and has, no doubt, joined those robbers – for robbers they must be – that he may fulfil his vow. It is fortunate that I have made the discovery, and I will send over immediately to the Intendant.' As soon as a clump of trees had shut out the thicket, and he had no longer any fear of being seen by these people, Humphrey went in the direction which the robber had mentioned and soon afterwards he perceived the oak scathed with lightning, which stood by itself on a green spot of about twenty acres. It had been a noble tree before it had been destroyed; now it spread its long, naked arms, covering a large space of ground, but without the least sign of vegetation or life remaining. The trunk was – many feet in diameter, and was apparently quite sound, although the tree was dead. Humphrey left Billy to feed on the herbage close by, and then, from the position of the sun in the heavens, ascertained the point at which he was to dig. First looking around him to see that he was not overlooked, he took his spade and pick-axe out of the cart and began his task. There was a spot not quite so green as the rest, which Humphrey thought likely to be the very place that he should dig at, as probably it was not green from the soil having been removed. He commenced at this spot, and after a few moments' labour his pickaxe struck upon something hard, which, on clearing away the earth, he discovered to be the wooden lid of a box. Satisfied that he was right, Humphrey now worked hard, and in a few minutes he had cleared away

154

sufficiently to be able to lift out the box and place it on the turf. He was about to examine it, when he perceived, at about five hundred yards' distance, three men coming towards him. 'They have discovered me,' thought Humphrey, 'and I must be off as soon as I can.' He ran to Billy, who was close to him, and bringing the cart to where the box lay, he lifted it in. As he was getting in himself, with the reins in his hands, he perceived that the three men were running towards him as fast as they could, and that they all had guns in their hands. They were not more than a hundred and fifty yards from him when Humphrey set off, putting Billy to a full trot.

The three men, observing this, called out to Humphrey to stop, or they would fire; but Humphrey's only reply was giving a lash to Billy, which set him off at a gallop. The men immediately fired, and the bullets whistled past Humphrey without doing any harm. Humphrey looked round, and finding that he had increased his distance, pulled up the pony, and went a more moderate pace. 'You'll not catch me,' thought Humphrey; 'and your guns are not loaded, so I'll tantalize you a little.' He made Billy walk, and turned round to see what the men were about. They had arrived at where he had dug out the box, and were standing round the hole, evidently aware that it was no use following him. 'Now,' thought Humphrey as he went along at a faster pace, 'those fellows will wonder what I have been digging up. The villains little think that I know where to find them, and they have proved what they are by firing at me. Now, what must I do? They may follow me to the cottage, for I have no doubt that they know where we live and that Edward is at the Intendant's. They may come and attack us, and I dare not leave the cottage tonight, or send Pablo away, in case they should; but I will tomorrow morning.' Humphrey considered, as he went along, all the circumstances and probabilities, and decided that he would act as he at first proposed to himself. In an hour he was at the cottage; and as soon as Alice had given him his dinner hour – he told her what had taken place.

'Where is Pablo?'

'He has been working in the garden with Edith all the day,' replied Alice.

'Well, dear, I hope they will not come tonight: tomorrow I will have them all in custody; but if they do come, we must do our best to beat them off. It is fortunate that Edward left the guns and pistols which he found in Clara's cottage, as we shall have no want of firearms; and we can barricade the doors and windows, so that they cannot get in in a hurry. But I must have Pablo to help me, for there is no time to be lost.'

'But cannot I help you, Humphrey?' said Alice. 'Surely I can do something?'

'We will see, Alice; but I think I can do without you. We have still plenty of daylight. I will take the box into your room.'

Humphrey, who had only taken the box out of the cart and carried it within the threshold of the door, now took it into his sister's bedroom, and then went out and called Pablo, who came running to him.

'Pablo,' said Humphrey, 'we must bring to the cottage some of the large pieces we sawed out for rafters, for I should not be surprised if the cottage were attacked this night.' He then told Pablo what had taken place. 'You see, Pablo, I dare not send to the Intendant tonight, in case the robbers should come here.'

'No, not send tonight,' said Pablo; 'stay here and fight them; first make door fast, then cut hole to fire through.'

'Yes, that was my idea. You don't mind fighting them, Pablo?' 'No; fight hard for Missy Alice and Missy Edith,' said Pablo; 'fight for you too, Massa Humphrey, and fight for myself,' added Pablo, laughing.

They then went for the pieces of squared timber, brought them from the sawpit to the cottage, and very soon fitted them to the doors and windows, so as to prevent several men, with using all their strength, from forcing them open.

'That will do,' said Humphrey; 'and now get me the small saw, Pablo, and I will cut a hole or two to fire through,'

It was dark before they had finished, and then they made all fast, and went to Pablo's room for the arms, which they got ready for service, and loaded.

'Now we are all ready, Alice, so let us have our supper,' said Humphrey. 'We will make a fight for it, and they shall not get in so easily as they think.'

After they had had their supper, Humphrey said the prayers, and told his sisters to go to bed.

'Yes, Humphrey, we will go to bed, but we will not undress; for if they come, I must be up to help you. I can load a gun, you know, and Edith can take them to you as fast as I load them. – Won't you, Edith?'

'Yes, I will bring you the guns, Humphrey, and you shall shoot them,' replied Edith.

Humphrey kissed his sisters, and they went to their room. He then put a light in the chimney, that he might not have to get one in case the robbers came, and then desired Pablo to go and lie down on his bed, as he intended to do the same. Humphrey remained awake till past three o'clock in the morning; but no robbers came. Pablo was snoring loud, and at last Humphrey fell asleep himself, and did not awake till broad daylight. He got up, and found Alice and Edith were already in the sitting-room, lighting the fire.

'I would not wake you, Humphrey, as you had been sitting up so long. The robbers have not made their appearance, that is clear. Shall you unbar the door and window-shutters now?'

'Yes, I think we may. – Here, Pablo!'

'Yes,' said Pablo, coming out half asleep; 'what the matter? Thief come?'

'No,' replied Edith, 'thief not come, but sun shine, and lazy Pablo not get up.'

'Up now, Missy Edith.'

'Yes, but not awake yet.'

'Yes, Missy Edith, quite awake.'

'Well, then, help me to undo the door, Pablo.'

They took down the barricades, and Humphrey opened the door cautiously, and looked out.

'They won't come now, at all events, I should think,' observed Humphrey; 'but there is no saying – they may be prowling about, and may think it easier to get in during daytime than at night. Go out, Pablo, and look about everywhere; take a pistol with you, and fire it off if there is any danger, and then come back as fast as you can.'

Pablo took the pistol, and then Humphrey went out of the door and looked well round in front of the cottage, but he would not leave the door till he was assured that no one was there. Pablo returned soon after, saying that he had looked round everywhere, and into the cow-house and yard, and there was nobody to be seen. This satisfied Humphrey, and they returned to the cottage.

'Now, Pablo, get your breakfast, while I write the letter to the Intendant,' said Humphrey; 'and then you must saddle Billy, and go over to him as fast as you can with the letter. You can tell him all I have not said in it. I shall expect you back at night, and some people with you.'

'I see,' said Pablo, who immediately busied himself with some cold meat which Alice put before him. Pablo had finished his breakfast and brought Billy to the door before Humphrey had finished his letter. As soon as it was written and folded, Pablo set off, as fast as Billy could go, to the other side of the forest.

Humphrey continued on the lookout during the whole day, with his gun on his arm, and his two dogs by his side; for he knew the dogs would give notice of the approach of anyone long before he might see them. But nothing occurred during the whole day; and when the evening closed in he barricaded the doors and windows, and remained on the watch with the dogs, waiting for the coming of the robbers, or for the coming of the party which he expected would be sent by the Intendant to take the robbers. Just as it was dark, Pablo returned with a note from Edward, saying that he would be over and at the cottage by ten o'clock with a large party.

Humphrey had said in his letter that it would be better that any force sent by the Intendant should not arrive till after dark, as the robbers might be near and perceive them, and then they might escape; he did not therefore expect them to come till some time after dark. Humphrey was reading a book, Pablo was dozing in the chimney-corner, the two girls had retired into their room and had lain down on the bed in their clothes, when the dogs both gave a low growl.

'Somebody come,' said Pablo, starting up.

Again the dogs growled, and Humphrey made a sign to Pablo to hold his tongue. A short time of anxious silence succeeded, for it was impossible to ascertain whether the parties were friends or enemies. The dogs now sprang up and barked furiously at the door, and as soon as Humphrey had silenced them a voice was heard outside, begging for admission to a poor, benighted traveller. This was sufficient: it could not be the party from the

Intendant's, but the robbers, who wished to induce them to open the door. Pablo put a gun into Humphrey's hand, and took another for himself; he then removed the light into the chimney, and on the application from outside being repeated, Humphrey answered, –

'That he never opened the door at that hour of the night, and that it was useless their remaining.'

No answer or repetition of the request was made; but as Humphrey retreated with Pablo into the fireplace a gun was fired into the lock of the door, which was blown off into the room; and had it not been for the barricades the door must have flown open. The robbers appeared surprised at such not being the case, and one of them inserted his arm into the hole made in the door, to ascertain what might be the further obstacle to open it, when Pablo slipped past Humphrey, and gaining the door, discharged his gun under the arm which had been thrust into the hole in the door. The party, whoever it might have been, gave a loud cry, and fell at the threshold outside.

'I think that will do,' said Humphrey; 'we must not take more life than is necessary. I had rather that you had fired through his arm; it would have disabled him, and that would have sufficed.'

'Kill much better,' said Pablo. 'Corbould shot through leg, come again to rob; suppose shot dead, never rob more.'

The dogs now flew to the back of the cottage, evidently pointing out that the robbers were attempting that side. Humphrey put his gun through the hole in the door, and discharged it.

'Why you do that, Massa Humphrey? Nobody there.'

'I know that, Pablo; but if the people are coming from the Intendant's, they will see the flash and perhaps hear the report, and it will let them know what is going on.'

'There is another gun loaded, Humphrey,' said Alice, who with Edith had joined them without Humphrey observing it.

'Thanks, love; but you and Edith must not remain here. Sit down on the hearth, and then you will be sheltered from any bullet which they may fire into the house. I have no fear of their getting in, and we shall have help directly, I have no doubt. – Pablo, I shall fire through the back door; they must be there, for the dogs have their noses under it, and are so violent. Do you fire another gun, as a signal, through the hole in the front door.'

Humphrey stood within four feet of the back door, and fired just above where the dogs held their noses and barked. Pablo discharged his gun as directed, and then returned to reload the guns. The dogs were now more quiet, and it appeared as if the robbers had retreated from the back door. Pablo blew out the light, which had been put more in the centre of the room when Alice and Edith took possession of the fireplace.

'No fear, Missy Edith; I know where find everything,' said Pablo, who now went and peered through the hole in the front door, to see if the robbers were coming to it again; but he could see and hear nothing for some time.

At last the attack was renewed; the dogs flew backwards and forwards, sometimes to one door and then to another, as if both were to be assailed; and at the same time a crash in Alice's bedchamber told them that the robbers had burst in the small window in that room, which Humphrey had not paid any attention to, as it was so small that a man could hardly introduce his body through it. Humphrey immediately called Holdfast and opened the door of the room; for he thought that a man forcing his way in would be driven back or held by the dog, and he and Pablo dared not leave the two doors. Watch, the other dog, followed Holdfast into the bedroom, and oaths and curses, mingled with the savage yells of the dogs, told them that a conflict was going on. Both doors were now battered with heavy pieces of timber at the same time, and Pablo said, –

'Great many robbers here.'

A moment or more had passed, during which Pablo and Humphrey had both again fired their guns through the door, when of a sudden other sounds were heard – shots fired outside, loud cries, and angry oaths and exclamations.

'The Intendant's people are come,' said Humphrey; 'I am sure of it.'

Shortly afterwards Humphrey heard his name called by Edward, and he replied, and went to the door and undid the barricades.

'Get a light, Alice, dear,' said Humphrey; 'we are all safe now. – I will open the door directly, Edward, but in the dark I cannot see the fastenings.'

'Are you all safe, Humphrey?'

'Yes, all safe, Edward. Wait till Alice brings a light.'

Alice soon brought one, and then the door was unfastened. Edward stepped over the body of a man which lay at the threshold, saying, –

'You have settled somebody there, at all events,' and then caught Edith and Alice in his arms.

He was followed by Oswald and some other men, leading in the prisoners.

'Bind that fellow fast, Oswald,' said Edward. – 'Get another light, Pablo; let us see who it is that lies outside the door.'

'First see who is in my bedroom, Edward,' said Alice, 'for the dogs are still there.'

'In your bedroom, dearest? Well, then, let us go there first.' Edward went in with Humphrey, and found a man half in the window and half out, held by the throat, and apparently suffocated by me two dogs. He took the dogs off, and desiring the men to secure the robber, and ascertain whether he was alive or not, he returned to the sitting-room, and then went to examine the body outside the door.

'Corbould, as I live!' cried Oswald.

'Yes,' replied Edward; 'he has gone to his account. God forgive him!'

On inquiry they found that of all the robbers, to the number of ten, not one had escaped: eight they had made prisoners; Corbould and the man whom the dogs had seized, and who was found to be quite dead, made up the number. The robbers were all bound and guarded; and then leaving them under the charge of Oswald and five of his men, Edward and Humphrey set off with seven more to Clara's cottage, to ascertain if there were any more to be found there. They arrived by two o'clock in the morning, and on knocking several times the door was opened, and they seized another man, the only one who was found in it. They then went back to the cottage with their prisoner, and by the time that they had arrived it was daylight. As soon as the party sent by the Intendant had been supplied with a breakfast, Edward bade farewell to Humphrey and his sisters, that he might return and deliver up his prisoners. Pablo went with him to bring back the cart which carried the two dead bodies. This capture cleared the forest of the robbers who had so long infested it, for they never had any more attempts made from that time.

Before Edward left, Humphrey and he examined the box which Humphrey had dug up from under the oak, and which had occasioned such danger to the inmates of the cottage; for one of the men stated to Edward that they suspected that the box which they had seen Humphrey dig out contained treasure, and that without they had seen him in possession of it they never should have attacked the cottage, although Corbould had often persuaded them so to do; but as they knew that he was only seeking revenge – and they required money to stimulate them – they had refused, as they considered that there was nothing to be obtained in the cottage worth the risk; as they knew that the inmates had firearms, and would defend themselves. On examination of its contents they found in the box a sum of forty pounds in gold, a bag of silver, and some other valuables in silver spoons, candlesticks, and ornaments for women. Edward took a list of the contents, and when he returned he stated to the Intendant all that had occurred, and requested to know what should be done with the money and other articles which Humphrey had found.

'I wish you had said nothing to me about it,' said the Intendant, 'although I am pleased with your open and fair dealing. I cannot say anything, except that you had better let Humphrey keep it till it is claimed – which, of course, it never will be. But, Edward, Humphrey must come over here and make his deposition, as I must report the capture of these robbers and send them to trial. You had better go with the clerk and take the depositions of Pablo and your sisters, while Humphrey comes here. You can stay till his return. Their depositions are not of so much consequence as Humphrey's, as they can only speak as to the attack; but Humphrey's I must take down myself.'

When Patience and Clara heard that Edward was going over, they obtained leave to go with him to see Alice and Edith, and were to be escorted back by Humphrey. This the Intendant consented to, and they had a very merry party. Humphrey remained two days at the Intendant's house, and then returned to the cottage, where Edward had taken his place during his absence.

CHAPTER 21

The winter set in very severe, and the falls of snow were very heavy and frequent. It was fortunate that Humphrey had been so provident in making so large a quantity of hay, or the stock would have been starved. The flock of goats in great part subsisted themselves on the bark of trees and moss; at night they had some hay given to them, and they did very well. It was hardly possible for Edward to come over to see his brother and sisters, for the snow was so deep as to render such a long journey too fatiguing for a horse. Twice or thrice after the snow fell he contrived to get over, but after that they knew that it was impossible, and they did not expect him. Humphrey and Pablo had little to do except attending to the stock, and cutting firewood to keep up their supply, for they now burnt it very fast. The snow lay several feet high round the cottage, being driven against it by the wind. They had kept a passage dear to the yard, and had kept the yard as clear of snow as possible; they could do no more. A sharp frost and clear weather succeeded to the snowstorms, and there appeared no chance of the snow melting away. The nights were dark and long, and their oil for their lamp was getting low. Humphrey was anxious to go to Lymington, as they required many things; but it was impossible to go anywhere except on foot, and walking was, from the depth of the snow, a most fatiguing exercise. There was one thing, however, that Humphrey had not forgotten, which was, that he had told Edward that he would try and capture some of the forest ponies; and during the whole of the time since the heavy fall of snow had taken place he had been making his arrangements. The depth of the snow prevented the animals from obtaining any grass, and they were almost starved, as they could find nothing to subsist upon except the twigs and branches of trees which they could reach. Humphrey went out with Pablo, and found the herd, which was about five miles from the cottage, and near to Clara's cottage. He and Pablo brought with them as much hay as they could carry, and strewed it about so as to draw the ponies nearer to them, and then Humphrey looked for a place which would answer his purpose. About three miles from the cottage he found what he thought would suit him. There was a sort of avenue between two thickets, about a hundred yards wide, and the wind blowing through this avenue during the snowstorm had drifted the snow at one end of it, and right across it raised a large mound several feet high. By strewing small bundles of hay he drew the herd of ponies into this avenue, and in the avenue he left them a good quantity to feed upon every night for several nights, till at last the herd of ponies went there every morning.

'Now, Pablo, we must make a trial,' said Humphrey. 'You must get your lassos ready, in case they should be required. We must go to the avenue before daylight with the two dogs, tie one upon one side of the avenue, and the other on the other, that they may bark and prevent the ponies from attempting to escape through the thicket. Then we must get the ponies between us and the drift of snow which lies across the avenue, and try if we cannot draw them into the drift. If so, they will plunge in so deep that some of them will not be able to get out before we have thrown the ropes round their necks.'

'I see,' said Pablo; 'very good – soon catch them.'

Before daylight they went with the dogs and a large bundle of hay,. which they strewed nearer to the mound of drift snow. They then tied the dogs up on each side, ordering them to lie down and be quiet. They then walked through the thicket so as not to be perceived, until they considered that they were far enough from the drift snow. About daylight the herd came to pick up the hay as usual, and after they had passed them Humphrey and Pablo followed in the thicket, not wishing to show themselves till the last moment. While the ponies were busy with the hay they suddenly ran out into the avenue and separated, so as to prevent the ponies from attempting to gallop past them, shouting as loud as they could, as they ran up to the ponies, and calling to the dogs, who immediately set up barking on each side. The ponies, alarmed at the noise and the appearance of Humphrey and Pablo, naturally set off in the only direction which appeared to them to be clear, and galloped away over the mound of drift snow, with their tails streaming, snorting and plunging in the snow as they hurried along. But as soon as they arrived at the mound of drift snow they plunged first up to their bellies, and afterwards, as they attempted to force their way where the snow was deeper, many of them stuck fast altogether, and attempted to clear themselves in vain. Humphrey and Pablo, who had followed them as fast as they could run, now came up with them and threw the lasso over the neck of one, and ropes with slip nooses over two more, which were floundering in the snow there together. The remainder of the herd, after great exertions, got clear of the snow by turning round and galloping back through the avenue. The three ponies captured made a furious struggle; but by drawing the ropes tight round their necks they were choked, and soon unable to move. They then tied their fore legs, and loosed the ropes round their necks, that they might recover their breath.

'Get them now, Massa Humphrey,' said Pablo.

'Yes. But our work is not yet over, Pablo: we must get them home. How shall we manage that?'

'Suppose they no eat today and tomorrow, get very tame.'

'I believe that will be the best way; they cannot get loose again, do all they can.'

'No, sir; but get one home today. This very fine pony; suppose we try him.'

Pablo then put the halter on, and tied the end short to the fore leg of the pony, so that it could not walk without keeping its head close to the ground; if it raised its head, it was obliged to lift up its leg. Then he put the lasso round its neck to choke it if it was too unruly; and having done that, he cast loose the ropes which had tied its fore legs together.

'Now, Massa Humphrey, we get him home somehow. First I go loose the dogs; he 'fraid of the dogs, and run t'other way.'

The pony, which was an iron-grey and very handsome, plunged furiously and kicked behind; but it could not do so without falling down, which it did several times before Pablo returned with the dogs. Humphrey held one part of the lasso on one side, and Pablo on the other, keeping the pony between them; and with the dogs barking at it behind, they contrived, with a great deal of exertion and trouble, to get the pony to the cottage. The poor animal, driven in this way on three legs, and every now and then choked with the lasso, was covered with foam before they arrived. Billy was turned out of his stable to make room for the newcomer, who was fastened securely to the manger, and then left without food, that he might become tame. It was too late then, and they were too tired themselves, to go for the other two ponies; so they were left lying on the snow all night, and the next morning they found they were much tamer than the first; and during the day, following the same plan, they were both brought to the stable and secured alongside of the other. One was a bay pony with black legs, and the other, a brown one. The bay pony was a mare, and the other two horses. Alice and Edith were delighted with the new ponies, and Humphrey was not a little pleased that he had succeeded in capturing them, after what had passed between Edward and him. After two days' fasting the poor animals were so tame that they ate out of Pablo's hand, and submitted to be stroked and caressed; and before they were a fortnight in the stable Alice and Edith could go up to them without danger. They were soon broken in, for the yard being full of muck, Pablo took them into it and mounted them. They plunged and kicked at first, and tried all they could to get rid of him, but they sank so deep into the muck that they were soon tired out; and after a month they were all three tolerably quiet to ride.

The snow was so deep all over the country that there was little communication with the metropolis. The Intendant's letter spoke of King Charles raising another army in Holland, and that his adherents in England were preparing to join him as soon as he marched southward.

'I think, Edward,' said the Intendant, 'that the King's affairs do now wear a more promising aspect; but there is plenty of time yet. I know your anxiety to serve your King, and I cannot blame it. I shall not prevent your going, although, of course, I must not be cognizant of your having so done. When the winter breaks up I shall send you to London. You will then be able better to judge of what is going on, and your absence will not create any suspicion; but you must be guided by me.'

'I certainly will, sir,' replied Edward. 'I should indeed like to strike one blow for the King, come what will.'

'All depends upon whether they manage affairs well in Scotland; but there is so much jealousy and pride, and I fear treachery also, that it is hard to say how matters may end.'

It was soon after this conversation that a messenger arrived from London with letters announcing that King Charles had been crowned in Scotland with great solemnity and magnificence.

'The plot thickens,' said the Intendant; 'and by this letter from my correspondent, Ashley Cooper, I find that the King's army is well appointed, and that David Lesley is lieutenant-general, Middleton commands the horse, and Wemyss the artillery. That Wemyss is certainly a good officer, but was not true to the late King; may he behave better to the present! Now, Edward, I shall send you to London, and I will give you letters to those who will advise you how to proceed. You may take the black horse; he will bear you well. You will, of course, write to me; for Sampson will go with you, and you can send him back when you consider that you do not require or wish for his presence. There is no time to be lost, for, depend upon it, Cromwell, who is still at Edinburgh, will take the field as soon as he can. Are you ready to start tomorrow morning?'

'Yes, sir, quite ready.'

'I fear that you cannot go over to the cottage to bid farewell to your sisters; but perhaps it is better that you should not.'

'I think so too, sir,' replied Edward. 'Now that the snow has nearly disappeared, I did think of going over, having been so long absent; but I must send Oswald over instead.'

'Well, then, leave me to write my letters, and do you prepare your saddle-bags. Patience and Clara will assist you. Tell Sampson to come to me.'

Edward went to Patience and Clara, and told them that he was to set off for London on the following morning, and was about to make his preparations.

'How long do you remain, Edward?' inquired Patience.

'I cannot tell. Sampson goes with me, and I must, of course, be guided by your father. Do you know where the saddle-bags are, Patience?'

'Yes; Phœbe shall bring them to your room.'

'And you and Clara must come and give me your assistance.'

'Certainly we will, if you require it; but I did not know that your wardrobe was so extensive.'

'You know that it is anything but extensive, Patience; but that is the reason why your assistance is more required. A small wardrobe ought at least to be in good order; and what I would require is that you would look over the linen, and where it requires a little repair you will bestow upon it your charity.'

'That we will do, Clara,' replied Patience. 'So get your needles and thread, and let us send him to London with whole linen. — We will come when we are ready, sir.'

'I don't like his going to London at all,' said Clara; 'we shall be so lonely when he has gone.'

Edward had left the room, and having obtained the saddlebags from Phœbe, had gone up to his chamber. The first thing that he laid hold of was his father's sword. He took it down, and having wiped it carefully, he kissed it, saying, 'God grant that I may do credit to it, and prove as worthy to wield it as was my brave father!' He had uttered these words aloud; and again taking the sword and laying it down on the bed, turned round, and perceived that Patience had, unknown to him, entered the room, and was standing close to him. Edward was not conscious that he had spoken aloud, and therefore merely said, 'I was not aware of your presence, Patience. Your foot is so light.'

'Whose sword is that, Edward?'

'It is mine; I bought it at Lymington.'

'But what makes you have such an affection for that sword?'

'Affection for it?'

'Yes; as I came into the room you kissed it as fervently as . . .'

'As a lover would his mistress, I presume you would say,' replied Edward.

'Nay, I meant not to use such vain words. I was about to say, as a Catholic would a relic. I ask you again, why so? A sword is but a sword. You are about to leave this on a mission of my father's. You are not a soldier, about to engage in strife and war; if you were, why kiss your sword?'

'I will tell you. I do love this sword. I purchased it, as I told you, at Lymington, and they told me that it belonged to Colonel Beverley. It is for his sake that I love it. You know what obligations our family were under to him.'

'This sword was, then, wielded by Colonel Beverley, the celebrated Cavalier, was it?' said Patience, taking it from off the bed and examining it.

'Yes, it was; and here, you see, are his initials upon the hilt.'

'And why do you take it to London with you? Surely it is not the weapon which should be worn by a secretary, Edward? It is too large and cumbrous, and out of character.'

'Recollect that till these last few months I have been a forester, Patience, and not a secretary. Indeed, I feel that I am more fit for active life than the situation which your father's kindness has bestowed upon me. I was brought up, as you have heard, to follow to the wars, had my patron lived.'

Patience made no reply. Clara now joined them, and they commenced the task of examining the linen; and Edward left the room, as he wished to speak with Oswald. They did not meet again till dinner-time. Edward's sudden departure had spread a gloom over them all; even the Intendant was silent and thoughtful. In the evening he gave Edward the letters which he had written, and a considerable sum of money, telling him where he was to apply if he required more for his expenses. The Intendant cautioned him on his behaviour in many points, and also relative to his dress and carriage during his stay in the metropolis.

'If you should leave London, there will be no occasion – nay, it would be dangerous to write to me. I shall take it for granted that you will retain

Sampson till your departure, and when he returns here I shall presume that you have gone north. I will not detain you longer, Edward. May Heaven bless and protect you!'

So saying, the Intendant went away to his own room,

'Kind and generous man!' thought Edward; 'how much did I mistake you when we first met!'

Taking up the letters and bag of money, which still remained on the table, Edward went to his room, and having placed the letters and money in the saddle-bag, he commended himself to the Divine Protector and retired to rest.

Before daylight the sound of Sampson's heavy travelling boots below roused up Edward, and he was soon dressed. Taking his saddle-bags on his arm, he walked softly downstairs, that he might not disturb any of the family; but when he was passing the sitting-room he perceived that there was a light in it, and on looking in, that Patience was up and dressed. Edward looked surprised, and was about to speak, when Patience said, –

'I rose early, Edward, because, when I took leave of you last night, I forgot a little parcel that I wanted to give you before you went. It will not take much room, and may beguile a weary hour. It is a little book of meditations. Will you accept it, and promise me to read it when you have time?'

'I certainly will, my dear Patience – if I may venture on the expression – read it, and think of you.'

'Nay, you must read it and think of what it contains,' replied Patience.

'I will, then. I shall not need the book to remind me of Patience Heatherstone, I assure you.'

'And now, Edward, I do not pretend to surmise the reason of your departure, nor would it be becoming in me to attempt to discover what my father thinks proper to be silent upon; but I must beg you to promise one thing.'

'Name it, dear Patience,' replied Edward. 'My heart is so full at the thought of leaving you that I feel I can refuse you nothing.'

'It is this: I have a presentiment, I know not why, that you are about to encounter danger. If so, be prudent – be prudent for the sake of your dear sisters – be prudent for the sake of all your friends, who would regret you; promise me that.'

'I do promise you most faithfully, Patience, that I will ever have my sisters and you in my thoughts, and will not be rash under any circumstances.'

'Thank you, Edward. May God bless you and preserve you!'

Edward first kissed Patience's hand, that was held in his own; but perceiving the tears starting in her eyes, he kissed them off, without any remonstrance on her part, and then left the room. In a few moments more he was mounted on a fine powerful black horse, and, followed by Sampson, on his road to London.

We will pass over the journey, which was accomplished without any event worthy of remark. Edward had from the commencement called

Sampson to his side, that he might answer the questions he had to make upon all that he saw, and which the reader must be aware was quite new to one whose peregrinations had been confined to the New Forest and the town adjacent. Sampson was a very powerful man, of a cool and silent character, by no means deficient in intelligence, and trustworthy withal. He had long been a follower of the Intendant, and had served in the army. He was very devout, and generally, when not addressed, was singing hymns in a low voice.

On the evening of the second day they were close to the metropolis, and Sampson pointed out to Edward St Paul's Cathedral and Westminster Abbey, and other objects worthy of note.

'And where are we to lodge, Sampson?' inquired Edward.

'The best hotel that I know of for man and beast is the "Swan with Three Necks", in Holborn. It is not over-frequented by roisterers, and you will there be quiet, and if your affairs demand it, unobserved.'

'That will suit me, Sampson. I wish to observe, and not be observed, during my stay in London.'

Before dark they had arrived at the hotel, and the horses were in the stable. Edward had procured an apartment to his satisfaction, and feeling fatigued with his two days travelling, had gone to bed.

The following morning he examined the letters which had been given to him by the Intendant, and inquired of Sampson if he could direct him on his way. Sampson knew London well, and Edward set out to Spring Gardens to deliver a letter, which the Intendant informed him was confidential, to a person of the name of Langton. Edward knocked and was ushered in, Sampson taking a seat in the hall while Edward was shown into a handsomely-furnished library, where he found himself in the presence of a tall, spare man, dressed after the fashion of the Roundheads of the time. He presented the letter. Mr Langton bowed, and requested Edward to sit down; and after Edward had taken a chair he then seated himself and opened the letter.

'You are right welcome, Master Armitage,' said Mr Langton. 'I find that, young as you appear to be, you are in the whole confidence of our mutual friend Master Heatherstone. He hints at your being probably obliged to take a journey to the north, and that you will be glad to take charge of any letters which I may have to send in that direction. I will have them ready for you; and in case of need they will be such as will give a colouring to your proceeding, provided you may not choose to reveal your true object. How wears our good friend Heatherstone and his daughter?'

'Quite well, sir.'

'And he told me in one of his former letters that he had the daughter of our poor friend Ratcliffe with him. Is it not so?'

'It is, Master Langton; and a gentle, pretty child as you wish to see.'

'When did you arrive in London?'

'Yesterday evening, sir.'

'And do you propose any stay?'

'That I cannot answer, sir. I must be guided by your advice. I have nought to do here, unless it be to deliver some three or four letters, given me by Mr Heatherstone.'

'It is my opinion, Master Armitage, that the less you are seen in this city the better. There are hundreds employed to find out newcomers, and to discover from their people, or by other means, for what purpose they may have come; for you must be aware, Master Armitage, that the times are dangerous and people's minds are various. In attempting to free ourselves from what we considered despotism, we have created for ourselves a worse despotism, and one that is less endurable. It is to be hoped that what has passed will make not only kings but subjects wiser than they have been. Now what do you propose – to leave this instantly?'

'Certainly, if you think it advisable.'

'My advice, then, is to leave London immediately. I will give you letters to some friends of mine in Lancashire and Yorkshire; in either county you can remain unnoticed, and make what preparations you think necessary. But do nothing in haste – consult well, and be guided by them, who will, if it is considered advisable and prudent, join with you in your project. I need say no more. Call upon me tomorrow morning, an hour before noon, and will have letters ready for you.'

Edward rose to depart, and thanked Mr Langton for his kindness.

'Farewell, Master Armitage,' said Langton. 'Tomorrow at the eleventh hour.'

Edward then quitted the house, and delivered the other letters of credence. The only one of importance at the moment was the one of credit; the others were to various members of the Parliament, desiring them to know Master Armitage as a confidential friend of the Intendant, and in case of need to exert their good offices in his behalf. The letter of credit was upon a Hamburg merchant, who asked Edward if he required money. Edward replied that he did not at present, but that he had business to do for his employer in the north, and might require some when there, if it was possible to obtain it so far from London.

'When do you set out, and to what town do you go?'

'That I cannot well tell till tomorrow.'

'Call before you leave this, and I will find some means of providing for you as you wish.'

Edward then returned to the hotel. Before he went to bed he told Sampson that he found that he had to leave London on Mr Heatherstone's affairs, and might be absent some time; he concluded by observing that he did not consider it necessary to take him with him, as he could dispense with his services, and Mr Heatherstone would be glad to have him back.

'As you wish, sir,' replied Sampson. 'When am I to go back?'

'You may leave tomorrow as soon as you please. I have no letter to send. You may tell them that I am well, and will write as soon as I have anything positive to communicate.'

Edward then made Sampson a present, and wished him a pleasant journey.

At the hour appointed on the following day Edward repaired to Mr Langton, who received him very cordially.

'I am all ready for you, Master Armitage. There is a letter to two Catholic ladies in Lancashire, who will take great care of you; and here is one to a friend of mine in Yorkshire. The ladies live about four miles from the town of Bolton, and my Yorkshire friend in the city of York. You may trust to either of them. And now farewell; and if possible, leave London before nightfall – the sooner the better. Where is your servant?'

'He has returned to Master Heatherstone this morning.'

'You have done right. Lose no time to leave London, and don't be in a hurry in your future plans. You understand me. If any one accosts you on the road, put no trust in any professions. You, of course, are going down to your relations in the north. Have you pistols?'

'Yes, sir; I have a pair which did belong to the unfortunate Mr Ratcliffe.'

'Then they are good ones, I'll answer for it. No man was more particular about his weapons, or knew how to use them better. Farewell, Master Armitage, and may success attend you!'

Mr Langton held out his hand to Edward, who respectfully took his leave.

Chapter 22

Edward was certain that Mr Langton would not have advised him to leave London if he had not considered that it was dangerous to remain. He therefore first called upon the Hamburg merchant, who, upon his explanation, gave him a letter of credit to a friend who resided in the city of York; and then returned to the hotel, packed up his saddle-bags, paid his reckoning, and, mounting his horse, set off on the northern road. As it was late in the afternoon before he was clear of the metropolis, he did not proceed farther than Barnet, where he pulled up at the inn. As soon as he had seen his horse attended to, Edward, with his saddle-bags on his arm, went into the room in the inn where all the travellers congregated. Having procured a bed, and given his saddle-bags into the charge of the hostess, he sat down by the fire, which, although it was warm weather, was nevertheless kept alight.

Edward had made no alteration in the dress which he had worn since he had been received in the house of Mr Heatherstone. It was plain, although of good materials. He wore a high-crowned hat, and altogether would, from his attire, have been taken for one of the Roundhead party.

His sword and shoulder-belt were indeed of more gay appearance than those usually worn by the Roundheads; but this was the only difference.

When Edward first entered the room there were three persons in it whose appearance was not very prepossessing. They were dressed in what had once been very gay attire, but which now exhibited tarnished lace, stains of wine, and dust from travelling. They eyed him as he entered with his saddle-bags, and one of them said, –

'That's a fine horse you were riding, sir. Has he much speed?'

'He has,' replied Edward as he turned away and went into the bar to speak with the hostess and give his property into her care.

'Going north, sir?' inquired the same person when Edward returned.

'Not exactly,' replied Edward, walking to the window to avoid further conversation.

'The Roundhead is on the stilts,' observed another of the party.

'Yes,' replied the first. 'It is easy to see that he has not been accustomed to be addressed by gentlemen. For half a pin I would slit his ears.'

Edward did not choose to reply; he folded his arms, and looked at the man with contempt.

The hostess, who had overheard the conversation, now called for her husband, and desired him to go into the room and prevent any further insults to the young gentleman who had just come in. The host, who knew the parties, entered the room, and said, –

'Now you'll clear out of this as fast as you can; be off with you, and go to the stables, or I'll send for somebody whom you will not like.'

The three men rose and swaggered, but obeyed the host's orders, and left the room.

'I am sorry, young master, that these roisterers should have affronted you, as my wife tells me that they have. I did not know that they were in the house. We cannot well refuse to take in their horses; but we know well who they are, and if you are travelling far you had better ride in company.'

'Thank you for your caution, my good host,' replied Edward. 'I thought that they were highwaymen, or something of that sort.'

'You have made a good guess, sir; but nothing has yet been proved against them, or they would not be here. In these times we have strange customers, and hardly know who we take in. You have a good sword there, sir, I have no doubt; but I trust that you have other arms.'

'I have,' replied Edward, opening his doublet, and showing his pistols.

'That's right, sir. Will you take anything before you go to bed?'

'Indeed I will, for I am hungry; anything will do, with a pint of wine.'

As soon as he had supped, Edward asked the hostess for his saddle-bags, and went up to his bed.

Early the next morning he rose and went to the stable to see his horse fed. The three men were in the stables, but they did not say anything to him. Edward returned to the inn, called for breakfast, and, as soon as he had finished, took out his pistols to renew the priming. While so occupied he happened to look up, and perceived one of the men with his face against the window, watching him. 'Well, now you see what you have to expect if you try your trade with me,' thought Edward. 'I am very glad that you have been spying.' Having replaced his pistols, Edward paid his reckoning, and went to the stable, desiring the hostler to saddle his horse and fix on his saddlebags. As soon as this was done he mounted and rode off. Before he was well clear of the town the highwaymen cantered past him on three well-bred active horses. 'I presume we shall meet again,' thought Edward, who for some time cantered at a gentle pace; and then, as his horse was very fresh, he put him to a faster pace, intending to do a long day's work. He had ridden about fifteen miles when he came to a heath, and as he continued at a fast trot he perceived the three highwaymen about a quarter of a mile in advance of him. They were descending a hill which was between them, and he soon lost sight of them again. Edward now pulled up his horse to let him recover his wind, and walked him gently up the hill. He had nearly gained the summit when he heard the report of firearms, and soon afterwards a man on horseback, in full speed, galloped over the hill towards him. He had a pistol in his hand, and his head turned back. The reason for this was soon evident, as immediately after him appeared the three highwaymen in pursuit. One fired his pistol at the man who fled, and missed him. The man then fired in return, and with true aim, as one of the highwaymen fell. All this was so sudden that Edward had hardly time to draw his pistol and put spurs to his horse before the parties were upon him and were passing him. Edward levelled at the second highwayman as he passed him, and the man fell. The third highwayman, perceiving this, turned his horse to the side of the road, cleared a ditch, and galloped away across the heath. The man who had been attacked had pulled up his horse when Edward came to his assistance, and now rode up to him, saying, –

'I have to thank you, sir, for your timely aid; for these rascals were too many for me.'

'You are not hurt, I trust, sir?' replied Edward.

'No, not the least; the fellow singed my curls, though, as you may perceive. They attacked me about half a mile from here. I was proceeding north when I heard the clatter of hoofs behind me; I looked round, and saw at once what they were, and I sprung my horse out of the road to a thicket close to it, that they might not surround me. One of the three rode forward to stop my passage, and the other two rode round to the back of the thicket to get behind me. I then saw that I had separated them, and could gain a start upon them by riding back again, which I did as fast as I could, and they immediately gave chase. The result you saw. Between us we have broken up the gang; for both these fellows seem dead, or nearly so.'

'What shall we do with them?'

'Leave them where they are,' replied the stranger. 'I am in a hurry to get on. I have important business at the city of York, and cannot waste my time in depositions and such nonsense. It is only two scoundrels less in the world, and there's an end of the matter.'

As Edward was equally anxious to proceed, he agreed with the stranger that it was best to do as he proposed.

'I am also going north,' replied Edward, 'and am anxious to get there as soon as I can. '

'With your permission we will ride together,' said the stranger. 'I shall be the gainer, as I shall feel that I have one with me who is to be trusted to in case of any further attacks during our journey.'

There was such a gentlemanlike, frank, and courteous air about the stranger that Edward immediately assented to his proposal of their riding in company for mutual protection. He was a powerful, well-made man, of apparently about one or two and twenty, remarkably handsome in person, dressed richly, but not gaudily, in the Cavalier fashion, and wore a hat with a feather. As they proceeded, they entered into conversation on indifferent matters for some time, neither party attempting by any question to discover who his companion might be. Edward had more than once, when the conversation flagged for a minute, considered what reply he should give in case his companion should ask him the cause of his journey, and at last had made up his mind what to say.

A little before noon they pulled up to bait their horses at a small village, the stranger observing that he avoided St Albans, and all other large towns, as he did not wish to satisfy the curiosity of people, or to have his motions watched; and therefore, if Edward had no objection, he knew the country so well that he could save time by allowing him to direct their path. Edward was, as may be supposed, very agreeable to this, and during their whole journey they never entered a town except they rode through it after dark, and put up at humble inns on the road-side, where, if not quite so well attended to, at all events they were free from observation.

It was, however, impossible that this reserve could continue long, as they became more and more intimate every day. At last the stranger said, –

'Master Armitage, we have travelled together for some time, inter-changing thoughts and feelings, but with due reserve as respects ourselves and our own plans. Is this to continue? If so, of course you have but to say so; but if you feel inclined to trust me, I have the same feeling towards you. By your dress I should imagine that you belonged to a party to which I am opposed; but your language and manners do not agree with your attire; and I think a hat and feathers would grace that head better than the steeple-crowned affair which now covers it. It may be that the dress is only assumed as a disguise – you know best. However, as I say, I feel confidence in you, to whatever party you may belong, and I give you credit for your prudence and reserve in these troubled times. I am a little older than you, and may advise you; and I am indebted to you, and cannot therefore betray you – at least I trust you believe so.'

'I do believe it,' replied Edward; 'and I will so far answer you, Master Chaloner, that this attire of mine is not the one which I would wear if I had my choice.'

172

'I believe that,' replied Chaloner; 'and I cannot help thinking you are bound north on the same business as myself – which is, I confess to you honestly, to strike a blow for the King. If you are on the same errand, I have two old relations in Lancashire who are staunch to the cause, and I am going to their house to remain until I can join the army. If you wish it, you shall come with me, and I will promise you kind treatment and safety while under their roof.'

'And the names of these relatives of yours, Master Chaloner?' said Edward.

'Nay, you shall have them; for when I trust I trust wholly. Their name is Conynghame.'

Edward took his letters from out of his side-pocket, and handed one of them to his fellow-traveller. The address was, 'To the worthy Mistress Conynghame of Portlake, near Bolton, county of Lancaster.'

'It is to that address that I am going myself,' said Edward, smiling. 'Whether it is the party you refer to, you best know.'

Chaloner burst out with a loud laugh.

'This is excellent! Two people meet, both bound on the same business, both going to the same rendezvous, and for three days do not venture to trust each other.'

'The times require caution,' replied Edward, as he replaced his letter.

'You are right,' answered Chaloner, 'and you are of my opinion. I know now that you have both prudence and courage. The first quality has been scarcer with us Cavaliers than the last; however now all reserve is over, at least on my part.'

'And on mine also,' replied Edward.

Chaloner then talked about the chances of the war. He stated that King Charles's army was in a good state of discipline, and well found in everything; that there were hundreds in England who would join it as soon as it had advanced far enough into England; and that everything wore a promising appearance.

'My father fell at the battle of Naseby, at the head of his retainers,' said Chaloner, after a pause; 'and they have contrived to fine the property, so that it has dwindled from thousands down to hundreds. Indeed, were it not for my good old aunts, who will leave me their estates, and who now supply me liberally, I should be but a poor gentleman.'

'Your father fell at Naseby?' said Edward. 'Were you there?'

'I was,' replied Chaloner.

'My father also fell at Naseby,' said Edward.

'Your father did?' replied Chaloner. 'I do not recollect the name – Armitage – he was not in command there, was he?' continued Chaloner.

'Yes, he was,' replied Edward.

'There was none of that name among the officers that I can recollect, young sir,' replied Chaloner, with an air of distrust. 'Surely you have been misinformed.'

'I have spoken the truth,' replied Edward, 'and have now said so much that I must, to remove your suspicion, say more than perhaps I should have done. My name is not Armitage, although I have been so called for some time. You have set me the example of confidence, and I will follow it. My father was Colonel Beverley, of Prince Rupert's troop.'

Chaloner started with astonishment.

'I'm sure that what you say is true,' at last said he; 'for I was thinking who it was that you reminded me of. You are the very picture of your father. Although a boy at the time, I knew him well, Master Beverley; a more gallant Cavalier never drew sword. Come, we must be sworn friends in life and death Beverley,' continued Chaloner, extending his hand, which was eagerly grasped by Edward, who then confided to Chaloner the history of his life. When he had concluded, Chaloner said, –

'We all heard of the firing of Arnwood, and it is at this moment believed that all the children perished. It is one of the tales of woe that our nurses repeat to the children, and many a child has wept at your supposed deaths. But tell me, now – had you not fallen in with me, was it your intention to have joined the army under your assumed name of Armitage?'

'I hardly know what I intended to do. I wanted a friend to advise me.'

'And you have found one, Beverley. I owe my life to you, and I will repay the debt as far as is in my power. You must not conceal your name to your sovereign; the very name of Beverley is a passport; but the son of Colonel Beverley will be indeed welcomed. Why, the very name will be considered as a harbinger of good fortune. Your father was the best and truest soldier that ever drew sword, and his memory stands unrivalled for loyalty and devotion. We are near to the end of our journey; yonder is the steeple of Bolton church. The old ladies will be out of their wits when they find that they have a Beverley under their roof.'

Edward was much delighted at this tribute paid to his father's memory, and the tears more than once started into his eyes as Chaloner renewed his praise.

Late in the evening they arrived at Portlake, a grand old mansion situated in a park crowded with fine old timber. Chaloner was recognized as they rode up the avenue by one of the keepers, who hastened forward to announce his arrival; and the domestics had opened the door for them before they arrived at it. In the hall they were met by the old ladies, who expressed their delight at seeing their nephew, as they had had great fear that something had happened to him.

'And something did very nearly happen to me,' replied Chaloner, 'had it not been for the timely assistance of my friend here, who, notwithstanding his Puritan attire, I hardly need tell you is a Cavalier devoted to the good cause, when I state that he is the son of Colonel Beverley, who fell at Naseby with my good father.'

'No one can be more welcome, then,' replied the old ladies, who extended their hands to Edward. They then went into a sitting-room, and supper was ordered to be sent up immediately.

'Our horses will be well attended to, Edward,' said Chaloner. 'We need not any longer look after them ourselves. – And now, good aunts, have you no letters for me?'

'Yes, there are several; but you had better eat first.'

'Not so; let me have the letters. We can read them before supper. and talk them over when at table.'

One of the ladies produced the letters, which Chaloner, as he read them, handed over to Edward for his perusal. They were from General Middleton and some other friends of Chaloner's who were with the army, giving him information as to what was going on, and what their prospects were supposed to be.

'You see that they have marched already,' said Chaloner, 'and I think the plan is a good one, and it has put General Cromwell in an awkward position. Our army is now between his and London, with three days' march in advance. And we shall now be able to pick up our English adherents, who can join us without risk as we go along. It has been a bold step, but a good one; and if they only continue as well as they have begun, we shall succeed. The Parliamentary army is not equal to ours in numbers as it is, and we shall add to ours daily. The King has sent to the Isle of Man for the Earl of Derby, who is expected to join tomorrow.'

'And where is the army at this moment?' inquired Edward.

'They will be but a few miles from us tonight, their march is so rapid. Tomorrow we will join if it pleases.'

'Most willingly,' replied Edward.

After an hour's more conversation, they were shown into their rooms, and retired for the night.

CHAPTER 23

The next morning, before they had quitted their beds, a messenger arrived with letters from General Middleton; and from him they found that the King's army had encamped on the evening before not six miles from Portlake. As they hastily dressed themselves, Chaloner proposed to Edward that a little alteration in his dress would be necessary; and taking him to a wardrobe in which had been put aside some suits of his own, worn when he was a younger and slighter made man than he now was, he requested Edward to make use of them. Edward, who was aware that Chaloner was right in his proposal, selected two suits of colours which pleased him most; and dressing in one, and changing his hat for one more befitting his new attire, was transformed into a handsome Cavalier. As soon as they had broken their fast they took leave of the old ladies, and mounting their horses, set off for the camp. An hour's ride brought them to the outposts; and communicating with the officer on duty, they were conducted by an orderly to the tent of General Middleton, who received Chaloner with great warmth as an old friend, and was very courteous to Edward as soon as he heard that he was the son of Colonel Beverley.

'I have wanted you, Chaloner,' said Middleton. 'We are raising a troop of horse. The Duke of Buckingham commands it, but Massy will be the real leader of it. You have influence in this county, and will, I have no doubt, bring us many good hands.'

'Where is the Earl of Derby?'

'Joined us this morning. We have marched so quick that we have not had time to pick our adherents up.'

'And General Leslie?'

'Is by no means in good spirits; why, I know not. We have too many ministers with his army, that is certain, and they do harm; but we cannot help ourselves. His Majesty must be visible by this time. If you are ready, I will introduce you; and when that is done, we will talk matters over.'

General Middleton then walked with them to the house in which the King had taken up his quarters for the night; and after a few minutes' waiting in the ante-room, they were admitted into his presence.

'Allow me, your Majesty,' said General Middleton, after the first salutations, 'to present to you Major Chaloner, whose father's name is not unknown to you.'

'On the contrary, well known to us,' replied the King, 'as a loyal and faithful subject, whose loss we must deplore. I have no doubt that his son inherits his courage and his fidelity.'

The King held out his hand, and Chaloner bent his knee and kissed it.

'And now your Majesty will be surprised that I should present to you one of a house supposed to be extinct – the eldest son of Colonel Beverley.'

'Indeed!' replied his Majesty. 'I heard that all his family perished at the ruthless burning of Arnwood. I hold myself fortunate, as a king, that even one son of so loyal and brave a gentleman as Colonel Beverley has escaped. – You are welcome, young sir – most welcome to us. You must be near us. The very name of Beverley will be pleasing to our ears by night or day.'

Edward knelt down and kissed his Majesty's hand, and the King said, –

'What can we do for a Beverley? Let us know, that we may show our feelings towards his father's memory.'

'All I request is mat your Majesty will allow me to be near you in the hour of danger,' replied Edward.

'A right Beverley reply,' said the King. – 'And so we shall see to it, Middleton.'

After a few more courteous words from his Majesty they withdrew; but General Middleton was recalled by the King for a minute or two to receive his commands. When he rejoined Edward and Chaloner, he said to Edward, –

'I have orders to send in for his Majesty's signature your commission as captain of horse, and attached to the King's personal staff. It is a high compliment to the memory of your father, sir, and, I may add, your own personal appearance. Chaloner will see to your uniforms and accoutrements. You are well mounted, I believe. You have no time to lose, as we march tomorrow for Warrington in Cheshire.'

'Has anything been heard of the Parliamentary army?'

'Yes; they are on the march towards London by the Yorkshire road, intending to cut us off if they can. And now, gentlemen, farewell; for I have no idle time, I assure you.'

Edward was soon equipped, and now attended upon the King. When they arrived at Warrington they found a body of horse drawn up to oppose their passage onwards. These were charged, and fled with a trifling loss; and as they were known to be commanded by Lambert, one of Cromwell's best generals, there was great exultation in the King's army. But the fact was that Lambert had acted upon Cromwell's orders, which were to harass and delay the march of the King as much as possible, but not to risk with his small force anything like an engagement. After this skirmish it was considered advisable to send back the Earl of Derby and many other officers of importance into Lancashire, that they might collect the King's adherents in that quarter and in Cheshire. Accordingly the earl, with about two hundred officers and gentlemen, left the army with that intention. It was then considered that it would be advisable to march the army direct to London; but the men were so fatigued with the rapidity of the march up to the present time, and the weather was so warm, that it was decided in the negative; and as Worcester was a town well affected to the King, and the country abounded with provisions, it was resolved that the army should march there and wait for English reinforcements. This was done. The city opened the gates with every mark of satisfaction, and supplied the army with all that it required. The first bad news which reached them was the dispersion and defeat of the whole of the Earl of Derby's party by a regiment of militia, which had surprised them at Wigan during the night, when they were all asleep, and had no idea that any enemy was near to them. Although attacked at such a disadvantage, they defended themselves till a large portion of them were killed, and the remainder were taken prisoners, and most of them brutally put to death. The Earl of Derby was made a prisoner, but not put to death with the others.

'This is bad news, Chaloner,' said Edward.

'Yes; it is more than bad,' replied the latter. 'We have lost our best officers, who never should have left the army; and now the consequences of the defeat will be that we shall not have any people come forward to join us. The winning side is the right side in this world. And there is more evil than that: the Duke of Buckingham has claimed the command of the army, which the King has refused; so that we are beginning to fight among ourselves. General Leslie is evidently dispirited, and thinks bad of the cause. Middleton is the only man who does his duty. Depend upon it, we shall have Cromwell upon us before we are aware of it; and we are in a state of sad confusion – officers quarrelling, men disobedient, much talking, and little doing. Here we have been five days, and the works which have been proposed to be thrown up as defences not yet begun.'

'I cannot but admire the patience of the King, with so much to harass and annoy him.'

'He must be patient perforce,' replied Chaloner; 'he plays for a crown, and it is a high stake. But he cannot command the minds of men, although he may the persons. I am no croaker, Beverley, but this I do say, that if we succeed with this army, as it is at present disorganized, we shall perform a miracle.'

'We must hope for the best,' replied Edward. 'Common danger may cement those who would otherwise be asunder; and when they have the army of Cromwell before them, they may be induced to forget their private quarrels and jealousies and unite in the good cause.'

'I wish I could be of your opinion, Beverley,' replied Chaloner; 'but I have mixed with the world longer than you have, and I think otherwise.'

Several more days passed, during which no defences were thrown up, and the confusion and quarrelling in the army continued to increase, until at last news arrived that Cromwell was within half a day's march of them, and that he had collected all the militia on his route, and was now in numbers nearly double to those in the King's army. All was amazement and confusion; nothing had been done, no arrangements had been made, and Chaloner told Edward that all was lost if immediate steps were not taken.

On the 3rd of October the army of Cromwell appeared in sight. Edward had been on horseback, attending the King for the best part of the night; the disposition of the troops had been made as well as it could; and it was concluded, as Cromwell's army remained quiet, that no attempt would be made on that day. About noon, the King returned to his lodging to take some refreshment after his fatigue. Edward was with him; but before an hour had passed the alarm came that the armies were engaged. The King mounted his horse, which was ready saddled at the door; but before he could ride out of the city he was met and nearly beaten back by the whole body almost of his own cavalry, who came running on with such force that he could not stop them. His Majesty called to several of the officers by name, but they paid no attention; and so great was the panic that both the King and his staff who attended him were nearly overthrown and trampled under foot.

Cromwell had passed a large portion of his troops over the river without the knowledge of the opponents, and when the attack was made in so unexpected a quarter a panic ensued. Where General Middleton and the Duke Hamilton commanded a very brave resistance was made; but Middleton being wounded, Duke Hamilton having his leg taken off by a round shot, and many gentlemen having fallen, the troops, deserted by the remainder of the army, at last gave way, and the rout was general, the foot throwing away their muskets before they were discharged.

His Majesty rode back into the town, and found a body of horse who had been persuaded by Chaloner to make a stand 'Follow me,' said his Majesty; 'we will see what the enemy are about. I do not think they pursue, and if so, we may yet rally from this foolish panic.'

His Majesty, followed by Edward, Chaloner, and several of his personal staff, then galloped out to reconnoitre; but to his mortification he found that the troops had not followed him, but gone out of the town by the other gate, and that the enemy's cavalry in pursuit were actually in the town. Under such circumstances, by the advice of Chaloner and Edward his Majesty withdrew, and turning his horse's head, he made all haste to leave Worcester. After several hours' riding the King found himself in company of about 4,000 of the cavalry who had so disgracefully fled; but they were still so panic-struck that he could put no confidence in them, and having advised with those about him, he resolved to quit them. This he did without mentioning his intentions to any of his staff, not even Chaloner or Edward, leaving at night with two of his servants, whom he dismissed as soon as it was daylight, considering that his chance of escape would be greater if he was quite alone.

It was not till the next morning that they discovered that the King had left them, and then they determined to separate, and, as the major portion were from Scotland, to make what haste they could back to that country. And now Chaloner and Edward consulted as to their plans.

'It appears to me,' said Edward, laughing, 'that the danger of this campaign of ours will consist in getting back again to our homes; for I can most safely assert that I have not as yet struck a blow for the King.'

'That is true enough, Beverley. When do you propose going back to the New Forest? I think, if you will permit me, I will accompany you,' said Chaloner. 'All the pursuit will be to the northward, to intercept and overtake the retreat into Scotland. I cannot, therefore, go to Lancashire; and indeed, as they know that I am out, they will be looking for me everywhere.'

'Then come with me,' said Edward. 'I will find you protection till you can decide what to do. Let us ride on away from this, and we will talk over the matter as we go; but depend upon it, the farther south we get the safer we shall be, but still not safe unless we can change our costume. There will be a strict search for the King to the south, as they will presume that he will try to get safe into France. Hark! what is that? I heard the report of arms. Let us ride up this hill and see what is going on.'

They did so, and perceived that there was a skirmish between a party of Cavaliers and some of the Parliamentary cavalry at about a quarter of a mile distant.

'Come, Chaloner, let us at all events have one blow,' said Edward.

'Agreed,' replied Chaloner, spurring his horse; and down they were at full speed, and in a minute were in the *mêlée* coming on the rear of the Parliamentary troops.

This sudden attack from behind decided the affair. The Parliamentary troopers, thinking that there were more than two coming upon them, made off after another minute's combat, leaving five or six of their men on the ground.

'Thanks, Chaloner! thanks, Beverley!' said a voice which they immediately recognized. It was that of Grenville, one of the King's pages. 'These fellows with me were just about to run if you had not come to our aid. I will remain with them no longer, but join you if you will permit me.'

'At all events remain here till they go away. I will send them off.'

'My lads, you must all separate, or there will be no chance of escape. No, more than two should ride together. Depend upon it, we shall have more of the troops here directly.'

The men, about fifteen in number, who had been in company with Grenville, considered that Chaloner's advice was good, and without ceremony set off, with their horses' heads to the northward, leaving Chaloner, Edward and Grenville together on the field of the affray. About a dozen men were lying on the ground, either dead or severely wounded; seven of them were of the King's party, and the other five of the Parliamentary troops.

'Now what I propose,' said Edward, 'is this: let us do what we can for those who are wounded, and then strip off the dresses and accoutrements of those Parliamentary dragoons who are dead, and dress ourselves in them, accoutrements and all. We can then pass through the country in safety, as we shall be supposed to be one of the parties looking for the King.'

'That is a good idea,' replied Chaloner, 'and the sooner it is done the better.'

'Well,' said Edward, wiping his sword, which he still held drawn, and then sheathing it, 'I will take the spoils of this fellow nearest to me. He fell by my hand, and I am entitled to them by all the laws of war and chivalry. But first let us dismount and look to the wounded.'

They tied their horses to a tree, and having given what assistance they could to the wounded men, they proceeded to strip three of the Parliamentary troopers; and then laying aside their own habiliments, they dressed themselves in the uniform of the enemy, and mounting their horses, made all haste from the place. Having gained about twelve miles, they pulled up their horses, and rode at a more leisurely pace. It was now eight o'clock in the evening, but still not very dark; they therefore rode on another five miles, till they came to a small village where they dismounted at an ale-house, and put their horses into the stable.

'We must be insolent and brutal in our manners, or we shall be suspected.'

'Very true,' said Grenville, giving the hostler a kick, and telling him to bestir himself if he did not want his ears cropped.

They entered the ale-house, and soon found out they were held in great terror. They ordered everything of the best to be produced, and threatened to set fire to the house if it was not – they turned the man and his wife out of their bed, and all three went to sleep in it; and, in short, they behaved in such an arbitrary manner that nobody doubted that they were Cromwell's horse. In the morning they set off again, by Chaloner's advice paying for nothing that they had ordered, although they had all of them plenty of money. They now rode fast, inquiring at the places which they passed through whether any fugitives had been seen, and if they came to a town, inquiring, before they entered, whether there were any Parliamentary troops. So well did they manage that after four days they had gained the skirts of the New Forest, and concealed themselves in a thicket till night-time, when Edward proposed that he should conduct his fellow-travellers to the cottage, where he would leave them till his plans were arranged.

Edward had already arranged his plans. His great object was to ward off any suspicion of where he had been, and, of course, any idea that the Intendant had been a party to his acts – and the fortunate change of his dress enabled him now to do so with success. He had decided to conduct his two friends to the cottage that night, and the next morning to ride over in his Parliamentary costume to the Intendant's house, and bring the first news of the success of Cromwell and the defeat at Worcester; by which stratagem it would appear as if he had been with the Parliamentary and not with the Jacobite army.

As they travelled along, they found that the news of Cromwell's success had not yet arrived. In those times there was not the rapidity of communication that we now have, and Edward thought it very probable that he would be the first to communicate the intelligence to the Intendant and those who resided near him.

As soon as it was dark the three travellers left their retreat, and, guided by Edward, soon arrived at the cottage. Their appearance at first created no little consternation, for Humphrey and Pablo happened to be in the yard, when they heard the clattering of the swords and accoutrements, and through the gloom observed, as they advanced, that the party were troopers. At first Humphrey was for running on and barring the door, but on a second reflection he felt that he could not do a more imprudent thing if there was danger; and he therefore contented himself with hastily imparting the intelligence to his sisters, and then remaining at the threshold to meet the coming of the parties. The voice of Edward calling him by name dissipated all alarm, and in another minute he was in the arms of his brother and sisters.

'First let us take our horses to the stable, Humphrey,' said Edward, after the first greeting was over, 'and then we will come and partake of anything that Alice can prepare for us, for we have not fared over well for the last three days.'

Accompanied by Humphrey and Pablo they all went to the stables, and turned out the ponies to make room for the horses; and as soon as they were all fed and littered down they returned to the cottage and Chaloner and Grenville were introduced. Supper was soon on the table, and they were too hungry to talk while they were eating, so that but little information was gleaned from them that night. However, Humphrey ascertained that all was lost, and that they had escaped from the field, previous to Alice and Edith leaving the room to prepare beds for the newcomers. When the beds were ready, Chaloner and Grenville retired, and then Edward remained half an hour with Humphrey, to communicate to him what had passed. Of course he could not enter into detail, but told him that he would get information from their new guests after he had left, which he must do early in the morning.

'And now, Humphrey, my advice is this. My two friends cannot remain in this cottage, for many reasons; but we have the key of Clara's cottage, and they can take up their lodging there, and we can supply them with all they want until they find means of going abroad, which is their intention. I must be off to the Intendant's tomorrow, and the day after I will come over to you. In the meantime our guests can remain here, while you and Pablo prepare the cottage for them; and when I return everything shall be settled, and we will conduct them to it. I do not think there is much danger of their being discovered while they remain there – certainly not so much as if they were here; for we must expect parties of troops in every direction now, as they were when the King's father made his escape from Hampton Court. And now to bed, my good brother; and call me early, for I much fear that I shall not wake up if you do not.'

The brothers then parted for the night.

The next morning, long before their guests were awake, Edward had been called by Humphrey, and found Pablo at the door with his horse. Edward, who had put on his Parliamentary accoutrements, bade a hasty farewell to them, and set off across the forest to the house of the Intendant, where he arrived before they had left their bedrooms. The first person he encountered was, very fortunately, Oswald, who was at his cottage door. Edward beckoned to him, being then about one hundred yards off, but Oswald did not recognize him at first, and advanced towards him in a very leisurely manner, to ascertain what the trooper might wish to inquire. But Edward called him Oswald, and that was sufficient. In few words Edward told him how all was lost, and how he had escaped by changing clothes with one of the enemy.

'I am now come to bring the news to the Intendant, Oswald. You understand me, of course?'

'Of course I do, Master Edward, and will take care that it is well known that you have been fighting by the side of Cromwell all this time. I should recommend you to show yourself in this dress for the remainder of the day and then everyone will be satisfied. Shall I go to the Intendant's, before you?'

'No, no, Oswald; the Intendant does not require me to be introduced to him, of course. I must now gallop up to his house and announce myself. Farewell for the present; I shall see you during the day.'

Edward put spurs to his horse, and arrived at the Intendant's at full speed, making no small clattering in the yard below as he went in, much to the surprise of Sampson, who came out to ascertain what was the cause, and who was not a little surprised at perceiving Edward, who threw himself off the horse, and desiring Sampson to take it to the stable, entered the kitchen, and disturbed Phœbe, who was preparing breakfast. Without speaking to her, Edward passed on to the Intendant's room, and knocked.

'Who is there?' said the Intendant.

'Edward Armitage,' was the reply, and the door was opened. The Intendant started back at the sight of Edward in the trooper's costume.

'My dear Edward, I am glad to see you in any dress; but this requires explanation. Sit down and tell me all.'

'All is soon told, sir,' replied Edward, taking off his iron skull-cap and allowing his hair to fall down on his shoulder.

He then, in a few words, stated what had happened, and by what means he had escaped, and the reason why he had kept on the trooper's accoutrements and made his appearance in them.

'You have done very prudently,' replied the Intendant, 'and you have probably saved me. At all events, you have warded off all suspicion, and those who are spies upon me will now have nothing to report except to my favour. Your absence has been commented upon and made known at high quarters, and suspicion has arisen in consequence. Your return as one of the Parliamentary forces will now put an end to all ill-natured remarks. My dear Edward, you have done me a service. As my secretary, and having been known to have been a follower of the Beverleys, your absence was considered strange, and it was intimated at high quarters that you had gone to join the King's forces, and that with my knowledge and consent. This I have from Langton, and it has in consequence injured me not a little; but now your appearance will make all right again. Now we will first to prayers, and then to breakfast, and after that we will have a more detailed account of what has taken place since your departure. Patience and Clara will not be sorry to recover their companion, but how they will like you in that dress I cannot pretend to say. However, I thank God that you have returned safe to us; and I shall be most happy to see you once more attend in the more peaceful garb of a secretary.'

'I will, with your permission, sir, not quit this costume for one day, as it may be as well that I should be seen in it.'

'You are right, Edward. For this day retain it; tomorrow you will resume your usual costume. Go down to the parlour; you will find Patience and Clara anxiously waiting for you, I have no doubt. I will join you there in ten minutes.'

Edward left the room, and went downstairs. It hardly need be said how joyfully he was received by Patience and Clara. The former, however, expressed her joy in tears, the latter in wild mirth.

We will pass over the explanations and the narrative of what had occurred which was given by Edward to Mr Heatherstone in his own room. The Intendant said as he concluded, –

183

'Edward, you must now perceive that for the present nothing more can be done. If it pleases the Lord, the time will come when the monarch will be reseated on his throne; at present we must bow to the powers that be. And I tell you frankly, it is my opinion that Cromwell aims at sovereignty, and will obtain it. Perhaps it may be better that we should suffer the infliction for a time, as for a time only can it be upheld, and it may be the cause of the King being more schooled and more fitted to reign than, by what you have told me in the course of your narrative, he at present appears to be.'

'Perhaps so, sir,' replied Edward. 'I must say that the short campaign I have gone through has very much opened my eyes. I have seen but little true chivalric feeling, and much of interested motives, in those who have joined the King's forces. The army collected was composed of most discordant elements, and were so discontented, so full of jealousy and ill-will, that I am not surprised at the result. One thing is certain, that there must be a much better feeling existing between all parties before such a man as Cromwell can ever be moved from his position; and for the present the cause may be considered as lost.'

'You are right, Edward,' replied the Intendant. 'I would they were better; but as they are, let us make the best of them. You have now seen enough to have subdued that fiery zeal for the cause which previously occupied your whole thoughts. Now let us be prudent, and try if we cannot be happy.'

CHAPTER 24

It was only to Oswald that Edward made known what had occurred; he knew that he was to be trusted. The next day Edward resumed his forester's dress, while another one was preparing for him, and went over to the cottage, where, with the consent of the Intendant, he proposed remaining for a few days. Of course Edward had not failed to acquaint the Intendant with his proposed plans relative to Chaloner and Grenville, and received his consent, at the same time advising that they should gain the other side of the Channel as soon as they possibly could. Edward found them all very anxious for his arrival. Humphrey and Pablo had been to the cottage, which they had found undisturbed since the capture of the robbers, and made everything ready for the reception of the two cavaliers, as on their first journey they took with them a cartload of what they knew would be necessary. Chaloner and Grenville appeared to be quite at home already, and not very willing to shift their quarters. They, of course, still retained their trooper's clothes, as they had no other to wear until they could be procured from Lymington; but, as we have before mentioned, they were in no want of money. They had been amusing the girls and Humphrey with a description of what had occurred during the campaign, and Edward found that he had but little to tell them as Chaloner had commenced his narrative with an account of his first meeting with Edward, when he had been attacked by the highwaymen. As soon as he could get away, Edward went out with Humphrey to have some conversation with him.

'Now, Humphrey, as you have pretty well heard all my adventures since our separation, let me hear what you have been doing.'

'I have no such tales of stirring interest to narrate as Chaloner has been doing as your deputy, Edward,' replied Humphrey. 'All I can say is that we have had no visitors, that we have longed for your return, and that we have not been idle since you quitted us.'

'What horses were those in the stable,' said Edward, 'that your turned out to make room for ours when we arrived?'

Humphrey laughed, and then informed Edward of the manner in which they had succeeded in capturing them.

'Well, you really deserve credit, Humphrey, and certainly were not born to be secluded in this forest.'

'I rather think that I have found that I was born for it,' replied Humphrey, 'although I must confess that since you have quitted us I have not felt so contented here as I did before. You have returned, and you have no idea what an alteration I see in you since you have mixed up with the world and have been a party in such stirring scenes.'

'Perhaps so, Humphrey,' replied Edward; 'and yet do you know that, although I so ardently wished to mix with the world and to follow the wars, I am anything but satisfied with what I have seen of it; and so far from feeling any inclination to return to it, I rather feel more inclined to remain here, and remain in quiet and in peace. I have been disappointed, that is the truth. There is a great difference between the world such as we fancy it when we are pining for it and the world when we actually are placed within the vortex and perceive the secrets springs of men's actions. I have gained a lesson, but not a satisfactory one, Humphrey; it may be told in a very few words. It is a most deceitful and hollow world, and that is all said in few words.'

'What very agreeable, pleasant young men are Master Chaloner and Grenville!' observed Humphrey.

'Chaloner I know well,' replied Edward. 'He is to be trusted, and he is the only one in whom I have been able to place confidence, and therefore I was most fortunate in falling in with him as I did on my first starting. Grenville I know little about. We met often, it is true, but it was in the presence of the King, being both of us on his staff. At the same time, I must acknowledge that I know nothing against him; and this I do know, which is that he is brave.'

Edward then narrated what had passed between the Intendant and him since his return, and how well satisfied the Intendant had been with his ruse in returning to him in the dress of a trooper.

'Talking about that, Edward, do you not think it likely that we shall have the troopers here in search of the King?'

'I wonder you have not had them already,' replied Edward.

'And what shall we do if they arrive?'

'That is all prepared for,' replied Edward, 'although till you mentioned it I had quite forgotten it. The Intendant was talking with me on the subject last night, and here is an appointment for you as verderer, signed by him, which you are to use as you may find necessary; and here is another missive, ordering you to receive into your house two of the troopers who may be sent down here, and find them quarters and victuals, but not to be compelled to receive more. Until the search is over, Chaloner and Grenville must retain their accoutrements and remain with us. And, Humphrey, if you have not made any use of the clothes which I left here – I mean the first dress I had made when I was appointed secretary, and which I thought rather too faded to wear any longer – I will put it on now, as, should any military come here as scouters to the Intendant, I shall have some authority over them.

'It is in your chest, where you left it, Edward. The girls did propose to make two josephs out of it for winter wear; but they never have thought of it since, or have not had time. By-the-by, you have not told me what you think of Alice and Edith after your long absence.'

'I think they are both very much grown and very much improved,' replied Edward; 'but I must confess to you that I think it is high time that they were, if possible, removed from their present homely occupations and instructed as young ladies should be.'

'But how, Edward, is that to be?'

'That I cannot yet tell, and it grieves me that I cannot; but still I see the necessity of it, if ever we are to return to our position in society.'

'And are we ever to return?'

'I don't know. I thought little of it before I went away and mixed in society, but since I have been in the world I have been compelled to feel that my dear sisters are not in their sphere, and I have resolved upon trying if I cannot find a more suitable position for them. Had we been successful, I should have had no difficulty, but now I hardly know what to do.'

'I have not inquired about Mistress Patience, brother. How is she?'

'She is as good and as handsome as ever, and very much grown. Indeed, she is becoming quite womanly.'

'And Clara?'

'Oh, I do not perceive any difference in her. I think she is grown, but I hardly observed her. Here comes Chaloner; we will tell him of our arrangements, in case we are disturbed by the military parties.'

'It is a most excellent arrangement,' said Chaloner, when Edward had made the communication; 'and it was a lucky day when I first fell in with you, Beverley.'

'Not Beverley, I pray you. That name is to be forgotten. It was only revived for the occasion.'

'Very true. Then, Master Secretary Armitage, I think the arrangement excellent. The only point will be to find out what troops are sent down in this direction, as we must, of course, belong to some other regiment, and have been pursued from the field of battle. I should think that Lambert's squadrons will not be this way.'

'We will soon ascertain that. Let your horses be saddled and accoutred, so that should any of them make their appearance the horses may be at the door. It is my opinion that they will be here some time today.'

'I fear that it will be almost impossible for the King to escape,' observed Chaloner. 'I hardly know what to think of his leaving us in that way.'

'I have reflected upon it,' replied Edward, 'and I think it was perhaps prudent. Some were to be trusted, and some not. It was impossible to know who were and who were not; he therefore trusted nobody. Besides, his chance of escape, if quite alone, is greater than if in company.'

'And yet I feel a little mortified that he did not trust me,' continued Edward; 'my life was at his service.'

'He could no more read your heart than he could mine or others,' observed Chaloner; 'and any selection would have been invidious. On the whole, I think he acted wisely, and I trust that it will prove so. One thing is certain, which is, that all is over now, and that for a long while – we may let our swords rest in their scabbards. Indeed, I am sickened with it after what I have seen, and would gladly live here with you, and help to till the land – away from the world and all its vexations. What say you, Edward? Will you and your brother take me as a labourer after all is quiet again?'

'You would soon tire of it, Chaloner; you were made for active exertion and bustling in the world.'

'Nevertheless, I think, under two such amiable and pretty mistresses, I could stay well contented here: it is almost Arcadian. But still it is selfish for me to talk in this way; indeed, my feelings are contrary to my words.'

'How do you mean, Chaloner?'

'To be candid with you, Edward, I was thinking what a pity it is that two such sweet girls as your sisters should be employed here in domestic drudgery, and remain in such an uncultivated state – if I may be pardoned for speaking so freely – but I do so because I am convinced that if in proper hands they would grace a court; and you must feel that I am right.'

'Do you not think that the same feelings have passed in my mind, Chaloner? Indeed, Humphrey will tell you that we were speaking on the same subject but an hour ago. You must, however, be aware of the difficulty I am in; were I in possession of Arnwood and its domain, then indeed – but that is all over now, and I presume I shall shortly see my own property, whose woods are now in sight of me, made over to some Roundhead, for good services against the Cavaliers at Worcester.'

'Edward,' replied Chaloner, 'I have this to say to you, and I can say it because you know that I am indebted to you for my life, and that is a debt that nothing can cancel. If at any time you determine upon removing your sisters from this, recollect my maiden aunts at Portlake. They cannot be in better hands, and they cannot be in the hands of any person who will more religiously do their duty towards them, and be pleased with the trust confided to them. They are rich, in spite of exactions; but in these times women are not fined and plundered as men are, and they have been well able to afford all that has been taken from them, and all that they have voluntarily given to the assistance of our party. They are alone, and I really believe that nothing would make them more happy than to have the care of the two sisters of Edward Beverley – be sure of that. But I will be more sure of it if you will find means of sending to them a letter, which I shall write to them. I tell you that you will do them a favour, and that if you do not accept the offer, you will sacrifice your sisters' welfare to your own pride – which I do not think you would do.'

'Most certainly I will not do that,' replied Edward; 'and I am fully sensible of your kind offer; but I can say no more until I hear what your good aunts may reply to your letter. You mistake me much, Chaloner, if you think that any sense of obligation would prevent me from seeing my sisters removed from a position so unworthy of them, but which circumstances have driven them to. That we are paupers is undeniable; but I never shall forget that my sisters are the daughters of Colonel Beverley.'

'I am delighted with your reply, Edward, and I fear not that of my good aunts. It will be a great happiness to me when I am wandering abroad to know that your sisters are under their roof, and are being educated as they ought to be.'

'What's the matter, Pablo?' said Humphrey to the former, who came running out of breath.

'Soldiers,' said Pablo; 'plenty of them; gallop this way – gallop every way.'

'Now, Chaloner, we must get ourselves out of this scrape; and I trust that afterwards all will be well,' said Edward. 'Bring the horses out to the door; and, Chaloner, you and Grenville must wait within; bring my horse out also, as it will appear as if I had just ridden over. I must in to change my dress. – Humphrey, keep a lookout and let us know when they come.'

Chaloner and Edward went in, and Edward put on his dress of secretary. Shortly afterwards a party of cavalry were seen galloping towards the cottage. They soon arrived there, and pulled up their horses. An officer who headed them addressed Humphrey in a haughty tone, and asked him who he was.

'I am one of the verderers of the forest, sir,' replied Humphrey respectfully.

'And whose cottage is that? And who have you there?'

'The cottage is mine, sir; two of the horses at the door belong to two troopers who have come in quest of those who fled from Worcester; the other horse belongs to the secretary of the Intendant of the forest, Master

188

Heatherstone, who has come over with directions from the Intendant as to the capture of the rebels.'

At this moment Edward came out and saluted the officer.

'This is the secretary, sir, Master Armitage,' said Humphrey, falling back. Edward saluted the officer, and said, –

'Master Heatherstone, the Intendant, has sent me over here to make arrangements for the capture of the rebels. This man is ordered to lodge two troopers as long as they are considered necessary to remain; and I have directions to tell any officer whom I may meet that Master Heatherstone and his verderers will take good care that none of the rebels are harboured in this direction; and that it will be better that the troops scour the southern edge of the forest, as it is certain that the fugitives will try all that they can to embark for France.'

'What regiment do the troopers belong to that you have here?'

'I believe to Lambert's troop, sir; but they shall come out and answer for themselves. – Tell those men to come out,' said Edward to Humphrey.

'Yes, sir; but they are hard to wake, for they have ridden from Worcester; but I will rouse them.'

'Nay, I cannot wait,' replied the officer. 'I know none of Lambert's troops, and they have no information to give.'

'Could you not take them with you, sir, and leave two of your men instead of them? for they are troublesome people to a poor man, and devour everything,' said Humphrey submissively.

'No, no,' replied the officer, laughing, 'we all know Lambert's people – a friend or enemy is much the same to them. I have no power over them, and you must make the best of it. – Forward, men!' continued the officer, saluting Edward as he passed on; and in a minute or two they were far in the distance.

'That's well over,' observed Edward. 'Chaloner and Grenville are too young-looking and too good-looking for Lambert's villains, and a sight of them might have occasioned suspicion. We must, however, expect more visits. – Keep a good lookout, Pablo.'

Edward and Humphrey then went in and joined the party inside the cottage, who were in a state of no little suspense during the colloquy outside.

'Why, Alice, dearest, you look quite pale?' said Edward as he came in.

'I feared for our guests, Edward. I'm sure that if they had come into the cottage Master Chaloner and Master Grenville would never have been believed to be troopers.'

'We thank you for the compliment, Mistress Alice,' said Chaloner; 'but I think, if necessary, I could ruffle and swear with the best, or rather the worst, of them. We passed for troopers very well on the road here.'

'Yes, but you did not meet any other troopers.'

'That's very true, and shows your penetration. I acknowledge that with troopers there would have been more difficulty; but still, among so many thousands there must be many varieties, and it would be an awkward

189

thing for an officer of one troop to arrest upon suspicion the men belonging to another. I think, when we are visited again, I shall sham intoxication – that will not be very suspicious.'

'No, not on either side,' replied Edward. – 'Come, Alice, we will eat what dinner you may have ready for us.'

For three or four days the Parliamentary forces continued to scour the forest, and another visit or two was paid to the cottage, but without suspicion being created, in consequence of the presence of Edward and his explanations. The parties were invariably sent in another direction. Edward wrote to the Intendant, informing him what had occurred, and requesting permission to remain a few days longer at the cottage; and Pablo, who took the letter, returned with one from the Intendant acquainting him that the King had not yet been taken, and requesting the utmost vigilance on his part to ensure his capture, with directions to search various places in company with the troopers who had been stationed at the cottage; or, if he did not like to leave the cottage, to show the letter to any officer commanding parties in search, that they might act upon the suggestions contained in it. This letter Edward had an opportunity of showing to one or two officers commanding parties who approached the cottage, and whom Edward went out to communicate with, thereby preventing their stopping there.

At last, in about a fortnight, there was not a party in the forest, all of them having gone down to the seaside to look out for the fugitives, several of whom were taken.

Humphrey took the cart to Lymington to procure clothes for Chaloner and Grenville, and it was decided that they should assume those of verderers of the forest, which would enable them to carry a gun. As soon as Humphrey had obtained what was requisite, Chaloner and Grenville were conducted to Clara's cottage, and took possession – of course never showing themselves outside the wood which surrounded it. Humphrey lent them Holdfast as a watch, and they took leave of Alice and Edith with much regret. Humphrey and Edward accompanied them to their new abode. It was arranged that the horses should remain under the care of Humphrey, as they had no stable at Clara's cottage.

On parting, Chaloner gave Edward the letter for his aunts; and then Edward once more bent his steps towards the Intendant's house, and found himself in the company of Patience and Clara.

Edward narrated to the Intendant all that had occurred, and the Intendant approved of what he had done, strongly advising that Chaloner and Grenville should not attempt to go to the Continent till all pursuit was over.

'Here's a letter I have received from the Government, Edward, highly commending my vigilance and activity in pursuit of the fugitives. It appears that the officers you fell in with have written up to state what admirable dispositions we had made. It is a pity, is it not, Edward, that we are compelled to be thus deceitful in this world? Nothing but the times, and the wish to do good, could warrant it. We meet the wicked, and fight them with their own weapons; but although it is treating them as they deserve, our conscience must tell us that it is not right.'

'Surely, sir, to save the lives of people who have committed no other fault except loyalty to their King will warrant our so doing – at least I hope so.'

'According to the Scriptures, I fear it will not; but it is a difficult question for us to decide. Let us be guided by our own consciences. If they do not reproach us, we cannot be far from right.'

Edward then produced the letter he had received from Chaloner, requesting that the Intendant would have the kindness to forward it.

'I see,' replied the Intendant; 'I can forward these through Langton. I presume it is to obtain credit for money. It shall go on Thursday.'

The conference was then broken up, and Edward went to see Oswald.

CHAPTER 25

For several days Edward remained at home, anxiously awaiting every news which arrived, expecting every time that the capture of the King would be announced, and with great joy finding that hitherto all efforts had been unsuccessful. But there was a question which now arose in Edward's mind, and which was the cause of deep reflection. Since the proposal of sending his sisters away had been started, he felt the great inconvenience of his still representing himself to the Intendant as the grandson of Armitage. His sisters, if sent to the ladies at Portlake, must be sent without the knowledge of the Intendant; and if so, the discovery of their absence would soon take place, as Patience Heatherstone would be constantly going over to the cottage; and he now asked himself the question whether, after all the kindness and confidence which the Intendant had shown him, he was right in any longer concealing from him his birth and parentage. He felt that he was doing the Intendant an injustice in not showing to him that confidence which he deserved.

That he was justified in so doing at first he felt; but since the joining the King's army, and the events which had followed, he considered that he was treating the Intendant ill, and he now resolved to take the first opportunity of making the confession. But to do it formally, and without some opportunity which might offer, he felt awkward. At last he thought that he would at once make the confession to Patience, under the promise of secrecy. That he might do at once; and after he had done so, the Intendant could not tax him with want of confidence altogether. He had now analysed his feelings towards Patience, and he felt how dear she had become to him. During the time he was with the army she had seldom been out of his thoughts; and although he was often in the society of well-bred women, he saw not one that, in his opinion, could compare with Patience Heatherstone. But still, what chance had he of supporting a wife? At present, at the age of nineteen, it was preposterous. Thoughts like these ran in his mind, chasing each other, and followed by others as vague and unsatisfactory; and in the end Edward came to the conclusion that he was without a penny, and that being known as the heir of Beverley would be to his disadvantage; that he was in love with Patience Heatherstone, and had no chance at present of obtaining her; and that he had done well up to the present time in concealing who he was from the Intendant, who could safely attest that he knew not that he was protecting the son of so noted a Cavalier; and that he would confess to Patience who he was, and give as a reason for not telling her father that he did not wish to commit him by letting him know who it was that was under his protection. How far the reader may be satisfied with the arguments which Edward was satisfied with, we cannot pretend to say; but Edward was young, and hardly knew how to extricate himself from the cloak which necessity had first compelled him to put on. Edward was already satisfied that he was not quite looked upon with indifference by Patience Heatherstone; and he was not yet certain whether it was not a grateful feeling that she had towards him more than any other. That she believed him to be beneath her in birth he felt convinced, and therefore she could have no idea that he was Edward Beverley. It was not till several days after he had made up his mind that he had an opportunity of being with her alone, as Clara Ratcliffe was their constant companion. However, one evening Clara went out, and stayed out so long carelessly wrapped up that she caught cold; and the following evening she remained at home, leaving Edward and Patience to take their usual walk unaccompanied by her. They had walked for some minutes in silence, when Patience observed, –

'You are very grave, Edward, and have been very grave ever since your return. Have you anything to vex you beyond the failure of the attempt?'

'Yes, I have, Patience. I have much on my conscience, and do not know how to act. I want an adviser and a friend, and know not where to find one.'

'Surely, Edward, my father is your sincere friend, and not a bad adviser.'

'I grant it; but the question is between your father and me, and I cannot advise with him for that reason.'

'Then advise with me, Edward, if it is not a secret of such moment that it is not to be trusted to a woman. At all events, it will be the advice of a sincere friend; you will give me credit for that.'

'Yes, and for much more; for I think I shall have good advice, and will therefore accept your offer. I feel, Patience, that although I was justified, on my first acquaintance with your father, in not making known to him a secret of some importance, yet now that he has put such implicit confi-

192

dence in me I am doing him and myself an injustice in not making the communication – that is, as far as confidence in him is concerned, I consider that he has a right to know all; and yet I feel that it would be prudent on my part that he should not know all, as the knowledge might implicate him with those with whom he is at present allied. A secret sometimes is dangerous; and if your father could not say that on his honour he knew not of the secret, it might harm him if the secret became afterwards known. Do you understand me?'

'I cannot say that I exactly do. You have a secret that you wish to make known to my father, and you think the knowledge of it may harm him. I cannot imagine what kind of secret that may be.'

'Well, I can give you a case in point. Suppose now that I knew that King Charles was hidden in your stable-loft. Such might be the case, and your father be ignorant of it, and his assertion of his ignorance would be believed. But if I were to tell your father that the King was there, and it was afterwards discovered, do you not see that, by confiding such a secret to him, I should do harm, and perhaps bring him into trouble?'

'I perceive now, Edward. Do you mean to say that you know where the King is concealed? For if you do, I must beg of you not to let my father know anything about it. As you say, it would put him in a difficult position, and must eventually harm him much. There is a great different between wishing well to a cause and supporting it in person. My father wishes the King well, I believe, but at the same time he will not take an active part, as you have already seen. At the same time, I am convinced that he would never betray the King if he knew where he was. I say, therefore, if that is your secret, keep it from him, for his sake and for mine, Edward, if you regard me.'

'You know not how much I regard you, Patience. I saw many high-born women when I was away, but none could I see equal to Patience Heatherstone, in my opinion; and Patience was ever in my thoughts during my long absence.'

'I thank you for your kind feelings towards me,' replied Patience; 'but, Master Armitage, we were talking about your secret.'

'Master Armitage!' rejoined Edward. 'How well you know how to remind me, by that expression, of my obscure birth and parentage, whenever I am apt to forget the distance which I ought to observe!'

'You are wrong,' replied Patience; 'but you flattered me so grossly that I called you Master Armitage to show that I disliked flattery – that was all. I dislike flattery from those who are above me in rank as well as those who are below me; and I should have done the same to any other person, whatever his condition might be. But forget what I said. I did not mean to vex you, only to punish you for thinking me so silly as to believe such nonsense.'

'Your humility may construe that into flattery which was said by me in perfect sincerity and truth – that I cannot help, ' replied Edward. 'I might have added much more, and yet have been sincere. If you had not reminded me of my not being of gentle birth, I might have had the presumption to have told you much more; but I have been rebuked.'

Edward finished speaking, and Patience made no reply. They walked on for several moments without exchanging another syllable. At last Patience said, –

'I will not say who is wrong, Edward; but this I do know, that the one who first offers the olive branch after a misunderstanding cannot but be right. I offer it now, and ask you whether we are to quarrel about one little word. Let me ask you, and give me a candid answer: Have I ever been so base as to treat as an inferior one to whom I have been so much obliged?'

'It is I who am in fault, Patience,' replied Edward. 'I have been dreaming for a long while, pleased with my dreams, and forgetting that they were dreams, and not likely to be realized. I must now speak plainly. I love you, Patience – love you so much that to part from you would be misery; to know that my love was rejected, as bitter as death. That is the truth, and I can conceal it no longer. Now I admit you have a right to be angry.'

'I see no cause for anger, Edward,' replied Patience. 'I have not thought of you but as a friend and benefactor; it would have been wrong to have done otherwise. I am but a young person, and must be guided by my father. I would not offend him by disobedience. I thank you for your good opinion of me, and yet I wish you had not said what you have.'

'Am I to understand from your reply that if your father raised no objection my lowly birth would be none in your opinion?'

'Your birth has never come into my head, except when reminded of it by yourself.'

'Then, Patience, let me return for the present to what I had to confide to you. I was –'

'Here comes my father, Edward,' said Patience.

'Surely I have done wrong, for I feel afraid to meet him.'

Mr Heatherstone now joined them, and said to Edward, –

'I have been looking for you. I have news from London which has rejoiced me much. I have at last obtained what I have some time been trying for – and, indeed, I may say that your prudence and boldness in returning home as a trooper, added to your conduct in the forest, has greatly advanced and ultimately obtained for me my suit. There was some suspense before that, but your conduct has removed it, and now we shall have plenty to do.'

They walked to the house, and the Intendant, as soon as he had gained his own room, said to Edward, –

'There is a grant to me of a property which I have long solicited for my services. Read it.'

Edward took up the letter, in which the Parliament informed Mr Heatherstone that his application for the property of Arnwood had been acceded to, and signed by the Commissioners, and that he might take immediate possession. Edward turned pale as he laid the document down on the table.

194

'We will ride tomorrow, Edward, and look it over. I intend to rebuild the house.'

Edward made no reply.

'Are you not well?' said the Intendant, with surprise.

'Yes, sir,' replied Edward, 'I am well, I believe; but I will confess to you that I am disappointed. I did not think that you would have accepted a property from such a source, and so unjustly sequestrated.'

'I am sorry, Edward,' replied the Intendant, 'that I should have fallen in your good opinion; but allow me to observe that you are so far right that I never would have accepted a property to which there were living claimants. But this is a different case. For instance, the Ratcliffe property belongs to little Clara, and is sequestrated. Do you think I would accept it? Never! But here is a property without an heir: the whole family perished in the flames of Arnwood! There is no living claimant! It must be given to somebody, or remain with the Government. This property, therefore, and this property only, out of all sequestrated, I selected, as I felt that in obtaining it I did harm to no one. I have been offered others, but have refused them. I would accept of this, and this only; and that is the reason why my applications have hitherto been attended with no success. I trust you believe me, Edward, in what I assert?'

'First answer me one question, Mr Heatherstone. Suppose it were proved that the whole of the family did not, as it is supposed, perish at the conflagration of Arnwood; suppose a rightful heir to it should at any time appear – would you then resign the property to him?'

'As I hope for heaven, Edward, I would!' replied the Intendant, solemnly raising his eyes upwards as he spoke. 'I then should think that I had been an instrument to keep the property out of other hands less scrupulous, and should surrender it as a trust which had been confided to me for the time only.'

'With such feelings, Mr Heatherstone, I can now congratulate you upon your having obtained possession of the property,' replied Edward.

'And yet I do not deserve so much credit, as there is little chance of my sincerity being put to the test, Edward. There is no doubt that the family all perished, and Arnwood will become the dower of Patience Heatherstone.'

Edward's heart beat quick. A moment's thought told him his situation. He had been prevented, by the interruption of Mr Heatherstone, from making his confession to Patience, and now he could not make it to anybody without a rupture with the Intendant, or a compromise, by asking what he so earnestly desired – the hand of Patience. Mr Heatherstone, observing to Edward that he did not look so well, said supper was ready, and that they had better go into the next room. Edward mechanically followed. At supper he was tormented by the incessant inquiries of Clara as to what was the matter with him. He did not venture to look at Patience, and made a hasty retreat to bed, complaining, as he well might do, of a severe headache.

Edward threw himself on his bed, but to sleep was impossible. He thought of the events of the day, over and over again. Had he any reason to believe that Patience returned his affection? No; her reply was too calm, too composed to make him suppose that. And now that she would be an heiress there would be no want of pretenders to her hand, and he would lose her and his property at the same time. It was true that the Intendant had declared that he would renounce the property if the true heir appeared, but that was easy to say upon the conviction that no heir would appear. And even if he did renounce it, the Parliament would receive it again rather than it should fall into the hands of a Beverley. 'Oh that I had never left the cottage!' thought Edward. 'I might then at least have become resigned and contented with my lot. Now I am miserable, and whichever way I turn I see no prospect of being otherwise. One thing only I can decide upon, which is that I will not remain any longer than I can help under this roof. I will go over and consult with Humphrey; and if I can only place my sisters as I want, Humphrey and I will seek our fortunes.'

Edward rose at daylight, and dressing himself, went down and saddled his horse. Desiring Sampson to tell the Intendant that he had gone over to the cottage and would return by the evening, he rode across the forest, and arrived just as they were sitting down to breakfast. His attempts to be cheerful before his sisters did not succeed, and they were all grieved to see him look so pale and haggard. As soon as breakfast was over Edward made a sign, and he and Humphrey went out.

'What is the matter, my dear brother?' said Humphrey.

'I shall tell you all. Listen to me,' replied Edward, who then gave him the detail of all that had passed, from the time he had walked out with Patience Heatherstone till he went to bed. 'Now, Humphrey, you know all; and what shall I do? Remain there I cannot!'

'If Patience Heatherstone had professed regard for you,' replied Humphrey, 'the affair would have been simple enough. Her father could have no objections to the match, and he would at the same time have acquitted his conscience as to the retaining of the property; but you say she showed none.'

'She told me very calmly that she was sorry that I had said what I did.'

'But do women always mean what they say, brother?' said Humphrey.

'She does, at all events,' replied Edward; 'she is truth itself. No, I cannot deceive myself. She feels a deep debt of gratitude for the service I rendered her, and that prevented her from being more harsh in her reply than what she was.'

'But if she knew that you were Edward Beverley, do you not think it would make a difference in her?'

'And if it did, it would be too humiliating to think that I was only married for my rank and station.'

'But considering you of mean birth, may she not have checked those feelings which she considered under the circumstances improper to indulge?'

'Where there is such a sense of propriety there can be little affection.'

196

'I know nothing about these things, Edward,' replied Humphrey. 'But I have been told that a woman's heart is not easily read; or if I have not been told it, I have read it or dreamt it. What do you propose to do?'

'What I fear you will not approve of, Humphrey: it is to break up our establishment altogether. If the answer is favourable from the Misses Conynghame, my sisters shall go to them; but that we had agreed upon already. Then for myself – I intend to go abroad, resume my name, and obtain employment in some foreign service. I will trust to the King for assisting me to that.'

'That is the worst part of it, Edward; but if your peace of mind depends upon it, I will not oppose it.'

'You, Humphrey, may come with me and share my fortunes, or do what you think more preferable.'

'I think then, Edward, that I shall not decide rashly. I must have remained here with Pablo if my sisters had gone to the Ladies Conynghame and you had remained with the Intendant. I shall therefore, till I hear from you, remain where I am, and I shall be able to observe what is going on here, and let you know.'

'Be it so,' replied Edward. 'Let me only see my sisters well placed, and I shall be off the next day. It is misery to remain there now.'

After some more conversation Edward mounted his horse and returned to the Intendant's. He did not arrive till late, for supper was on the table. The Intendant gave him a letter for Mr Chaloner, which was enclosed in one from Mr Langton, and further informed Edward that news had arrived of the King having made his escape to France.

'Thank God for that!' exclaimed Edward. 'With your leave, sir, I will tomorrow deliver this letter to the party to whom it is addressed, as I know it to be of consequence.'

The Intendant having given his consent, Edward retired without having exchanged a word with Patience or Clara beyond the usual civilities of the table.

The following morning Edward, who had not slept an hour during the night, set off for Clara's cottage, and found Chaloner and Grenville still in bed. At the sound of his voice the door was opened, and he gave Chaloner the letter. The latter read it, and then handed it to Edward. The Misses Conynghame were delighted at the idea of receiving the two daughters of Colonel Beverley, and would treat them as their own. They requested that they might be sent to London immediately, where the coach would meet them to convey them down to Lancashire. They begged to be kindly remembered to Captain Beverley, and to assure him that his sisters should be well cared for.

'I am much indebted to you, Chaloner,' said Edward. 'I will send my brother off with my sisters as soon as possible. You will soon think of returning to France; and if you will permit me, I will accompany you. '

'You, Edward! That will be delightful. But you had no idea of the kind when last we met. What has induced you to alter your mind?'

'I will tell you by-and-by; I do not think I shall be here again for some days. I must be a great deal at the cottage when Humphrey is away, for Pablo will have a great charge upon him – what with the dairy, and horses, and breed of goats, and other things – more than he can attend to; but as soon as Humphrey returns I will come to you and make preparations for our departure. Till then farewell, both of you. We must see to provision you for three weeks or a month before Humphrey starts.'

Edward bade them a hearty farewell, and then rode to the cottage.

Although Alice and Edith had been somewhat prepared for leaving the cottage, yet the time was so very uncertain that the blow fell heavily upon them. They were to leave their brothers, whom they loved so dearly, to go to strangers; and when they understood that they were to leave in two days, and that they should not see Edward again, their grief was very great. But Edward reasoned with Alice and consoled her, although with Edith it was a more difficult task. She not only lamented her brothers, but her cow, her pony and her kids; all the dumb animals were friends and favourites of Edith, and even the idea of parting with Pablo was the cause of a fresh burst of tears.

Having made every arrangement with Humphrey, Edward once more took his leave, promising to come over and assist Pablo as soon as he could.

The next day Humphrey was busied in his preparations. They supplied the provisions to Clara's cottage, and when Pablo took them over in the cart, Humphrey rode to Lymington and provided a conveyance to London for the following day. We may as well observe that they set off at the hour appointed, and arrived safely at London in three days. There, at an address given in the letter, they found the coach waiting, and having given his sisters into the charge of an elderly waiting-woman, who had come up in the coach to take charge of them, they quitted him with many tears, and Humphrey hastened back to the New Forest.

On his return he found to his surprise that Edward had not called at the cottage as he had promised; and with a mind foreboding evil, he mounted a horse and set off across the forest to ascertain the cause. As he was close to the Intendant's house he was met by Oswald, who informed him that Edward had been seized with a violent fever, and was in a very dangerous state, having been delirious for three or four days.

Humphrey hastened to dismount, and knocked at the door of the house. It was opened by Sampson, and Humphrey requested to be shown up to his brother's room. He found Edward in the state described by Oswald, and wholly unconscious of his presence; the maid Phœbe was by his bedside.

'You may leave,' said Humphrey, rather abruptly. 'I am his brother.'

Phœbe retired, and Humphrey was alone with his brother.

'It was, indeed, an unhappy day when you came to this house,' exclaimed Humphrey, as the tears rolled down his cheeks. 'My poor, poor Edward!'

Edward now began to talk incoherently, and attempted to rise from the bed, but his efforts were unavailing – he was too weak; but he raved of Patience Heatherstone, and he called himself Edward Beverley more than once, and he talked of his father and of Arnwood.

'If he has raved in this manner,' thought Humphrey, 'he has not many secrets left to disclose. I will not leave him, and will keep others away if I can.'

Humphrey had been sitting an hour with his brother, when the surgeon came to see his patient. He felt his pulse, and asked Humphrey if he was nursing him.

'I am his brother, sir,' replied Humphrey.

'Then, my good sir, if you perceive any signs of perspiration – and I think now that there is a little – keep the clothes on him and let him perspire freely. If so, his life will be saved.'

The surgeon withdrew, saying that he would return again late in the evening.

Humphrey remained for another two hours at the bedside, and then feeling that there was a sign of perspiration, he obeyed the injunctions of the surgeon, and held on the clothes against all Edward's endeavours to throw them off. For a short time the perspiration was profuse, and the restlessness of Edward subsided into a deep slumber.

'Thank heaven! there are then hopes.'

'Did you say there were hopes?' repeated a voice behind him.

Humphrey turned, and perceived Patience and Clara behind him, who had come in without his observing it.

'Yes,' replied Humphrey, looking reproachfully at Patience, 'there are hopes, by what the surgeon said to me – hopes that he may yet be able to quit this house, which he was so unfortunate as to enter.'

This was a harsh and rude speech of Humphrey's; but he considered that Patience Heatherstone had been the cause of his brother's dangerous state, and that she had not behaved well to him.

Patience made no reply, but falling down on her knees by the bedside, prayed silently; and Humphrey's heart smote him for what he had said to her. 'She cannot be so bad,' thought Humphrey, as Patience and Clara quitted the room without the least noise.

Shortly afterwards the Intendant came up into the room, and offered his hand to Humphrey, who pretended not to see it, and did not take it.

'He has got Arnwood – that is enough for him,' thought Humphrey; 'but my hand in friendship he shall not receive.'

The Intendant put his hand within the clothes, and feeling the high perspiration in which Edward was in, said,—

'I thank thee, O God, for all thy mercies, and that Thou hast been pleased to spare this valuable life. – How are your sisters, Master Humphrey?' said the Intendant; 'my daughter bade me inquire. I will send over to them and let them know that your brother is better, if you do not leave this for the cottage yourself after the surgeon has called again.'

'My sisters are no longer at the cottage, Master Heatherstone,' replied Humphrey; 'they have gone to some friends who have taken charge of them. I saw them safe to London myself, or I should have known of my brother's illness and have been here before this.'

'You indeed tell me news, Master Humphrey,' replied the Intendant. 'With whom, may I ask, are your sisters placed, and in what capacity are they gone?'

This reply of the Intendant's reminded Humphrey that he had somewhat committed himself, as, being supposed to be the daughters of a forester, it was not to be thought that they had gone up to be educated; and he therefore replied, –

'They found it lonely in the forest, Master Heatherstone, and wished to see London; so we have taken them there, and put them into the care of those who have promised that they shall be well placed.'

The Intendant appeared to be much disturbed and surprised, but he said nothing, and soon afterwards quitted the room. He almost immediately returned with the surgeon, who, as soon as he felt Edward's pulse, declared that the crisis was over, and that when he awoke he would be quite sensible. Having given directions as to the drink of his patient, and some medicine which he was to take, the surgeon then left, stating that he should not call until the next evening, unless he was sent for, as he considered all danger over.

Edward continued in a quiet slumber for the major portion of the night. It was just break of day when he opened his eyes. Humphrey offered him some drink, which Edward took greedily, and seeing Humphrey, said, –

'O Humphrey, I had quite forgotten where I was – I'm so sleepy!' and with these words his head fell on the pillow, and he was again asleep.

When it was broad daylight Oswald came into the room.

'Master Humphrey, they say that all danger is over now, but that you have remained here all night. I will relieve you now, if you let me. Go and take a walk in the fresh air; it will revive you.'

'I will, Oswald, and many thanks. My brother has woke up once, and, I thank God, is quite sensible. He will know you when he wakes again, and then do you send for me.'

Humphrey left the room, and was glad, after a night of close confinement in a sickroom, to feel the cool morning air fanning his cheeks. He had not been long out of the house before he perceived Clara coming towards him.

'How d'ye do, Humphrey?' said Clara; 'and how is brother this morning?'

'He is better, Clara, and I hope now out of danger.'

'But, Humphrey,' continued Clara, 'when we came into the room last night, what made you say what you did?'

'I do not recollect that I said anything.'

'Yes, you did: you said that there were now hopes that your brother would be able soon to quit this house, which he had been so unfortunate as to enter. Do you recollect?'

'I may have said so, Clara,' replied Humphrey; 'it was only speaking my thoughts aloud.'

'But why do you think so, Humphrey? Why has Edward been unfortunate in entering this house? That is what I want to know. Patience cried so much after she left the room because you said that. Why did you say so? You did not think so a short time ago.'

'No, my dear Clara, I did not, but I do now, and I cannot give you my reasons; so you must say no more about it.' –

Clara was silent for a time, and then said, –

'Patience tells me that your sisters have gone away from the cottage. You told her father so.'

'It is very true; they have gone.'

'But why have they gone? What have they gone for? Who is to look after the cows, and goats, and poultry? Who is to cook your dinner, Humphrey? What can you do without them, and why did you send them away without letting me or Patience know that they were going, so that at least we might have bid them farewell?'

'My dear Clara,' replied Humphrey – who, feeling no little difficulty in replying to all these questions, resolved to cut the matter short by appearing to be angry – 'you know that you are the daughter of a gentleman, and so is Patience Heatherstone. You are both of gentle birth; but my sisters, you know, are only the daughters of a forester, and my brother Edward and I are no better. It does not become Mistress Patience and you to be intimate with such as we are, especially now that Mistress Patience is a great heiress; for her father has obtained the large property of Arnwood, and it will be hers after his death. It is not fit that the heiress of Arnwood should mix herself up with foresters' daughters; and as we had friends near Lymington who offered to assist us, and take our sisters under their charge, we thought it better that they should go; for what would become of them if any accident was to happen to Edward or to me? Now they will be provided for. After they have been taught, they will make very nice tire-women to some lady of quality added Humphrey, with a sneer. 'Don't you think they will, my pretty Clara?'

Clara burst into tears.

'You are very unkind, Humphrey,' sobbed she. 'You had no right to send away your sisters. I don't believe you – what's more!' and Clara ran away into the house.

CHAPTER 26

Our readers may think that Humphrey was very unkind; but it was to avoid being questioned by Clara, who was evidently sent for the purpose, that he was so harsh. At the same time, it must be admitted that Mr Heatherstone having obtained possession of Arnwood rankled no doubt in the minds of both the brothers, and every act now on the part of him or his family was viewed in a false medium. But our feelings are not always at our control, and Edward was naturally impetuous, and Humphrey so much attached, and so much alarmed at his brother's danger, that he was even more excited. The blow fell doubly heavy, as it appeared that at the very same time Patience had rejected his brother, and taken possession of their property, which had been held by the family for centuries. What made the case more annoying was that explanation, if there was any to offer on either side, was, under present circumstances, almost impossible.

Soon after Clara left him Humphrey returned to his brother's room. He found him awake, and talking to Oswald. Ardently pressing his brother's hand, Edward said, –

'My dear Humphrey, I shall soon be well now, and able, I trust, to quit this house. What I fear is that some explanation will be asked for by the Intendant, not only relative to my sisters having left us, but also upon other points. This is what I wish to avoid, without giving offence. I do not think that the Intendant is so much to blame in having obtained my property, as he does not know that a Beverley existed; but I cannot bear to have any further intimacy with him, especially after what has taken place between me and his daughter. What I have to request is that you will never quit this room while I am still here, unless you are relieved by Oswald; so that the Intendant or anybody else may have no opportunity of having any private communication with me, or forcing me to listen to what they may have to say. I made this known to Oswald before you came in.'

'Depend upon it, it shall be so, Edward; for I am of your opinion. Clara came to me just now, and I had much trouble, and was compelled to be harsh, to get rid of her importunity.'

When the surgeon called he pronounced Edward out of danger, and that his attendance would be no longer necessary. Edward felt the truth of this. All that he required was strength, and that he trusted in a few days to obtain.

Oswald was sent over to the cottage to ascertain how Pablo was going on by himself. He found that everything was correct, and that Pablo, although he felt proud of his responsibility, was very anxious for Humphrey's return, as he found himself very lonely. During Oswald's absence on this day Humphrey never quitted the room; and although the Intendant came up several times, he never could find an opportunity of speaking to Edward, which he evidently wished to do.

To inquiries made as to how he was Edward always complained of great weakness, for a reason which will soon be understood. Several days elapsed, and Edward had often been out of bed during the night, when not likely to be intruded upon, and he now felt himself strong enough to be removed; and his object was to leave the Intendant's house without his knowledge, so as to avoid any explanation.

One evening Pablo came over with the horses after it was dark. Oswald put them into the stable, and, the morning proving fine and clear, a little before break of day Edward came softly downstairs with Humphrey, and mounting the horses, set off for the cottage, without any one in the Intendant's house being aware of their departure.

It must not be supposed, however, that Edward took this step without some degree of consideration as to the feelings of the Intendant. On the contrary, he left a letter with Oswald, to be delivered after his departure, in which he thanked the Intendant sincerely for all the kindness and compassion he had shown towards him; assured him of his gratitude and kind feelings towards him and his daughter, but said that circumstances had occurred of which no explanation could be given without great pain to all parties, which rendered it advisable that he should take such an apparently unkind step as to leave without bidding them farewell in person; that he was about to embark immediately for the Continent to seek his fortune in the wars; and that he wished all prosperity to the family, which would ever have his kindest wishes and remembrances.

'Humphrey,' said Edward, after they had ridden about two miles across the forest, and the sun had risen in an unclouded sky, 'I feel like an emancipated slave. Thank God! my sickness has cured me of all my complaints, and all I want now is active employment. And now, Humphrey, Chaloner and Grenville are not a little tired of being mured up in the cottage, and I am as anxious as they are to be off. What will you do? Will you join us, or will you remain at the cottage?'

'I have reflected upon it, Edward, and I have come to the determination of remaining at the cottage. You will find it expensive enough to support one where you are going, and you must appear as a Beverley should do. We have plenty of money saved to equip you, and maintain you well for a year or so; but after that you may require more. Leave me here. I can make money, now that the farm is well stocked, and I have no doubt that I shall be able to send over a trifle every year, to support the honour of the family. Besides, I do not wish to leave this for another reason. I want to know what is going on, and watch the motions of the Intendant and the heiress of Arnwood. I also do not wish to leave the country until I know how my sisters get on with the Ladies Conynghame; it is my duty to watch over them. I have made up my mind, so do not attempt to dissuade me.'

'I shall not, my dear Humphrey, as I think you have decided properly; but I beg you will not think of laying by money for me – a very little will suffice my wants.'

'Not so, good brother; you must and shall, if I can help you, ruffle it with the best. You will be better received if you do; for though poverty is no sin, as the saying is, it is scouted as sin should be, while sins are winked at. You know that I require no money, and therefore you must and shall, if you love me, take it all.'

'As you will, my dear Humphrey. Now, then, let us put our horses to speed, for, if possible, we will tomorrow morning leave the forest.'

By this time all search for the fugitives from Worcester had long been over, and there was no difficulty in obtaining the means of embarkation. Early the next morning everything was ready, and Edward, Humphrey, Chaloner, Genville, and Pablo set off for Southampton, one of the horses carrying the little baggage which they had with them. Edward, as we have before mentioned, with the money he had saved, and the store at the cottage, which had been greatly increased, was well supplied with cash; and that evening they embarked, with their horses, in a small sailing vessel, and with a favourable light wind arrived at a small port of France on the following day. Humphrey and Pablo returned to the cottage, we need hardly now say, very much out of spirits at the separation.

'O Massa Humphrey,' said Pablo as they rode along, 'Missy Alice and Missy Edith go away; I wish go with them. Massa Edward go away; I wish go with him. You stay at cottage; I wish stay with you. Pablo cannot be in three places.'

'No, Pablo; all you can do is to stay where you can be most useful.'

'Yes, I know that. You want me at cottage very much. Missy Alice and Edith and Massa Edward no want me; so I stay at cottage.'

'Yes, Pablo, we will stay at the cottage; but we can't do everything now. I think we must give up the dairy, now that my sisters are gone. I'll tell you what I have been thinking of, Pablo. We will make a large enclosed place, to coax the ponies into during the winter; pick out as many as we think are good, and sell them at Lymington. That will be better than churning butter.'

'Yes, I see; plenty of work for Pablo.'

'And plenty for me too, Pablo; but you know, when the enclosure is once made it will last for a long while, and we will get the wild cattle into it if we can.'

'Yes, I see,' said Pablo. 'I like that very much; only not like trouble to build place.'

'We shan't have much trouble, Pablo: if we fell the trees inside the wood at each side, and let them lie one upon the other, the animals will never break through them.'

'That very good idea – save trouble,' said Pablo. 'And what you do with cows, suppose no make butter?'

'Keep them, and sell their calves; keep them, to entice the wild cattle into the pen.'

'Yes, that good. And turn out old Billy to 'tice ponies into pen,' continued Pablo, laughing.

'Yes, we will try it.'

We must now return to the Intendant's house. Oswald delivered the letter to the Intendant, who read it with much astonishment.

'Gone! is he actually gone?' said Mr Heatherstone.

'Yes, sir, before daylight this morning.'

'And why was I not informed of it?' said Mr Heatherstone; 'why have you been a party to this proceeding, being my servant? May I inquire that?'

'I knew Master Edward before I knew you, sir,' replied Oswald.

'Then you had better follow him,' rejoined the Intendant in an angry tone.

'Very well, sir,' replied Oswald, who quitted the room.

'Good Heaven, how all my plans have been frustrated!' exclaimed the Intendant, when he was alone. He then read the letter over more carefully than he had done at first. '"Circumstances had occurred of which no explanation could be given by him." I do not comprehend that; I must see Patience.'

Mr Heatherstone opened the door and called to his daughter.

'Patience,' said Mr Heatherstone, 'Edward has left the house this morning; here is a letter which he has written to me. Read it, and let me know if you can explain some portion of it which to me is incomprehensible. Sit down and read it attentively.'

Patience, who was much agitated, gladly took the seat and perused Edward's letter. When she had done so she let it drop in her lap and covered all her face, the tears trickling through her fingers. After a time the Intendant said, –

'Patience, has anything passed between you and Edward Armitage?'

Patience made no reply, but sobbed aloud. She might not have shown so much emotion, but it must be remembered that for the last three weeks since Edward had spoken to her, and during his subsequent illness, she had been very unhappy. The reserve of Humphrey, the expressions he had made use of, his repulse of Clara, and her not having seen anything of Edward during his illness, added to his sudden and unexpected departure without a word to her, had broken her spirits, and she sank beneath the load of sorrow.

The Intendant left her to recover herself before he again addressed her. When she had ceased sobbing her father spoke to her in a very kind voice, begging her that she would not conceal anything from him, as it was most important to him that the real facts should be known.

'Now tell me, my child, what passed between Edward and you.'

'He told me, just before you came up to us that evening, that he loved me.'

'And what was your reply?'

'I hardly know, my dear father, what it was that I said. I did not like to be unkind to one who saved my life, and I did not choose to say what I thought, because – because – because he was of low birth; and how could I give encouragement to the son of a forester without your permission?'

'Then you rejected him?'

'I suppose I did, or that he considered that I did so. He had a secret of importance that he would have confided to me, had you not interrupted us.'

'And now, Patience, I must request you to answer me one question candidly. I do not blame you for your conduct, which was correct under the circumstances. I also had a secret which I perhaps ought to have confided; but I did consider that the confidence and paternal kindness with which I treated Edward would have been sufficient to point out to you that I could not have been very averse to an union – indeed, the freedom of communication which I allowed between you must have told you so; but your sense of duty and propriety has made you act as you ought to have done, I grant, although contrary to my real wishes.'

'Your wishes, my father?' said Patience.

'Yes – my wishes. There is nothing I so ardently desired as an union between you and Edward; but I wished you to love him for his own merits.'

'I have done so, father,' replied Patience, sobbing again, 'although I did not tell him so.'

The Intendant remained silent for some time, and then said, –

'There is no cause for further concealment, Patience; I have only to regret that I was not more explicit sooner. I have long suspected, and have since been satisfied, that Edward Armitage is Edward Beverley, who, with his brother and sisters, were supposed to have been burnt to death at Arnwood.'

Patience removed her handkerchief from her face, and looked at her father with astonishment.

'I tell you that I had a strong suspicion of it, my dear child first, from the noble appearance, which no forest garb could disguise; but what gave me further conviction was that when at Lymington I happened to fall in with one Benjamin, who had been a servant at Arnwood, and interrogated him closely. He really believed that the children were burnt. 'It is true that I asked him particularly relative to the appearance of the children – how many were boys and how many were girls, their ages, etc.; but the strongest proof was that the names of the four children corresponded with the names of the Children of the Forest, as well as their ages, and I went to the church register and extracted them. Now this was almost amounting to proof; for it was not likely that four children in the forest cottage should have the same ages and names as those of Arnwood. After I had ascertained this point, I engaged Edward, as you know, wishing to secure him; for I was once acquainted with his father, and at all events well acquainted with the colonel's merits. You remained in the house together, and it was with pleasure that I watched the intimacy between you; and then I exerted myself to get Arnwood restored to him. I could not ask it for him, but I prevented it being given to any other by laying claim to it myself. Had Edward remained with us, all might have succeeded as I wished; but he would join in the unfortunate insurrection, and I knew it useless to prevent him, so I let him go. I found that he took the name of Beverley during the time he was with the King's army, and when I was last in town I was told so by the Commissioners, who wondered where he had come from; but the effect was that it was now useless for me to request the estate for him, as I had wished to do – his having served in the royal army rendered it impossible. I therefore claimed it for myself, and succeeded. I had made up my mind that he was attached to you, and you were equally so to him; and as soon as I had the grant sent down, which was on the evening he addressed you, I made known to him that the property was given to me; and I added, on some dry questions being put to me by him, relative to the possibility of there being still existing an heir to the estate, that there was no chance of that, and that you would be the mistress of Arnwood. I threw it out as a hint to him, fancying that, as far as you were concerned, all would go well, and that I would explain to him my knowledge of who he was after he had made known his regard for you.'

'Yes, I see it all now,' replied Patience. 'In one hour he is rejected by me, and in the next he is told that I have obtained possession of his property. No wonder that he is indignant, and looks upon us with scorn. And now he had left us; we have driven him into danger, and may never see him again. O father, I am very, very miserable!'

'We must hope for the best, Patience. It is true that he has gone to the wars, but it does not therefore follow that he is to be killed. You are both very young – much too young to marry – and all may be explained. I must see Humphrey, and be candid with him.'

'But Alice and Edith – where are they gone, father?'

'That I can inform you. I have a letter from Langton on the subject, for I begged him to find out. He says that there are two young ladies of the name of Beverley who have been placed under the charge of his friends the Ladies Conynghame, who is aunt to Major Chaloner, who has been for some time concealed in the forest. – But I have letters to write, my dear Patience. Tomorrow, if I live and do well, I will ride over to the cottage to see Humphrey Beverley.'

The Intendant kissed his daughter, and she left the room.

Poor Patience! she was glad to be left to herself and think over this strange communication. For many days she had felt how fond she had been of Edward – much more so than she had believed herself to be. 'And now,' she thought, 'if he really loves me, and hears my father's explanation, he will come back again.' By degrees she recovered her serenity, and employed herself in her quiet domestic duties.

Mr Heatherstone rode over to the cottage the next day, where he found Humphrey busily employed as usual, and, what was very unusual, extremely grave. It was not a pleasant task for Mr Heatherstone to have to explain his conduct to so very young a man as Humphrey; but he felt that he could not be comfortable until the evil impression against him was removed, and he knew that Humphrey had a great deal of sterling good sense. His reception was cool; but when the explanation was made Humphrey was more than satisfied, as it showed that the Intendant had been their best friend, and that it was from a delicacy on the part of Patience, rather than from any other cause, that the misunderstanding had occurred. Humphrey inquired if he had permission to communicate the substance of their conversation to his brother, and Mr Heatherstone stated that such was his wish and intention when he confided it to Humphrey. It is hardly necessary to say that Humphrey took the earliest opportunity of writing to Edward at the direction which Chaloner had left with him.

CHAPTER 27

But we must follow Edward for a time. On his arrival at Paris he was kindly received by King Charles, who promised to assist his views in joining the army.

'You have to choose between two generals, both great in the art of war – Condé and Turenne. I have no doubt that they will be opposed to each other soon. That will be the better for you, as you will learn tactics from such great players.'

'Which would your Majesty recommend me to follow?' inquired Edward.

'Condé is my favourite, and he will soon be opposed to this truculent and dishonest court, who have kept me here as an instrument to accomplish their own wishes, but who have never intended to keep their promises and place me on the English throne. I will give you letters to Condé; and recollect that whatever general you take service under, you will follow him without pretending to calculate how far his movements may be right or wrong – that is not your affair. Condé is now just released from Vincennes; but, depend upon it, he will be in arms very soon.'

As soon as he was furnished with the necessary credentials from the King, Edward presented himself at the levee of the Prince of Condé.

'You are here highly spoken of,' said the prince, 'for so young a man. So you were at the affair of Worcester? We will retain you, for your services will be wanted by-and-by. Can you procure any of your countrymen?'

'I know but of two that I can recommend from personal knowledge; but these two officers I can venture to pledge myself for.'

'Any more?'

'That I cannot at present reply to, your Highness, but I should think it very possible.'

'Bring me the officers tomorrow at this hour, Monsieur Beverley. *Au revoir.*'

The Prince of Condé then passed on to speak to other officers and gentlemen who were waiting to pay their respects.

Edward went to Chaloner and Grenville, who were delighted with the intelligence which he brought them. The next day they were at the prince's levee, and introduced by Edward.

'I am fortunate, gentlemen,' said the prince, 'in securing the services of such fine young men. You will oblige me by enlisting as many of your countrymen as you may consider likely to do good service, and then follow me to Guienne, to which province I am now about to depart. Be pleased to put yourself into communication with the parties named in this paper, and after my absence you will receive from them every assistance and necessary supplies which may be required.'

A month after this interview, Condé, who had been joined by a great number of nobles, and had been reinforced by troops from Spain, set up the standard of revolt. Edward and his friends joined them, with about three hundred English and Scotchmen, which they had enlisted, and very soon afterwards Condé obtained the victory at Blenan, and in April 1652 advanced to Paris.

Turenne, who had taken the command of the French army, followed him, and a severe action was fought in the streets of the suburb D'Antoine, in which neither party had the advantage. But eventually Condé was beaten back by the superior force of Turenne, and not receiving the assistance he expected from the Spaniards, he fell back to the frontiers of Champagne.

Previous to his departure from Paris Edward had received Humphrey's letter, explaining away the Intendant's conduct, and the contents removed a heavy load from Edward's mind; but he now thought of nothing but war, and although he cherished the idea of Patience Heatherstone, he was resolved to follow the fortunes of the prince as long as he could. He wrote a letter to the Intendant, thanking him for his kind feelings and intentions towards him, and he trusted that he might one day have the pleasure of seeing him again. He did not, however, think it advisable to mention the name of his daughter, except in inquiring after her health and sending his respects. 'It may be years before I see her again,' thought Edward, 'and who knows what may happen?'

The Prince of Condé now had the command of the Spanish forces in the Netherlands, and Edward with his friends followed his fortunes and gained his goodwill: they were rapidly promoted.

Time flew on, and in the year 1654 the court of France concluded an alliance with Cromwell, and expelled King Charles from the French frontiers. The war was still carried on in the Netherlands. Turenne bore down Condé, who had gained every campaign; and the court of Spain, wearied with reverses, made overtures of peace, which were gladly accepted by the French.

During these wars Cromwell had been named Protector, and had shortly afterwards died.

Edward, who but rarely heard from Humphrey, was now anxious to quit the army and go to the King, who was in Spain; but to leave his colours while things were adverse was impossible.

After the peace and the pardon of Condé by the French king the armies were disbanded, and the three adventurers were free. They took their leave of the prince, who thanked them for their long and meritorious services; and they then hastened to King Charles, who had left Spain and come to the Low Countries. At the time of their joining the King, Richard, the son of Cromwell, who had been nominated Protector, had resigned, and everything was ready for the Restoration.

On the 15th of May 1660 the news arrived that Charles had been proclaimed King on the 8th, and a large body of gentlemen went to invite him over. The King sailed from Scheveling, was met at Dover by General Monk, and conducted to London, which he entered amidst the acclamations of the people on the 29th of the same month.

We may leave the reader to suppose that Edward, Chaloner, and Grenville were among the most favoured of those in his train. As the procession moved slowly along the Strand, through a countless multitude, the windows of all the houses were filled with well-dressed ladies, who waved their white kerchiefs to the King and his attendant suite. Chaloner, Edward, and Grenville, who rode side by side as gentlemen-in-waiting, were certainly the most distingiushed among the King's retinue.

'Look, Edward,' said Chaloner, 'at those two lovely girls at yon window. Do you recognize them?'

'Indeed, I do not. Are they any of our Paris beauties?'

'Why, thou insensible and unnatural animal, they are thy sisters Alice and Edith! And do you recognize behind them my good aunts Conynghame?'

'It is so, I believe,' replied Edward. 'Yes, now that Edith smiles I'm sure it is them.'

'Yes,' replied Grenville, 'there can be no doubt of that. But will they, think you, recognize us?'

'We shall see,' replied Edward, as they now approached within a few yards of the window; for while they had been speaking the procession had stopped.

'Is it possible,' thought Edward, 'that these can be the two girls in russet gowns that I left at the cottage? And yet it must be. Well, Chaloner, to all appearance your good aunts have done justice to their charge.'

'Nature has done more, Edward. I never thought that they would have grown into such lovely girls as they have, although I always thought that they were handsome.'

As they passed, Edward caught the eye of Edith, and smiled.

'Alice, that's Edward!' said Edith, so loud as to be heard by the King and all near him.

Alice and Edith rose and waved their handkerchiefs, but they were obliged to cease and put them to their eyes.

'Are those your sisters, Edward?' said the King.

'They are, your Majesty.'

The King rose in his stirrups, and made a low obeisance to the window where they were standing.

'We shall have some court beauties, Beverley,' said the King, looking at him over his shoulder.

As soon as the ceremonies were over and they could escape from their personal attentions, Edward and his two friends went to the house in which resided the Ladies Conynghame and his sisters.

We pass over the joy of this meeting after so many years' absence, and the pleasure which it gave to Edward to find his sisters grown such accomplished and elegant young women. That his two friends, who were, as the reader will recollect, old acquaintances of Alice and Edith, were warmly received, we hardly need say.

'Now, Edward, who do you think was here today? The reigning belle, and the toast of all the gentlemen.'

'Indeed! I must be careful of my heart. Dear Edith, who is she?'

'No less than one with whom you were formerly well acquainted, Edward – Patience Heatherstone.'

'Patience Heatherstone!' cried Edward, 'the toast of all London!'

'Yes; and deservedly so, I can assure you. But she is as good as she is handsome, and, moreover, treats all the gay gallants with perfect indifference. She is staying with her uncle, Sir Ashley Cooper; and her father is also in town, for he called here with her today.'

'When did you hear from Humphrey, Edith?'

'A few days back. He has left the cottage now altogether.'

'Indeed! Where does he reside then?'

'At Arnwood. The house has been rebuilt, and I understand is a very princely mansion. Humphrey has charge of it until it is ascertained to whom it is to belong.'

'It belongs to Mr Heatherstone, does it not?' replied Edward.

'How can you say so, Edward? You received Humphrey's letters a long while ago.'

'Yes, I did. But let us not talk about it any more, my dear Edith; I am in great perplexity.'

'Nay, dear brother, let us talk about it,' said Alicè, who had come up and overheard the latter portion of the conversation. 'What is your perplexity?'

'Well,' replied Edward, 'since it is to be so, let us sit down and talk over the matter. I acknowledge the kindness of Mr Heatherstone, and feel that all he asserted to Humphrey is true; still I do not like that I should be indebted to him for a property which is mine, and that he has no right to give. I acknowledge his generosity, but I do not acknowledge his right of possession. Nay, much as I admire – and, I may say, fond as I am for time has not effaced the feeling of his daughter, it still appears to be that, although not said, it is expected that she is to be included in the transfer; and I will accept no wife on such conditions.'

'That is to say, because all you wish for – your property and a woman you love – are offered you in one lot, you will not accept them. They must be divided and handed over to you in two,' said Alice, smiling.

'You mistake, dearest; I am not so foolish. But I have a certain pride, which you cannot blame. Accepting the property from Mr Heatherstone is receiving a favour, were it given as a marriage portion with his daughter. Now, why should I accept as a favour what I can claim as a right? It is my intention of appealing to the King and demanding the restoration of my property. He cannot refuse it.'

'Put not your trust in princes, brother,' replied Alice. 'I doubt if the King or his council will consider it advisable to make so many discontented as to restore property which has been so long held by others, and by so doing create a host of enemies. Recollect also that Mr Heatherstone and his brother-in-law, Sir Ashley Cooper, have done the King much more service than you ever have or can do. They have been most important agents in his restoration, and the King's obligations to them are much greater than they are to you. Besides, merely for what may be called a point of honour, for it is no more, in what an unpleasant situation will you put his Majesty! At all events, Edward, recollect you do not know what are the intentions of Mr Heatherstone. Wait and see what he proffers first.'

'But, my dear sister, it appears to me that his intentions are evident. Why has he rebuilt Arnwood? He is not going to surrender my property and make me a present of the house.'

'The reason for rebuilding the mansion was good. You were at the wars; it was possible that you might not or that you might not return. He said this to Humphrey, who has all along been acting as his factotum in the business; and recollect, at the time that Mr Heatherstone commenced the rebuilding of the mansion, what prospect was there of the restoration of the King, or of your ever being in a position to apply for the restoration of your property? I believe, however, that Humphrey knows more of Mr Heatherstone's intentions than he has made known to us; and I therefore say again, my dear Edward, make no application till you ascertain what Mr Heatherstone's intentions may be.'

'Your advice is good, my dear Alice, and I will be guided by it,' replied Edward.

'And now let me give you some advice for your friends, Masters Chaloner and Grenville. That much of their property has been given away and put into other hands I know; and probably they expect it will be restored upon their application to the King. Those who hold the property think so too, and so far it is fortunate. Now, from wiser heads than mine, I have been told that these applications will not be acceded to, as is supposed; but at the same time, if they were to meet the parties, and close with them at once, before the King's intentions are known, they would recover their property at a third or a quarter of the value. Now is their time; even a few days' delay may make a difference. They can easily obtain a delay for the payment of the moneys. Impress that upon them, my dear

Edward, and let them, if possible, be off to their estates tomorrow and make the arrangements.'

'That is advice which must be followed,' replied Edward. 'We must go now, and I will not fail to communicate it to them this very night.'

We may as well here inform the reader that the advice was immediately acted upon, and that Chaloner and Grenville recovered all their estates at about five years' purchase.

Edward remained at court several days. He had written to Humphrey, and had dispatched a messenger with the letter, but the messenger had not yet returned. The court was now one continual scene of fétes and gaiety. On the following day a drawing-room was to be held, and Edward's sisters were to be presented. Edward was standing, with many others of the suite, behind the chair of the King, amusing himself with the presentations as they took place, and waiting for the arrival of his sisters. Chaloner and Grenville were not with him – they had obtained leave to go into the country, for the object we have before referred to – when his eyes caught, advancing towards the King, Mr Heatherstone, who led his daughter Patience. That they had not perceived him was evident; indeed, her eyes were not raised once, from the natural timidity felt by a young woman in the presence of royalty. Edward half concealed himself behind one of his companions, that he might gaze upon her without reserve. She was indeed a lovely young person, but little altered, except having grown taller and more rounded and perfect in her figure; and her court dress displayed proportions which her humble costume at the New Forest had concealed, or which time had not matured. There was the same pensive, sweet expression in her face, which had altered little; but the beautiful rounded arms, the symmetrical fall of the shoulders, and the proportion of the whole figure was a surprise to him; and Edward in his own mind agreed that she might well be the reigning toast of the day.

Mr Heatherstone advanced and made his obeisance, and then his daughter was led forward and introduced by a lady unknown to Edward. After he had saluted her, the King said, loud enough for Edward to hear, –

'My obligations to your father are great. I trust that the daughter will often grace our court.'

Patience made no reply, but passed on; and soon afterwards Edward lost sight of her in the crowd.

If there ever had been any check to Edward's feelings towards Patience – and time and absence have their effect upon the most ardent of lovers – the sight of her so resplendent in beauty acted upon him like magic; and he was uneasy till the ceremony was over, and he was enabled to go to his sisters.

When he entered the room he found himself in the arms of Humphrey, who had arrived with the messenger. After the greetings were over Edward said, –

'Alice and I have seen Patience, and I fear I must surrender at discretion. Mr Heatherstone may make his own terms; I must waive all pride rather

213

than lose her. I thought that I had more control over myself; but I have seen her, and feel that my future happiness depends upon obtaining her as a wife. Let her father but give me her, and Arnwood will be but a trifle in addition.'

'With respect to the conditions upon which you are to possess Arnwood,' said Humphrey, 'I can inform you what they are. They are wholly unshackled, further than that you are to repay by instalments the money expended in the building of the house. This I am empowered to state to you, and I think you will allow that Mr Heatherstone has fully acted up to what he stated were his views when he first obtained a grant of the property.'

'He has indeed,' replied Edward.

'As for his daughter, Edward, you have yet to "win her and wear her", as the saying is. Her father will resign the property to you as yours by right; but you have no property in his daughter, and I suspect that she will not be quite so easily handed over to you.'

'But why should you say so, Humphrey? Have we not been attached from our youth?'

'Yes, it was a youthful passion, I grant; but recollect, nothing came of it, and years have passed away. It is now seven years since you quitted the forest, and in your letters to Mr Heatherstone you made no remark upon what had passed between you and Patience. Since that you have never corresponded or sent any messages; and you can hardly expect that a girl, from the age of seventeen to twenty-four, will cherish the image of one who, to say the least, had treated her with undifference. That is my view of the matter, Edward; it may be wrong.'

'And it may be true,' replied Edward mournfully.

'Well, my view is different,' replied Edith. 'You know, Humphrey, how many offers Patience Heatherstone has had, and has every day, I may say. Why has she refused them all? In my opinion, because she has been constant to a proud brother of mine, who does not deserve her!'

'It may be so, Edith,' replied Humphrey. 'Women are riddles. I only argued upon the common sense of the thing.'

'Much you know about women,' replied Edith. 'To be sure, you do not meet many in the New Forest, where you have lived all your life.'

'Very true, my dear sister. Perhaps that is the reason that the New Forest has had such charms for me.'

'After that speech, sir, the sooner you get back again the better!' retorted Edith. But Edward made a sign to Humphrey, and they beat a retreat.

'Have you seen the Intendant, Humphrey?'

'No; I was about to call upon him, but I wanted to see you first.'

'I will go with you. I have not done him justice,' replied Edward, 'and yet I hardly know how to explain to him –'

'Say nothing, but meet him cordially: that will be explanation sufficient.'

'I shall meet him as one whom I shall always revere, and feel that I owe a deep debt of gratitude. What must he think of my not having called upon him?'

'Nothing. You hold a place at court. You may not have known that he was in London, as you have never met him. Your coming with me will make it appear so. Tell him that I have just made known to you his noble and disinterested conduct.'

'You are right – I will. I fear, however, Humphrey, that you are right, and Edith wrong, as regards his daughter.'

'Nay, Edward, recollect that I have, as Edith observed, passed my life in the woods.'

Edward was most kindly received by Mr Heatherstone. Edward, on Mr Heatherstone repeating to him his intentions relative to Arnwood, expressed his sense of that gentleman's conduct, simply adding, –

'You may think me impetuous, sir, but I trust you will believe me grateful.'

Patience coloured up and trembled when Edward first saw her. Edward did not refer to the past for some time after they had renewed their acquaintance. He wooed her again, and won her. Then all was explained.

About a year after the Restoration there was *fête* at Hampton Court, given in honour of three marriages taking place – Edward Beverley to Patience Heatherstone, Chaloner to Alice and Grenville to Edith; and as his Majesty himself said as he gave away the brides, 'Could loyalty be better rewarded?'

But our young readers will not be content if they do not hear some particulars about the other personages who have appeared in our little history. Humphrey must take the first place. His love of farming continued. Edward gave him a large farm, rent free; and in a few years Humphrey saved up sufficient to purchase a property for himself. He then married Clara Ratcliffe, who has not appeared lately on the scene, owing to her having been, about two years before the Restoration, claimed by an elderly relation, who lived in the country, and whose infirm state of health did not permit him to quit the house. He left his property to Clara, about a year after her marriage to Humphrey. The cottage in the New Forest was held by, and eventually made over to, Pablo, who became a very steady character, and in the course of time married a young girl from Arnwood, and had a houseful of young gipsies. Oswald, so soon as Edward came down to Arnwood, gave up his place in the New Forest, and lived entirely with Edward, as his steward; and Phœbe also went to Arnwood, and lived to a good old age, in the capacity of housekeeper, her temper becoming rather worse than better as she advanced in years.

This is all that we have been able to collect relative to the several parties, and so now we must say farewell.